PLAYER
PIANO

KURT VONNEGUT

Delta
Trade Paperbacks

A Delta Book
Published by
Dell Publishing
a division of
Random House, Inc.
1540 Broadway
New York, New York 10036

Cover design: Carin Goldberg
Cover illustration: Gene Greif
Book design: Nancy Field

ISBN: 0-385-33378-1

Reprinted by arrangement with Delacorte Press/Seymour Lawrence

Manufactured in the United States of America
Published simultaneously in Canada

January 1999

10 9 8 7 6 5

BVG

For Jane—God Bless Her

Consider the lilies of the field, how they grow:
They toil not, neither do they spin;
And yet I say unto you,
That even Solomon in all his glory
Was not arrayed like one of these. . . .

—MATTHEW 6:28

FOREWORD

This book is not a book about what is, but a book about what could be. The characters are modeled after persons as yet unborn, or, perhaps, at this writing, infants.

It is mostly about managers and engineers. At this point in history, 1952 A.D., our lives and freedom depend largely upon the skill and imagination and courage of our managers and engineers, and I hope that God will help them to help us all stay alive and free.

But this book is about another point in history, when there is no more war, and . . .

1

Ilium, New York, is divided into three parts.

In the northwest are the managers and engineers and civil servants and a few professional people; in the northeast are the machines; and in the south, across the Iroquois River, is the area known locally as Homestead, where almost all of the people live.

If the bridge across the Iroquois were dynamited, few daily routines would be disturbed. Not many people on either side have reasons other than curiosity for crossing.

During the war, in hundreds of Iliums over America, managers and engineers learned to get along without their men and women, who went to fight. It was the miracle that won the war—production with almost no manpower. In the patois of the north side of the river, it was the know-how that won the war. Democracy owed its life to know-how.

Ten years after the war—after the men and women had come home, after the riots had been put down, after thousands had been jailed under the antisabotage laws—Doctor Paul Proteus was petting a cat in his office. He was the most important, brilliant person in Ilium, the manager of the Ilium Works, though only thirty-five. He was tall, thin, nervous, and dark, with the gentle good looks of his long face distorted by dark-rimmed glasses.

He didn't feel important or brilliant at the moment, nor had he for some time. His principle concern just then was that the black cat be contented in its new surroundings.

Those old enough to remember and too old to compete

said affectionately that Doctor Proteus looked just as his father had as a young man—and it was generally understood, resentfully in some quarters, that Paul would someday rise almost as high in the organization as his father had. His father, Doctor George Proteus, was at the time of his death the nation's first National Industrial, Commercial, Communications, Foodstuffs, and Resources Director, a position approached in importance only by the presidency of the United States.

As for the Proteus genes' chances of being passed down to yet another generation, there were practically none. Paul's wife, Anita, his secretary during the war, was barren. Ironically as anyone would please, he had married her after she had declared that she was certainly pregnant, following an abandoned office celebration of victory.

"Like that, kitty?" With solicitousness and vicarious pleasure, young Proteus ran a roll of blueprints along the cat's arched back. "Mmmmm-aaaaah—good, eh?" He had spotted her that morning, near the golf course, and had picked her up as a mouser for the plant. Only the night before, a mouse had gnawed through the insulation on a control wire and put buildings 17, 19, and 21 temporarily out of commission.

Paul turned on his intercom set. "Katharine?"

"Yes, Doctor Proteus?"

"Katharine, when's my speech going to be typed?"

"I'm doing it now, sir. Ten, fifteen minutes, I promise."

Doctor Katharine Finch was his secretary, and the only woman in the Ilium Works. Actually, she was more a symbol of rank than a real help, although she was useful as a stand-in when Paul was ill or took a notion to leave work early. Only the brass—plant managers and bigger—had secretaries. During the war, the managers and engineers had found that the bulk of secretarial work could be done—as could most lower-echelon jobs—more quickly and efficiently and cheaply by machines. Anita was about to be dismissed when Paul had

married her. Now, for instance, Katharine was being annoyingly unmachine-like, dawdling over Paul's speech, and talking to her presumed lover, Doctor Bud Calhoun, at the same
time.

Bud, who was manager of the petroleum terminal in
Ilium, worked only when shipments came or went by barge
or pipeline, and he spent most of his time between these
crises—as now—filling Katharine's ears with the euphoria of
his Georgia sweet talk.

Paul took the cat in his arms and carried her to the
enormous floor-to-ceiling window that comprised one wall.
"Lots and lots of mice out there, kitty," he said.

He was showing the cat an old battlefield at peace.
Here, in the basin of the river bend, the Mohawks had over-
powered the Algonquins, the Dutch the Mohawks, the British the Dutch, the Americans the British. Now, over bones
and rotten palings and cannon balls and arrowheads, there lay
a triangle of steel and masonry buildings, a half-mile on each
side—the Illium Works. Where men had once howled and
hacked at one another, and fought nip-and-tuck with nature
as well, the machines hummed and whirred and clicked, and
made parts for baby carriages and bottle caps, motorcycles
and refrigerators, television sets and tricycles—the fruits of
peace.

Paul raised his eyes above the rooftops of the great triangle to the glare of the sun on the Iroquois River, and beyond—to Homestead, where many of the pioneer names still
lived: van Zandt, Cooper, Cortland, Stokes . . .

"Doctor Proteus?" It was Katharine again.

"Yes, Katharine."

"It's on again."

"Three in Building 58?"

"Yessir—the light's on again."

"All right—call Doctor Shepherd and find out what
he's doing about it."

"He's sick today. Remember?"

"Then it's up to me, I guess." He put on his coat, sighed with ennui, picked up the cat, and walked into Katharine's office. "Don't get up, don't get up," he said to Bud, who was stretched out on a couch.

"Who was gonna get up?" said Bud.

Three walls of the room were solid with meters from baseboard to molding, unbroken save for the doors leading into the outer hall and into Paul's office. The fourth wall, as in Paul's office, was a single pane of glass. The meters were identical, the size of cigarette packages, and stacked like masonry, each labeled with a bright brass plate. Each was connected to a group of machines somewhere in the Works. A glowing red jewel called attention to the seventh meter from the bottom, fifth row to the left, on the east wall.

Paul tapped the meter with his finger. "Uh-huh—here we go again: number three in 58 getting rejects, all right." He glanced over the rest of the instruments. "Guess that's all, eh?"

"Just that one."

"Whatch goin' do with thet cat?" said Bud.

Paul snapped his fingers. "Say, I'm glad you asked that. I have a project for you, Bud. I want some sort of signaling device that will tell this cat where she can find a mouse."

"Electronic?"

"I should hope so."

"You'd need some kind of sensin' element thet could smell a mouse."

"Or a rat. I want you to work on it while I'm gone."

As Paul walked out to his car in the pale March sunlight, he realized that Bud Calhoun *would* have a mouse alarm designed—one a cat could understand—by the time he got back to the office. Paul sometimes wondered if he wouldn't have been more content in another period of history, but the rightness of Bud's being alive now was beyond question. Bud's mentality was one that had been remarked upon as being peculiarly American since the nation had been born—

the restless, erratic insight and imagination of a gadgeteer. This was the climax, or close to it, of generations of Bud Calhouns, with almost all of American industry integrated into one stupendous Rube Goldberg machine.

Paul stopped by Bud's car, which was parked next to his. Bud had shown off its special features to him several times, and, playfully, Paul put it through its paces. "Let's go," he said to the car.

A whir and a click, and the door flew open. "Hop in," said a tape recording under the dashboard. The starter spun, the engine caught and idled down, and the radio went on.

Gingerly, Paul pressed a button on the steering column. A motor purred, gears grumbled softly, and the two front seats lay down side by side like sleepy lovers. It struck Paul as shockingly like an operating table for horses he had once seen in a veterinary hospital—where the horse was walked alongside the tipped table, lashed to it, anesthetized, and then toppled into operating position by the gear-driven table top. He could see Katharine Finch sinking, sinking, sinking, as Bud, his hand on the button, crooned. Paul raised the seats with another button. "Goodbye," he said to the car.

The motor stopped, the radio winked off, and the door slammed. "Don't take any wooden nickels," called the car as Paul climbed into his own. "Don't take any wooden nickels, don't take any wooden nickels, don't take any—"

"I won't!"

Bud's car fell silent, apparently at peace.

Paul drove down the broad, clean boulevard that split the plant, and watched the building numbers flash by. A station wagon, honking its horn, and its occupants waving to him, shot past in the opposite direction, playfully zigzagging on the deserted street, heading for the main gate. Paul glanced at his watch. That was the second shift just coming off work. It annoyed him that sophomoric high spirits should be correlated with the kind of young men it took to keep the plant going. Cautiously, he assured himself that when he,

5

Finnerty, and Shepherd had come to work in the Ilium Works thirteen years before, they had been a good bit more adult, less cock-sure, and certainly without the air of belonging to an elite.

Some people, including Paul's famous father, had talked in the old days as though engineers, managers, and scientists were an elite. And when things were building up to the war, it was recognized that American know-how was the only answer to the prospective enemy's vast numbers, and there was talk of deeper, thicker shelters for the possessors of know-how, and of keeping this cream of the population out of the front-line fighting. But not many had taken the idea of an elite to heart. When Paul, Finnerty, and Shepherd had graduated from college, early in the war, they had felt sheepish about not going to fight, and humbled by those who did go. But now this elite business, this assurance of superiority, this sense of rightness about the hierarchy topped by managers and engineers—this was instilled in all college graduates, and there were no bones about it.

Paul felt better when he got into Building 58, a long, narrow structure four blocks long. It was a pet of his. He'd been told to have the north end of the building torn down and replaced, and he'd talked Headquarters out of it. The north end was the oldest building in the plant, and Paul had saved it—because of its historical interest to visitors, he'd told Headquarters. But he discouraged and disliked visitors, and he'd really saved Building 58's north end for himself. It was the original machine shop set up by Edison in 1886, the same year in which he opened another in Schenectady, and visiting it took the edge off Paul's periods of depression. It was a vote of confidence from the past, he thought—where the past admitted how humble and shoddy it had been, where one could look from the old to the new and see that mankind really had come a long way. Paul needed that reassurance from time to time.

Objectively, Paul tried to tell himself, things really were

better than ever. For once, after the great bloodbath of the war, the world really was cleared of unnatural terrors—mass starvation, mass imprisonment, mass torture, mass murder. Objectively, know-how and world law were getting their long-awaited chance to turn earth into an altogether pleasant and convenient place in which to sweat out Judgment Day.

Paul wished he had gone to the front, and heard the senseless tumult and thunder, and seen the wounded and dead, and maybe got a piece of shrapnel through his leg. Maybe he'd be able to understand then how good everything now was by comparison, to see what seemed so clear to others—that what he was doing, had done, and would do as a manager and engineer was vital, above reproach, and had, in fact, brought on a golden age. Of late, his job, the system, and organizational politics had left him variously annoyed, bored, or queasy.

He stood in the old part of Building 58, which was now filled with welding machines and a bank of insulation braiders. It soothed him to look up at the wooden rafters, uneven with ancient adze marks beneath flaking calcimine, and at the dull walls of brick soft enough for men—God knows how long ago—to carve their initials in: "KTM," "DG," "GP," "BDH," "HB," "NNS." Paul imagined for a moment—as he often imagined on visits to Building 58—that he was Edison, standing on the threshold of a solitary brick building on the banks of the Iroquois, with the upstate winter slashing through the broomcorn outside. The rafters still bore the marks of what Edison had done with the lonely brick barn: bolt holes showed where overhead shafts had once carried power to a forest of belts, and the wood-block floor was black with the oil and scarred by the feet of the crude machines the belts had spun.

On his office wall, Paul had a picture of the shop as it had been in the beginning. All of the employees, most of them recruited from surrounding farms, had stood shoulder to shoulder amid the crude apparatus for the photograph, almost fierce with dignity and pride, ridiculous in stiff collars and derbies. The photographer had apparently been accustomed to taking pictures of athletic teams and fraternal organizations, for the picture had the atmosphere, after the fashion of the day, of both. In each face was a defiant promise of physical strength, and at the same time, there was the attitude of a secret order, above and apart from society by virtue of participating in important and moving rites the laity could only guess about—and guess wrong. The pride in strength and important mystery showed no less in the eyes of the sweepers than in those of the machinists and inspectors, and in those of the foreman, who alone was without a lunchbox.

A buzzer sounded, and Paul stepped to one side of the aisle as the sweeping machine rattled by on its rails, whooshing up a cloud of dust with spinning brooms, and sucking up the cloud with a voracious snout. The cat in Paul's arms clawed up threads from his suit and hissed at the machine.

Paul's eyes began to nag him with a prickling sensation, and he realized that he'd been gazing into the glare and sputter of the welding machines without protecting his eyes. He clipped dark glasses over his spectacles, and strode through the antiseptic smell of ozone toward lathe group three, which was in the center of the building, in the new part.

He paused for a moment by the last welding-machine group, and wished Edison could be with him to see it. The old man would have been enchanted. Two steel plates were stripped from a pile, sent rattling down a chute; were seized by mechanical hands and thrust under the welding machine. The welding heads dropped, sputtered, and rose. A battery of electric eyes balefully studied the union of the two plates, signaled a meter in Katharine's office that all was well with welding-machine group five in Building 58, and the welded plates skittered down another chute into the jaws of the punch-press group in the basement. Every seventeen seconds, each of the twelve machines in the group completed the cycle.

Looking the length of Building 58, Paul had the impression of a great gymnasium, where countless squads practiced precision calisthenics—bobbing, spinning, leaping, thrusting, waving. . . . This much of the new era Paul loved: the machines themselves were entertaining and delightful.

Cursorily, he opened the control box for the welding-machine group, and saw that the machines were set to run for three more days. After that, they would shut down automatically until Paul received new orders from headquarters and relayed them to Doctor Lawson Shepherd, who was second-in-command and responsible for Buildings 53 through 71. Shepherd, who was sick today, would then set the controls for a new batch of refrigerator backs—however many backs EPICAC, a computing machine in Carlsbad Caverns, felt the economy could absorb.

Paul, calming the anxious cat with his long, slender fingers, wondered indifferently if Shepherd really was sick. Probably not. More likely, he was seeing important people, trying to get transferred out from under Paul.

Shepherd, Paul, and Edward Finnerty had all come to Ilium together as youngsters. Now Finnerty had moved on to bigger things in Washington; Paul had been given the highest job in Ilium; and Shepherd, sulky and carping, but efficient, had, in his own eyes, been humiliated by being named second-in-command to Paul. Transfers were an upper-echelon decision, and Paul hoped to God that Shepherd got one.

Paul arrived at lathe group three, the troublemaker he had come to see. He had been agitating a long time for permission to junk the group, without much luck. The lathes were of the old type, built originally to be controlled by men, and adapted during the war, clumsily, to the new techniques. The accuracy was going out of them, and, as the meter in Katharine's office had pointed out, rejects were showing up in quantity. Paul was willing to bet that the lathe group was ten per cent as wasteful as it had been in the days of human control and mountainous scrap heaps.

The group, five ranks of ten machines each, swept their tools in unison across steel bars, kicked out finished shafts onto continuous belts, stopped while raw bars dropped between their chucks and tailstocks, clamped down, and swept their tools across the bars, kicked out the finished shafts onto . . .

Paul unlocked the box containing the tape recording that controlled them all. The tape was a small loop that fed continuously between magnetic pickups. On it were recorded the movements of a master machinist turning out a shaft for a fractional horsepower motor. Paul counted back—eleven, twelve, thirteen years ago, he'd been in on the making of the tape, the master from which this one had been made. . . .

He and Finnerty and Shepherd, with the ink hardly dry on their doctorates, had been sent to one of the machine shops to make the recording. The foreman had pointed out his best man—what *was* his name?—and, joking with the puzzled machinist, the three bright young men had hooked up the recording apparatus to the lathe controls. Hertz! That had been the machinist's name—Rudy Hertz, an old-timer, who had been about ready to retire. Paul remembered the name now, and remembered the deference the old man had shown the bright young men.

Afterward, they'd got Rudy's foreman to let him off, and, in a boisterous, whimsical spirit of industrial democracy, they'd taken him across the street for a beer. Rudy hadn't understood quite what the recording instruments were all about, but what he had understood, he'd liked: that he, out of thousands of machinists, had been chosen to have his motions immortalized on tape.

And here, now, this little loop in the box before Paul, here was Rudy as Rudy had been to his machine that afternoon—Rudy, the turner-on of power, the setter of speeds, the controller of the cutting tool. This was the essence of Rudy as far as his machine was concerned, as far as the economy was concerned, as far as the war effort had been concerned. The tape was the essence distilled from the small, polite man with the big hands and black fingernails; from the man who thought the world could be saved if everyone read a verse from the Bible every night; from the man who adored a collie for want of children; from the man who . . . What else had Rudy said that afternoon? Paul supposed the old man was dead now—or in his second childhood in Homestead.

Now, by switching in lathes on a master panel and feeding them signals from the tape, Paul could make the essence of Rudy Hertz produce one, ten, a hundred, or a thousand of the shafts.

Paul closed the box's door. The tape seemed in good condition, and so were the pickups. Everything, in fact, was as ship-shape as could be expected, considering the antiquity of the machines. There were just going to have to be rejects, and that was that. The whole group belonged in a museum, not a production setup. Even the box was archaic—a vaultlike affair bolted to the floor, with a steel door and lock. At the time of the riots, right after the war, the master tapes had all been locked up in this way. Now, with the antisabotage laws as rigidly enforced as they were, the only protection the controls needed was from dust, cockroaches, and mice.

At the door, in the old part of the building once more, Paul paused for a moment to listen to the music of Building 58. He had had it in the back of his mind for years to get a composer to do something with it—*the Building 58 Suite*. It was wild and Latin music, hectic rhythms, fading in and out of phase, kaleidoscopic sound. He tried to separate and identify the themes. There! The lathe groups, the tenors: *"Furrazz-ow-ow-ow-ow-ow-ak! ting! Furr-azz-ow-ow . . ."* The welders, the baritones: *"Vaaaaaaa-zuzip! Vaaaaaaa-zuzip!"* And, with the basement as a resonating chamber, the punch presses, the basses: *"Aw-grumph! tonka-tonka. Aw-grump! tonka-tonka . . ."* It was exciting music, and Paul, flushed, his vague anxieties gone, gave himself over to it.

Out of the corner of his eye, a crazy, spinning movement caught his fancy, and he turned in his delight to watch a cluster of miniature maypoles braid bright cloth insulation about a black snake of cable. A thousand little dancers whirled about one another at incredible speeds, pirouetting, dodging one another, unerringly building their snug snare about the cable. Paul laughed at the wonderful machines, and had to look away to keep from getting dizzy. In the old days, when women had watched over the machines, some of the more simple-hearted had been found sitting rigidly at their posts, staring, long after quitting time.

His gaze fell upon an asymmetrical heart scratched into the old brick, and in its center, "K.L.–M.W.", and the date, "1931." K.L. and M.W. had taken a liking to one another, then, in the same year that Edison had died. Paul thought again of the fun of showing the old man around Building 58, and suddenly realized that most of the machinery would be old stuff, even to Edison. The braiders, the welders, the punch presses, the lathes, the conveyers—everything in sight, almost, had been around in Edison's time. The basic parts of the automatic controls, too, and the electric eyes and other elements that did and did better what human senses had once done for industry—all were familiar enough in scientific circles even in the nineteen-twenties. All that was new was the combination of these elements. Paul reminded himself to bring that out in his talk at the Country Club that night.

The cat arched her back and clawed at Paul's suit again. The sweeper was snuffling down the aisle toward them once more. It sounded its warning buzzer, and Paul stepped out of its path. The cat hissed and spat, suddenly raked Paul's hand with her claws, and jumped. With a bouncing, stiff-legged gait, she fled before the sweeper. Snatching, flashing, crashing, shrieking machines kept her in the middle of the aisle, yards ahead of the sweeper's whooshing brooms. Paul looked frantically for the switch that would stop the sweeper, but before he found it, the cat made a stand. She faced the oncoming sweeper, her needle-like teeth bared, the tip of her tail snapping back and forth. The flash of a welder went off inches from her eyes, and the sweeper gobbled her up and hurled her squalling and scratching into its galvanized tin belly.

Winded after a quarter-mile run through the length of the building, Paul caught the sweeper just as it reached a chute. It gagged, and spat the cat down the chute and into a freight car outside. When Paul got outside, the cat had scrambled up the side of the freight car, tumbled to the ground, and was desperately clawing her way up a fence.

"No, kitty, no!" cried Paul.

The cat hit the alarm wire on the fence, and sirens screamed from the gate house. In the next second the cat hit the charged wires atop the fence. A pop, a green flash, and the cat sailed high over the top strand as though thrown. She dropped to the asphalt—dead and smoking, but outside.

An armored car, its turret nervously jerking its brace of machine guns this way and that, grumbled to a stop by the small corpse. The turret hatch clanged open, and a plant guard cautiously raised his head. "Everything all right, sir?"

"Turn off the sirens. Nothing but a cat on the fence." Paul knelt, and looked at the cat through the mesh of the fence, frightfully upset. "Pick up the cat and take her to my office."

"Beg your pardon, sir?"

"The cat—I want her taken to my office."

"She's dead, sir."

"You heard me."

"Yessir."

Paul was in the depths again as he climbed into his car in front of Building 58. There was nothing in sight to divert him, nothing but asphalt, a perspective of blank, numbered façades, and wisps of cold cirrus clouds in a strip of blue sky. Paul glimpsed the only life visible through a narrow canyon between Buildings 57 and 59, a canyon that opened onto the river and revealed a bank of gray porches in Homestead. On the topmost porch an old man rocked in a patch of sunlight. A child leaned over the railing and launched a square of paper in a lazy, oscillating course to the river's edge. The youngster looked up from the paper to meet Paul's gaze. The old man stopped rocking and looked, too, at the curiosity, a living thing in the Ilium Works.

As Paul passed Katharine Finch's desk on his way into his office, she held out his typewritten speech. "That's very good, what you said about the Second Industrial Revolution," she said.

"Old, old stuff."

"It seemed very fresh to me—I mean that part where you say how the First Industrial Revolution devalued muscle work, then the second one devalued routine mental work. I was fascinated."

"Norbert Wiener, a mathematician, said all that way back in the nineteen-forties. It's fresh to you because you're too young to know anything but the way things are now."

"Actually, it is kind of incredible that things were ever any other way, isn't it? It was so ridiculous to have people stuck in one place all day, just using their senses, then a reflex, using their senses, then a reflex, and not really thinking at all."

"Expensive," said Paul, "and about as reliable as a putty ruler. You can imagine what the scrap heap looked like, and what hell it was to be a service manager in those days. Hangovers, family squabbles, resentments against the boss, debts, the war—every kind of human trouble was likely to show up in a product one way or another." He smiled. "And happiness, too. I can remember when we had to allow for holidays, especially around Christmas. There wasn't anything to do but take it. The reject rate would start climbing around the fifth of December, and up and up it'd go until Christmas. Then the holiday, then a horrible reject rate; then New Year's, then a ghastly reject level. Then things would taper down to normal—which was plenty bad enough—by January fifteenth or so. We used to have to figure in things like that in pricing a product."

"Do you suppose there'll be a Third Industrial Revolution?"

Paul paused in his office doorway. "A third one? What would that be like?"

"I don't know exactly. The first and second ones must have been sort of inconceivable at one time."

"To the people who were going to be replaced by machines, maybe. A third one, eh? In a way, I guess the third one's been going on for some time, if you mean thinking machines. That would be the third revolution, I guess—machines that devaluate human thinking. Some of the big computers like EPICAC do that all right, in specialized fields."

"Uh-huh," said Katharine thoughtfully. She rattled a pencil between her teeth. "First the muscle work, then the routine work, then, maybe, the real brainwork."

"I hope I'm not around long enough to see that final step. Speaking of industrial revolutions, where's Bud?"

"A barge was coming in, so he had to get back to work. He left this for you." She handed him a crumpled laundry slip with Bud's name on it.

Paul turned the slip over and found, as he had expected, a circuit diagram for a mouse detector and alarm system that might very well work. "Astonishing mind, Katharine."

She nodded uncertainly.

Paul closed his door, locked it silently, and got a bottle from under papers in a bottom drawer. He blacked out for an instant under the gloriously hot impact of a gulp of whisky. He hid the bottle again, his eyes watering.

"Doctor Proteus, your wife is on the phone," said Katharine on the intercom.

"Proteus speaking." He started to sit, and was distressed to find a small wicker basket in his chair, containing a dead black cat.

"This is me, darling, Anita."

"Hello, hello, hello." He set the basket on the floor gently, and sank into his chair. "How are you, sweetheart?" he said absently. His mind was still on the cat.

"All set to have a good time tonight?" It was a theatrical contralto, knowing and passionate: Ilium's Lady of the Manor speaking.

"Been jumpy all day about the talk."

"Then you'll do it brilliantly, darling. You'll get to Pittsburgh yet. I haven't the slightest doubt about that, Paul, not the slightest. Just wait until Kroner and Baer hear you tonight."

"Kroner and Baer accepted, did they?" These two were manager and chief engineer, respectively, of the entire Eastern Division, of which the Ilium Works was one small part. It was Kroner and Baer who would decide who was to get the most important job in their division, a job left vacant two weeks ago by death—the managership of the Pittsburgh Works. "How gay can a party get?"

"Well, if you don't like that, I have some news you will like. There's going to be another very special guest."

"Hi ho."

"And you have to go to Homestead for some Irish whisky for him. The club hasn't got any."

"Finnerty! Ed Finnerty!"

"Yes, Finnerty. He called this afternoon and was very specific about your getting some Irish for him. He's on his way from Washington to Chicago, and he's going to stop off here."

"How long has it been, Anita? Five, six years?"

"Not since before you got to be manager. *That* long." She was hale, enthusiastic about Finnerty's coming. It annoyed Paul, because he knew very well that she didn't care for Finnerty. She was crowing, not because she was fond of Finnerty but because she enjoyed the ritual attitudes of friendships, of which she had none. Also, since he'd left Ilium, Ed Finnerty had become a man of consequence, a member of the National Industrial Planning Board; and this fact no doubt dulled her recollections of contretemps with Finnerty in the past.

"You're right about that being good news, Anita. It's wonderful. Takes the edge off Kroner and Baer."

"Now, you're going to be nice to them, too."

"Oh yes. Pittsburgh, here we come."

"If I tell you something for your own good, promise not to get mad?"

"No."

"All right, I'll tell you anyway. Amy Halporn said this morning she'd heard something about you and Pittsburgh. Her husband was with Kroner today, and Kroner had the impression that you didn't *want* to go to Pittsburgh."

"How does he want me to tell him—in Esperanto? I've told him I wanted the job a dozen different ways in English."

"Apparently Kroner doesn't feel you really mean it. You've been too subtle and modest, darling."

"Kroner's a bright one, all right."

"How do you mean?"

"I mean he's got more insight into me than I do."

"You mean you don't want the Pittsburgh job?"

"I'm not sure. He apparently knew that before I did."

"You're tired, darling."

"I guess."

"You need a drink. Come home early."

"All right."

"I love you, Paul."

"I love *you*, Anita. Goodbye."

Anita had the mechanics of marriage down pat, even to the subtlest conventions. If her approach was disturbingly rational, systematic, she was thorough enough to turn out a creditable counterfeit of warmth. Paul could only suspect that her feelings were shallow—and perhaps that suspicion was part of what he was beginning to think of as his sickness.

His head was down, his eyes closed, when he hung up. When he opened his eyes, he was looking at the dead cat in the basket.

"Katharine!"

"Yessir."

"Will you have somebody bury this cat."

"We wondered what you wanted to do with it."

"God knows what I had in mind." He looked at the corpse and shook his head. "God knows. Maybe a Christian burial; maybe I hoped she'd come around. Get rid of it right away, would you?"

He stopped by Katharine's desk on his way home and told her not to worry about the glowing jewel on the seventh meter from the bottom, fifth row from the left, on the east wall.

"Beyond help," he said. Lathe group three, Building 58, had been good in its day, but was showing wear and becoming a misfit in the slick, streamlined setup, where there was no place for erratic behavior. "Basically, it wasn't built for the job it's doing anyway. I look for the buzzer to go off any day now, and that'll be the end."

In each meter box, in addition to the instrument, the jewel, and the warning lamp, was a buzzer. The buzzer was the signal for a unit's complete breakdown.

2

THE SHAH OF BRATPUHR, spiritual leader of 6,000,000 members of the Kolhouri sect, wizened and wise and dark as cocoa, encrusted with gold brocade and constellations of twinkling gems, sank deep into the royal-blue cushions of the limousine—like a priceless brooch in its gift box.

On the other side of the limousine's rear seat sat Doctor Ewing J. Halyard, of the United States Department of State, a heavy, florid, urbane gentleman of forty. He wore a flowing sandy mustache, a colored shirt, a boutonniere, and a waistcoat contrasting with his dark suit, and wore them with such poise that one was sure he'd just come from a distinguished company where everyone dressed in this manner. The fact was that only Doctor Halyard did. And he got away with it beautifully.

Between them, nervous, grinning, young, and forever apologetic for his own lack of éclat or power, was Khashdrahr Miasma, the interpreter, and nephew of the Shah, who had learned English from a tutor, but had never before been outside of the Shah's palace.

"Khabu?" said the Shah in his high, frail voice.

Halyard had been with the Shah for three days now and was able to understand, without Khashdrahr's help, five of the Shah's expressions. *"Khabu"* meant "where?" *"Siki"* meant "what?" *"Akka sahn"* meant "why?" *"Brahous brahouna, houna saki"* was a combination of blessing and thanks, and *Sumklish* was the sacred Kolhouri drink which Khashdrahr carried in a hip flask for the Shah.

The Shah had left his military and spiritual fastness in the mountains to see what he could learn in the most power-

ful nation on earth for the good of his people. Doctor Halyard was his guide and host.

"Khabu?" said the Shah again, peering out at the city.

"The Shah wishes to know, please, where we are now,"
said Khashdrahr.

"I know," said Halyard, smiling wanly. It had been
khabu and *siki* and *akka sahn* until he was half out of his
mind. He leaned forward. "Ilium, New York, your highness. We are about to cross the Iroquois River, which di-
vides the town in two. Over there on the opposite bank is
the Ilium Works."

The limousine came to a halt by the end of the bridge,
where a large work crew was filling a small chuckhole. The
crew had opened a lane for an old Plymouth with a broken
headlight, which was coming through from the north side of
the river. The limousine waited for the Plymouth to get
through, and then proceeded.

The Shah turned to stare at the group through the back
window, and then spoke at length.

Doctor Halyard smiled and nodded appreciatively, and
awaited a translation.

"The Shah," said Khashdrahr, "he would like, please,
to know who owns these slaves we see all the way up from
New York City."

"Not slaves," said Halyard, chuckling patronizingly.
"Citizens, employed by government. They have same rights
as other citizens—free speech, freedom of worship, the right
to vote. Before the war, they worked in the Ilium Works,
controlling machines, but now machines control themselves
much better."

"Aha!" said the Shah, after Khashdrahr had translated.

"Less waste, much better products, cheaper products
with automatic control."

"Aha!"

"And any man who cannot support himself by doing a
job better than a machine is employed by the government,

either in the Army or the Reconstruction and Reclamation Corps."

"Aha! *Khabu bonanza-pak?*"

"Eh?"

"He says, 'Where does the money come from to pay them?' " said Khashdrahr.

"Oh. From taxes on the machines, and taxes on personal incomes. Then the Army and the Reconstruction and Reclamation Corps people put their money back into the system for more products for better living."

"Aha!"

Doctor Halyard, a dutiful man with a bad conscience about the size of his expense accounts, went on explaining America, though he knew very little was getting through. He told the Shah that advances had been most profound in purely industrial communities, where the bulk of the population—as in Ilium—had made its living tending machines in one way or another. In New York City, for instance, there were many skills difficult or uneconomical to mechanize, and the advances hadn't liberated as high a percentage of people from production.

"Kuppo!" said the Shah, shaking his head.

Khashdrahr blushed, and translated uneasily, apologetically. "Shah says, 'Communism.' "

"No *Kuppo!*" said Halyard vehemently. "The government does not own the machines. They simply tax that part of industry's income that once went into labor, and redistribute it. Industry is privately owned and managed, and co-ordinated—to prevent the waste of competition—by a committee of leaders from private industry, not politicians. By eliminating human error through machinery, and needless competition through organization, we've raised the standard of living of the average man immensely."

Khashdrahr stopped translating and frowned perplexedly. "Please, this *average man*, there is no equivalent in our language, I'm afraid."

"You know," said Halyard, "the ordinary man, like, well, anybody—those men working back on the bridge, the man in that old car we passed. The little man, not brilliant but a good-hearted, plain, ordinary, everyday kind of person."

Khashdrahr translated.

"Aha," said the Shah, nodding, *"Takaru."*

"What did he say?"

"Takaru," said Khashdrahr. "Slave."

"No *Takaru,"* said Halyard, speaking directly to the Shah. *"Ci-ti-zen."*

"Ahhhhh," said the Shah. *"Ci-ti-zen."* He grinned happily. *"Takaru—citizen. Citizen—Takaru."*

"No *Takaru!"* said Halyard.

Khashdrahr shrugged. "In the Shah's land are only the Elite and the *Takaru.*"

Halyard's ulcer gave him a twinge, the ulcer that had grown in size and authority over the years of his career as an interpreter of America to provincial and ignorant notables from the backwaters of civilization.

The limousine came to a stop again, and the driver honked his horn at a crew of Reconstruction and Reclamation Corpsmen. They had left their wheelbarrows blocking the road, and were throwing rocks at a squirrel on a branch a hundred feet overhead.

Halyard rolled down his window. "Get these damn wheelbarrows out of the way!" he shouted.

"Ci-ti-zen!" piped the Shah, smiling modestly at his newly acquired bilinguality.

"Drop dead," called one of the rock throwers. Reluctantly, surlily, he came down to the road and moved two wheelbarrows very slowly, studying the car and its occupants as he did it. He stepped to one side.

"Thanks! It's about time!" said Halyard as the limousine eased past the man.

"You're welcome, Doc," said the man, and he spat in Halyard's face.

Halyard sputtered, manfully regained his poise, and wiped his face. "Isolated incident," he said bitterly.

"Takaru yamu brouha, pu dinka bu," said the Shah sympathetically.

"The Shah," said Khashdrahr gravely, "he says it is the same with *Takaru* everywhere since the war."

"No *Takaru*," said Halyard apathetically, and let it go.

"Sumklish," sighed the Shah.

Khashdrahr handed him the flask of sacred liquor.

3

DOCTOR PAUL PROTEUS, the man with the highest income in Ilium, drove his cheap and old Plymouth across the bridge to Homestead. He had had the car at the time of the riots, and among the bits of junk in the glove compartment— match cards, registration, flashlight, and face tissues—was the rusty pistol he had been issued then. Having a pistol where some unauthorized person might get at it was very much against the law. Even members of the huge standing army did without firearms until they'd disembarked for occupation duty overseas. Only the police and plant guards were armed. Paul didn't want the pistol but was forever forgetting to turn it in. Over the years, as it had accumulated a patina of rust, he'd come to regard it as a harmless antique. The glove compartment wouldn't lock, so Paul covered the pistol with tissues.

The engine wasn't working properly, now and then

hesitating, catching again, slowing suddenly, catching again. His other cars, a new station wagon and a very expensive sedan, were at home, as he put it, for Anita. Neither of the good cars had ever been in Homestead, and neither had Anita for many years. Anita never needled him about his devotion to the old car, though she did seem to think some sort of explanation to others was in order. He had overheard her telling visitors that he had had it rebuilt in such a way that it was far better mechanically than what was coming off the automatic assembly lines at Detroit—which simply wasn't true. Nor was it logical that a man with so special a car would put off and put off having the broken left headlamp fixed. And he wondered how she might have explained, had she known, that he kept a leather jacket in the trunk, and that he exchanged his coat for this and took off his necktie before crossing the Iroquois. It was a trip he made only when he had to—for, say, a bottle of Irish whisky for one of the few persons he had ever felt close to.

He came to a stop at the Homestead end of the bridge. About forty men, leaning on crowbars, picks, and shovels, blocked the way, smoking, talking, milling about something in the middle of the pavement. They looked around at Paul with an air of sheepishness and, as though there were nothing but time in the world, they moved slowly to the sides of the bridge, leaving an alley barely wide enough for Paul's car. As they separated, Paul saw what it was they had been standing around. A small man was kneeling beside a chuckhole perhaps two feet in diameter, patting a fresh fill of tar and gravel with the flat of his shovel.

Importantly, the man waved for Paul to go *around* the patch, not *over* it. The others fell silent, and watched to make sure that Paul did go around it.

"Hey, Mac, your headlamp's busted," shouted one of the men. The others joined in, chorusing the message earnestly.

Paul nodded his thanks. His skin began to itch, as though he had suddenly become unclean. These were members of the Reconstruction and Reclamation Corps, in their own estimate the "Reeks and Wrecks." Those who couldn't compete economically with machines had their choice, if they had no source of income, of the Army or the Reconstruction and Reclamation Corps. The soldiers, with their hollowness hidden beneath twinkling buttons and buckles, crisp serge, and glossy leather, didn't depress Paul nearly as much as the Reeks and Wrecks did.

He eased through the work crew, past a black government limousine, and into Homestead.

A saloon was close to the end of the bridge. Paul had to park his car a half-block away, for another crew was flushing out the storm sewers with an opened fire hydrant. This seemed to be a favorite undertaking. Whenever he had come to Homestead when the temperature had been above freezing, he'd found a hydrant going.

One big man, with an air of proprietorship, kept his hands on the wrench that controlled the flow. Another stood by as second-in-command of the water. All around them, and along the course of the water to the sewer mouth, a crowd stood watching. A dirty little boy caught a scrap of paper skittering along the sidewalk, fashioned it into a crude boat, and launched it in the gutter. All eyes followed the craft with interest, seeming to wish it luck as it shot perilous rapids, as it snagged on a twig, spun free, shot into the swift, deep main flow, mounted a crest for a triumphant instant, and plunged into the sewer.

"Uh!" grunted a man standing by Paul, as though he had been aboard the boat.

Paul worked his way through the crowd, which was continuous with the clientele of the saloon, and got to within one rank of the bar. His back was against an old player piano. No one seemed to have recognized him. It would have been surprising if someone had, for, in line with policy, he kept pretty much to his own side of the river and never permitted his name or picture to appear in the Ilium *Star-Tribune*.

Around the bar were old men, pensioners, too old for the Army or the Reeks and Wrecks. Each had before him a headless beer in a glass whose rim was opaqued by hours of slow, thoughtful sipping. These oldsters probably arrived early and left late, and any other business had to be done over their heads. On the screen of the television set behind the bar, a large earth mother of a woman, her voice shut off by the volume knob, beamed, moved her lips excitedly, and broke eggs into a mixing bowl. The old men watched, occasionally clicking their dentures or licking their lips.

"Excuse me," said Paul self-consciously.

No one made a move to let him get to the bar. A fat, whitening collie, curled beneath the barstool of an old man blocking Paul's way, showed its toothless gums and growled fuzzily.

Futilely, Paul waved his hand for the bartender's attention. As he shifted from one foot to the other, he recalled the fully mechanized saloon he, Finnerty, and Shepherd had designed when they'd been playful young engineers. To their surprise, the owner of a restaurant chain had been interested enough to give the idea a try. They'd set up the experimental unit about five doors down from where Paul now stood, with coin machines and endless belts to do the serving, with germicidal lamps cleaning the air, with uniform, healthful light, with continuous soft music from a tape recorder, with seats scientifically designed by an anthropologist to give the average man the absolute maximum in comfort.

The first day had been a sensation, with a waiting line extending blocks. Within a week of the opening, curiosity had been satisfied, and it was a boom day when five customers stopped in. Then this place had opened up almost next door, with a dust-and-germ trap of a Victorian bar, bad light, poor ventilation, and an unsanitary, inefficient, and probably dishonest bartender. It was an immediate and unflagging success.

He caught the bartender's eye at last. When the bartender saw Paul, he dropped his role of high-handed supervisor of morals and settler of arguments and became an obsequious host, like the bartender at the Country Club. Paul was afraid for a moment that he'd been recognized. But when the bartender failed to call him by name, he supposed that only his class had been recognized.

There were a few men in Homestead—like this bartender, the police and firemen, professional athletes, cab drivers, specially skilled artisans—who hadn't been displaced by machines. They lived among those who had been displaced, but they were aloof and often rude and overbearing with the mass. They felt a camaraderie with the engineers and managers across the river, a feeling that wasn't, incidentally, reciprocated. The general feeling across the river was that these persons weren't too bright to be replaced by machines; they were simply in activities where machines weren't economical. In short, their feelings of superiority were unjustified.

Now, the bartender had sensed that Paul was a personage, and he made a show of letting everyone else go to hell while he gave service to Paul. The others noticed, and turned to stare at the privileged newcomer.

Paul ordered the bottle of Irish in a quiet voice, and tried to become inconspicuous by bending over and petting the aged collie. The dog barked, and its owner turned on his barstool to confront Paul. The old man was as toothless as the dog. Paul's first impression was of red gums and huge hands—as though everything were sapped of color and strength but these.

"He wouldn't hurt nobody," said the old man apologetically. "Just kind of edgy about being old and blind, and never sure of what's going on, is all." He ran his big hands along the dog's fat sides. "He's a good old dog." He looked thoughtfully at Paul. "Say, I bet I know you."

Paul looked anxiously after the bartender, who had disappeared into the cellar after the whisky. "Really? I've been in here once or twice before."

"No, not here," said the old man loudly. "The plant, the plant. You're young Doctor Proteus."

A lot of people heard, and those closest to the two studied Paul with disturbing candor, and fell silent in order to hear whatever was being said.

The old man was apparently quite deaf, for his voice was erratically loud, then soft. "Don't recognize my face, Doctor?" He wasn't mocking, he was frankly admiring, and proud that he could prove himself on speaking terms with this distinguished man.

Paul colored. "I can't say I remember. The old welding shop, was it?"

The old man swept his hand over his face deprecatingly. "Aaaah, not enough left of the old face for my best friend to recognize," he said good-humoredly. He thrust out his hands, palms up. "But look at those, Doctor. Good as ever, and there's not two like them anywhere. You said so yourself."

"Hertz," said Paul. "You're Rudy Hertz."

Rudy laughed, and looked about the room triumphantly, as though to say, "See, by God, Rudy Hertz does know Doctor Proteus, and Proteus knows Hertz! How many of you can say that?"

"And this is the dog you were telling me about—ten, fifteen years ago?"

"Son of the dog, Doctor." He laughed. "I wasn't no pup then, though, was I?"

"You were a damn fine machinist, Rudy."

"I say so myself. Knowing that, knowing smart men like you say that about Rudy, that means a lot. It's about all I got, you know, Doctor? That and the dog." Rudy shook the arm of the man next to him, a short, heavy, seemingly soft man, middle-aged, with a homely, round face. His eyes were magnified and fogged by extremely thick glasses. "Hear what Doctor Proteus here said about me?" Rudy gestured at Paul. "Smartest man in Ilium says that about Rudy. Maybe he's the smartest man in the country."

Paul wished to God the bartender would hurry up. The man Rudy had shaken was now studying Paul sullenly. Paul glanced quickly about the room and saw hostility all around him.

Addled Rudy Hertz thought he was doing a handsome thing by Paul, showing him off to the crowd. Rudy was senile, remembering only his prime, incapable of remembering or understanding what had followed his retirement. . . .

But these others, these men in their thirties, forties, and fifties—*they* knew. The youngsters in the booth, the two soldiers and three girls, they were like Katharine Finch. They couldn't remember when things had been different, could hardly make sense of what had been, though they didn't necessarily like what was. But these others who stared now, they remembered. They had been the rioters, the smashers of machines. There was no threat of violence in their looks now, but there was resentment, a wish to let him know that he had intruded where he was not liked.

And still the bartender did not return. Paul limited his field of vision to Rudy, ignoring the rest. The man with thick glasses, whom Rudy had invited to admire Paul, continued to stare.

Paul talked inanely now about the dog, about Rudy's remarkable state of preservation. He was helplessly aware that he was hamming it up, proving to anyone who might still have doubts that he was indeed an insincere ass.

"Let's drink to old times!" said Rudy, raising his glass. He didn't seem to notice that silence greeted his proposal, and that he drank alone. He made clucking noises with his tongue, and winked in fond reminiscence, and drained his glass with a flourish. He banged it on the bar.

Paul, smiling glassily, decided to say nothing more,

since anything more would be the wrong thing. He folded his arms and leaned against the keyboard of the player piano. In the silence of the saloon, a faint discord came from the piano, hummed to nothingness.

"Let's drink to our sons," said the man with thick glasses suddenly. His voice was surprisingly high for so resonant-looking a man. Several glasses were raised this time. When the toast was done, the man turned to Paul with the friendliest of smiles and said, "My boy's just turned eighteen, Doctor."

"That's nice."

"He's got his whole life ahead of him. Wonderful age, eighteen." He paused, as though his remark demanded a response.

"I'd like to be eighteen again," said Paul lamely.

"He's a good boy, Doctor. He isn't what you'd call real bright. Like his old man—his heart's in the right place, and he wants to do the most he can with what he's got." Again the waitful pause.

"That's all any of us can do," said Paul.

"Well, as long as such a smart man as you is here, maybe I could get you to give me some advice for the boy. He just finished his National General Classification Tests. He just about killed himself studying up for them, but it wasn't any use. He didn't do nearly well enough for college. There were only twenty-seven openings, and six hundred kids trying for them." He shrugged. "I can't afford to send him to a private school, so now he's got to decide what he's going to do with his life, Doctor: what's it going to be, the Army or the Reeks and Wrecks?"

"I suppose there's a lot to be said for both," said Paul uncomfortably. "I really don't know much about either one. Somebody else, like Matheson, maybe, would . . ." His sentence trailed off. Matheson was Ilium's manager in charge of testing and placement. Paul knew him slightly, didn't like him very well. Matheson was a powerful bureaucrat who went about his job with the air of a high priest. "I'll call Matheson, if you like, and ask him, and let you know what he says."

"Doctor," said the man, desperately now, with no tinge of baiting, "isn't there something the boy could do at the Works? He's awfully clever with his hands. He's got a kind of instinct with machines. Give him one he's never seen before, and in ten minutes he'll have it apart and back together again. He loves that kind of work. Isn't there someplace in the plant—?"

"He's got to have a graduate degree," said Paul. He reddened. "That's policy, and I didn't make it. Sometimes we get Reconstruction and Reclamation people over to help put in big machines or do a heavy repair job, but not very often. Maybe he could open a repair shop."

The man exhaled, slumped dejectedly. "Repair shop," he sighed. "Repair shop, he says. How many repair shops you think Ilium can support, eh? Repair shop, sure! I was going to open one when I got laid off. So was Joe, so was Sam, so was Alf. We're all clever with our hands, so we'll all open repair shops. One repairman for every broken article in Il- ium. Meanwhile, our wives clean up as dressmakers—one dressmaker for every woman in town."

Rudy Hertz had apparently missed all the talk and was still celebrating in his mind the happy reunion with his great and good friend, Doctor Paul Proteus. "Music," said Rudy grandly. "Let's have music!" He reached over Paul's shoulder and popped a nickel into the player piano.

Paul stepped away from the box. Machinery whirred importantly for a few seconds, and then the piano started clanging away at *"Alexander's Ragtime Band"* liked cracked carillons. Mercifully, conversation was all but impossible. Mercifully, the bartender emerged from the basement and handed Paul a dusty bottle over the old heads.

Paul turned to leave, and a powerful hand closed on his upper arm. Rudy, his expansive host, held him.

31

"I played this song in your honor, Doctor," shouted Rudy above the racket. "Wait till it's over." Rudy acted as though the antique instrument were the newest of all wonders, and he excitedly pointed out identifiable musical patterns in the bobbing keys—trills, spectacular runs up the keyboard, and the slow, methodical rise and fall of keys in the bass. "See—see them two go up and down, Doctor! Just the way the feller hit 'em. Look at 'em go!"

The music stopped abruptly, with the air of having delivered exactly five cents worth of joy. Rudy still shouted. "Makes you feel kind of creepy, don't it, Doctor, watching them keys go up and down? You can almost see a ghost sitting there playing his heart out."

Paul twisted free and hurried out to his car.

4

"DARLING, YOU LOOK as though you've seen a ghost," said Anita. She was already dressed for the party at the Country Club, already dominating a distinguished company she had yet to join.

As she handed Paul his cocktail, he felt somehow inadequate, bumbling, in the presence of her beautiful assurance. Only things that might please or interest her came to mind—all else submerged. It wasn't a conscious act of his mind, but a reflex, a natural response to her presence. It annoyed him that the feeling should be automatic, because he fancied himself in the image of his father, and, in this situation, his father would

PLAYER PIANO

have been completely in charge—taking the first, last, and best lines for himself.

The expression "armed to the teeth" occurred to Paul as he looked at her over his glass. With an austere dark gown that left her tanned shoulders and throat bare, a single bit of jewelry on her finger, and very light make-up, Anita had successfully combined the weapons of sex, taste, and an aura of masculine competence.

She quieted, and turned away under his stare. Inadvertently, he'd gained the upper hand. He had somehow communicated the thought that had bobbed up in his thoughts unexpectedly: that her strength and poise were no more than a mirror image of his own importance, an image of the power and self-satisfaction the manager of the Ilium Works could have, if he wanted it. In a fleeting second she became a helpless, bluffing little girl in his thoughts, and he was able to feel real tenderness toward her.

"Good drink, sweetheart," he said. "Finnerty upstairs?"

"I sent him on over to the club. Kroner and Baer got there early, and I sent Finnerty over to keep them company while you get dressed."

"How does he look?"

"How did Finnerty always look? Awful. I swear he was wearing the same baggy suit he wore when he said goodbye to us seven years ago. And I'll swear it hasn't been cleaned since then, either. I tried to get him to wear your old tuxedo, and he wouldn't hear of it. Went right over the way he was. I suppose a stiff shirt would have been worse in a way. It would have showed how dirty his neck is."

She pulled the neck of her dress lower, looked at herself in a mirror, and raised it slightly again—a delicate compromise. "Honestly," she said, talking to Paul's image in the mirror, "I'm crazy about that man—you *know* I am. But he just looks awful all the time. I mean, after all, a man in his position, and not even clean."

Paul smiled and shook his head. It was true. Finnerty

33

had always been shockingly lax about his grooming, and some of his more fastidious supervisors in the old days had found it hard to believe that a man could be so staggeringly competent, and at the same time so unsanitary-looking. Occasionally, the tall, gaunt Irishman would surprise everyone—usually between long stretches of work—by showing up with his cheeks gleaming like wax apples, and with new shoes, socks, shirt, tie, and suit, and, presumably, underwear. Engineers' and managers' wives would make a big fuss over him, to show him that such care of himself was important and rewarding; and they declared that he was really the handsomest thing in the Ilium industrial fold. Quite possibly he was, in a coarse, weathered way: grotesquely handsome, like Abe Lincoln, but with a predatory, defiant cast to his eyes rather than the sadness of Lincoln's. After Finnerty's periodic outbursts of cleanliness and freshness, the wives would watch with increasing distress as he wore the entire celebrated outfit day in and day out, until the sands and soot and grease of time had filled every seam and pore.

And Finnerty had other unsavory aspects. Into the resolutely monogamous and Eagle Scout-like society of engineers and managers, Finnerty often brought women he'd picked up in Homestead a half-hour before. When it came time, after supper, to play games, Finnerty and the girl would generally take a highball in either hand and wander off to the shrub-walled first tee, if it was warm, or out to his car, if it was cold.

His car—in the old days, anyway—had been more disreputable than Paul's was today. In this direction, at least—the most innocuous direction, socially—Paul had imitated his friend. Finnerty had claimed that his love of books and records and good whisky kept him too broke to buy a car and clothes commensurate with his position in life. Paul had computed the value of Finnerty's record, book, and bottle collections and concluded that the Irishman would still have plenty left for even two new cars. It was then that Paul began to suspect that Finnerty's way of life wasn't as irrational as it seemed; that it was, in fact, a studied and elaborate insult to the managers and engineers of Ilium, and to their immaculate wives.

Why Finnerty had seen fit to offend these gentle people was never clear to Paul, who supposed the aggressiveness, like most aggressiveness, dated back to some childhood muddle. The only intimation as to what that childhood had been like had come not from Finnerty but from Kroner, who took a breeder's interest in his engineers' bloodlines. Kroner had once remarked, confidingly and with a show of sympathy, that Finnerty was a mutant, born of poor and stupid parents. The only insight Finnerty had ever permitted Paul was in a moment of deep depression, during a crushing hangover, when he'd sighed and said he'd never felt he belonged anywhere.

Paul wondered about his own deep drives as he realized how much pleasure he was getting from recollections of Finnerty's socially destructive, undisciplined antics. Paul indulged himself in the wistful sensation of feeling that he, Paul, might be content, if only—and let the thought stop there, as though he knew vaguely what lay beyond. He didn't.

Paul envied Finnerty's mind, for Finnerty could be anything he wanted to be, and be brilliant at it. Whatever the times might have called for, Finnerty would have been among the best. If this had been the age of music, Finnerty would have been, and in fact was, a top-flight pianist—or he might have been an architect or physician or writer. With inhuman intuition, Finnerty could sense the basic principles and motives of almost any human work, not just engineering.

Paul could have been only what he was, he thought. As he filled his glass again, he supposed that he could only have come to this moment, this living room, into the presence of Anita.

It was an appalling thought, to be so well-integrated into the machinery of society and history as to be able to

KURT VONNEGUT

move in only one plane, and along one line. Finnerty's arrival was disturbing, for it brought to the surface the doubt that life should be that way. Paul had been thinking of hiring a psychiatrist to make him docile, content with his lot, amiable to all. But now, here was Finnerty, pushing him in the other direction. Finnerty had seemed to see something in Paul he hadn't seen in the others, something he'd liked—possibly a rebellious streak that Paul was only now beginning to suspect. For *some reason* Finnerty had made Paul his only friend.

"In a way, I wish Finnerty'd picked another day," said Anita. "It raises all sorts of problems. Baer's supposed to be on my left, and Kroner on my right; but now, with a member of the National Industrial Planning Board blowing in unexpectedly, I'm not sure who goes where. Is Ed Finnerty bigger brass than Kroner and Baer?" she asked incredulously.

"Look in the *Organization Directory*, if you want," said Paul. "I think you'll find the N.I.P.B. is listed ahead of the regional people—but it's more brain trust than brass. Finnerty won't care. He'll probably eat with the help."

"If he sets foot in the kitchen, the Board of Health will throw him in jail." She laughed uneasily. It was evident that she found it trying to be a good sport about Finnerty, to pretend that his eccentricities were amusing. She changed the subject. "Tell me about today."

"Nothing about today. One more, like all the rest."

"You got the whisky?"

"Yes. I had to go across the river to get it."

"Was it such an awful ordeal?" she chided. She couldn't understand why he hated to run errands into Homestead, and teased him about it. "Was it so awful?" she said again, bordering on baby talk, as though he were a lazy little boy coaxed into doing a small favor for his mother.

"Pretty bad."

"Really?" She was surprised. "Nothing violent, I hope."

"No. Everybody was very polite, in fact. One of the

36

pensioners recognized me from the old days and threw an impromptu party for me."

"Well, that sounds like downright fun."

"Does, doesn't it? His name is Rudy Hertz." Without describing his own reactions, he told her what had happened. He found himself watching her closely, experimenting.

"And that upset you?" She laughed. "You *are* a sensitive darling, aren't you? You tell me you've been through a nightmare, and nothing happened at all."

"They hate me."

"They proved they loved and admired you. And, what's more, they should."

"The man with the thick glasses as much as said his son's life wasn't worth living on account of me."

"You said that. He didn't. And I won't have you saying ridiculous things like that. Do you get some sort of pleasure out of making things up to feel guilty about? If his son isn't bright enough for anything but the Reeks and Wrecks or the Army, is that your fault?"

"No; but if it hadn't been for men like me, he might have a machine in the plant—"

"Is he starving?"

"Of course not. Nobody starves."

"And he's got a place to live and warm clothes. He has what he'd have if he were running a stupid machine, swearing at it, making mistakes, striking every year, fighting with the foreman, coming in with hangovers."

"You're right, you're right." He held up his hands. "Of course you're right. It's just a hell of a time to be alive, is all—just this goddamn messy business of people having to get used to new ideas. And people just don't, that's all. I wish this were a hundred years from now, with everybody used to the change."

"You're tired. I'm going to tell Kroner you need a month off."

"I'll tell him, if I feel like it."

"I wasn't trying to run your life, darling. But you never ask for anything."

"Let me do the asking, if you don't mind."

"I don't. I promise you I don't mind at all."

"Did you lay my things out?"

"On your bed," she said primly. She'd been hurt. "Tuxedo, shirt, socks, studs, cuff links, and a new tie."

"New tie?"

"Dubonnet."

"Dubonnet! For Christ's sake."

"Kroner and Baer are wearing dubonnet ties."

"And is my underwear like theirs?"

"I'm sure I didn't notice."

"I'm wearing a black tie."

"Pittsburgh, darling—remember? You said you wanted to go there."

"Hi ho, dubonnet." He climbed the stairs to their bedroom, stripping off his coat and shirt as he went.

"Ed!" Finnerty was stretched out on Anita's bed.

"So there you are," said Finnerty. He pointed at the tuxedo laid out on Paul's bed. "I thought this was you. I've been talking to it for half an hour."

"Anita said you'd gone to the club."

"Anita expelled me out the front door, so I came in the back and up here."

"Well, I'm glad you did. How are things?"

"Worse than ever, but there's hope."

"Fine," said Paul, laughing uncertainly. "Married?"

"Never. Shut the door."

Paul closed it. "How's the Washington job?"

"I've quit."

"Really? Something bigger yet?"

"I think so, or I wouldn't have quit."

"Where?"

"No place. No job at all."

"Not enough pay, or worn out, or what?"

"Sick of it," he said slowly. "The pay was fantastically good, ridiculously good—paid like a television queen with a forty-inch bust. But when I got this year's invitation to the Meadows, Paul, something snapped. I realized I couldn't face another session up there. And then I looked around me and found out I couldn't face anything about the system any more. I walked out, and here I am."

Paul's invitation to the Meadows was carelessly displayed by Anita in the front-hall mirror, where no one could fail to notice it. The Meadows was a flat, grassy island in the St. Lawrence, in Chippewa Bay, where the most important men, and the most promising men ("Those whose development within the organization is not yet complete," said the *Handbook*) in the Eastern and Middle-Western Divisions spent a week each summer in an orgy of morale building— through team athletics, group sings, bonfires and skyrockets, bawdy entertainment, free whisky and cigars; and through plays, put on by professional actors, which pleasantly but unmistakably made clear the nature of good deportment within the system, and the shape of firm resolves for the challenging year ahead.

Finnerty took a crumpled pack of cigarettes from his pocket, offered one bent at almost a right angle. Paul straightened it out, his fingers unsteady. "Got the shakes?" said Finnerty.

"I'm chief speaker tonight."

"Oh?" He seemed disappointed. "Then you don't ordinarily have the shakes these days? What's the occasion?"

"Thirteen years ago today, the Ilium Works was placed under the National Manufacturing Council."

"Like every other plant in the country."

"Ilium was a little earlier than most." The union of the country's manufacturing facilities under one council had taken place not long after Finnerty, Paul, and Shepherd came to work in Ilium. It had been done because of the war. Similar councils had been formed for the transportation, raw materials, food, and communications industries, and over them all had been Paul's father. The system had so cut waste and duplication that it was preserved after the war, and was, in fact, often cited as one of the few concrete benefits of the war.

"Does that make you happy, that this has been going on thirteen years?"

"It calls for comment, anyway. I'm going to keep it factual. It isn't going to be like Kroner's evangelism."

Finnerty fell silent, apparently uninterested in pursuing the subject. "Funny," he said at last, "I thought you'd be pretty close to the edge by now. That's why I came here."

Paul twisted his face as he struggled to get his collar button moored. "Well, you weren't completely wrong. There's talk of my chatting with a psychiatrist."

"So you *are* in rough shape. Wonderful! Let's get out of this damn party. We've got to talk."

The bedroom door opened, and Anita looked in from the hall. "Oh! Ed. Who's with Baer and Kroner?"

"Kroner's with Baer, Baer's with Kroner," said Finnerty. "Close the door, please, Anita."

"It's time to go to the club."

"It's time for *you* to go to the club," said Finnerty. "Paul and I'll be along later."

"We're going together, and now, Ed. We're ten minutes late as it is. And I won't be bullied by you. I refuse." She smiled unconvincingly.

"Let's go," said Paul.

"Anita," said Finnerty, "if you don't show more respect for men's privacy, I'll design a machine that's everything you are, and *does* show respect."

She colored. "I can't say I find you screamingly funny."

"Stainless steel," said Finnerty. "Stainless steel, covered with sponge rubber, and heated electrically to 98.6 degrees."

"Now, look—" said Paul.

"And blushes at will," said Finnerty.

"And I could make a man like you out of a burlap bag filled with mud," said Anita. "Anybody who tries to touch you comes away dirty!" She slammed the door, and Paul listened to her heels clicking down the staircase.

"Now, why in hell did you do that?" said Paul. "Do you mind telling me?"

Finnerty lay motionless on the bed, staring at the ceiling. "I don't know," he said slowly, "but I'm not sorry. Go on with her."

"What are your plans?"

"Go on!" He said it as though Paul had suddenly intruded just as he was giving form to an important, difficult thought.

"There's Irish whisky for you in a brown bag in the front hall," said Paul, and he left Finnerty lying there.

5

PAUL OVERTOOK ANITA in the garage, where she was starting the station wagon. Without looking directly at him, she waited for him to climb in beside her. They drove to the club in silence, with Paul feeling let down by the coarse, irrational reality of Finnerty. Over the years, he supposed bitterly, he must have created a wise and warm Finnerty in his imagination, an image that had little to do with the real man.

At the club door, Anita straightened Paul's tie, pulled her cape down to bare her shoulders, smiled, and pushed into the brightly lighted foyer.

The far end of the foyer opened into the bar, and there two dozen of the Ilium Works' bright young men, identical in their crew cuts and the tailoring of their tuxedos, surrounded two men in their middle fifties. One of the older men, Kroner, tall, heavy, and slow, listened to the youngsters with ponderous affectionateness. The other, Baer, slight and nervous, noisily and unconvincingly extroverted, laughed, nudged, and clapped shoulders, and maintained a continuous commentary on whatever was being said: "Fine, fine, right, sure, sure, wonderful, yes, yes, exactly, fine, good."

Ilium was a training ground, where fresh graduates were sent to get the feel of industry and then moved on to bigger things. The staff was young, then, and constantly renewing itself. The oldest men were Paul, and his second-in-command, Lawson Shepherd. Shepherd, a bachelor, stood by the bar, somewhat apart from the rest, looking wise, and faintly amused by the naïveté of some of the youngsters' remarks.

The wives had congregated in two adjacent booths, and there spoke quietly and uneasily, and turned to look whenever the volume of voices rose above a certain level, or whenever the bass voice of Kroner rumbled through the haze of small talk with three or four short, wise, wonderfully pregnant words.

The youngsters turned to greet Paul and Anita effusively, with playful obsequiousness, with the air of having proprietorship over all good times, which they generously encouraged their elders to share in.

Baer waved and called to them in his high-pitched voice. Kroner nodded almost imperceptibly, and stood perfectly still, not looking directly at them, waiting for them to come up so that greetings could be exchanged quietly and with dignity.

Kroner's enormous, hairy hand closed about Paul's, and

Paul, in spite of himself, felt docile, and loving, and childlike. It was as though Paul stood in the enervating, emasculating presence of his father again. Kroner, his father's closest friend, had always made him feel that way, and seemingly wanted to make him feel that way. Paul had sworn a thousand times to keep his wits about him the next time he met Kroner. But it was a matter beyond his control, and at each meeting, as now, the power and resolve were all in the big hands of the older man.

Though Paul was especially aware of the paternal aura about Kroner, the big man tried to make the feeling general. He spoke of himself as father to all of the men under him, and more vaguely, to their wives; and it was no pose. His administration of the Eastern Division had an emotional flavor about it, and it seemed unlikely that he could have run the Division any other way. He was cognizant of every birth or major illness, and heaped blame on himself in the rare instances that any of his men went wrong. He could also be stern—again, paternally.

"How are you, Paul?" he said warmly. The quizzical set of his thick eyebrows indicated that this was a question, not a salutation. The tone was one Kroner used when inquiring into someone's condition after a siege of pneumonia or worse.

"He's never been better," said Anita briskly.

"Glad to hear it. That's fine, Paul." Kroner continued to hold onto his hand and to stare into his eyes.

"Feel good, do you, eh? Good? Good, eh? Wonderful," said Baer, clapping him on the shoulder several times. "Wonderful." Baer, the Eastern Division's chief engineer, turned to Anita. "And, oh my! Don't you look nice. My, yes. Oh! I should say so." He grinned.

Baer was a social cretin, apparently unaware that he was anything but suave and brilliant in company. Someone had once mentioned his running commentary on conversations to him, and he hadn't known what they were talking about.

Technically, there wasn't a better engineer in the East, including Finnerty. There was little in the Division that hadn't
been master-minded by Baer, who here seemed to Kroner
what a fox terrier seems to a St. Bernard. Paul had thought
often of the peculiar combination of Kroner and Baer, and
wondered if, when they were gone, higher management
could possibly duplicate it. Baer embodied the knowledge
and technique of industry; Kroner personified the faith, the
near-holiness, the spirit of the complicated venture. Kroner,
in fact, had a poor record as an engineer and had surprised
Paul from time to time with his ignorance or misunderstanding of technical matters; but he had the priceless quality of
believing in the system, and of making others believe in it,
too, and do as they were told.

The two were inseparable, though their personalities
met at almost no point. Together, they made an approxi-
mately whole man.

"Did someone tell you Paul had been sick?" said Anita,
laughing.

"I'd heard Paul's nerves had been bothering him," said
Kroner.

"Not true," said Paul.

Kroner smiled. "Glad to hear it, Paul. You're one of our
best men." He looked at him fondly. "In the footsteps of
your father, Paul."

"Where did you hear about Paul's nerves?" said Anita.

"Can't imagine," said Kroner.

"Doctor Shepherd told us," said Baer brightly. "I was
there this morning. Remember? It was Shepherd."

"Now listen," said Kroner with unaccustomed quick-
ness, "that was something else Shepherd was talking about.
You know it was, if you'll just think back."

"Oh sure, that's right, that's right; something else,
something else," said Baer, looking puzzled. He clapped Paul
on the shoulder again. "So you're feeling better, eh? Well,
that's what counts. Wonderful, wonderful."

Doctor Shepherd, his neck blazing red above his stiff collar, moved quietly away from the bar toward the French doors that opened onto the golf course.

"By the way," said Kroner heartily, "where's your friend Finnerty? What does Ed look like? I imagine he's found life in Washington a little less—" he searched for a word "—informal than here."

"If you mean, does he wash?—the answer is still no," said Anita.

"That's what I meant," said Kroner. "Well, none of us are perfect, and darn few of us perfect enough to get a place on the National Industrial Planning Board. Where is he?"

"He may be along later," said Paul. "He's a little tired from his trip."

"Why, where's Mom?" said Anita, ditching the subject of Finnerty. Mom was Kroner's wife, whom he always brought to social functions, deposited with other wives, and ignored until the affectionate moment when it was time to retrieve her and cart her hundred and eighty pounds home.

"That intestinal thing that's been making the rounds," said Kroner gravely.

Everyone within hearing shook his or her head compassionately.

"Dinner," said a Philippino waiter. There had once been a movement to have the service done by machines, but the extremists who'd proposed this had been voted down by an overwhelming majority.

As Paul, Kroner, Baer, and Anita walked into the candlelit dining room, followed by the rest, four of the youngest engineers, the most recent arrivals, brushed past and turned to block the way.

Fred Berringer, a short, heavy, slit-eyed blond, seemed to be their leader. He was a wealthy, extroverted, dull boy from a good family of engineers and managers in Minneapolis. He had squeaked through college, and was just barely acceptable to the personnel machines. Ordinarily, nobody would have hired him. But Kroner, who knew his bloodlines, had taken him on anyway and sent him to Ilium to be trained. The break had done anything but teach him humility. He took it as evidence that his money and name could beat the system any time and, paraphrased, he'd said as much. The hell of it was that his attitude won grudging admiration from his fellow engineers, who had got their jobs the hard way. Paul supposed, gloomily, that beaters of systems had always been admired by the conventional. At any rate, Kroner still believed in the boy, so Paul had no choice but to keep him on, and to pair a smarter man with him to backstop his mental apparatus.

"What is this, Fred, a stickup?" said Paul.

"Checker champion," said Fred, "I hereby challenge you for the championship immediately after dinner."

Kroner and Baer seemed delighted. They were forever suggesting that teams be formed and games be played as a method for building morale in the Eastern Division's family.

"Just you, or all four of you?" said Paul. He was in fact the club checker champion, though there had never been any sort of official playoff. No one could beat him, and, wearily as often as not, he had had to prove his invincibility to each new group of engineers—like these four. It was a custom, and the close little society on the north side of the river seemed to feel the need of customs, of private jokes, of building up social characteristics to distinguish themselves—in their own eyes—from the rest of society. The checker game of the new engineers with Paul was one of the hoariest traditions, now in its seventh year.

"Me, mostly," said Berringer. "But all of us, in a way." The others laughed like conspirators. Apparently something special had been cooked up, and one or two of the older engineers seemed to be sharing in the high expectations.

"All right," said Paul good-humoredly; "if there were ten of you, and each one blowing cigar smoke in my face, I'd still win."

The four parted to let Paul, Anita, and the two guests of honor get to the table.

"Oh," said Anita, studying the place cards at the head of the table, "there's been a mistake." She picked up the card to her left, wadded it up, and handed it to Paul. She moved another card into the vacant position and sat down, flanked by Kroner and Baer. She called a waiter to take away the now extra place setting. Paul looked at the card and saw it was Finnerty's.

The assemblage was a practical, earthy one, and the shrimp cocktails, consommé, creamed chicken, peas, and mashed potatoes were enjoyed for their own sake. There was little talk, and much pantomimed savoring and beaming to show the hostess that everything tasted first rate.

Periodically, Kroner would comment on this dish or that, and he would be echoed by Baer, and then by nods about the table. Once, an argument broke out in loud whispers at the far end of the table, among the four youngsters who had challenged Paul to the checker game. When all eyes turned in their direction, they shut up. Berringer frowned, sketched a diagram of some sort on a napkin, and thrust it at the other three. One of them made a slight correction and handed it back. Understanding, then admiration, showed on Berringer's face. He nodded vigorously and went back to eating.

Paul counted around the table—twenty-seven managers and engineers, the staff of the Ilium Works and their wives, less the evening shift. There were two vacant places: one, the bare square of tablecloth once reserved for Finnerty; the other, the untouched setting for Shepherd, who had not come back from his hurried trip onto the golf course.

Finnerty was probably still lying in the bedroom, staring at the ceiling, perhaps talking to himself. Maybe he'd left soon after they had and gone on a bender or whoring expedition in Homestead. Paul hoped they'd seen the last of him for another few years. The brilliant liberal, the iconoclast, the freethinker he had admired in his youth now proved to be no more than sick, repellent. The quitting, the uninvited attack on Anita, the glorying in neuroses—all had a frightening cast to them. It was an awful disappointment. Paul had expected that Finnerty would be able to give him something—what, he didn't know—to assuage the nameless, aching need that had been nagging him almost, as Shepherd had apparently told Kroner, to the point of distraction.

As for Shepherd, Paul felt completely charitable, and even embarrassed that the man should be so upset at having been discovered as an informer. Paul stood.

"Where are you going, dear?" said Anita.

"To get Shepherd."

"He didn't say you were having a breakdown," said Baer.

Kroner frowned at Baer. "No, really he didn't, Paul. If you like, I'll go after him. It was my fault, bringing up the subject. It wasn't Shepherd, and the poor boy—"

"I just *thought* it was Shepherd," said Baer.

"I think it's up to me," said Paul.

"I'll come, too," said Anita. There was a promise of vengeance in her voice.

"No, I'd rather you wouldn't."

Paul headed through the bar quickly, and heard her coming after him.

"I wouldn't miss this for anything."

"There isn't going to be anything to miss," said Paul. "I'm simply going to tell him everything's O.K., I understand. And I do understand."

"He wants that Pittsburgh job, Paul. That's why he told Kroner you were having a breakdown. Now he's scared stiff for fear of losing his job. Good!"

"I'm not going to get him fired."

"You could keep him worrying for a while. It'd serve him right."

"Please, Anita—this is between Shepherd and me."

They stood on the turf of the golf course now, in a muffled world of blues and blacks under the frail light of a new moon. Seated on the bench by the first tee, his legs stretched out and far apart, was Shepherd, with three cocktail glasses lined up beside him.

"Shep," called Paul softly.

"Hello." It was flat, with nothing behind it.

"Beat it," whispered Paul to Anita. She stayed, clenching and unclenching her hands.

"Soup's getting cold," said Paul, as kindly as possible. He sat down on the bench, with the three glasses between them. "I don't give a damn whether you told them I was going to pieces or not." Anita stood a dozen yards away, silhouetted against the French doors.

"I'd rather you'd get sore as hell about it," said Sheperd. "I told them, all right. Go ahead and can me."

"Oh, for Christ's sake, Shep, nobody's going to can you."

Paul had never known what to make of Shepherd, had found it hard to believe that any man really thought as Shepherd did. When Shepherd had first arrived in Ilium, he had announced to his fellow new arrivals, Paul and Finnerty, that he intended to compete with them. Baldly, ridiculously, he talked of competitiveness and rehashed with anyone who would listen various crises where there had been a showdown between his abilities and those of someone else, crises that the other participants had looked upon as being routine, unremarkable, and generally formless. But, to Shepherd, life seemed to be laid out like a golf course, with a series of beginnings, hazards, and ends, and with a definite summing up—for comparison with others scores—after each hole. He was variously grim or elated over triumphs or failures no one else seemed to notice, but always stoical about the laws that governed the game. He asked no quarter, gave no quarter, and made very little difference to Paul, Finnerty, or any of his other associates. He was a fine engineer, dull company, and doggedly master of his fate and *not* his brother's keeper.

Paul, fidgeting silently on the bench, tried to put himself in Shepherd's place. Shepherd had lost a round, and now, grimly respectful of the mechanics of the competitive system, he wanted to pay the forfeit for losing and get on to the next episode, which he was, as always, determined to win. It was a hard world he lived in, but he wouldn't have it any other way. God knows why.

"Wanted to do me out of the Pittsburgh job, eh?" said Paul.

"I think I'm a better man for it," said Shepherd. "But what difference does that make now? I'm out of it."

"You lost."

"I *tried* and lost," said Shepherd. It was a vital distinction. "Go ahead and fire me."

The surest way to needle Shepherd was to refuse to compete. "I don't know," said Paul, "I think you'd be a good man for the Pittsburgh spot. If you like, I'll write a recommendation."

"Paul!" said Anita.

"Go back in, Anita," said Paul. "We'll be back in a minute." Anita seemed to be itching to give Shepherd just what he wanted, a rousing fight, something he could use as a starting point for another, as he saw it, cycle of play.

"I forgive you," said Paul. "I want you to go on working for me, if you will. There isn't a better man in the world for your job."

"You'd like to keep me right under your thumb, wouldn't you?"

Paul laughed bleakly. "No. It'd be just as before. Under my thumb? How could—"

"If you won't fire me, I want a transfer."

"All right. You know that isn't up to me. But let's go

inside, shall we?" He held out his hand as Shepherd stood. Shepherd refused it, and brushed by.

Anita stopped him. "If you have any opinions on my husband's health, perhaps he or his doctor should be the first to hear them," she said huskily.

"Your husband and his doctor have known for months what I told Kroner and Baer. He isn't in any shape to be trusted with a foot-treadle sewing machine, let alone Pittsburgh." He was warming up now, getting his spirit back, and perhaps seeing the possibilities of having their voices carry into the dining room.

Paul seized them both by their arms and propelled them into the bar and in view of the dinner party. All were looking questioningly in their direction. Paul, Anita, and Shepherd smiled, and crossed the bar to the dining room, arm in arm.

"Under the weather?" said Kroner to Shepherd kindly.

"Yessir. Scallops for lunch did it, I think."

Kroner nodded sympathetically and turned to the waiter. "Could the boy have milk toast, do you suppose?" Kroner was willing to go to any lengths to preserve harmony in his family, to give a man in a tight spot a way out. For the rest of the evening, Paul supposed, Kroner would be keeping alive—as with the milk toast now—the polite fiction of Shepherd's illness.

After coffee and a liqueur, Paul gave a brief talk on the integration of the Ilium Works with other industry under the National Manufacturing Council fourteen years before. And then he went into the more general subject of what he called the Second Industrial Revolution. He read the talk, rather, taking pains to look up from his manuscript at regular intervals. It was, as he had told Katharine Finch in the office that afternoon, old stuff—a progress report, a reaffirmation of faith in what they were doing and had done with industry. Machines were doing America's work far better than Americans had ever done it. There were better goods for more people at less cost, and who could deny that that was magnificent and gratifying? It was what everyone said when he had to make a talk.

At one point, Kroner raised his big hand and asked if he might make a comment. "Just to sort of underline what you're saying, Paul, I'd like to point out something I thought was rather interesting. One horsepower equals about twenty-two manpower—*big* manpower. If you convert the horsepower of one of the bigger steel-mill motors into terms of manpower, you'll find that the motor does more work than the entire slave population of the United States at the time of the Civil War could do—and do it twenty-four hours a day." He smiled beatifically. Kroner was the rock, the fountainhead of faith and pride for all in the Eastern Division.

"That *is* an interesting figure," said Paul, searching for his place in the manuscript. "And that, of course, simply applies to the First Industrial Revolution, where machines devalued muscle work. The second revolution, the one we're now completing, is a little tougher to express in terms of work saved. If there were some measure like horsepower in which we could express annoyance or boredom that people used to experience in routine jobs—but there isn't."

"You can measure rejects, I'm here to tell you," said Baer, "and the darnedest, stupidest mistakes imaginable. The waste, the stoppages, the lemons! You can express it in dollars all right, dollars that went into bad workmanship."

"Yes," said Paul, "but I was thinking of it from the worker's point of view. The two industrial revolutions eliminated two kinds of drudgery, and I was looking for some way of estimating just how much the second revolution had relieved men of."

"I work," said Baer. Everyone laughed.

"The others—across the river," said Paul.

"They never did work," said Kroner, and again everyone laughed.

"And they're reproducing like rabbits," said Anita.

"Somebody telling dirty jokes about rabbits reproducing?" said Finnerty, standing in the doorway. He swayed slightly, and his breathing was shallow. He had evidently found the whiskey. "Which one was it? Where the little girl rabbit went into the rabbit hardware store, and the clerk—"

Kroner was on his feet. "Well, Finnerty—how are you, my boy?" He summoned the waiter. "You're just in time for coffee, my boy—a big cup of black coffee." He put his huge arm around Finnerty and steered him to the place that Anita had had cleared. Finnerty picked up the place card of the engineer next to him, squinted at it, then at the man. "Where's *my* goddamn place card?"

"Give him his place card, for heaven's sakes," said Anita.

Paul took it from his pocket, smoothed it out, and set it before Finnerty. Finnerty nodded, and fell into a morose silence.

"We were just talking about the Second Industrial Revolution," said Kroner, as though nothing were amiss. "Paul was talking about how there is no real measure of the kind of drudgery it has eliminated. I think the story can be told in terms of a curve, perhaps—as most stories can be presented most clearly."

"Not the one about the little girl rabbit in the rabbit hardware store," said Finnerty.

Everyone, following Kroner's example, ignored him. "If we plot man hours worked against the number of vacuum tubes in use, the man hours worked drop as the tubes increase."

"Like rabbits," said Finnerty.

Kroner smiled. "As you say, like rabbits. Incidentally, Paul, another interesting sidelight your father probably told you about is how people didn't pay much attention to this, as you call it, Second Industrial Revolution for quite some time. Atomic energy was hogging the headlines, and everybody talked as though peacetime uses of atomic energy were going to remake the world. The Atomic Age, that was the big thing to look forward to. Remember, Baer? And meanwhile, the tubes increased like rabbits."

"And dope addiction, alcoholism, and suicide went up proportionately," said Finnerty.

"Ed!" said Anita.

"That was the war," said Kroner soberly. "It happens after every war."

"And organized vice and divorce and juvenile delinquency, all parallel the growth of the use of vacuum tubes," said Finnerty.

"Oh, come on, Ed," said Paul, "you can't prove a logical connection between those factors."

"If there's the slightest connection, it's worth thinking about," said Finnerty.

"I'm sure there isn't enough connection for us to be concerned with here," said Kroner severely.

"Or enough imagination or honesty," said Finnerty.

"Oh, honestly! What are you talking about?" said Anita. She wadded her napkin nervously. "Come on—shall we leave this gloomy place and have the checker championship?"

The response was sighs and grateful nods all around the table. With little regret, Paul laid the remainder of his speech aside. The party, save for Finnerty, swept into the club's game room, where a checkerboard had already been set up, and where a battery of floor lamps ringed the table on which it rested, immaculate and glaring.

The four challengers trotted ahead, held a hurried conference, and three of them went to the checkroom. The fourth, Fred Berringer, sat down at the board and grinned mysteriously.

Paul took the chair opposite. "Play much?" he said.

"A little, a little."

"Let's see, Fred, you're from Minnesota, aren't you? Is

the Minnesota checker championship by any chance at stake, Fred?"

"Sorry, I've got the club championship to win, and nothing to lose."

"You're going to lose, going to lose," said Baer. "They all do, all do, all of them do, eh Paul? All lose to you."

"Modesty forbids that I answer," said Paul. "My record speaks for itself." He permitted himself a mild sort of elation over his invincibility. There would be some bizarre twist to tonight's game, judging from the activity in the checkroom, but he wasn't worried.

"Make way for Checker Charley! Make way for Checker Charley!" shouted Berringer's seconds from the foyer.

The crowd in the gameroom parted, and the three rolled in a man-high box that was shrouded in a bedsheet and grumbled along on casters.

"There's a man in there?" said Kroner.

"A brain, a brain," said Berringer triumphantly. "Checker Charley, world's champion checker player, and looking for new planets to conquer." He grabbed a corner of the bedsheet, and unveiled Charley—a gray steel box with a checkerboard painted on its front panel. In each square that could be occupied by a checkerpiece were a red and a green jewel, each with a lamp behind it.

"Pleased to meet you, Charley," said Paul, trying to smile. When he realized what was going on, he felt himself reddening and getting a little mad. His first inclination was to walk the hell out.

Baer had the back of the box open. "Oh, oh, my, yes indeed," he said. "Look, look, look, and that goes over to there—and oh! Ha! Oh, my, I believe it's even got a memory. Isn't that what the tape's for, boys, huh? Memory? Tape memory?"

"Yessir," said Berringer uncertainly. "I guess so."

"You built this?" said Kroner incredulously.

"Nossir," said Berringer, "my father. His hobby."

"Berringer, Berringer, Berringer," said Baer, frowning.

"You know—*Dave* Berringer; this is Dave's boy," said Kroner.

"Oh!" Baer looked at Checker Charley with new admiration. "By George, no wonder, no wonder, no wonder." Fred's father, one of the top computing-machine men in the country, had built it.

Paul slouched in his chair resignedly and waited for the comedy to begin. He looked at young Berringer's dull, complacent face, and was sure that the youngster didn't know much more about the machine than its external switches and signals.

Finnerty strolled in from the dining room, eating from a plate he held at chin level. He set his plate atop the cabinet and stuck his head into the back, alongside Baer's. "Any money on this?" he said.

"Are you crazy?" said Paul.

"Anything you say, boy; anything you say," said Berringer. He laid his fat billfold on the table.

The other three youngsters had plugged a cord from Checker Charley into an outlet in the baseboard; and now, as they flicked switches on and off, the box hummed and clicked, and lights on the front panel winked off and on.

Paul stood. "I concede," he said. He patted the box. "Congratulations, Charles, you're a better man than I am. Ladies and gentlemen, I give you the new club champion." He started out toward the bar.

"Darling," said Anita, catching his sleeve. "Oh, come on now, that isn't like you."

"I can't win against the damn thing. It can't make a mistake."

"You can at least play against it."

"And prove what?"

"Come on, Paul," said Finnerty, "I've looked Charley

over, and he doesn't look so all-fired bright to me. I've got fifty dollars on you with Goldilocks here, and I'll cover anybody else who thinks Checker Charley's got a chance."

Eagerly, Shepherd slapped down three twenties. Finnerty covered him.

"Bet the sun won't rise tomorrow," said Paul.

"Play," said Finnerty.

Paul settled into his chair again. Dispiritedly, he pushed a checkerpiece forward. One of the youngsters closed a switch, and a light blinked on, indicating Paul's move on Checker Charley's bosom, and another light went on, indicating the perfect countermove for Berringer.

Berringer smiled and did what the machine told him to do. He lit a cigarette and patted the pile of currency beside him.

Paul moved again. A switch was closed, and the lights twinkled appropriately. And so it went for several moves.

To Paul's surprise, he took one of Berringer's pieces without, as far as he could see, laying himself open to any sort of disaster. And then he took another piece, and another. He shook his head in puzzlement and respect. The machine apparently took a long-range view of the game, with a grand strategy not yet evident. Checker Charley, as though confirming his thoughts, made an ominous hissing noise, which grew in volume as the game progressed.

"As of now, I am offering odds of three to one against Checker Charley," said Finnerty. Berringer and Shepherd both took him up on it for another twenty apiece.

Paul exchanged one man for three.

"Say—now wait just a minute," said Berringer.

"Wait for what?" said Finnerty.

"Something's wrong."

"You and Checker Charley are being beaten is all. Somebody always wins, and somebody always loses," said Finnerty. "That's the way it goes."

"Sure, but if Checker Charley was working right he couldn't lose." Berringer arose unsteadily. "Listen, we'd better call this thing off while we find out what's wrong." He tapped the front panel experimentally. "Jesus Christ, he's hot as a frying pan!"

"Finish the game, Junior. I want to know who's champ," said Finnerty.

"Don'tcha see!" said Berringer furiously. "It isn't working right." He looked pleadingly around the room.

"Your move," said Paul.

Berringer looked helplessly at the lights, slid a man forward.

Paul took two more of Berringer's pieces and made his own piece a king. "This must be the trickiest booby trap in history," he laughed. He was enjoying himself immensely.

"Any minute now, Checker Charley's going to see his opening, and then it's going to be bye-bye championship," said Finnerty. "Hop, hop, hop, hoppity hop. Curtains, Paul."

"Calculus is a wonderful thing," said Paul. He sniffed. The air was getting heavy with a smell like burning paint, and his eyes were beginning to smart.

One of Berringer's seconds jerked open the back of the box, and smoke, colored a poisonous green by the glare from within, poured into the room.

"Fire!" cried Baer.

A waiter came running with a fire extinguisher and sent a jet of fluid into Checker Charley's entrails. Steam billowed up as the jet fizzed and sputtered on the glowing parts.

The lights on Charley's steel bosom were skittering about the board wildly now, playing a demoniacal and swift game according to rules only the machine could understand. All the lights went on at once, a hum swelled louder and louder, until it sounded like a thunderous organ note, and suddenly died. One by one, the little lamps winked out, like a village going to sleep.

"Oh my, my, oh my," murmured Baer.

"Fred, I'm so sorry," said Anita. She looked reproach-fully at Paul.

The engineers crowded around Checker Charley, and those in the front rank probed through the ashes, melted tubes, and blackened wires. Tragedy was in every face. Something beautiful had died.

"Such a lovely thing," said Kroner sadly, resting his hand on Berringer's shoulder. "If you like, perhaps things would go easier if I told your father what happened."

"It was practically his life—away from the laboratory," said Berringer. He was shocked and scared. "Years and years. Why did it have to happen?" It was one more hollow echo to the question humanity had been asking for millenniums, the question men were seemingly born to ask.

"The Lord giveth, and the Lord taketh away," said Finnerty.

Berringer bit his lip and nodded, until it began to dawn on him just who it was that had spoken. His round, stupid face slowly took on a mean, threatening cast. "Uh-huh," he said, licking his lips, "the wise guy. Almost forgot about you."

"Well, you'd better not. I've got a lot of money bet on who's going to win."

"Now, see here, Finnerty," said Kroner placatingly, "let's call it a draw, shall we? I mean, after all, the boy's got a right to be upset, and—"

"Draw, hell," said Finnerty. "Paul beat Checker Charley fair and square."

"I'm beginning to see, I think," said Berringer menacingly. He gathered Finnerty's lapels in his hands. "What'd you do to Checker Charley, wise guy?"

"Ask Baer. His head was in there with mine. Baer, did I do anything to Charley?"

"What, eh? Do anything, do anything? Damage, you mean? No, no, no," said Baer.

"So sit down and finish the game, fat boy," said Finnerty. "Or concede. Either way, I want my money."

"If you didn't do anything to Charley, how come you were so sure he'd lose?"

"Because my sympathy's with any man up against a machine, especially a machine backing up a knucklehead like you against a man like Paul. Besides, Charley had a loose connection."

"Then you should have said so!" said Berringer. He gestured at the ruins of the machine. "Look—just look, will you? Look what you did by not telling me about the connection. I ought to mop this place up with your dirty face."

"Now, now, now—there, there," said Kroner, stepping between the two. "You should have said something about that connection, Ed. This is a shame, a real shame."

"If Checker Charley was out to make chumps out of men, he could damn well fix his own connections. Paul looks after his own circuits; let Charley do the same. Those who live by electronics, die by electronics. *Sic semper tyrannis.*" He gathered up the bills from the table. "Good night."

Anita dug her fingernails into Paul's arm. "Oh Paul, Paul, he's ruined the whole evening."

On his way out, Finnerty paused by Paul and Anita. "Nice going, champ."

"Please give them their money back," said Anita. "The machine wasn't working right. Be fair. Isn't that right, Paul?"

To the amazement of the whole somber group, Paul lost control and burst out laughing.

"That's the spirit, champ," said Finnerty. "I'm going home now, before these gentlemen sportsmen find a rope."

"Home? Washington?" said Anita.

"Your house, dear. I haven't got a place in Washington any more."

Anita closed her eyes. "Oh, I see."

6

"Wʜᴀᴛ ᴡᴀs ʜɪs expression like when he said it?" said Anita.

Paul had the comforter pulled up over his face and was trying to get to sleep tightly curled in the dark, muffled womb he made of his bed each night. "He looked sad," he murmured. "But he always looks sad—real sweet and sad."

For three hours they had been going over the events of the evening at the club, coming back again and again to what Kroner had said by way of farewell.

"And he didn't take you aside for a couple of words at any time?" She was wide awake.

"Scout's honor, Anita, all he said was what he said at the last."

She repeated Kroner's words judiciously, " 'I want you to come see me and Mom sometime next week, Paul.' "

"That's all."

"Nothing about Pittsburgh?"

"No," he said patiently. "I tell you, no." He tucked the comforter more snugly around his head and pulled his knees up higher. "No."

"Haven't I got a right to be interested?" she said. He'd evidently hurt her. "Is that what you're telling me, that I haven't the right to care?"

"Gladja care," he said thickly. "Fine, wonderful, thanks." In the quasi nightmare of being only half asleep, he visualized the notion of man and wife as one flesh—a physical monstrosity, pathetic, curious, and helpless Siamese twins.

"Women *do* have insight into things that men don't have," she was saying. "We notice important things that men let go by. Kroner wanted *you* to break the ice about Pittsburgh tonight, and you just—"

"We'll find out what Kroner has on his mind when I call on him. Now, please, let's sleep."

"Finnerty!" she said. "He's the one who threw a monkey wrench into things. Honestly! How long is he going to stay?"

"He'll get sick of us in a couple of days, the way he gets sick of anything."

"The N.I.P.B. mustn't leave him much time to go traipsing over the country to insult old friends."

"He quit. Hasn't got a job."

She sat up in bed. "They fired him! Well, good for them."

"Quit. They offered him a raise to stay. His idea." He found himself awakened by a subject that interested him. Anita's hammering at the subject of Pittsburgh had tended to make him curl up tighter and tighter. Now he felt himself relaxing somewhat, straightening out like a man. Finnerty was a magical name again; Paul's feelings about him had swung a full circle. Morale and *esprit de corps*, which Paul hadn't felt in any undertaking for years, had sprung up between them in the course of the exhilarating humiliation of Checker Charley. Moreover—Paul's thoughts were coming alive as though refreshed by a cool wind—there was enchantment in what Finnerty had done, a thing almost as inconceivable and beautifully simple as suicide: he'd quit.

"Paul . . ."

"Hmmmm?"

"Your father thought you'd be manager of Pittsburgh someday. If he were alive, nothing would make him happier than to know you got the job."

"Umm hmmmm." He remembered how Anita, shortly after their marriage, had dug up a picture of his father from a trunk and had had it enlarged and framed as her first birthday present to him. The picture was over on his bureau now, where she had put it—where he could see it the first thing in the morning and the last thing at night. She had never met Paul's father, and he hadn't said much about him to her; yet she'd built up a kind of mythology about the man that could keep her talking knowingly for hours. The myth had it that Paul's father in his youth had been just as easygoing as Paul, and that the strength that got him to the top job in the economy came in the middle years of his life—came in the years Paul was just beginning.

Kroner, too, kept alive the notion that Paul could be expected to follow in his father's footsteps. This faith of Kroner's had had a lot to do with Paul's getting to be manager of Ilium; and now that faith might get him the managership of Pittsburgh. When Paul thought about his effortless rise in the hierarchy, he sometimes, as now, felt sheepish, like a charlatan. He could handle his assignments all right, but he didn't have what his father had, what Kroner had, what Shepherd had, what so many had: the sense of spiritual importance in what they were doing; the ability to be moved emotionally, almost like a lover, by the great omnipresent and omniscient spook, the corporate personality. In short, Paul missed what made his father aggressive and great: the capacity to really give a damn.

"What are you going to do about Shepherd?" said Anita.

Paul started to curl up again. "Do? I've already done it. Nothing."

"If somebody doesn't clip his wings, he's going right over everybody's heads one of these days."

"Welcome to."

"You don't mean that."

"I mean I want to sleep."

Her bedsprings creaked as she lay down once more. She shifted her weight about restlessly for several minutes. "You know, it's a funny thing," she said.

"Hmmmm?"

"I've always noticed that when Shepherd turned his face a certain way, he looked an awful lot like somebody else. And it wasn't until tonight that I figured out who it was."

"Mmmm."

"When you see him at just the right angle, he's the spitting image of your father."

7

PRIVATE FIRST CLASS ELMO C. HACKETTS, JR., approached the Shah of Bratpuhr, Doctor Ewing J. Halyard, of the State Department, Khashdrahr Miasma, their interpreter, General of the Armies Milford S. Bromley, General William K. Corbett, camp commander, Major General Earl Pruitt, division commander, and their aides.

Private First Class Hacketts was in the middle of the First Squad of the Second Platoon of B Company of the First Battalion of the 427th Regiment of the 107th Infantry Division of the Ninth Corps of the Twelfth Army, and he stayed right there, and put his left foot down every time the drummer hit the bass drum.

"Dee-veesh-ee-own—" cried the Division Commander through a loudspeaker.

"Reg-ee-ment—" bawled four regimental commanders.

" 'Tal-ee-own—" cried twelve battalion commanders.

"Cump-neee—" shouted thirty-six company commanders.

"Batt-reeee—" shouted twelve battery commanders.

"P'toon—" muttered a hundred and ninety-two platoon commanders.

"Hacketts," said Private First Class Hacketts to himself. "Halt!"

And Hacketts did, hut, two.

"Ri-yut—" said the loudspeaker.

"Right, right, right, right, right, right . . ." echoed two hundred and fifty-six voices.

"Right," said Private First Class Hacketts to himself. "Fay-yuss!"

Hacketts faced right, hut, two. And he stared into the small, bright eyes of the Shah of Bratpuhr, spiritual leader of 6,000,000 people somewhere else.

The Shah bowed slightly from the waist.

Hacketts did not bow back because he wasn't supposed to and he wasn't going to do a goddamn thing he wasn't supposed to do and he had only twenty-three more years to go on his hitch and then he was through with the Army and the hell with it, and in twenty-three years if some sonofabitching colonel or lieutenant or general came up to him and said, "Salute me," or "Pick up that butt," or "Shine your shoes," or something like that he'd say, "Kiss my ass, sonny," and whip out the old discharge and spit in his eye and walk away laughing like crazy because his twenty-five years was up and all he had to do was hang around with the old gang in Hooker's in Evansville and wait for the old pension check and to hell with you buddy because I don't have to take no crap from nobody no more because I'm through and—

The Shah clapped his hands delightedly and continued to stare at Private First Class Hacketts, who was a huge, healthy man. *"Niki Takaru!"* he cried, exhaling a strong effluvium of *Sumklish.*

"No *Takaru!*" said Doctor Halyard. "Sol-dee-yers."

"No Takaru?" said the Shah in puzzlement.

"What's he say?" said General of the Armies Bromley.

"Said they're a fine bunch of slaves," said Halyard. He turned to the Shah again and waggled his finger at the small, dark man. "No *Takaru*. No, no, no."

Khashdrahr seemed baffled, too, and offered Halyard no help in clarifying the point.

"Sim koula Takaru, akka sahn salet?" said the Shah to Khashdrahr.

Khashdrahr shrugged and looked questioningly at Halyard. "Shah says, if these not slaves, how you get them to do what they do?"

"Patriotism," said General of the Armies Bromley sternly. "Patriotism, damn it."

"Love of country," said Halyard.

Khashdrahr told the Shah, and the Shah nodded slightly, but his look of puzzlement did not disappear. *"Sidi ba—"* he said tentatively.

"Eh?" said Corbett.

"Even so—" translated Khashdrahr, and he looked as doubtful as the Shah.

"Lay-eft—" shouted the loudspeaker.

"Left, left, left, left, left, left . . ."

"Left," said Hacketts to himself.

And Hacketts thought of how he was going to be left alone in the barracks this week end when everybody else was out on pass because of what happened in inspection that morning after he'd mopped and squeegeed the floor and washed the windows by his bunk and tightened up his blankets and made sure the tooth-paste tube was to the *left* of the shaving-cream tube and the tube caps both pointed *away* from the aisle and that the cuffs on his rolled-up socks pointed *up* in his footlocker and that his mess kit and mess cup and mess spoon and mess fork and mess knife and canteen were shining and that his wooden rifle was waxed and its simulated metalwork blackened and his shoes shined and that the extra pair under his bunk were laced to the *top* and tied and that the clothes on his hangers went: two shirts, O.D.;

two pants, O.D.; three shirts, khaki; three pants, khaki; two shirts, herringbone twill; two pants, herringbone twill; field jacket; dress blouse, O.D.; raincoat, O.D.; and that all the pockets were empty and buttoned and then the inspecting officer came through and said, "Hey soldier, your fly's open and no pass for you," and—

"Fay-yuss."

"Hut, two," said Hacketts.

"For'd—"

"For'd, for'd, for'd, for'd, for'd for'd . . ."

"For'd," said Hacketts to himself.

And Hacketts wondered where the hell he'd go in the next twenty-three years and thought it'd be a relief to get the hell out of the States for a while and go occupy someplace else and maybe be somebody in some of those countries instead of a bum with no money looking for an easy lay and not getting it in his own country or not getting a good lay anyway but still a pretty good lay compared to no lay at all but anyway there was more to living than laying and he'd like a little glory by God and there might be laying *and* glory overseas and while there wasn't any shooting and wasn't going to be none either probably for a good long while still you got a real gun and bullets and there was a little glory in that and sure as hell it was more grownup than marching up and down with a wooden one and he'd sure like a little rank too but he knew what his I.Q. was and everybody else did too and especially the machines so that was that for twenty-three more years unless one of the machines burned out a tube and misread his card and sent him to O.C.S. and that happened now and then and there was old Mulcahy who got ahold of his card and doctored it with an icepick so the machines would think he was qualified for a big promotion but he got restricted to barracks instead for having clap twenty-six times and then transferred to the band as a trombone player when he couldn't even whistle "Hot Cross Buns" and anyway it was better than the frigging Reeks and Wrecks any day and

no big worries and a nice-looking suit only the pants ought
to have zippers and in only twenty-three more years he could
go up to some sonofabitching general or colonel or something and say, "Kiss my—"

"Harch!"

"Boom!" went the bass drum, and down came Hack-
etts' left foot, and off he went in the midst of the vast, tracta-
ble human avalanche.

"Takaru," said the Shah to Khashdrahr above the din.

Khashdrahr nodded and smiled agreement. *"Takaru."*

"What the hell am I supposed to do?" said Halyard
unhappily to General of the Armies Bromley. "This guy
thinks of everything he sees in terms of his own country, and
his own country must be a Goddamn mess."

*"Amerikka vagga bouna, ni houri manko Salim da vagga
dinko,"* said the Shah.

"What's eating him now?" said Halyard impatiently.

"He say Americans have changed almost everything on
earth," said Khashdrahr, "but it would be easier to move the
Himalayas than to change the Army."

The Shah was waving goodbye to the departing troops.
"Dibo, Takaru, dibo."

8

PAUL BREAKFASTED ALONE, while Anita and Finnerty,
in widely separated beds, slept late after a busy evening.

He had difficulty starting his Plymouth and finally realized that it was out of gas. There had been almost a half-tank the afternoon before. Finnerty, then, had gone for a long ride in it after they'd left him alone on the bed and gone to the Country Club without him.

Paul rummaged about the glove compartment for a siphon hose, and found it. He paused, sensing that something was missing. He stuck his hand into the glove compartment again and felt around inside. The old pistol was gone. He looked on the floor and searched behind the seat cushion without finding it. Perhaps some urchin had taken it while he'd been in Homestead after the whisky. He'd have to tell the police about it right away, and there'd be all sorts of forms to fill out. He tried to think of a lie that would get him out of accusations of negligence and not get anybody else in trouble.

He dipped the siphon hose into the station wagon's tank, sucked and spat, and plunged the other end of the hose into the Plymouth's empty tank. As he waited for the slow transfer to take place, he stepped out of the garage and into a warm patch of sunlight.

The bathroom window above clattered open, and he looked up to see Finnerty staring at himself in the medicine-cabinet mirror. Finnerty didn't notice Paul. He had a bent cigarette in his mouth, and there it remained while he washed his face with a cursory and random dabbing motion. The ash on the cigarette grew longer and longer, and, incredibly, longer, until the coal was almost at his lips. He removed the cigarette from his mouth, and the long ash fell. Finnerty flipped the butt in the direction of the toilet, replaced it with another, and proceeded to shave. And the ash grew longer and longer. He leaned close to the mirror, and the ash broke against it. He pressed a pimple between his thumb and forefinger, seemingly without results. Still squinting in the mirror at the reddened spot, he groped for a towel with one hand, seized one without looking at it, and swept Anita's stockings from the towel rack and into the bathtub. Finnerty, his toilet complete, said something to his reflection, grimaced, and made his exit.

Paul returned to the garage, coiled the siphon hose in the glove compartment, and drove off. The car was hesitating again—catching and slowing, catching and slowing. At any rate, it took his mind momentarily from the inconvenient matter of the missing pistol. On the long grade past the golf course, the engine seemed to be hitting on no more than three cylinders, and a squad from the Reconstruction and Reclamation Corps, putting in a spruce windbreak to the north of the clubhouse, turned to watch the car's enervated struggle with gravity.

"Hey! Headlamp's busted," called one of the men.

Paul nodded and smiled his thanks. The car faltered, and came to a stop, just short of the summit. Paul set his emergency brake and got out. He lifted the hood and tested various connections. Tools being laid against the side of the car made a clattering noise, and a half-dozen Reeks and Wrecks stuck their heads under the hood with his.

"It's his plugs," said a small, bright-eyed, Italian-looking man.

"Aaaaaaah, in a pig's ass it's his plugs," said a tall, ruddy-faced man, the oldest of the group. "Lemme show you where the real trouble is. Here, that wrench, that's the ticket." He went to work on the fuel pump, soon had the top off of it. He pointed to the gasket beneath the cap. "There," he said soberly, like an instructor in surgery, "there's your trouble. Sucking air. I knew that the minute I heard you coming a mile off."

"Well," said Paul, "guess I'd better call somebody to come and get it. Probably take a week to order a new gasket."

"Five minutes," said the tall man. He took off his hat and, with an expression of satisfaction, ripped out the sweatband. He took a penknife from his pocket, laid the cap of the fuel pump over the sweatband, and cut out a leather disk just the right size. Then he cut out the disk's center, dropped the new gasket in place, and put the pump back together. The others watched eagerly, handed him tools, or offered to hand him tools, and tried to get into the operation wherever they could. One man scraped the green and white crystals from a battery connection. Another one went around tightening the valve caps on the tires.

"Now try her!" said the tall man.

Paul stepped on the starter, the motor caught, roared fast and slow without a miss as he pumped the accelerator. He looked up to see the profound satisfaction, the uplift of creativity, in the faces of the Reeks and Wrecks.

Paul took out his billfold and handed two fives to the tall man.

"One'll do," he said. He folded it carefully and tucked it into the breast pocket of his blue workshirt. He smiled sardonically. "First money I've earned in five years. I oughta frame that one, eh?" He looked closely at Paul, for the first time aware of the man and not his motor. "Seems like I know you from somewhere. What's your line?"

Something made Paul want to be someone other than who he was. "Got a little grocery store," he said.

"Need a guy who's handy with his hands?"

"Not just now. Things are pretty slow."

The man was scrawling something on a piece of paper. He held the paper against the hood, and twice punched his pencil through the paper as the pencil crossed a crack. "Here—here's my name. If you've got machines, I'm the guy that can keep them going. Put in eight years in the works as a millwright before the war, and anything I don't know, I pick up fast." He handed the paper to Paul. "Where you going to put it?"

Paul slipped the paper under the transparent window in his billfold, over his driver's license. "There—right on top." He shook the man's hand and nodded to the others. "Thanks."

The motor took hold with assurance and swept Paul over the hilltop and up to the gate of the Ilium Works. A watchman waved from his pillbox, a buzzer sounded, and the iron, high-spiked gate swung open. He came now to the solid inner door, honked, and looked expectantly at a thin slit in the masonry, behind which another guard sat. The door rumbled upward, and Paul drove up to his office building.

He went up the steps two at a time—his only exercise—and unlocked two outer doors that led him into Katharine's office, and beyond that, his own.

Katharine hardly looked up when he came in. She seemed lost in melancholy, and, on the other side of the room, on the couch that was virtually his, Bud Calhoun was staring at the floor.

"Can I help?" said Paul.

Katharine sighed. "Bud wants a job."

"Bud wants a job? He's got the fourth-highest-paid job in Ilium now. I couldn't equal what he gets for running the depot. Bud, you're crazy. When I was your age, I didn't make half—"

"Ah want a job," said Bud. "Any job."

"Trying to scare the National Petroleum Council into giving you a raise? Sure, Bud, I'll make you an offer better than what you're getting, but you've got to promise not to take me up on it."

"Ah haven't got a job any more," said Bud. "Canned."

Paul was amazed. "Really? What on earth for? Moral turpitude? What about the gadget you invented for—"

"Thet's it," said Bud with an eerie mixture of pride and remorse. "Works. Does a fine job." He smiled sheepishly. "Does it a whole lot better than Ah did it."

"It runs the whole operation?"

"Yup. Some gadget."

"And so you're out of a job."

"Seventy-two of us are out of jobs," said Bud. He

slumped even lower in the couch. "Ouah job classification has been eliminated. Poof." He snapped his fingers.

Paul could see the personnel manager pecking out Bud's job code number on a keyboard, and seconds later having the machine deal him seventy-two cards bearing the names of those who did what Bud did for a living—what Bud's machine now did better. Now, personnel machines all over the country would be reset so as no longer to recognize the job as one suited for men. The combination of holes and nicks that Bud had been to personnel machines would no longer be acceptable. If it were to be slipped into a machine, it would come popping right back out.

"They don't need P-128's any more," said Bud bleakly, "and nothing's open above or below. Ah'd take a cut, and go back to P-129 or even P-130, but it's no dice. Everything's full up."

"Got any other numbers, Bud?" said Paul. "The only P-numbers we're authorized are—"

Katharine had the *Manual* open before her. She'd already looked the numbers up. "P-225 and P-226—lubrication engineers," she said. "And Doctor Rosenau's got both of those."

"That's right, he does," said Paul. Bud was in a baffling mess, and Paul didn't see how he could help him. The machines knew the Ilium Works had its one allotted lubrication engineer, and they wouldn't tolerate a second. If Bud were recorded as a lubrication engineer and introduced into the machines, they'd throw him right out again.

As Kroner often said, eternal vigilance was the price of efficiency. And the machines tirelessly riffled through their decks again and again and again in search of foot draggers, free riders, and misfits.

"You know it isn't up to me, Bud," said Paul. "I haven't got any real say about who's taken on."

"He knows that," said Katharine. "But he has to start

somewhere, and we thought maybe you'd know of some opening, or who to see."

"Oh, it makes me sore," said Paul. "Whatever got into them to give you a Petroleum Industries assignment, anyway? You should be in design."

"Got no aptitude for it," said Bud. "Tests proved that."

That would be on his ill-fated card, too. All his aptitude-test grades were on it—irrevocably, immutable, and the card knew best. "But you *do* design," said Paul. "And you do it with a damn sight more imagination than the prima donnas in the Lab." The Lab was the National Research and Development Laboratory, which was actually a war-born conglomeration of all the country's research and development facilities under a single headquarters. "You're not even paid to design, and still you do a better job of it than they do. That telemetering arrangement for the pipeline, your car, and now this monster that runs the depot—"

"But the test says no," said Bud.

"So the machines say no," said Katharine.

"So that's that," said Bud. "Ah guess."

"You might see Kroner," said Paul.

"Ah tried, and didn't get past his secretary. Ah told her Ah was after a job, and she called up Personnel. They ran mah card through the machines while she held the phone; and then she hung up, and looked sad, and said Kroner had meetings all month."

"Maybe your university can help," said Paul. "Maybe the grading machine needed new tubes when it went over your development aptitude test." He spoke without conviction. Bud was beyond help. As an old old joke had it, the machines had all the cards.

"Ah've written, asking them to check my grades again. No matter what Ah say, Ah get the same thing back." He threw a piece of graph paper on Katharine's desk. "Theah. Ah've written three letters, and gotten three of these back."

"Uh-huh," said Paul, looking at the familiar graph with

distaste. It was a so-called Achievement and Aptitude Profile, and every college graduate got one along with his sheepskin. And the sheepskin was nothing, and the graph was everything. When time for graduation came, a machine took a student's grades and other performances and integrated them into one graph—the profile. Here Bud's graph was high for theory, there low for administration, here low for creativity, and so on, up and down across the page to the last quality—*personality*. In mysterious, unnamed units of measure, each graduate was credited with having a high, medium, or low personality. Bud, Paul saw, was a strong medium, as the expression went, personality-wise. When the graduate was taken into the economy, all his peaks and valleys were translated into perforations on his personnel card.

"Well, thanks anyway," said Bud suddenly, gathering up his papers, as though embarrassed at having been so weak as to bother anyone with his troubles.

"Something will turn up," said Paul. He paused at his office door. "How are you fixed for money?"

"They're keepin' me on a few more months, until all the new equipment gets installed. And Ah've got the award from the suggestion system."

"Well, thank God you got something out of it. How much?"

"Five hundred. It's the biggest one this year."

"Congratulations. Is that on your card?"

Bud held the rectangle of cardboard up to the window and squinted at the nicks and perforations. "Think thet little devil raht there's it."

"That's for your smallpox vaccination," said Katharine, looking over his shoulder. "I've got one of those."

"No, the little triangle next to thet one."

Katharine's phone rang. "Yes?" She turned to Paul. "A Doctor Finnerty is at the gate and wants in."

"If it's just to shoot the bull, tell him to wait until late this afternoon."

"He says he wants to see the plant, not you."

"All right; let him in."

"They're shorthanded at the gate," said Katharine. "One of the guards is down with flu. What'll they do about an escort for him?"

The few visitors that did get admitted to the Ilium Works were taken about by guides, who only incidentally pointed out the wonders of the place. The guides were armed, and their main job was to see that no one got close enough to vital controls to knock them out. The system was a holdover from the war, and from the postwar riot period, but it still made sense. Every so often, antisabotage laws not-withstanding, someone got it into his head to jimmy some-thing. It hadn't happened in Ilium for years, but Paul had heard reports from other works—reports of a visitor with a crude bomb in a briefcase in Syracuse; of an old lady in Buffalo stepping from a group of sightseers to jam her um-brella into some vital clockwork. . . . Things like that still happened, and Kroner had stipulated that visitors to plants should be watched every second. The saboteurs had come from every walk of life—including, in at least one hushed-up instance, the brass. As Kroner had said, you never could tell who was going to try it next.

"Oh, what the hell, let Finnerty in without an escort," said Paul. "He's a special case—an old Ilium man."

"The directive said no exceptions," said Katharine. She knew all of the directives—and there were thousands of them—cold.

"Let him roam."

"Yessir."

Bud Calhoun watched the interchange with far more interest than it merited, Paul thought. It was as though they had been putting on an absorbing drama. When Katharine hung up she mistook his gaze for adoration and returned it warmly.

"Six minutes," said Bud.

"Six minutes for what?" said Katharine.

"Six minutes foah nothin'," said Bud. "It took thet long to get a man in through the gate."

"Well?"

"Three of you tied up for six minutes—you two and the guard. Eighteen man minutes in all. Hell, it cost over two bucks to let him in. How many people come to the gate a year?"

"Ten a day, maybe," said Paul.

"Twenty-seven hundred and fifty-eight a year," said Katharine.

"And you pass on each one?"

"Katharine usually does," said Paul. "That's the biggest part of her job."

"At a dollah a head, thet's twenty-seven hundred dollahs a year," said Bud reproachfully. He pointed at Katharine. "This is ridiculous! If policy is iron-clad, why not let a machine make the decisions? Policy isn't thinkin', it's a reflex. You could even build a gadget with an exception for Finnerty and still get away foah less than a hundred dollahs."

"There are all sorts of special decisions I have to make," said Katharine defensively. "I mean, all sorts of things come up that require more than routine thought—more than any old machine could do."

Bud wasn't listening. He held his palms apart, marking the size of the box being born in his imagination. "Either a visitor is a nonentity, a friend, an employee, small brass, or big brass. The guard presses one of five buttons in the top row on the box. See it? Either the visitor is sight-seein', inspectin', makin' a personal call, or here on business. The guard pushes one of four buttons in thet row. The machine has two lights, a red one for no, and a green one for yes. Whatever the policy is, bingo!—the lights tell him what to do."

"Or we could tack a memo about policy on the guardhouse wall," said Paul.

Bud looked startled. "Yes," he said slowly, "you *could*

do thet." It was clear he thought it was a pretty drab man who would think much of *that* solution.

"I'm mad," said Katharine, her voice small. "You have no right to go around saying a machine can do what I do."

"Aw, now honey—there wasn't anything personal in it."

She was crying now, and Paul slipped into his office and shut the door.

"Your wife's on the phone," said Katharine brokenly on the intercom set.

"All right. Yes, Anita?"

"Have you heard from Kroner?"

"No. I'll let you know if I do."

"I hope he had a good time last night."

"He did—or firmly believes he did."

"Is Finnerty there?"

"In the plant somewhere."

"You should see the bathroom."

"I saw it in the making."

"He had four cigarettes going, and forgot about every one of them. One on top of the medicine cabinet, one on the window sill, one on the top of the john, and one on the toothbrush rack. I couldn't eat my breakfast. He's got to go."

"I'll tell him."

"What are you going to tell Kroner?"

"I don't know yet. I don't know what he's going to say."

"Pretend I'm Kroner and I've just said, sort of casually, 'Well, Paul, the Pittsburgh spot is still open.' Then what do you say?"

This was the game she never tired of—one that took every bit of Paul's patience to play. She was forever casting herself as a person of influence and making Paul play dialogues with her. There would then be a critique, in which his responses were analyzed, edited, and polished by her. No real dialogues ever came close to her phantasies, which served chiefly to show how primitive a notion she had of men of affairs and of how business was done.

"Go on," she prodded.

"Pittsburgh, eh?" said Paul. "Holy smokes! Wow!"

"No, now, I'm serious," she said firmly. "What will you say?"

"Darling, I'm busy now."

"All right; you think it over and call me back. You know what I think you should say?"

"I'll call you back."

"All right. Goodbye. I love you."

"I love *you*, Anita. Goodbye."

"Doctor Shepherd is on the phone," said Katharine.

Paul picked up the now moist instrument again. "What's the matter now, Shep?"

"There's an unauthorized man in Building 57! Get the guards down here."

"Is it Finnerty?"

"An unauthorized man," said Shepherd stubbornly.

"All right. Is it an unauthorized Finnerty?"

"Yes—but that's beside the point. It makes no difference what his name is. He's roaming around without an escort, and you know how Kroner feels about that."

"I gave him permission. I know he's down there."

"You're putting *me* in a sweet spot."

"I don't get you."

"I mean I'm responsible for these buildings, and now you're telling me to ignore very specific orders from Kroner. Am I supposed to be left holding the bag if word gets out?"

"Look, just forget it. It's all right. I'll take the responsibility."

"In other words, you *order* me to let Finnerty go through unescorted."

"Yes—that's it. I *order* you."

"O.K., I just wanted to make sure I had it straight. Berringer wondered about it, too, so I had him listen in."

"Berringer?" said Paul.

"Yeah!" said Berringer.

"Just keep this under your hat is all."

"You're the boss," said Berringer flatly.

"All squared away now, Shepherd?" said Paul.

"I guess. And are we to understand that you've authorized him to make drawings, too?"

"Drawings?"

"Layouts."

At this point Paul realized that his judgment had been pushed into the background by more emotional matters, but he decided it was too late to do anything about it gracefully. "Let him do what he wants. He may come up with some useful ideas. All right?"

"You're the boss," said Shepherd. "Isn't that right, Berringer?"

"He's the boss," said Berringer.

"I'm the boss," said Paul, and he let the telephone clatter into its cradle.

Bud Calhoun was still trying to patch things up with Katharine in the next office. His voice had become wheedling and penetrating. Paul could understand snatches of it.

"As far as thet goes," Bud was saying, "it wouldn't be much of a trick to replace *him* with a gadget." Paul had a good idea where Bud's stubby index finger was pointing.

9

FINNERTY APPARENTLY FOUND plenty to entertain himself with in the Ilium Works. He didn't appear in Paul's office until late in the afternoon. When he did arrive, Katharine Finch gave a small cry of surprise. He'd let himself in through two locked doors with keys he'd presumably failed to turn in when he left the plant for Washington years before.

Paul's door was ajar, and he heard the conversation.

"Don't go for your rod, lady. The name's Finnerty."

Katharine did have a gun somewhere in her desk, though no ammunition. That secretaries should be armed was a regulation held over from the old days, too; one Kroner thought well enough of to revive in a directive.

"You're not authorized to have those keys," she said coldly.

"Have you been crying?" said Finnerty.

"I'll see if Doctor Proteus can see you."

"What is there to cry about? See—none of the red lights are on, no buzzers going off, so all's well with the world."

"Send him in, Katharine," called Paul.

Finnerty walked in and sat on the edge of Paul's desk. "What's the matter with Miss Policy out there?"

"Broken engagement. What's on your mind?"

"Thought we'd have a couple of drinks—if you feel like listening."

"All right. Let me call Anita and tell her we'll be late for supper."

Katharine got Anita on the line, and Paul told his wife what he was up to.

"Have you thought out what you'd say to Kroner if he told you Pittsburgh was still open?"

"No—it's been a hell of a day."

"Well, I've been thinking about it, and—"

"Anita, I've got to go."

"All right. I love you."

"I love *you*, Anita. Goodbye." He looked up at Finnerty. "O.K., let's go." He felt somehow conspiratorial, and got a small lift from the feeling. Being with Finnerty had often had that effect. Finnerty had an air of mysteriousness about him, an implication that he knew of worlds unsuspected by anyone else—a man of unexplained absences and shadowy friends. Actually, Finnerty let Paul in on very little that was surprising, and only gave him the illusion of sharing in mysteries—if, indeed, there were any. The illusion was enough. It filled a need in Paul's life, and he went gladly for a drink with the odd man.

"Is there somewhere I can reach you?" said Katharine.

"No, I'm afraid not," said Paul. He planned to go to the Country Club, where he could be reached easily enough. But, on an impulse, he indulged his appetite for secretiveness.

Finnerty had come over in Paul's station wagon. They left it at the Works and took Paul's old car.

"Across the bridge," said Finnerty.

"I thought we'd go to the club."

"This is Thursday, isn't it? Do the civic managers still have their big dinner there on Thursdays?"

The civic managers were the career administrators who ran the city. They lived on the same side of the river as the managers and engineers of the Ilium Works, but the contact between the two groups was little more than perfunctory and, traditionally, suspicious. The schism, like so many things, dated back to the war, when the economy had, for efficiency's sake, become monolithic. The question had arisen: who was to run it, the bureaucrats, the heads of business and industry, or the military? Business and bureaucracy had stuck together long enough to overwhelm the military and had since then worked side by side, abusively and suspiciously, but, like Kroner and Baer, each unable to do a whole job without the other.

"Not much changes in Ilium," said Paul. "The civic managers will be there all right. But if we get over there this early, we can get a booth in the bar."

"I'd rather share a bed in a leprosarium."

"All right; over the bridge it is. Let me put on something more comfortable." Paul stopped his car just short of the bridge, and traded his coat for the jacket in the trunk.

"I wondered if you still did that. That's even the same jacket, isn't it?"

"Habit."

"What would a psychiatrist say about it?"

"He'd say it was a swat at my old man, who never went anywhere without a Homburg and a double-breasted suit."

"Think he was a bastard?"

"How do I know what my father was? The editor of *Who's Who* knows about as much as I do. The guy was hardly ever home."

They were driving through Homestead now. Paul suddenly snapped his fingers in recollection and turned down a side street. "I've got to stop by police headquarters for a minute. Mind waiting?"

"What's the trouble?"

"Almost slipped my mind. Somebody swiped the gun from the glove compartment, or it fell out, or something."

"Keep driving."

"It'll just take a minute, I hope."

"I took it."

"You? Why?"

"Had an idea I might want to shoot myself." He said it matter-of-factly. "Even had the barrel in my mouth for a while, and the hammer back—for maybe ten minutes."

"Where is it now?"

"Bottom of the Iroquois somewhere." He licked his lips. "Tasted oil and metal all through dinner. Turn left."

Paul had learned to listen with outward calm when Finnerty spoke of his morbid moments. When he was with Finnerty he liked to pretend that he shared the man's fantastic and alternately brilliant or black inner thoughts—almost as though he were discontent with his own relative tranquility. Finnerty had spoken dispassionately of suicide often; but, seemingly, he did it because he got pleasure from savoring the idea. If he'd felt driven to kill himself, he would have been dead long ago.

"You think I'm insane?" said Finnerty. Apparently he wanted more of a reaction than Paul had given him.

"You're still in touch. I guess that's the test."

"Barely—*barely*."

"A psychiatrist could help. There's a good man in Albany."

Finnerty shook his head. "He'd pull me back into the center, and I want to stay as close to the edge as I can without going over. Out on the edge you see all kinds of things you can't see from the center." He nodded. "Big, undreamed-of things—the people on the edge see them first." He laid his hand on Paul's shoulder, and Paul fought a reflex that suddenly made him want to get as far away as possible. "Here's the place we want," said Finnerty. "Park here."

They had circled several blocks and were back at the head of the bridge, by the same saloon Paul had visited for the whisky. Paul, with uncomfortable memories of the place, wanted to go somewhere else, but Finnerty was already out of the car and on his way in.

Gratefully, Paul saw that the street and saloon were almost deserted, so there was a good chance he wouldn't see any of the people who'd watched his confusion the day before. No hydrants were going, but from far away, from the direction of Edison Park, came faint band music—a clue as to where everyone might be.

"Hey, your headlamp's busted," said a man, peering through the doorway of the saloon.

Paul passed him quickly, without getting a good look at him. "Thanks."

Only when he'd overtaken Finnerty in the damp twilight of the inside did he turn for another look at the man—at his short, broad back. The man's neck was thick and red, and glinting behind his ears were the hooks of steel spectacles. It was the same man, Paul realized, the same man who had been sitting by Rudy Hertz—the man whose son had just turned eighteen. Paul remembered that he had promised this man, in the panic of the moment, to speak to Matheson, the placement director, about the son. Perhaps he hadn't recognized Paul. Paul slid into a booth with Finnerty, in the darkest corner of the room.

The man turned and smiled, his eyes lost behind the milky, thick lenses of his glasses. "You're entirely welcome, Doctor Proteus," he called. "It isn't often that anyone can do a favor for anyone in your position."

Paul pretended he hadn't heard, and turned his attention to Finnerty, who dug a spoon around and around and around in a sugar bowl. Some of the white grains spilled over, and Finnerty absently drew the mathematical symbol for infinity in them with the tip of his finger.

"Funny what I expected from this reunion, what I guess everybody expects from affectionate reunions. I thought seeing you would somehow clear up all sorts of problems, get me thinking straight," said Finnerty. He had a candor about his few emotional attachments that Paul found disquieting. He used words to describe his feelings that Paul could never bring himself to use when speaking of a friend: love, affection, and other words generally consigned to young and inexperienced lovers. It wasn't homosexual; it was an archaic expression of friendship by an undisciplined man in an age when most men seemed in mortal fear of being mistaken for pansies for even a split second.

"I guess I looked forward to some sort of rebirth too," said Paul.

"But you find out quick enough that old friends are old friends, and nothing more—no wiser, no more help than anyone else. Well, what the hell, that doesn't mean I'm not damned pleased to see you again."

"No booth service until eight," called the bartender.

"I'll get them," said Finnerty. "What'll it be?"

"Bourbon—plain water. Make it a weak one. Anita's expecting us in an hour."

Finnerty came back with two strong highballs.

"Is there any water in it?" said Paul.

"There was enough water in it as it was." Finnerty swept the sugar from the table with his palm. "It's the loneliness," he said, as though picking up the thread of a conversation that had been interrupted. "It's the loneliness, the not belonging anywhere. I just about went crazy with loneliness here in the old days, and I figured things would be better in Washington, that I'd find a lot of people I admired and belonged with. Washington is worse, Paul—Ilium to the tenth power. Stupid, arrogant, self-congratulatory, unimaginative, humorless men. And the women, Paul—the dull wives feeding on the power and glory of their husbands."

"Oh, now listen, Ed," said Paul, smiling, "they're good-hearted people."

"Who isn't? I'm not, I guess. Their superiority is what gets me, this damn hierarchy that measures men against machines. It's a pretty unimpressive kind of man that comes out on top."

"Here come some more!" called the man with the thick glasses from the door. From far off came the sound of marching, and the thump of a bass drum. The noise came closer, a whistle blew, and a brass band exploded with music.

Paul and Finnerty hurried to the door.

"Who are they?" shouted Finnerty at the man in thick glasses.

The man smiled. "Don't think they want anybody to know. Secret."

At the head of the procession, surrounded by four trumpeters dressed as Arabs, was a florid, serious old man in a turban and pantaloons, carefully cradling in his arms an elephant tusk inscribed with mysterious symbols. Behind him came an enormous square banner, held aloft by a staggering giant, and steadied in the wind, maypole fashion, by a dozen Arabs tugging at colored ropes. The banner, which from a distance had given promise of explaining all, was embroidered with four lines of long-forgotten—or perhaps recently invented—script, and with four green owls against a field of apricot. After it came the band, which carried out the Arabian motif. There were owl-bearing pennants hung from the brasses, and the banner's message was repeated, in case anyone had missed it, on a cart-borne bass drum perhaps twelve feet in diameter.

"Hooray," said the man in thick glasses mildly.

"Why are you cheering?" said Finnerty.

"Don't you think something's called for? Cheering Luke Lubbock mostly. He's the one with the tusk."

"Doing a swell job," said Finnerty. "What's he represent?"

"Secret. He couldn't be it any more, if he told."

"Looks like he's about the most important thing."

"Next to the tusk."

The parade turned a corner, the whistle blew again, and the music stopped. Down the street, another whistle shrilled, and the whole business began again as a company of kilted bagpipers swung into view.

"Parade competition down at the park," said the man with the glasses. "They'll be coming by for hours. Let's go in and have a drink."

"On us?" said Finnerty.

"Who else?"

"Wait," said Paul, "this should be interesting."

An automobile had just come from the north side of the river, and its driver honked irritably at the marchers, who blocked his way. The horn and the bagpipes squalled at one another until the last rank of marchers had turned down the side street. Paul recognized the driver too late to get out of sight. Shepherd looked at him with puzzlement and mild censure, waved vaguely, and drove on. Peering through the back window were the small eyes of Fred Berringer.

Paul refused to attach any importance to the incident. He sat down in the booth with the short, heavy man, while Finnerty went after more drinks.

"How's your son?" said Paul.

"Son, Doctor? Oh, oh, of course—my son. You said you were going to talk to Matheson about him, didn't you? What did the good Matheson say?"

"I haven't seen him yet. I've been meaning to, but the opportunity hasn't come up."

The man nodded. "Matheson, Matheson—beneath that cold exterior, there beats a heart of ice. Well, it's just as well. There's no need to talk to him now. My boy's all set."

"Oh, really? I'm glad to hear that."

"Yes, he hanged himself this morning in the kitchen."

"Lord!"

"Yes, I told him what you said yesterday, and it was so discouraging that he just gave up. It's the best way. There *are* too many of us. Upps! You're spilling your drink!"

"What's going on here?" said Finnerty.

"I was just telling the Doctor here that my son couldn't find any good reason for being alive, so he quit it this morning—with an ironing cord."

Paul covered his eyes. "Jesus, oh Jesus I'm sorry."

The man looked up at Finnerty with a mixture of bewilderment and exasperation. "Now, hell, why'd I have to go and do that? Have a drink, Doctor, and pull yourself together. I haven't got a son, never had one." He shook Paul's arm. "Hear me? It's a lot of crap."

"Then why don't I bust your stupid head open?" said Paul, half standing in the booth.

"Because you're wedged in too tightly," said Finnerty, pushing him back down. He set the drinks before them.

"Sorry," said the man to Paul. "I just wanted to see how one of those superbrains worked. What's your I.Q., Doctor?"

"It's a matter of record. Why don't you go look it up?" It was a matter of record. Everyone's I.Q., as measured by the National Standard General Classification Test, was on public record—in Ilium, at the police station. "Go on," he said acidly, "experiment with me some more. I love it."

"You picked a bad specimen if you're out to find out what the rest of them across the river are like," said Finnerty. "This guy's an odd one."

"You're an engineer too."

"Until I quit."

The man looked surprised. "You know, this is really very illuminating, if you're not kidding me. There are malcontents, eh?"

"Two that we know of," said Finnerty.

"Well, you know, in a way I wish I hadn't met you two. It's much more convenient to think of the opposition as a nice homogeneous, dead-wrong mass. Now I've got to muddy my thinking with exceptions."

"How have you got yourself typed," said Paul, "as an upstate Socrates?"

"The name is Lasher, the Reverend James J. Lasher, R-127 and SS-55. Chaplain, Reconstruction and Reclamation Corps."

"The first number's for Protestant minister. What's the second, that SS thing?" said Finnerty.

"Social scientist," said Lasher. "The 55 designates an anthropologist with a master's degree."

"And what does an anthropologist do these days?" said Paul.

"Same thing a supernumerary minister does—becomes a public charge, a bore, or possibly a rum-dum, or a bureaucrat." He looked back and forth between Paul and Finnerty. "You, I know, Doctor Proteus. And you?"

"Finnerty, Edward Francis Finnerty, Ph.D., one-time EC-002."

"There's a collector's item—a double-o-two number!" said Lasher. "I've known several single-o men, but never a double-o. I guess you're the highest classification I ever had friendly words with. If the Pope set up shop in this country, he'd be only one notch up—in the R-numbers of course. He'd be an R-001. I heard somewhere that the number was being held for him, over the objections of Episcopal bishops who want R-001 themselves. Delicate business."

"They could give him a negative number," said Paul.

"That the Episcopalians would go along with. My glass is empty."

"What was this business about the people across the river being the opposition?" said Paul. "You think they do the Devil's work, do you?"

"That's pretty strong. I will say you've shown up what thin stuff clergymen were peddling, most of them. When I had a congregation before the war, I used to tell them that the life of their spirit in relation to God was the biggest thing in their lives, and that their part in the economy was nothing by comparison. Now, you people have engineered them out of their part in the economy, in the market place, and they're finding out—most of them—that what's left is just about zero. A good bit short of enough, anyway. My glass is empty."

Lasher sighed. "What do you expect?" he said. "For generations they've been built up to worship competition and the market, productivity and economic usefulness, and the envy of their fellow men—and boom! it's all yanked out from under them. They can't participate, can't be useful any more. Their whole culture's been shot to hell. My glass is empty."

"I just had it filled again," said Finnerty.

"Oh, so you did." Lasher sipped thoughtfully. "These displaced people need something, and the clergy can't give it to them—or it's impossible for them to take what the clergy offers. The clergy says it's enough, and so does the Bible. The people say it isn't enough, and I suspect they're right."

"If they were so fond of the old system, how come they were so cantankerous about their jobs when they had them?" said Paul.

"Oh, this business we've got now—it's been going on for a long time now, not just since the last war. Maybe the actual jobs weren't being taken from the people, but the sense of participation, the sense of importance was. Go to the library sometime and take a look at magazines and newspapers clear back as far as World War II. Even then there was a lot of talk about know-how winning the war of production—*know-how*, not people, not the *mediocre* people running most of the machines. And the hell of it was that it was pretty much true. Even then, half the people or more didn't understand much about the machines they worked at or the things they were making. They were participating in the economy all right, but not in a way that was very satisfying to the ego. And then there was all this let's-not-shoot-Father-Christmas advertising."

"How's that?" said Paul.

"You know—those ads about the American system, meaning managers and engineers, that made America great. When you finished one, you'd think the managers and engineers had given America everything: forests, rivers, minerals, mountains, oil—the works.

"Strange business," said Lasher. "This crusading spirit of the managers and engineers, the idea of designing and manufacturing and distributing being sort of a holy war: all that folklore was cooked up by public relations and advertising men hired by managers and engineers to make big business popular in the old days, which it certainly wasn't in the beginning. Now, the engineers and managers believe with all their hearts the glorious things their forebears hired people to say about them. Yesterday's snow job becomes today's sermon."

"Well," said Paul, "you'll have to admit they did some pretty wonderful things during the war."

"Of course!" said Lasher. "What they did for the war effort really was something like crusading; but"—he shrugged—"so was what everybody else did for the war effort. Everybody behaved wonderfully. Even I."

"You keep giving the managers and engineers a bad time," said Paul. "What about the scientists? It seems to me that—"

"Outside the discussion," said Lasher impatiently. "They simply add to knowledge. It isn't knowledge that's making trouble, but the uses it's put to."

Finnerty shook his head admiringly. "So what's the answer right now?"

"That is a frightening question," said Lasher, "and also my favorite rationalization for drinking. This is my last drink, incidentally; I don't like being drunk. I drink because I'm scared—just a little scared, so I don't have to drink much. Things, gentlemen, are ripe for a phony Messiah, and when he comes, it's sure to be a bloody business."

"Messiah?"

"Sooner or later someone's going to catch the imagination of these people with some new magic. At the bottom of it will be a promise of regaining the feeling of participation, the feeling of being needed on earth—hell, *dignity*. The police are bright enough to look for people like that, and lock them up under the antisabotage laws. But sooner or later someone's going to keep out of their sight long enough to organize a following."

Paul had been watching his expression closely, and de-

cided that, far from being in horror of the impending upris-
ing, Lasher was rather taken by the idea. "And then what?"
said Paul. He picked up his glass and rattled the ice cubes
against his teeth. He'd finished his second drink and wanted
another.

Lasher shrugged. "Oh, hell—prophecy's a thankless
business, and history has a way of showing us what, in retro-
spect, are very logical solutions to awful messes."

"Prophesy anyway," said Finnerty.

"Well—I think it's a grave mistake to put on public
record everyone's I.Q. I think the first thing the revolutionar-
ies would want to do is knock off everybody with an I.Q.
over 110, say. If I were on your side of the river, I'd have the
I.Q. books closed and the bridges mined."

"Then the 100's would go after the 110's, the 90's after
the 100's, and so on," said Finnerty.

"Maybe. Something like that. Things are certainly set
up for a class war based on conveniently established lines of
demarkation. And I must say that the basic assumption of the
present setup is a grade-A incitement to violence: the smarter
you are, the better you are. Used to be that the richer you
were, the better you were. Either one is, you'll admit, pretty
tough for the have-not's to take. The criterion of brains is
better than the one of money, but"—he held his thumb and
forefinger about a sixteenth of an inch apart—"about *that*
much better."

"It's about as rigid a hierarchy as you can get," said
Finnerty. "How's somebody going to up his I.Q.?"

"Exactly," said Lasher. "And it's built on more than just
brain power—it's built on special kinds of brain power. Not
only must a person be bright, he must be bright in certain
approved, useful directions: basically, management or engineering."

"Or marry someone who's bright," said Finnerty.

"Sex can still batter down all sorts of social structures—
you're right," Lasher agreed.

"Big tits will get you in anywhere," said Finnerty.

"Well, it's comforting to know that something hasn't changed in centuries, isn't it?" Lasher smiled.

There was a mild commotion at the bar, and Lasher leaned out of the booth to see what was going on. "Hey," he called, "Luke Lubbock—come over here."

Luke, the serious old man who had borne the elephant tusk at the head of the parade, came over from the bar, gulping his beer as he came, and looking nervously at the clock. He was perspiring and short of breath, like a man who'd been running. He had a large parcel wrapped in brown paper under his arm.

Paul welcomed the opportunity to study Luke's magnificent costume more closely. Like a stage set, it was designed to impress at a distance. Nearness showed that the splendor was a fraud of cheap cloth, colored glass, and radiator paint. At his waist was a jeweled poniard, basically plywood, with an owl on its hilt. Counterfeit rubies as big as robin's eggs, mounted in golden sunbursts, were hung at random on the front of his lavender blouse. About the cuffs of his blouse and jade-green pantaloons were circlets of tiny bells, and—again—perched at the upturned tips of his golden slippers were a pair of miniature owls.

"Luke, you look wonderful," said Lasher.

Luke's eyes flashed agreement, but he was an important man, in too much of a hurry to respond to flattery. "It's too much, too much," he said. "Now I got to change so's I can march with the Parmesans. They're waiting up the street, and I got to change, and some damn fool's locked hisself in the can, so I got no place to change." He looked around quickly. "Would you let me do it in the booth, and kind of screen me?"

"You bet," said Finnerty.

They let Luke squirm into the shadows of the booth, and Paul found himself keeping a playful, leering lookout for women.

Muttering, Luke started to disrobe. He dropped his belt and poniard on the table, where they struck with an impressive thump. The glittering heap grew and grew, until, from a distance, it might have looked good enough to be at the end of a rainbow.

Paul relaxed his vigil for an instant to glance at Luke, and he was shocked at the transformation. The man was in his underwear now, ragged and drab, and none-too-clean. And Luke had somehow shrunk and saddened and was knobbed and scarred and scrawny. He was subdued now, talking not at all, and meeting no one's eyes. Almost desperately, hungrily, he ripped open the brown parcel and took from it a pale-blue uniform, encrusted with gold embroidery and piped in scarlet. He pulled on the trousers and black boots, and the jacket with its ponderous epaulets. Luke was growing again, getting his color back, and as he strapped on his saber he was talkative again—important and strong. He bundled up his other costume in the brown paper, left the parcel with the bartender, and rushed into the street, waving naked steel.

A whistle blew, and the Parmesans fell in behind him, to be led to glorious exploits in a dreamworld those on the sidewalk could only speculate about.

"Harmless magic: good, old-fashioned bunkum," laughed Lasher. "Talk about your hierarchies: Luke, with an I.Q. of about 80, has titles that'd make Charlemagne sound like a cook's helper. But that sort of business wears thin pretty quick for everybody but a few Luke Lubbocks. The lodge turnover is terrific." He stood. "No more for me, thanks." He rapped on the table. "But someday, gentlemen, someone is going to give them something to sink their teeth in—probably you, and maybe me."

"We'll give them something to sink their teeth in?" said Paul. He noticed he was getting somewhat thick of speech.

"You'll be what they'll get to sink their teeth in." Lasher laid his hand on Paul's shoulder. "One more thing: I want to be sure you understand that men really *do* worry about what there is for their sons to live for; and some sons *do* hang themselves."

"And this is as old as life itself," said Paul.

"Well?" said Lasher.

"Well, it's too bad. I'm certainly not overjoyed about it."

"You figure to be the new Messiah?" said Finnerty.

"Sometimes I think I'd like to be—if only in self-defense. Also, it'd be a swell way to get rich. Trouble is, I can be sold or unsold on anything too easily. I enjoy being talked into something. Pretty shaky outlook for a Messiah. Besides, who ever heard of a short, fat, middle-aged Messiah with bad eyesight? And I haven't got that common touch. Frankly, the masses give me a pain in the tail, and I guess I show it." He made clucking sounds with his tongue. "I'm going to get myself a uniform, so I'll know what I think and stand for."

"Or two—like Luke Lubbock," said Paul.

"All right, two. But that's the absolute maximum any self-respecting human being ought to permit himself." He sipped from Paul's highball. "Well, good night."

"Have another," said Finnerty.

"No—I mean it. I don't like getting tight."

"All right. I want to see you again, anyway. Where can I find you?"

"Here, most likely." He wrote an address on a paper napkin. "Or try here." He looked closely at Finnerty. "You know, wash your face, and you might do real well as a Messiah."

Finnerty looked startled, and didn't laugh.

Lasher picked up a hard-boiled egg at the bar, crackled its shell by rolling it along the keyboard of the player piano, and walked out into the evening.

"Magnificent, wasn't he?" said Finnerty raptly. His gaze returned reluctantly from the door to Paul. Paul saw his eyes take on a glaze of ennui, of letdown, and he knew that Finnerty had found a new friend who made Paul look very pale indeed.

"Your orders, gentlemen?" said a short, dark waitress, with a hard, trim figure. She looked at the television screen while waiting for them to reply. The sound never seemed to be turned on, only the video. An anxious young man in a long sports coat jiggled up and down on the screen, and blew through a saxophone.

The saloon was filling up, and many of the flamboyantly and enigmatically costumed marchers had come in for refreshment, giving the place an atmosphere of international unrest and intrigue.

One small young man in mufti, with immensely wise and large eyes, leaned back against the table in Paul's and Ed's booth and watched the television screen with what seemed to be more than routine interest. He turned casually to Paul. "What you think he's playing?"

"Beg pardon?"

"The guy on television—what's the name of the song?"

"I can't hear it."

"I know," he said impatiently, "that's the *point*. Guess from just seeing."

Paul frowned at the screen for a moment, tried to jiggle as the saxophonist jiggled, and to fit a song to the rhythm. Suddenly his mind clicked, and the tune was flowing in his imagination as surely as though the sound had been turned on. " 'Rosebud.' The song is 'Rosebud,' " said Paul.

The young man smiled quietly. " 'Rosebud,' eh? Just for laughs, want to put a little money on it? I'll say it's—um, ah, well—'Paradise Moon,' maybe."

"How much?"

The young man studied Paul's jacket, and then, with slight surprise, his expensive trousers and shoes. "Ten?"

"Ten, by God. 'Rosebud'!"

"What's he say it is, Alfy?" called the bartender.

"He says 'Rosebud,' I say 'Paradise Moon.' Turn her on."

The last notes of "Paradise Moon" blared from the loudspeaker, the saxophonist grimaced and backed off the screen. The bartender winked admiringly at Alfy and turned down the volume again.

Paul handed Alfy the ten. "Congratulations."

Alfy sat down in the booth without being invited. He looked at the screen, blew smoke through his nose, and closed his eyes reflectively. "What you figure they're playing now?"

Paul decided to buckle down and get his money back. He looked hard at the screen, and took his time. The whole orchestra was in view now, and, once he thought he'd picked up the thread of a melody, he looked from musician to musician for confirmation. "An old, old one," he said. " 'Stardust.' "

"For ten it's 'Stardust'?"

"For ten."

"What is it, Alfy?" called the bartender.

Alfy jerked a thumb at Paul. "This kid's fair. He says 'Stardust,' and I can see where he gets it. He's right about the oldy, but he picked the wrong one. 'Mood Indigo' is the name." He looked sympathetically at Paul. "It's a tough one all right." He snapped his fingers.

The bartender twisted the volume knob, and "Mood Indigo" filled the air.

"Wonderful!" said Paul, and he turned to Finnerty for confirmation. Finnerty was lost in his own thoughts, and his lips moved slightly, as though in an imaginary conversation. Despite the noise and excitement of Alfy's performances, he apparently hadn't noticed them.

"A knack," said Alfy modestly. "Like anything else: you know, keep at it long enough, and you surprise yourself. Couldn't tell you—in real detail, you know—how I did it. Gets to be another sense—you kind of *feel* it."

The bartender, the waitress, and several other bystanders had fallen silent in order to hear Alfy's words.

"Oh, there's some tricks," said Alfy. "Watch the bass drum quiver instead of what the guy's doing with the traps. Get the basic beat that way. Lot of people watch the traps, see, and the guy may be going off on a tangent. Things like that you can learn. And, you gotta know instruments—how they make a high note, how they make a low one. But that ain't enough." His voice took on a respectful, almost reverent tone. "It's kind of spooky what else it takes."

"He does classical stuff too," said the bartender eagerly. "Oughta see him with the Boston Pops on Sunday nights."

Alfy ground out his cigarette impatiently. "Yeah, yeah—classics," he said, frowning, mercilessly airing his inner doubts about himself. "Yeah, I was lucky last Sunday when you saw me. But I ain't got the repertory for that. I'm over my head, and you can't pick up in the middle of the classics. And you play hell building a repertory of that stuff, when you gotta wait sometimes a year, two years, to see the thing twice." He rubbed his eyes, as though remembering hours of concentration before a video screen. "You gotta see 'em plugged and plugged and plugged. And all the time new ones—and lots of 'em steals from oldies."

"Tough, eh?" said Paul.

Alfy raised his eyebrows. "Yeah, it's tough—like anything else. Tough to be the best."

"There's punks trying to break in, but they can't touch Alfy," said the bartender.

"They're good in their specialties—usually the quick killings," said Alfy. "You know, the minute a new number's out, they try and cash in on it before everybody's seen it. But none of 'em's making a living at it, I'll tell you that. Got no repertory, and that's what it takes to keep going day in, day out."

"This is your living?" said Paul. He hadn't succeeded in

keeping the sense of whimsey out of his voice, and quick resentment was all about him.

"Yeah," said Alfy coldly, "this is my living. A buck here, ten cents there—"

"Twenty bucks here," said Paul. This seemed to soften most of the expressions.

The bartender was anxious to maintain a friendly atmosphere. "Alfy started out as a pool shark, eh, Alfy?" he said briskly.

"Yeah. But the field's crowded. Maybe room for ten, twenty guys going at it steady. There must of been a couple of hundred of us trying to make a go of it with pool. The Army and the Reeks and Wrecks were on my tail, so I started looking around for something else. Funny, without thinking much about it, I'd been doing this since I was a kid. It's what I should of gone into right from the first. Reeks and Wrecks," he said contemptuously, apparently recalling how close he came to being drafted into the R and R Corps. "Army!" He spat.

A couple of soldiers and a large number of men from the Reeks and Wrecks heard him insult their organizations, and they did nothing but nod, sharing his contempt.

Alfy looked at the screen. " 'Baby, Dear Baby, Come Home With Me Now,' " he said. "A newy." He hurried to the bar to study the movements of the band more closely. The bartender rested his hand on the volume knob and watched anxiously for Alfy's signals. Alfy would raise an eyebrow, and the bartender would turn up the volume. It would be on for a few seconds, Alfy would nod, and off it would go again.

"What'll it be, boys?" said the waitress.

"Hmmm?" said Paul, still fascinated by Alfy. "Oh—bourbon and water." He was experimenting with his eyes, and finding that they didn't work too well.

"Irish and water," said Finnerty. "Hungry?"

"Yeah—give us a couple of hard-boiled eggs, please."

Paul felt wonderful, at one with the saloon, and, by extension, with all humanity and the universe. He felt witty, and
on the verge of a splendid discovery. Then he remembered.
"Holy God! Anita!"

"Where?"

"At home—waiting." Unsteadily, mumbling cheery
greetings to all he passed, Paul got to the telephone booth,
which reeked with a previous occupant's cigar smoke. He
called home.

"Look, Anita—I won't be home for supper. Finnerty
and I got to talking, and—"

"It's all right, dear. Shepherd told me not to wait."

"Shepherd?"

"Yes—he saw you down there, and told me you didn't
look like a man on his way home."

"When did you see him?"

"He's here now. He came to apologize for last night.
Everything's all ironed out, and we're having a very nice
time."

"Oh? You accepted his apology?"

"Let's say we arrived at an understanding. He's worried
that you'll turn in a bad report on him to Kroner, and I did
everything I could to make him think you were considering
it seriously."

"Oh, now listen, I'm not going to turn in any bad
report on that—"

"It's the way *he* plays. Fight fire with fire. I got him to
agree not to spread any more tales about you. Aren't you
proud of me?"

"Yeah, sure."

"Now you've got to keep working on him, keep him
worried."

"Uh-huh."

"Now, you just go ahead and have a good time. It does
you good to get away now and then."

"Yes'm."

"And please try to get Finnerty to move out."

"Yes'm."

"Do you think I nag you?"

"No'm."

"Paul! Would you like it if I didn't take an interest?"

"No'm."

"All right. You just go ahead and get drunk. It'll do you good. Eat something, though. I love you."

"I love *you*." He hung up, and turned to face the world through the steamy window of the phone booth. Along with his feeling of dizziness was a feeling of newness—the feeling of fresh, strong identity growing within him. It was a generalized love—particularly for the little people, the common people, God bless them. All his life they had been hidden from him by the walls of his ivory tower. Now, this night, he had come among them, shared their hopes and disappointments, understood their yearnings, discovered the beauty of their simplicities and their earthy values. This was *real*, this side of the river, and Paul loved these common people, and wanted to help, and let them know they were loved and understood, and he wanted them to love him too.

When he got back to the booth, two young women were sitting with Finnerty, and Paul loved them instantly.

"Paul—I'd like you to meet my cousin Agnes from Detroit," said Finnerty. He rested his hand on the knee of a fat and determinedly cheerful redhead sitting next to him. "And this," he said, pointing across the table at a tall, homely brunette, "is *your* cousin Agnes."

"How do you do, Agnes and Agnes."

"Are you as crazy as he is?" said the brunette suspiciously. "If you are, I'm going home."

"Good, clean, fun-loving American type, Paul is," said Finnerty.

"Tell me about yourself," said Paul expansively.

"My name isn't Agnes, it's Barbara," said the brunette. "And she's Martha."

"What'll it be?" said the waitress.

"Double Scotch and water," said Martha.

"Same," said Barbara.

"That'll be four dollars for the ladies' drinks," said the waitress.

Paul handed her a five.

"Holy smokes!" said Barbara, staring at the identification card in Paul's billfold. "This guy's an engineer!"

"You from *across* the river?" said Martha to Finnerty.

"Deserters."

Both girls moved away, and with their backs against the wall of the booth, they looked at Paul and Finnerty with puzzlement. "I'll be go to hell," said Martha at last. "What you want to talk about? I had algebra in high school."

"We're just plain folks," said Paul.

"What'll it be?" said the waitress.

"Scotch, double," said Martha.

"Same," said Barbara.

"Come here, damn it," said Finnerty, pulling Martha to his side again.

Barbara still kept her distance from Paul and looked at him distastefully. "What are you doing over here—having a good laugh at the dumb bunnies?"

"I like it over here," said Paul earnestly.

"You're making fun of me."

"Honest, I'm not at all. Did I say anything that sounded like I was?"

"You're thinking it," she said.

"That'll be four dollars for the ladies' drinks," said the waitress.

Paul paid again. He didn't know what to say next to Barbara. He didn't want to make a pass at her. He simply wanted her to be friendly and companionable, and to see that he wasn't a stuffed shirt at all. Far from it.

"They don't castrate you when they give you an engineering degree," Finnerty was saying to Martha.

"They might as well," said Martha. "Some of the kids that come over from across the river—you'd think they were."

"After our time," said Finnerty. "I meant they didn't *use* to."

To build up more of an atmosphere of intimacy, rapport, Paul casually picked up one of the shot-glasses before Barbara and sipped at it. It then dawned on him that the shots of expensive Scotch, which had been arriving as though by bucket brigade, were no more than brown water. "Smooth," he said.

"So what am I supposed to do, have a nervous breakdown?" said Barbara. "Let me out."

"No, please, that's all right. Just talk to me is all. I understand."

"What'll it be?" said the waitress.

"Scotch, double, with water," said Paul.

"Trying to make me feel bad?"

"I want you to feel good. If you need money, I want to help." He meant it with all his heart.

"Suit yourself, plunger," said Barbara. She looked restlessly about the room.

Paul's eyelids grew heavier and heavier and heavier as he tried to think of the phrase that would break the ice with Barbara. He folded his arms on the table top and, for just an instant's rest, he laid his head on them.

When he opened his eyes again, Finnerty was shaking him, and Barbara and Martha had gone. Finnerty helped him out onto the sidewalk for air.

The out-of-doors was a nightmare of light and noise, and Paul could see that some sort of torchlight parade was under way. He burst into a cheer as he recognized Luke Lubbock, who was being borne by in a sedan chair.

When Finnerty had established him back in the booth, a speech, the nugget of the whole evening's nebulous impressions, composed itself in Paul's mind, took on form and polish inspirationally, with no conscious effort on his part. He had only to deliver it to make himself the new Messiah and Ilium the new Eden. The first line was at his lips, tearing at them to be set free.

Paul struggled to stand on the bench, and from there he managed to step to the table. He held his hands over his head for attention.

"Friends, my friends!" he cried. "We must meet in the middle of the bridge!" The frail table suddenly lurched beneath him. He heard the splitting of wood, cheers, and again—darkness.

The next voice was the bartender's. "Come on—closing time. Gotta lock up," said the bartender gently.

Paul sat up and groaned. His mouth was dry, and his head ached. The table was gone from the booth, and there were only cracked plaster and boltheads to show where it had once been moored to the wall.

The saloon seemed deserted, but the air was filled with a painful clangor. Paul peered out of the booth and saw a man mopping the floor. Finnerty sat at the player piano, savagely improvising on the brassy, dissonant antique.

Paul shuffled over to the piano and laid his hand on Finnerty's shoulder. "Let's go home."

Finnerty continued to lash at the keys. "Staying!" he shouted above the music. "Go home!"

"Where you going to stay?"

Then Paul saw Lasher, who sat unobtrusively in the shadows, leaning against the wall in a chair. Lasher tapped his thick chest. "With me," he said with his lips.

Finnerty shook off Paul's hand and wouldn't answer.

"O.K.," said Paul fuzzily. "So long."

He stumbled into the street and found his car. He paused for a moment to listen to Finnerty's hellish music echoing from the façades of the sleeping town. The bartender stood respectfully at a distance from the frenzied pianist, afraid to interrupt.

10

AFTER THE NIGHT with Finnerty and Lasher, and with the good little people, Alfy, Luke Lubbock, the bartender, and Martha and Barbara, Doctor Paul Proteus slept until late in the afternoon. When he awoke, Anita was out of the house, and with a dry mouth, burning eyes, and a stomach that felt as though it were stuffed with cat fur, he went to his responsible post in the Ilium Works.

The eyes of Doctor Katharine Finch, his secretary, were bloodshot for another reason, a reason so all-consuming that she took little note of the condition of Paul.

"Doctor Kroner called," she said mechanically.

"Oh? He wants me to call back?"

"Doctor Shepherd took the message."

"He did, eh? Anything else?"

"The police?"

"Police? What did they want?"

"Doctor Shepherd took the message."

"All right." Everything seemed hot and bright and soporific. He sat on the edge of her desk, and rested. "Get Dog-Eat-Dog on the phone."

"That won't be necessary. He's in your office now."

Wondering bleakly what grievance or slight or infraction of rules Shepherd wanted to see him about, Paul pushed open his office door gingerly.

Shepherd sat at Paul's desk, absorbed in signing a stack of reports. He didn't look up. Briskly, his eyes still on the papers, he flicked on the intercom set. "Miss Finch—"

"Yessir."

"On this monthly security report: did Doctor Proteus

tell you how he planned to handle Finnerty's admission without escort yesterday?"

"I planned to keep my big mouth shut about it," said
Paul.

Shepherd looked up with seeming pleasure and surprise. "Well, speak of the Devil." He made no move to get
out of Paul's chair. "Say," he said with hearty camaraderie,
"I guess you were really hung over, eh, boy? Should have
taken the whole day off. I know my way around well enough
to fill in for you."

"Thanks."

"No trouble. There really isn't a heck of a lot to the
job."

"I expected Katharine to watch over things for me, and
call for help if she needed it."

"You know what Kroner would think of *that*. It doesn't
take a whole lot more trouble to do things right, Paul."

"Do you mind telling me what Kroner wanted?"

"Oh, yes—he wants to see you tonight instead of
Thursday. He's got to be in Washington tomorrow night, and
for the rest of the week."

"Wonderful. And what's the good news from the police?"

Shepherd laughed richly. "Some foul-up. They were all
excited about a pistol they found down by the river. They
claimed the serial numbers were for a gun checked out to
you. I told them to check again—that no man who's bright
enough to be manager of the Ilium Works is dumb enough to
leave a pistol around loose."

"That's a nice tribute, Shep. Mind if I use my phone?"

Shepherd pushed the phone across the desk and went
back to signing: "Lawson Shepherd, in absence of P. Proteus."

"Did you tell him I had a hangover?"

"Hell no, Paul. I covered up for you all right."

"What did you say was wrong?"

"Nerves."

"Great!" Katharine was getting Kroner's office on the line for Paul.

"Doctor Proteus in Ilium would like to speak to Doctor Kroner. He's returning Doctor Kroner's call," said Katharine.

It wasn't a day for judging proportions. Paul had been able to take the disturbances of Kroner, Shepherd, and the police with something bordering on apathy. Now, however, he found himself enraged by the ceremony of official telephone etiquette—time-consuming pomp and circumstance lovingly preserved by the rank-happy champions of efficiency.

"Is Doctor Proteus on?" said Kroner's secretary. "Doctor Kroner is in."

"Just a moment," said Katharine. "Doctor Proteus, Doctor Kroner is in and will speak to you."

"All right, I'm on."

"Doctor Proteus is on the line," said Katharine.

"Doctor Kroner, Doctor Proteus is on the line."

"Tell him to go ahead," said Kroner.

"Tell Doctor Proteus to go ahead," said Kroner's secretary.

"Doctor Proteus, please go ahead," said Katharine.

"This is Paul Proteus, Doctor Kroner. I'm returning your call." A little bell went *"tink-tink-tink,"* letting him know his conversation was being recorded.

"Shepherd said you'd been having trouble with your nerves, my boy."

"Not quite right. A touch of some kind of virus."

"Lot of that floating around. Well, do you feel well enough to come over to my house tonight?"

"Love it. Is there anything I should bring—anything in particular you want to discuss?"

"Like Pittsburgh?" said Shepherd in a stage whisper.

"No, no, purely social, Paul—just good talk is all. We

haven't had a good, friendly talk for a long while. Mom and I would just like to see you socialwise."

Paul thought back. He hadn't been invited to Kroner's socialwise for a year, since he'd been sized up for his last raise. "Sounds like fun. What time?"

"Eight, eight-thirty."

"And Anita's invited too?" It was a mistake. It slipped out without his thinking about it.

"Of course! You never go anywhere socially without her, do you?"

"Oh, no, sir."

"I should hope not." He laughed perfunctorily. "Well, goodbye."

"What did he say?" said Shepherd.

"He said you had no damn business signing those reports for me. He said Katharine Finch was to take off your name with ink-eradicator at once."

"Say, now just hold on," said Shepherd, standing.

Paul saw that all of the desk drawers were ajar. In the bottom drawer the neck of the empty whisky bottle was in plain view. He slammed each of the drawers shut in quick succession. When he came to the bottom one, he took out the bottle and held it out to Shepherd. "Here—want this? Might be valuable sometime. It's got my fingerprints all over it."

"Are you going to get me canned—is that it?" said Shepherd eagerly. "You want to make an issue of it in front of Kroner? Let's go. I'm ready any time. Let's see if you can make it stick."

"Get down where you belong. Go on. Clear out of this office, and don't come back unless I tell you to come back. Katharine!"

"Yes?"

"If Doctor Shepherd comes in this office again without permission, you're to shoot him."

Shepherd slammed the door, railed against Paul to Katharine, and left.

"Doctor Proteus, the police are on the phone," said Katharine.

Paul stalked out of the office and went home.

It was the maid's day off, and Paul found Anita in the kitchen, the picture, minus children, of domesticity.

The kitchen was, in a manner of speaking, what Anita had given of herself to the world. In planning it, she had experienced all the anguish and hellfire of creativity—tortured by doubts, cursing her limitations, at once hungry for and fearful of the opinions of others. Now it was done and admired, and the verdict of the community was: Anita was *artistic*.

It was a large, airy room, larger than most living rooms. Rough-hewn rafters, taken from an antique barn, were held against the ceiling by concealed bolts fixed in the steel framing of the house. The walls were wainscoted in pine, aged by sandblasting, and given a soft yellow patina of linseed oil.

A huge fireplace and Dutch oven of fieldstone filled one wall. Over them hung a long muzzle-loading rifle, powder horn, and bullet pouch. On the mantel were candle molds, a coffee mill, an iron and trivet, and a rusty kettle. An iron cauldron, big enough to boil a missionary in, swung at the end of a long arm in the fireplace, and below it, like so many black offspring, were a cluster of small pots. A wooden butter churn held the door open, and clusters of Indian corn hung from the molding at aesthetic intervals. A colonial scythe stood in one corner, and two Boston rockers on a hooked rug faced the cold fireplace, where the unwatched pot never boiled.

Paul narrowed his eyes, excluding everything from his field of vision but the colonial tableau, and imagined that he and Anita had pushed this far into the upstate wilderness, with the nearest neighbor twenty-eight miles away. She was making soap, candles, and thick wool clothes for a hard winter ahead, and he, if they weren't to starve, had to mold bullets and go shoot a bear. Concentrating hard on the illusion, Paul was able to muster a feeling of positive gratitude for Anita's presence, to thank God for a woman at his side to help with the petrifying amount of work involved in merely surviving. As, in his imagination, he brought home a bear to Anita, and she cleaned it and salted it away, he felt a tremendous lift—the two of them winning by sinew and guts a mountain of strong, red meat from an inhospitable world. And he would mold more bullets, and she would make more candles and soap from the bear fat, until late at night, when Paul and Anita would tumble down together on a bundle of straw in the corner, dog-tired and sweaty, make love, and sleep hard until the brittle-cold dawn. . . .

"Urdle-urdle-urdle," went the automatic washing machine. *"Urdle-urdle-ur dull!"*

Reluctantly, Paul let his field of vision widen to include the other side of the room, where Anita sat on a ladder-back chair before the cherry breakfront that concealed the laundry console. The console had been rolled from the breakfront, whose façade of drawers and doors was one large piece, making the breakfront sort of a small garage for the laundry equipment. The doors of a corner cabinet were open, revealing a television screen, which Anita watched intently. A doctor was telling an old lady that her grandson would probably be paralyzed from the waist down for the rest of his life.

"Urdle-urdle-urdle," went the console. Anita paid no attention. *"Znick. Bazz-wap!"* Chimes sounded. Still Anita ignored it. *"Azzzzzzzzzzzzzz. Froomp!"* The top of the console popped open, and a basket of dry laundry burst from it like a great chrysanthemum, white, fragrant, and immaculate.

"Hello," said Paul.

Anita motioned for him to be silent, and wait until the program was over, which meant the commercial too. "All right," she said at last and turned down the volume. "Your blue suit is laid out on the bed."

"Oh? What for?"

"What do you mean, what for? For going over to Kroner's."

"How did you know that?"

"Lawson Shepherd called to tell me."

"Deuced nice of him."

"Nice of someone to tell me what's going on, since you won't."

"What else'd he say?"

"He supposed you and Finnerty must have had a wonderful time, judging from how terrible you looked this afternoon."

"He knows as much about it as I do."

Anita lit a cigarette, shook out the match with a flourish, and squinted through the smoke she let out through her nose. "Were there girls, Paul?"

"In a manner of speaking. Martha and Barbara. Don't ask me who had who."

"Had?"

"Sat with."

She hunched in the chair, looked out the window soberly, and kept her cigarette hot with quick, shallow puffs, and her eyes watered in the dramatic gusts from her nose. "You don't have to tell me about it, if you don't want to."

"I won't, because I can't remember." He started to laugh. "One was called Barbara, and the other was called Martha, and beyond that, as the saying goes, everything went black."

"Then you don't know what happened? I mean, anything could have happened?"

His smile withered. "I mean everything really went black, and nothing could have happened. I was clay curled up in a booth."

"And you remember nothing?"

"I remember a man named Alfy, who makes his living

as a television shark, a man named Luke Lubbock, who can be whatever his clothes are, a minister who gets a kick out of seeing the world go to hell, and—"

"And Barbara and Martha."

"And Barbara and Martha. And parades—my God, parades."

"Feel better?"

"No. But you should, because I think Finnerty's found a new home and a new friend."

"Thank God for that. I want you to make it clear to Kroner tonight that he forced himself on our hospitality, that we were as upset by him as anyone was."

"That isn't quite true."

"Well then, keep it to yourself, if you like him so much."

She lifted the lid of the schoolmaster's desk, where she made out the daily menus and compared her stubs with the bank statements, and took from it three sheets of paper. "I know you think I'm silly, but it's worth a little trouble to do things right, Paul."

The papers contained some sort of an outline, with major divisions set off by Roman numerals, and with sub-sub-sub-sub-sub-divisions as small as (a). At random, and with his headache taking on new vitality, he chose item III., A., I., a.: "Don't smoke. Kroner is trying to break the habit."

"Maybe it would help to read it aloud," said Anita.

"Maybe it'd be better if I read it alone, where there aren't any distractions."

"It took most of the afternoon."

"I expect it did. It's the most thorough job you've done yet. Thanks, darling, I appreciate it."

"I love you, Paul."

"I love *you*, Anita."

"Darling—about Martha and Barbara—"

"I promise you, I didn't touch them."

"I was going to ask, did anybody see you with them?"

"I guess they did, but nobody of any importance. Not Shepherd, certainly."

"If it ever got back to Kroner, I don't know what I'd do. He might laugh off the drinking, but the women—"

"I went to bed with Barbara," said Paul suddenly.

"I thought you did. That's your affair." She was tiring of the conversation, apparently, and she looked restively at the television screen.

"And Shepherd saw me coming downstairs with her."

"Paul!"

"Joke."

She put her hand over her heart. "Oh—thank the Lord."

" 'Summer Loves,' " said Paul, looking at the television screen judiciously.

"What's that?"

"The band—they're playing 'Summer Loves.' " He whistled a few bars.

"How can you tell, with the volume off?"

"Go ahead, turn it up."

Apathetically, she turned the knob, and "Summer Loves," as sweet and indigestible as honey cake, oozed into the air.

Humming along with the orchestra, Paul went up the steps to his bedroom, reading the outline as he went:

"IV., A., I. If Kroner asks you why you want Pittsburgh, say it is because you can be of greater service . . . a. Soft-pedal bigger house and raise and prestige."

Fuzzily, Paul was beginning to see that he had made an ass of himself in the eyes of those on both sides of the river. He remembered his cry of the night before: "We must meet in the middle of the bridge!" He decided that he would be about the only one interested in the expedition, the only one who didn't feel strongly about which bank he was on.

If his attempt to become the new Messiah had been

successful, if the inhabitants of the north and south banks had met in the middle of the bridge with Paul between them, he wouldn't have had the slightest idea of what to do next. He knew with all his heart that the human situation was a frightful botch, but it was such a logical, intelligently arrived-at botch that he couldn't see how history could possibly have led anywhere else.

Paul did a complicated sum in his mind—his savings account plus his securities plus his house plus his cars—and wondered if he didn't have enough to enable him simply to quit, to stop being the instrument of any set of beliefs or any whim of history that might raise hell with somebody's life. To live in a house by the side of a road. . . .

11

THE SHAH OF BRATPUHR, looking as tiny and elegant as a snuffbox in one end of the vast cavern, handed the *Sumklish* bottle back to Khashdrahr Miasma. He sneezed, having left the heat of summer above a moment before, and the sound chattered along the walls to die whispering in bat roosts deep in Carlsbad Caverns.

Doctor Ewing J. Halyard was making his thirty-seventh pilgrimage to the subterranean jungle of steel, wire, and glass that filled the chamber in which they stood, and thirty larger ones beyond. This wonder was a regular stop on the tours Halyard conducted for a bizarre variety of foreign potentates, whose common denominator was that their people represented untapped markets for America's stupendous industrial output.

A rubber-wheeled electric car came to a stop by the elevator, where the Shah's party stood, and an Army major, armed with a pistol, dismounted and examined their credentials slowly, thoroughly.

"Couldn't we speed this up a little, Major?" said Halyard. "We don't want to miss the ceremony."

"Perhaps," said the major. "But, as officer of the day, I'm responsible for nine billion dollars worth of government property, and if something should happen to it somebody might be rather annoyed with me. The ceremony has been delayed, anyway, so you won't miss anything. The President hasn't showed up yet."

The major was satisfied at last, and the party boarded the open vehicle.

"Siki?" said the Shah.

"This is EPICAC XIV," said Halyard. "It's an electronic computing machine—a brain, if you like. This chamber alone, the smallest of the thirty-one used, contains enough wire to reach from here to the moon four times. There are more vacuum tubes in the entire instrument than there were vacuum tubes in the State of New York before World War II." He had recited these figures so often that he had no need for the descriptive pamphlet that was passed out to visitors.

Khashdrahr told the Shah.

The Shah thought it over, snickered shyly, and Khashdrahr joined him in the quiet, Oriental merriment.

"Shah said," said Khashdrahr, "people in his land sleep with smart women and make good brains cheap. Save enough wire to go to moon a thousand times."

Halyard chuckled appreciatively, as he was paid to do, wiped aside the tears engendered by his ulcer, and explained that cheap and easy brains were what was wrong with the world in the bad old days, and that EPICAC XIV could consider simultaneously hundreds or even thousands of sides of a question utterly fairly, that EPICAC XIV was wholly free of reason-muddying emotions, that EPICAC XIV never forgot anything—that, in short, EPICAC XIV was dead right about everything. And Halyard added in his mind that the procedure described by the Shah had been tried about a trillion times, and had yet to produce a brain that could be relied upon to do the right thing once out of a hundred opportunities.

They were passing the oldest section of the computer now, what had been the whole of EPICAC I, but what was now little more than an appendix or tonsil of EPICAC XIV. Yet, EPICAC I had been intelligent enough, dispassionate enough, retentive enough to convince men that he, rather than they, had better do the planning for the war that was approaching with stupifying certainty. The ancient phrase used by generals testifying before appropriation committees, "all things considered," was given some validity by the ruminations of EPICAC I, more validity by EPICAC II, and so on, through the lengthening series. EPICAC could consider the merits of high-explosive bombs as opposed to atomic weapons for tactical support, and keep in mind at the same time the availability of explosives as opposed to fissionable materials, the spacing of enemy foxholes, the labor situation in the respective processing industries, the probable mortality of planes in the face of enemy antiaircraft technology, and on and on, if it seemed at all important, to the number of cigarettes and Cocoanut Mound Bars and Silver Stars required to support a high-morale air force. Given the facts by human beings, the war-born EPICAC series had offered the highly informed guidance that the reasonable, truth-loving, brilliant, and highly trained core of American genius could have delivered had they had inspired leadership, boundless resources, and two thousand years.

Through the war, and through the postwar years to the present, EPICAC's nervous system had been extended outward through Carlsbad Caverns—intelligence bought by the foot and pound and kilowatt. With each addition, a new, unique individual had been born, and now Halyard, the Shah, and Khashdrahr were arriving at the bunting-covered platform, where the President of the United States of America, Jonathan Lynn, would dedicate to a happier, more efficient tomorrow, EPICAC XIV.

The trio sat down on folding chairs and waited quietly with the rest of the distinguished company. Whenever there was a break in the group's whispering, EPICAC's hummings and clickings could be heard—the sounds attendant to the flow of electrons, now augmenting one another, now blocking, shuttling through a maze of electromagnetic crises to a condition that was translatable from electrical qualities and quantities to a high grade of truth.

EPICAC XIV, though undedicated, was already at work, deciding how many refrigerators, how many lamps, how many turbine-generators, how many hub caps, how many dinner plates, how many door knobs, how many rubber heels, how many television sets, how many pinochle decks—how many everything America and her customers could have and how much they would cost. And it was EPICAC XIV who would decide for the coming years how many engineers and managers and research men and civil servants, and of what skills, would be needed in order to deliver the goods; and what I.Q. and aptitude levels would separate the useful men from the useless ones, and how many Reconstruction and Reclamation Corps men and how many soldiers could be supported at what pay level and where, and . . .

"Ladies and Gentlemen," said the television announcer, "the President of the United States."

The electric car pulled up to the platform, and President Jonathan Lynn, born Alfred Planck, stood and showed his white teeth and frank gray eyes, squared his broad shoulders, and ran his strong, tanned hands through his curly hair.

The television cameras dollied and panned about him like curious, friendly dinosaurs, sniffing and peering. Lynn was boyish, tall, beautiful, and disarming, and, Halyard thought bitterly, he had gone directly from a three-hour television program to the White House.

"Is this man the spiritual leader of the American people?" asked Khashdrahr.

Halyard explained the separation of Church and State, and met, as he had expected to meet, with the Shah's usual disbelief and intimations that he, Halyard, hadn't understood the question at all.

The President, with an endearing, adolescent combination of brashness and shyness, and with the barest trace of a Western drawl, was now reading aloud a speech someone had written about EPICAC XIV. He made it clear that he wasn't any scientist, but just plain folks, standing here, humble before this great new wonder of the world, and that he was here because American plain folks had chosen him to represent them at occasions like this, and that, looking at this modern miracle, he was overcome with a feeling of deep reverence and humility and gratitude . . .

Halyard yawned, and was annoyed to think that Lynn, who had just read "order out of chaos" as "order out of koze," made three times as much money as he did. Lynn, or, as Halyard preferred to think of him, Planck, hadn't even finished high school, and Halyard had known smarter Irish setters. Yet, here the son-of-a-bitch was, elected to more than a hundred thousand bucks a year!

"You mean to say that this man governs without respect to the people's spiritual destinies?" whispered Khashdrahr.

"He has no religious duties, except very general ones, token ones," said Halyard, and then he started wondering just what the hell Lynn did do. EPICAC XIV and the National Industrial, Commercial, Communications, Foodstuffs, and Resources Board did all the planning, did all the heavy thinking. And the personnel machines saw to it that all governmental jobs of any consequence were filled by top-notch civil servants. The more Halyard thought about Lynn's fat pay check, the madder he got, because all the gorgeous dummy had to do was read whatever was handed to him on state occasions: to be suitably awed and reverent, as he said, for all the ordinary, stupid people who'd elected him to office, to run wisdom from somewhere else through that resonant voicebox and between those even, pearly choppers.

And Halyard suddenly realized that, just as religion and government had been split into disparate entities centuries before, now, thanks to the machines, politics and government lived side by side, but touched almost nowhere. He stared at President Jonathan Lynn and imagined with horror what the country must have been like when, as today, any damn fool little American boy might grow up to be President, but when the President had had to actually run the country!

President Lynn was explaining what EPICAC XIV would do for the millions of plain folks, and Khashdrahr was translating for the Shah. Lynn declared that EPICAC XIV was, in effect, the greatest individual in history, that the wisest man that had ever lived was to EPICAC XIV as a worm was to that wisest man.

For the first time the Shah of Bratpuhr seemed really impressed, even startled. He hadn't thought much of EPICAC XIV's physical size, but the comparison of the worm and the wise man struck home. He looked about himself apprehensively, as though the tubes and meters on all sides were watching every move.

The speech was over, and the applause was dying, and Doctor Halyard brought the Shah to meet the President, and the television cameras nuzzled about them.

"The President is now shaking hands with the Shah of Bratpuhr," said the announcer. "Perhaps the Shah will give us the fresh impressions of a visitor from another part of the world, from another way of life."

"Allasan Khabou pillan?" said the Shah uncertainly.

"He wonders if he might ask a question," said Khashdrahr.

"Sure, you bet," said the President engagingly. "If I don't know the answers, I can get them for you."

Unexpectedly, the Shah turned his back to the President and walked alone, slowly, to a deserted part of the platform.

"Wha'd I do wrong?" said Lynn.

"Ssssh!" said Khashdrahr fiercely, and he placed himself, like a guard, between the puzzled crowd and the Shah.

The Shah dropped to his knees on the platform and raised his hands over his head. The small, brown man suddenly seemed to fill the entire cavern with his mysterious, radiant dignity, alone there on the platform, communing with a presence no one else could sense.

"We seem to be witnessing some sort of religious rite," said the announcer.

"Can't you keep your big mouth shut for five seconds?" said Halyard.

"Quiet!" said Khashdrahr.

The Shah turned to a glowing bank of EPICAC's tubes and cried in a piping singsong voice:

> *"Allakahi baku billa,*
> *Moumi a fella nam;*
> *Serani assu tilla,*
> *Touri serin a sam."*

"The crazy bastard's talking to the machine," whispered Lynn.

"Ssssh!" said Halyard, strangely moved by the scene.

"Siki?" cried the Shah. He cocked his head, listening. *"Siki?"* The word echoed and died—lonely, lost.

"Mmmmmm," said EPICAC softly. *"Dit, dit. Mmmmm. Dit."*

The Shah sighed and stood, and shook his head sadly, terribly let down. *"Nibo,"* he murmured. *"Nibo."*

"What's he say?" said the President.

" *'Nibo'*—'nothing.' He asked the machine a question, and the machine didn't answer," said Halyard. *"Nibo."*

"Nuttiest thing I ever heard of," said the President. "You have to punch out the questions on that thingamajig, and the answers come out on tape from the whatchamacallits. You can't just talk to it." A doubt crossed his fine face. "I mean, you can't, can you?"

"No sir," said the chief engineer of the project. "As you say, not without the thingamajigs and whatchamacallits."

"What'd he say?" said Lynn, catching Khashdrahr's sleeve.

"An ancient riddle," said Khashdrahr, and it was plain that he didn't want to go on, that something sacred was involved. But he was also a polite man, and the inquiring eyes of the crowd demanded more of an explanation. "Our people believe," he said shyly, "that a great, all-wise god will come among us one day, and we shall know him, for he shall be able to answer the riddle, which EPICAC could not answer. When he comes," said Khashdrahr simply, "there will be no more suffering on earth."

"All-wise god, eh?" said Lynn. He licked his lips and patted down his unruly forelock. "How's the riddle go?"

Khashdrahr recited:

> "Silver bells shall light my way,
>   And nine times nine maidens fill my day,
>   And mountain lakes will sink from sight,
>   And tigers' teeth will fill the night."

President Lynn squinted at the cavern roof thoughtfully. "Mmm. Silver bells, eh?" He shook his head. "That's a stinker, you know? A real stinker. I give up."

1

"I'm not surprised," said Khashdrahr. "I'm not surprised. I expect you do."

Halyard helped the Shah, who seemed to have been
aged and exhausted by the emotional ordeal, into the electric
car.

As they rode to the foot of the elevator, the Shah came
back to life somewhat and curled his lip at the array of electronics about them. *"Baku!"* he said.

"That's a new one on me," said Halyard to Khashdrahr,
feeling warmly toward the little interpreter, who had squared
away Jonathan Lynn so beautifully. "What's *Baku?*"

"Little mud and straw figures made by the Surrasi, a
small infidel tribe in the Shah's land."

"This looks like mud and straw to him?"

"He was using it in the broader sense, I think, of false
god."

"Um," said Halyard. "Well, how are the Surrasi doing?"

"They all died of cholera last spring." He added after a
moment, "Of course." He shrugged, as though to ask what
else people like that could possibly expect. *"Baku."*

12

THE KRONER HOME, just outside Albany, was a Victorian mansion, perfectly restored and maintained down to the
filigree along the eaves, and the iron spikes along the roof
peak. The archprophet of efficiency, Kroner, preferred it to

the gracile, wipe-clean-with-a-damp-cloth steel and glass machines almost all of the engineers and managers lived in. Though Kroner had never accounted for his having bought the place—beyond saying that he liked lots of room—it was so in keeping with him that no one gave the anachronism more than passing thought.

A portrait painter had sensed the rightness of the setting, with no clues other than Kroner's face. The painter had been commissioned to do portraits of all the district managers. He did them from photographs, since the managers were too busy—or prudently claimed to be—to sit. Intuitively, the painter had depicted Kroner in a red plush chair, with a massive wedding ring prominently displayed, and with a background of heavy velvet drapes.

The mansion was one more affirmation of Kroner's belief that nothing of value changed; that what was once true is always true; that truths were few and simple; and that a man needed no knowledge beyond these truths to deal wisely and justly with any problem whatsoever.

"Come in," rumbled Kroner gently, answering the door himself. He seemed to fill the whole house with his slow strength and rock-bound calm. He was as informal as he ever became, having replaced his double-breasted suit coat with a single-breasted one of a slightly lighter shade and with suede patches at the elbows. The coat, he explained to visitors, was something his wife had given him years ago, something which he'd only recently mustered nerve enough to wear.

"I love your house more every time I see it," said Anita.

"You must tell Janice that." Janice was Mrs. Kroner, who smiled sweetly from the living room. She was a fat repository of truisms, adages, and homilies, and was usually addressed by the young engineers and managers as "Mom."

Mom, Paul recalled, had never liked that Finnerty boy, who would never call her Mom nor confide in her. Once, after she'd prodded him to unburden himself and feel better, he'd rather testily told her that he'd already fled one mother. Paul she liked, because Paul, as a youngster, *had* confided in her now and then. He would never do it again, but his demeanor before her conveyed that his failure to confide recently wasn't due to revulsion, but to a lack of problems.

"Hello, Mom," said Paul.

"Hello, Mom," said Anita.

"You children take a load off your feet," said Mom. "Now just tell me all about yourselves."

"Well, we've redone the kitchen," said Anita.

Mom was thrilled, eager for details.

Kroner hung his huge head, as though listening intently to the small talk, or, more likely, Paul thought, counting away the seconds before it would be polite to separate the men and women—a custom of the house.

As Anita paused for breath, Kroner stood, beamed, and suggested that Paul come into his study to see the guns. It was the same gambit every time—the men were to see the guns. Years ago, Anita had made the mistake of saying she was interested in guns, too. Kroner had politely told her that his weren't the kind women liked.

Mom's response was always the same, too: "Oh guns—I hate them. I can't see why men want to go around shooting sweet little animals."

The fact was, Kroner never fired his guns. His pleasure seemed to be in owning and handling them. He also used them for props, to give an air of informality to his man-to-man talks. He announced raises and promotions, demotions and firings, and praised or warned, always in seemingly casual asides made while swabbing a bore.

Paul followed him into the dark-paneled study, and waited for him to choose his weapon from the gunrack that filled one wall. Kroner ran his index finger along the collection, like a stick along a picket fence. It had been a matter of speculation among Kroner's underlings as to whether there was any significance in the guns he chose for a particular discussion. For a while the rumor was current that shotguns were bad news, rifles were good news. But it hadn't withstood the test of time. Kroner finally chose a ten-gauge shotgun, broke open the breach, and squinted through the bore at a streetlight outside.

"Wouldn't dare shoot modern ammunition in this one," said Kroner. "Twist barrel—thing'd go all to pieces. But look at that inlay work, Paul."

"Beautiful. Priceless."

"Some man spent maybe two years on it. Time didn't mean anything in those days. The industrial dark ages, Paul."

"Yessir."

He selected a cleaning rod and lined up on his desk top a can of oil, a jar of grease, and several cloth patches. "Got to keep after a bore, or it'll pit on you just like that." He snapped his fingers. He oiled a patch, twisted it about the tip of the cleaning rod. "Especially in this climate."

"Yessir." Paul started to light a cigarette, and then remembered Anita's warning in the outline.

Kroner drove the cleaning rod downward. "Where's Ed Finnerty, by the way?"

"Don't know, sir."

"Police are looking for him."

"Really?"

Kroner slid the patch back and forth and didn't look at Paul. "Uh-huh. Now that he's out of a job, he's got to register with the police, and he hasn't."

"I left him downtown in Homestead last night."

"I know that. I thought maybe you knew where he went."

Kroner had a habit of saying he already knew what he'd just been told. Paul was sure the old man didn't really know anything about the night before. "I haven't any idea." He didn't want to make trouble for anyone. Let the police find out that Finnerty was with Lasher, if they could.

"Umm hmmm. See that pit right there?" He held the

muzzle of the gun a few inches from Paul's face and pointed out a tiny flaw. "That's what happens if you let a bore go for even a month. They'll run right away with you."

"Yessir."

"He isn't to be trusted any more, Paul. He isn't right in his head, and it wouldn't do to take chances with him, would it?"

"Nossir."

Kroner dabbed at the pit with the corner of a patch. "I supposed you saw it that way. That's why it's a little difficult for me to understand why you let him wander around the plant unescorted."

Paul reddened. No words came.

"Or why you'd let him have your gun. He isn't authorized for firearms any more, you know. Yet they tell me they found your pistol covered with his fingerprints."

Before Paul could order his thoughts, Kroner clapped him on his knee and laughed like Santa Claus. "I'm so sure you've got a good explanation, I don't even want to hear it. Got a lot of faith in you, my boy. Don't want to see you get into any trouble. Now that your father's gone, I feel it's sort of up to me to watch out for you."

"That's nice of you, sir."

Kroner turned his back to Paul, assumed a ready stance with the shotgun, and picked off an imaginary bird flushed from behind the desk. "Kaplowie!" He ejected an imaginary shell. "These are dangerous times—more dangerous than you'd suspect from the surface. Kaplowie! But it's also the Golden Age, isn't it, Paul?"

Paul nodded.

Kroner turned to look at him. "I said, isn't this the Golden Age?"

"Yessir. I nodded."

"Pull!" said Kroner, apparently imagining clay pigeons now. "Kaboom! There have always been doubters, criers of doom, stoppers of progress."

"Yessir. About Finnerty and the pistol, I—"

"Behind us now, forgotten," said Kroner impatiently. "The slate is clean. As I was about to say, look where we are now, because men went right ahead and took forward steps with stout hearts, in spite of the people telling them not to."

"Yessir."

"Kaplowie! Some men try to make light of what we're doing, what men like your father did, by saying it's just gadgeteering, blind tinkering. It's more than that, Paul."

Paul leaned forward, eager to hear what this extra quality might be. He'd felt for some time that everyone else in the system must be seeing something he was missing. Perhaps this was it, perhaps the beginning of an overwhelming fervor like his father's.

"It's a sight more than gadgeteering, I'll tell you, Paul."

"Yessir?"

"It's strength and faith and determination. Our job is to open new doors at the head of the procession of civilization. That's what the engineer, the manager does. There is no higher calling."

Dejectedly, Paul let his spine sag back in the chair.

Kroner put a fresh patch on the cleaning rod and began swabbing the bore again. "Paul—Pittsburgh is still open. The field has been narrowed down to two men."

It was somewhat startling that he said it just that way, the way Anita had said he would. He wondered what it was she thought he should say in response. He'd never given her a chance to say, and hadn't read the outline. "It's a wonderful chance to be of real service," he said. He supposed that was pretty close to what she had in mind.

Paul felt lightheaded, having borrowed Anita's thoughts for want of enthusiasm of his own. He was being offered the Pittsburgh job, lots more money, and, since he would have risen so high with the greater portion of his life still ahead, the assurance that he would almost certainly go clear to the top. The moment of his arrival at this point of immense good fortune was curiously bland. He had known it was coming for a long time. Kroner had wanted it for him and had come close to promising it to him often—always in the name of his father. When advances had come, as now, there had been a vestigal sort of ritual of surprise and congratulation, as though Paul, like his ancestors, had arrived by cunning, tenacity, and God's will or the Devil's laxness.

"It's a tough decision, Paul, between you and Fred Garth." Garth was a much older man, nearly Kroner's age, manager of the Buffalo Works. "Frankly, Garth hasn't got your technical imagination, Paul. As a manager he's excellent, but if it wasn't for prodding, the Buffalo Works would be just as it was when he took over five years ago. But he's steady and reliable, Paul, and there's never been any question that he was one of us, that he put progress and the system ahead of his own interests."

"Garth's a fine man," said Paul. Garth was, too: foursquare, desperate to please, and he seemed to have an anthropomorphic image of the corporate personality. Garth stood in relation to that image as a lover, and Paul wondered if this prevalent type of relationship had ever been given the consideration it deserved by sexologists. On second thought, he supposed that it had—the general phenomenon of a lover's devotion to the unseen—in studies of nuns' symbolic marriages to Christ. At any rate, Paul had seen Garth at various stages of his love affair, unable to eat for anxiety, on a manic crest, moved to maudlin near-crying at recollections of the affair's tender beginnings. In short, Garth suffered all the emotional hazards of a perennial game of she-loves-me, she-loves-me-not. To carry out directions from above—an irritating business for Paul—was, for Garth, a favor to please a lady. "I'd like to see him get the job."

"I'd like to see you get the job, Paul." Kroner's expression indicated that the mention of Garth had been so much window dressing. "You've got imagination and spirit and ability—"

"Thank you, sir."

"Let me finish. Imagination, spirit, and ability, and, for all I know, I may be completely wrong in calling your loyalty into question."

"Loyalty?"

Kroner laid the shotgun aside and pulled up a chair to face Paul's. He laid his big hands on Paul's knees and lowered his thick brows. The situation had the quality of a séance, with Kroner as the medium. Again, as he had felt when Kroner took his hand at the Country Club, Paul felt his strength and will dwarfed by the old man. "Paul, I want you to tell me what's on your mind."

The hands on his knees tightened. Paul struggled resentfully against the urge to pour his heart out to this merciful, wise, gentle father. But his sullenness decayed. Paul began to talk.

His formless misgivings and disquiet of a week before, he realized, had shape now. The raw material of his discontent was now cast in another man's molds. He was saying what Lasher had said the night before, talking about the spiritual disaster across the river, about the threat of revolution, about the hierarchy that was a nightmare to most. The way he phrased it, it wasn't a condemnation, it was a plea for refutation.

Kroner, his hands still on Paul's knees, hung his head lower and lower.

Paul came to the end, and Kroner stood and turned his back to stare out of the window. The spell was still in force, and Paul looked expectantly at the broad back, waiting for wisdom.

Kroner turned suddenly. "So you're against us."

"I didn't mean to say that, certainly. They're questions that deserve some sort of answer."

"Keep to your own side of the river, Paul! Your job is management and engineering. I don't know what the answers are to Lasher's questions. I do know that it's far easier to ask questions than to answer them. I know that there have always been questions, and men like Lasher ready to make trouble by asking them."

"You know about Lasher?" Paul hadn't mentioned his name.

"Yes, I've known about him for quite some time. And, as of this noon, I know what you and Lasher and Finnerty were up to last night." He looked sad. "As district industrial security officer, there isn't much I don't know, Paul. And sometimes, like now, I wish I didn't know so much."

"And Pittsburgh?"

"I still think you're the man for the job. I'm going to pretend that you didn't do last night what you did, didn't say just now what you said. I don't believe it came from your heart."

Paul was amazed. By some freakish circumstance he'd apparently clinched the job—after having arrived with the vague intention of disqualifying himself.

"This is the main stretch, Paul. Now it's all up to you."

"I could go on the wagon, I suppose."

"It's a little more complicated than that, I'm afraid. In a very short while you managed to pile up a fairly impressive police dossier: the pistol, letting Finnerty into the plant, last night's indiscretions—and, well, I've got to be able to explain it all away to the satisfaction of Headquarters. You could go to prison, you know."

Paul laughed nervously.

"I want to be able to say, Paul, that you were doing special security work for me, and I'd like to prove it."

"I see." Paul didn't.

"You'll agree that both Lasher and Finnerty are danger-ous men, potential saboteurs who should be put where they can't do any harm." He took the shotgun down from the rack again and distorted his face as he cleaned around the ejector with a toothpick. "So," he said after a few moments of silence, "I'll want you to testify that they tried to get you into a plot to sabotage the Ilium Works."

The door flew open, and Baer came in, grinning. "Congratulations, my boy. Congratulations. Wonderful, wonderful, wonderful."

"Congratulations?" said Paul.

"Pittsburgh, my boy, Pittsburgh!"

"It hasn't quite been settled," said Kroner.

"But you said yesterday—"

"A little something's come up since then." Kroner winked at Paul. "Nothing very serious, though, eh, Paul? A little hurdle."

"Um, oh, I see, uh-huh; a hurdle, a hurdle. I see. Um."

Paul was shaken and confused by what had just happened to him, and he hid his lack of composure behind a vacuous smile. He wondered if Baer had come in on cue.

"Paul here had some questions," said Kroner.

"Questions? Questions, my boy?"

"He wanted to know if we weren't doing something bad in the name of progress."

Baer sat on the desk and began taking kinks out of the telephone cord. He was thinking very hard, and from the man's expression Paul could only conclude that the question had never come to Baer's attention before. Now that it had, he was giving it his earnest consideration. "Is progress bad? Uh-huh—good question." He looked up from the cord. "I don't know, don't know. Maybe progress is bad, eh?"

Kroner looked at him with surprise. "Look, you know darn good and well history's answered the question a thousand times."

"It has? Has it? You know; I wouldn't. Answered it a thousand times, has it? That's good, good. All I know is, you've got to act like it has, or you might as well throw in the towel. Don't know, my boy. Guess I should, but I don't. Just do my job. Maybe that's wrong."

It was Kroner's turn to be dismayed. "Well, what say to a refresher?" he said briskly.

"I say yes to a refresher," said Paul gratefully.

Kroner chuckled. "There, there; it wasn't so rough, now was it?"

"Nope."

"That's my boy. Chin up."

As Baer, Paul, and Kroner filed into the living room, Mom was telling Anita sadly that it took all kinds of people to make a world.

"I just want to make sure everybody understands he invited himself," said Anita. "Mom, there wasn't a thing we could do about it."

Kroner dusted his hands. "Well, what say to a pick-me-up?"

"Wonderful, wonderful, wonderful," said Baer.

"Did you men have a good time with those awful guns?" said Mom, wrinkling her nose.

"Swell, Mom," said Paul.

Anita caught Paul's eyes, and raised her brows questioningly.

Paul nodded slightly.

She smiled and lay back in her chair, exhausted, satisfied.

Mom handed out small glasses of port, while Kroner tinkered with the phonograph. "Where is it?" he said.

"Now, now—right where it always is, on the turntable," said Mom.

"Oh yes—here it is. I thought maybe somebody else had been playing something since I used it."

"No. Nobody's been near the phonograph since last night."

Kroner held the tone arm over the spinning record. "This is for you, Paul. When I said pick-me-up I really had this in mind more than the wine. This is meat for the spirit. This can pull me out of a slump like nothing I can think of."

"I gave it to him last month, and I can't think of anything that's ever pleased him as much," said Mom.

Kroner lowered the needle into the groove and hurried
to a chair and covered his eyes before the music began.

The volume was turned way up, and suddenly the loudspeaker howled:

*"Ooooooooooooh, give me some men, who are stout-hearted
men, who will fight for the right they adore . . ."*

Paul looked around the room. Kroner was clumping his
feet up and down and jerking his head from side to side.
Mom was jerking her head, too, and so were Baer and
Anita—Anita more violently than any of them.

Paul sighed, and began to jerk his head, too.

*"Shoulder to shoulder, and bolder and bolder, they grow as
they go to the fore! Ooooooooooooh . . ."*

13

Lying abed after the stout-hearted men's evening at
the Kroner's, Doctor Paul Proteus, son of a successful man,
himself rich with prospects of being richer, counted his material blessings. He found that he was in excellent shape to
afford integrity. He was worth, without having to work another day in his life, almost three-quarters of a million dollars.

For once, his dissatisfaction with his life was specific.
He was reacting to an outrage that would be regarded as such
by almost any man in any period in history. He had been told
to turn informer on his friend, Ed Finnerty. This was about

as basic as an attack on integrity could be, and Paul received it with the same sort of relief that was felt when the first shots of the last war were fired—after decades of tension.

Now he could damn well lose his temper and quit.

Anita slept—utterly satisfied, not so much by Paul as by the social orgasm of, after years of the system's love play, being offered Pittsburgh.

She had delivered a monologue on the way home from Albany—a recitation that might have come from Shepherd. She'd reviewed Paul's career from the instant of their marriage onward, and Paul was surprised to learn that his path was strewn with bodies—men who had tried to best him, only to be chagrined and ruined.

She made the carnage so vivid that he was obliged for a moment to abandon his own thoughts, to see if there was the slightest truth in what she was saying. He went over the scalps she was counting one by one—men who had competed with him for this job or that—and found that they all had done well for themselves and were quite unbroken either financially or in spirit. But to Anita they were dead men, shot squarely between the eyes, and good riddance of bad rubbish.

Paul hadn't told Anita the conditions he would have to meet before he could have Pittsburgh. And he didn't intimate that he was going to do anything but take the job proudly, joyfully.

Now, lying beside her, he congratulated himself on his calm, on his being wily for the first time in his life, really. He wasn't going to tell Anita that he was quitting for a long time, not until she was ready. He would subtly re-educate her to a new set of values, and *then* quit. Otherwise the shock of being the wife of a nobody might do tragic things. The only grounds on which she met the world were those of her husband's rank. If he were to lose the rank it was frighteningly possible that she would lose touch with the world altogether, or, worse for Paul, leave him.

And Paul didn't want either of those things to happen.

She was what fate had given him to love, and he did his best to love her. He knew her too well for her conceits to be offensive most of the time, to be anything but pathetic.

She was also more of a source of courage than he cared to admit.

She also had a sexual genius that gave Paul his one un-qualified enthusiasm in life.

And Anita had also made possible, by her dogged atten-tion to details, the luxury of his detached, variously amused or cynical outlook on life.

She was also all he had.

A vague panic welled up cold in his chest, driving away drowsiness when he would most have welcomed it. He began to see that he, too, would be in for a shock. He felt oddly disembodied, an insubstantial wisp, nothingness, a man who declined to be any more. Suddenly understanding that he, like Anita, was little more than his station in life, he threw his arms around his sleeping wife, and laid his head on the breast of his fellow wraith-to-be.

"Mmmmm?" said Anita. "Mmmmmmm?"

"Anita—"

"Mmm?"

"Anita, I love you." The compulsion was upon him to tell her everything, to mingle his consciousness with hers. But as he momentarily raised his head from the drugging warmth and fragrance of her bosom, cool, fresh air from the Adirondacks bathed his face, and wisdom returned. He said nothing more to her.

"I love *you*, Paul," she murmured.

14

DOCTOR PAUL PROTEUS was a man with a secret. Most of the time it was an exhilarating secret, and he extracted momentary highs of joy from it while dealing with fellow members of the system in the course of his job. At the beginning and close of each item of business he thought, "To hell with you."

It was to hell with them, to hell with everything. This secret detachment gave him a delightful sense of all the world's being a stage. Waiting until the time when he and Anita would be in mental shape to quit and start a better life, Paul acted out his role as manager of the Ilium Works. Outwardly, as manager, he was unchanged; but inwardly he was burlesquing smaller, less free souls who would have taken the job seriously.

He had never been a reading man, but now he was developing an appetite for novels wherein the hero lived vigorously and out-of-doors, dealing directly with nature, dependent upon basic cunning and physical strength for survival—woodsmen, sailors, cattlemen. . . .

He read of these heroes with a half-smile on his lips. He knew his enjoyment of them was in a measure childish, and he doubted that a life could ever be as clean, hearty, and satisfying as those in the books. Still and all, there was a basic truth underlying the tales, a primitive ideal to which he could aspire. He wanted to deal, not with society, but only with Earth as God had given it to man.

"Is that a good book, Doctor Proteus?" said Doctor Katharine Finch, his secretary. She'd come into his office carrying a large gray cardboard box.

"Oh—hello, Katharine." He laid the book down with a smile. "Not great literature; I'll promise you that. Pleasant relaxation is all. All about bargemen on the old Erie Ship Canal." He tapped the broad, naked chest of the hero on the book jacket. "Don't make men like that any more. Well, what's in the box? That for me?"

"It's your shirts. They just came by mail."

"Shirts?"

"For the Meadows."

"Oh, *those* things. Open them up. What color are they?"

"Blue. You're on the Blue Team this year." She laid the shirts on the desk.

"Oh, no!" Paul stood and held one of the deep blue T-shirts at arm's length. "Dear God in heaven—no!" Across the chest of each of the shirts, in blazing gold letters, was the word "Captain." "Katharine, they can't do this to me."

"It's an honor, isn't it?"

"Honor!" He exhaled noisily and shook his head. "For fourteen days, Katharine, I, Queen of the May and captain of the Blue Team, am going to have to lead my men in group singing, marches, greased-pole climbing, volley ball, horse-shoes, softball, golf-ball driving, badminton, trapshooting, capture the flag, Indian wrestling, touch football, shuffle-board, and trying to throw the other captains into the lake. Agh!"

"Doctor Shepherd was very pleased."

"He always has been fond of me."

"No—I mean he was pleased about being a captain himself."

"Oh? Shepherd is a captain?" Paul's raised eyebrows were part of an old reflex, the wary reaction of a man who has been in the system for a good many years. Being chosen to captain one of the four teams *was* an honor, if a man gave a damn about such things. It was a way the higher brass had of showing favor, and, politically, Shepherd's having been chosen a captain was a striking business. Shepherd had always been a nobody at the Meadows, whose chief fame was as a pretty fair softball pitcher. Now, suddenly, he was a captain. "Which team?"

"Green. His shirts are on my desk. Green with orange lettering. Very vivid."

"Green, eh?" Well, if one cared about such things, Green was the lowest in the unofficial hierarchy of teams. It was one of those things that was understood without anyone's saying anything about it. Having looked this far into the piddling matter, Paul congratulated himself for having been named captain of the Blue, which, again, everybody seemed to feel was the team with the most tone. Not that it made any difference at all any more. Made none. Silly. To hell with it.

"They certainly give you enough shirts," said Katharine, counting. "Nine, ten, eleven, twelve."

"Nothing like enough. For two weeks you drink and sweat, drink and sweat, drink and sweat, until you feel like a sump pump. This is a day's supply at the outside."

"Uh-huh. Well, sorry, that's all there is in the box except this book." She held up the volume, which looked like a hymnal.

"Hi ho—*The Meadows Songbook*," said Paul wearily. He leaned back and closed his eyes. "Pick a song, Katharine, any song, and read it aloud."

"Here's the song for the Green Team, Doctor Shepherd's team. To the tune of the *William Tell Overture*."

"The whole overture?"

"That's what it says here."

"Well, go ahead and give it a try."

She cleared her throat, started to sing softly, thought better of it, and lapsed into plain reading:

"Green oh Green oh Green's the team!
Mightiest e'er the world has seen!
Red, Blue, White will scream,

When
They see the great Green Team!"

"That'll put hair on your chest, Katharine."

"Oh, gosh but it'll be fun! You *know* you'll love it when you get up there."

Paul opened his eyes to see that Katharine was reading another song, and her eyes shone with excitement and she rocked her head from side to side. "What's that you're reading now?"

"Oh, I wish I were a man! I was just reading your song."

"My song?"

"The Blue Team's song."

"Oh—*my* song. By all means, let's hear it."

She whistled a few bars of "Indiana," and then sang, this time heartily:

"Oh you Blue Team, you tried and true team,
There are no teams as good as you!
You will smash Green, also the Red Team,
And the White Team you'll batter, too.
They'd better scurry before your fury,
And in a hurry, without a clue;
Because the Blue Team's a tried and true team,
And there's no team as good as you!"

"Hmmm."

"And you *will* win, too. I know you will," said Katharine.

"You going to be at the Mainland?" The Mainland was a camp for wives and children, and women employees whose development wasn't yet complete, across the water from the Meadows, the island where the men went.

"That's as close as I can get to the real thing," said Katharine wistfully.

"That's close enough, believe me. Tell me, is Bud Calhoun going to be there?"

She colored, and he was instantly sorry he'd asked. "He had an invitation, I know," she said, "but that was before—" She shrugged unhappily. "And you know what the *Manual* says."

"The machines can't stand him any more," said Paul heavily. "Why don't they build in a gimmick that will give a man a free drink before he gets the ax? Do you know what he's up to now?"

"I haven't talked to him or seen him, but I did call up Matheson's office to find out what was going to be done with him. They said he was going to be a project supervisor for the—" her voice caught "—for the Reeks and Wrecks." Emotion was giving her a rough going-over now, and she left Paul's office hurriedly.

"I'm sure he'll do well," Paul called after her. "I'll bet we won't know our city a year from now, with him thinking up things for the Reeks and Wrecks to do."

Her phone rang, and she relayed the information to Paul that Doctor Edward Finnerty was at the gate, wanting in.

"Bind his hands and feet, put a bag over his head, and have four men bring him up. Fixed bayonets, of course. And be sure and get a picture of it for Shepherd."

Ten minutes later, Finnerty was escorted into Paul's office by an armed guard.

"For heaven's sake—look at you!" said Paul. Finnerty's hair was cut and combed, his face was pink, shining, and shaved, and his seersucker suit, while worn and a poor fit, was crisp and sanitary-looking.

Finnerty looked at him blankly, as though he couldn't guess what the fuss was about. "I'd like to borrow your car."

"Promise to wipe off the fingerprints when you're through?"

"Oh—you're sore about that pistol business, I suppose. Sorry. I meant to throw it in the river."

"You know about it, then?"

"Sure—and about how Shepherd turned in a report on you, too, telling how you let me in the plant without an escort. Tough." Finnerty, after less than a week in Homestead, had taken on rough, swashbuckling mannerisms—glaringly synthetic. He also seemed to be getting a real kick out of being a liability as an associate for anyone respectable.

Paul was amazed, as he had been amazed at Kroner's, by how much others knew about his affairs. "How do you know so much?"

"You'd be surprised who knows what, and how they find out. Surprise the pants off you to know what goes on in this world. My eyes are just opening." He leaned forward earnestly. "And, Paul—I'm finding myself. At last I'm finding myself."

"What do you look like, Ed?"

"Those dumb bastards across the river—they're *my* kind of people. They're real, Paul, real!"

Paul had never doubted that they were real, and so found himself without any sort of comment or emotional response for Finnerty's important announcement. "Well, I'm glad you've found yourself after all these years," he said. Finnerty had been finding himself ever since Paul had known him. And, weeks later, he'd always deserted that self with angry cries of impostor, and discovered another. "That's swell, Ed."

"Well, anyway, how about the keys to the car?"

"Is it fair to ask what for?"

"This is a milk run. I want to pick up my clothes and stuff at your house and run them over to Lasher's."

"You're living with Lasher?"

Finnerty nodded. "Surprising how well we hit it off, right from the first." His tone implied the barest trace of contempt for Paul's shallow way of life. "Keys?"

Paul threw them to him. "How do you plan to use the rest of your life, Ed?"

"With the people. That's my place."

"You know the cops are after you for not registering?"

"Spice of life."

"You can be jailed, you know."

"You're afraid to live, Paul. That's what's the matter with you. You know about Thoreau and Emerson?"

"A little. About as much as you did before Lasher primed you, I'll bet."

"Anyway, Thoreau was in jail because he wouldn't pay a tax to support the Mexican War. He didn't believe in the war. And Emerson came to jail to see him. 'Henry,' he said, 'why are you here?' And Thoreau said, 'Ralph, why *aren't* you here?' "

"I should want to go to jail?" said Paul, trying to get some sort of message for himself out of the anecdote.

"You shouldn't let fear of jail keep you from doing what you believe in."

"Well, it doesn't." Paul reflected that the big trouble, really, was finding something to believe in.

"All right, so it doesn't." There was weary disbelief in Finnerty's voice. He was apparently getting bored with his convention-ridden former friend from the north side of the river. "Thanks for the car."

"Any time." Paul was relieved when the door closed behind the new—this week's—Finnerty.

Katharine opened the door again. "He scares me," she said.

"You needn't be scared. He wastes all his energy on games with himself. There goes your phone."

"It's Doctor Kroner," said Katharine. "Yes," she said into the telephone, "Doctor Proteus is in."

"Would you please put him on," said Kroner's secretary.

"Doctor Proteus speaking."

"Doctor Proteus is on," said Katharine.

"Just a moment. Doctor Kroner wishes to speak with him. Doctor Kroner, Doctor Proteus in Ilium is on the line."

"Hello, Paul."

"How do you do, sir."

"Paul, about this Finnerty and Lasher business—" His playfully conspiratorial tone implied that the proposed prosecution of these two was sort of a practical joke. "Just wanted to tell you that I called Washington about it, to let them in on what we're going to do, and they say we should hold off for a while. They say the whole thing ought to be well planned at the top level. It's apparently bigger stuff than I thought." His voice dropped to a whisper. "It's beginning to look like a problem nationwise, not just Iliumwise."

Paul was pleased that there was to be a delay, but the reason for it was a surprise. "How could Finnerty get to be a problem nationwise or even Iliumwise? He's only been here a few days."

"Idle hands do the Devil's work, Paul. He's probably been getting into bad company, and it's the bad company we're really after. Anyway, the top brass wants in on whatever we do, and they want to have a meeting about it at the Meadows. Let's see—sixteen days from now."

"Fine," said Paul, and added, in his mind, the imaginary seal he affixed to all official business these days—"And to hell with you." He had no intention of turning informer on anyone. He would simply stall until he and Anita were fully prepared to say, "To hell with you, to hell with everything," aloud.

"We think the world of you over here, Paul."

"Thank you, sir."

Kroner was silent for a moment. Suddenly he shouted into the phone, almost rupturing Paul's eardrum.

"Beg your pardon, sir?" The message had been so loud as to be all pain and no sense.

PLAYER PIANO

Kroner chuckled, and lowered his voice a little. "I said, who's going to win, Paul?"

"Win?"

"The Meadows, the Meadows! Who's going to win?"

"Oh—the Meadows," said Paul. It was a nightmarish conversation, with Kroner vehement and happy, and with Paul devoid of the vaguest notion as to what was being discussed.

"What team?" said Kroner, a shade peevishly.

"Oh. Oh! The *Blue Team* is going to win!" He filled his lungs. "Blue!" he shouted.

"You bet your life we're going to win!" Kroner shouted back. "The Blues are behind you, Cap'n!" Kroner, then, was on the Blue Team, too. He started to sing in his rumbling basso:

"Oh you Blue Team, you tried and true team,
    There are no teams as good as you!
    You will smash Green, also the Red Team,
    And the White Team you'll batt—"

The song was interrupted by a cry: "White's going to win! Go, White!" It was Baer, yelling in the background. "So you think Blue's going to win, do you, do you, eh? Win? Think Blue's going to win, eh, eh? The White Team will trim you, trim you—aha, aha—trim the daylights out of the Blue Team."

There was the sound of laughter and banter and scuffling, and Kroner picked up the Blue Team's song where he'd left off:

"They'd better scurry before your fury,
    And in a hurry, without a clue;
    Because the—"

145

Baer's piercing voice cut through Kroner's bass with the White Team's song, to the tune of "Tramp, Tramp, Tramp":

"White, White, White's the one to watch for.
Blue, Green, Red will come to grief.
Before the fury of the White
They'll get knocked clear out of—"

The scuffling grew louder, and the songs degenerated into panting laughter. There was a clatter in Paul's receiver, a cry, a click, and then the dial tone.

Paul restored the receiver to its cradle with a limp hand. There was no quitting before the Meadows, he told himself glumly—no re-educating Anita and quitting in the few days remaining. The Meadows would have to be endured, and, worse luck, he would have to endure it as captain of the Blue Team.

His glance passed over the hairy tan chest, frank gray eyes, and keg-sized biceps of the man on the book jacket, and his thoughts slid easily, gratefully, into the fantasy of the new, good life ahead of him. Somewhere, outside of society, there was a place for a man—a man and wife—to live heartily and blamelessly, *naturally*, by hands and wits.

Paul studied his long, soft hands. Their only callus was on the large finger of his right hand. There, stained a dirty orange by cigarette tars, a tough hump had grown over the years, protecting his finger against the attrition of pen and pencil shafts. Skills—that was what the hands of the heroes in the novels had, skills. To date, Paul's hands had learned to do little save grip a pen, pencil, toothbrush, hair brush, razor, knife, fork, spoon, cup, glass, faucet, doorknob, switch, handkerchief, towel, zipper, button, snap, bar of soap, book, comb, wife, or steering wheel.

He recalled his college days, and was sure he'd learned some sort of manual skill there. He'd learned to make mechanical drawings. That was when the lump on his finger had begun to grow. What else? He'd learned to bounce a ball off several walls with skill, and to the consternation of most of his squash opponents. He'd been good enough to make the quarter-finals of the Regional Collegiate Squash Tournament two years in a row. He used to be able to do *that* with his hands.

What else?

Again uneasiness crept up on him—the fear that there was far too little of him to get along anywhere outside the system, to get along at all contentedly. He might go into some small business, such as the one he claimed to be in when he didn't want to be recognized—wholesale groceries. But he would still be caught in the mesh of the economy and its concomitant hierarchy. The machines wouldn't let him into that business, anyway, and even if they would, there'd be no less nonsense and posturing. Moreover, despite the fact that Paul was saying to hell with the whole system, he was aware that the relatively unskilled and dull business of buying and selling was beneath him. So to hell with it. The only thing worse would be complete idleness, which Paul could afford, but which, he was sure, was as amoral as what he was quitting.

Farming—now *there* was a magic word. Like so many words with little magic from the past still clinging to them, the word "farming" was a reminder of what rugged stock the present generation had come from, of how tough a thing a human being could be if he had to. The word had little meaning in the present. There were no longer farmers, but only agricultural engineers. In the rich Iroquois Valley in Ilium County, thousands of settlers had once made their living from the soil. Now Doctor Ormand van Curler managed the farming of the whole county with a hundred men and several million dollars' worth of machinery.

Farming. Paul's pulse quickened, and he daydreamed of living a century before—living in one of the many farmhouses now crumbling into their foundations over the valley.

He chose one farmhouse in particular for his fantasy, one close to the edge of town that he'd often admired. He suddenly realized that the farm, the little patch of the past, *wasn't* a part of van Curler's farm system. He was almost sure it wasn't.

"Katharine," he called excitedly, "get me the Ilium Real Estate Manager on the phone."

"Ilium Real Estate Office. Doctor Pond speaking." Pond's speech was effeminate, lisping.

"Doctor Pond, this is Doctor Proteus at the Works."

"Well! What can I do for *you*, Doctor Proteus?"

"You know that farmhouse out on King Street, just outside the city limits?"

"Mmmm. Just a moment." Paul heard a machine shuffling through cards, and then a bell announced that the card had been found. "Yes, the Gottwald place. I have the card right here."

"What's being done with it?"

"A good question! What can be done with it? I wish I knew. It was a hobby with Gottwald, you know, keeping it just like an old-fashioned farm. When he died, the heirs wanted to get van Curler to take it over, but he said it wasn't worth bothering with. Two hundred acres is all, and he'd have to cut down the windbreaks to connect it with other fields so he could farm it efficiently. Then the heirs found out that they couldn't have sold it to the Farm System anyway. It's in the deed that the place has to be kept old-fashioned." He laughed bitterly. "So all old Gottwald left his heirs was a nice headache, a white elephant."

"How much?"

"Are you serious? The thing's a museum exhibit, Doctor. I mean, almost nothing mechanical on the place. Even if you could beat the restrictions in the deed, it'd cost you thousands to get it in shape."

"How much?" The farm was looking better and better.

"Eighteen thousand, it says on the card." Before Paul

could close the deal that instant, Pond added, "but you can get it for fifteen, I'm sure. How would twelve suit you?"

"Would five hundred hold it until I can look it over?"

"It's been holding itself for almost fourteen years. Go on out and have a look, if you really feel you have to. After you've thrown up, there are some really nice things I'd like to show you." The machine riffled through its cards again. "For instance, there's a nice Georgian house on Griffin Boulevard. Electronic door openers, thermostatically controlled windows, radar range, electrostatic dust precipitators, ultrasonic clothes washer built in, forty-inch television screens in the master bedroom, guest room, living room, kitchen, and rumpus rooms, and twenty-inch screens in the maids' rooms and the kiddies' rooms, and—"

"Where can I get the key to the farm?"

"Oh, *that* thing. Well, to give you an idea of what you're getting into, there is no lock. There's a latchstring."

"Latchstring?"

"Yes, latchstring. I had to go out myself to find out what the darn thing is. There's a latch on the inside of the door, with a string tied to it. When you want to let somebody just walk in, you stick the little string through a hole in the door, so the string dangles outside. If you don't want people walking in, you pull the string in through the hole. Ghastly?"

"I'll survive somehow. Is the latchstring out?"

"There's a caretaker there, detailed from the Reeks and Wrecks. I'll call him and tell him to put it out. Confidentially, I'm sure they'll take eight."

15

THE LATCHSTRING AT the Gottwald house was out for Doctor Paul Proteus.

He tugged at it, listened with satisfaction as the latch disengaged itself inside, and walked in. The living room was dimly lit through tiny-paned, dusty windows, and what light did get in died without reflection on dull, dark antique surfaces. The floor rose and fell like a springboard beneath Paul's feet.

"The house breathes *with* you, like good underwear," said a lisping voice from the shadows. Paul looked in the direction from which it had come. The man sucked on his cigarette, lighting his moon face with a pink glow. "Doctor Proteus?"

"Yes."

"I'm Doctor Pond. Would you like me to turn on the lights?"

"Please, Doctor."

"Well, there aren't any. Kerosene lanterns throughout. Want to wash your hands or something?"

"Well, not—"

"Because, if you do, there's a pump in the back yard, and an outhouse by the chicken coop. Would you like to see the termites, the dry rot, the hog pen, and the manure-spreader, or shall we go to see that Georgian on Griffin Boulevard?" He walked to where they could see each other. Doctor Pond was very young, fat, and earnest, and plainly distressed by his surroundings.

"You're certainly eager to sell me the place," said Paul, laughing. With each new inconvenience, the place became more irresistible. It was a completely isolated backwater, cut off from the boiling rapids of history, society, and the economy. Timeless.

"I have a certain responsibility," said Doctor Pond carefully. "An administrator without a certain awareness, above and beyond the *Manual*, is like a ship without a rudder."

"He is?" said Paul absently. He was peering through a back window into the barnyard, and beyond that, through an opened barn door, where he could see the firm buff flank of a cow.

"Yes," said Doctor Pond, "like a ship without a rudder. For example, while the *Manual* doesn't tell me to do it, I make very sure that every man gets a house suited to his station on the ladder of life. The way a man lives can destroy or increase the stature of his job—can increase or decrease the stability and prestige of the entire system."

"You say I can get this whole farm for eight?"

"Please, Doctor—you put me in an uncomfortable position. I was excited when you first called, because this place has been such a headache for so long. But then my conscience started to work on me, and, well, I simply can't let you do it."

"I'll take it. Do the animals go with it?"

"Everything goes with it. That's in Gottwald's will and in the deed. It has to be kept just as it is and it must be farmed. See how impossible it is? Now, shall we go to Griffin Boulevard, where there's just the right house for the Manager of the Ilium Works?" When he spoke the title, his voice sounded like a choir of French horns.

"I want this."

"If you try to force me to sell it, I'll quit." Doctor Pond reddened. "My classification number may be twice what yours is, but I have a certain amount of integrity."

The word, coming from Pond, struck Paul as ridiculous at first, and he started to smile about it. Then he saw how tense the man was, and realized that what Pond was talking about was, by God, integrity. This pipsqueak of a man in a pipsqueak job had pipsqueak standards he was willing to lay his pipsqueak life down for. And Paul had a vision of civilization as a vast and faulty dike, with thousands of men like Doctor Pond in a rank stretching to the horizon, each man grimly stopping a leak with his finger.

"This would be a hobby, of course—a plaything," Paul lied. "I'd go on living where I'm living now."

Doctor Pond sighed and sank into a chair. "Oh—thank the Lord! Oh! You have no idea how much better I feel." He laughed in nervous relief. "Of course, of course, of course. And you'd keep Mr. Haycox on?"

"Who is Mr. Haycox?"

"The Reek and Wreck who's assigned to keep the place going. He's under orders from the Reeks and Wrecks, but of course the Gottwald estate pays him. You'd have to do the same."

"I'd like to meet him."

"He's an antique too." He threw his hands over his head. "What a place. I think you're mad, simply mad. But he who pays the piper calls the tune."

"As long as he doesn't threaten to disgrace the system."

"Exactly! That's almost good enough to carve over your mantel, but I doubt if the deed will let you."

"How about, 'After us the deluge,' " said Paul.

"Hmm?" Doctor Pond tried to make sense of the quotation, seemingly decided that it was some archaic, pleasant sentiment for those who understood poetry, and smiled. "That's nice too." Apparently the word "deluge" stuck in his mind. "Now, about the cellar here: it has an earth floor and *is* damp." He leaned out of the back door, wrinkled his nose in the sweet, stringent odor of manure cooking in the sunlight, and shouted, "Mr. Haycox! Oh, Mr. Haycox!"

Paul had opened the back of a grandfather clock. "I'll be damned," he said under his breath. "Wooden works." He checked his own watch, the shock-proof, waterproof, antimagnetic, glow-in-the-dark, self-winding chronometer Anita had given him for Christmas, and found that the grandfather clock was off by about twelve minutes. Indulging an atavistic whim, he set his watch to correspond with the hands of the relic, which grated and creaked away the seconds, sounding like a wooden ship straining in a strong wind.

The house was certainly one of the oldest in the valley. The rough rafters were inches above Paul's head, and the fireplace was sooted black, and there wasn't a true right angle anywhere. The house seemed to have twisted and stretched on its foundations until it had found a position of comfort for all of its parts—like a sleeping dog.

More remarkable than the way the house had relieved its stresses was the way it conformed to Paul's particular, not to say peculiar, needs. Here was a place where he could work with his hands, getting life from nature without being disturbed by any human beings other than his wife. Not only that, but Anita, with her love for things colonial, would be enchanted, stunned, even, by this completely authentic microcosm of the past.

"Ah," said Doctor Pond, "Mr. Haycox at last. When you yell for him, he never yells back. Just starts coming, taking his own sweet time."

Paul watched Mr. Haycox's heavy-footed progress across the hard-packed earth of the barnyard. The caretaker was an old man, with close-cropped white hair, coarse, tanned skin, and, like Rudy Hertz, with remarkably big hands. Unlike Rudy, Mr. Haycox wasn't desiccated. His flesh was firm, hard, and well colored. The chief toll he seemed to have paid time was in teeth, of which he had few. He might have been part of a pageant recalling farm life as it had once been. He wore old-fashioned blue denim overalls, a wide-brimmed straw hat, and heavy, crusty work shoes.

As though to point up the anachronism of Mr. Haycox and the Gottwald place for Paul, one of Doctor Ormand van Curler's men, riding on a tractor, appeared on the other side

KURT VONNEGUT

of the windbreak, snappy in spotless white coveralls, a red baseball cap, cool sandals which almost never touched the ground, and white gloves which, like Paul's hands, rarely touched anything but steering wheels, levers, and switches.

"What do *you* want?" said Mr. Haycox. "What's the matter now?" His voice was strong. He had none of the sheepishness or obsequiousness Paul had seen so frequently in Reeks and Wrecks. Mr. Haycox bore himself as though he owned the place, wanted the talk to be as brief and pithy as possible, and doubted that whatever was wanted of him could possibly be more important than what he had been doing.

"Doctor Proteus—this is Mr. Haycox."

"How are you?" said Paul.

" 'Do," said Mr. Haycox. "What kind of doctor?"

"Doctor of Science," said Paul.

Mr. Haycox seemed annoyed and disappointed. "Don't call that kind a doctor at all. Three kinds of doctors: dentists, vets, and physicians. You one of those?"

"No. Sorry."

"Then you ain't a doctor."

"He *is* a doctor," said Doctor Pond earnestly. "He knows how to keep machines healthy." He was trying to build up the importance of graduate degrees in the mind of this clod.

"Mechanic," said Mr. Haycox.

"Well," said Doctor Pond, "you can go to college and learn to be a specialist in all sorts of things besides making people or animals well. I mean, after all. The modern world would grind to a halt if there weren't men with enough advanced training to keep the complicated parts of civilization working smoothly."

"Um," said Mr. Haycox apathetically. "What do you keep working so smoothly?"

Doctor Pond smiled modestly. "I spent seven years in the Cornell Graduate School of Realty to qualify for a Doctor of Realty degree and get this job."

154

"Call yourself a doctor, too, do you?" said Mr. Haycox.

"I think I can say without fear of contradiction that I earned that degree," said Doctor Pond coolly. "My thesis was the third longest in any field in the country that year—eight hundred and ninety-six pages, double-spaced, with narrow margins."

"Real-estate salesman," said Mr. Haycox. He looked back and forth between Paul and Doctor Pond, waiting for them to say something worth his attention. When they'd failed to rally after twenty seconds, he turned to go. "I'm doctor of cowshit, pigshit, and chickenshit," he said. "When you doctors figure out what you want, you'll find me out in the barn shoveling *my* thesis."

"Mr. Haycox!" said Doctor Pond, furious. "You'll stay here until we're through with you!"

"Thought you was." He stopped, and stood perfectly motionless.

"Doctor Proteus is buying the farm."

"*My* farm?" Mr. Haycox turned slowly to face them, and real concern was in his eyes.

"The farm you've been taking care of," said Doctor Pond.

"*My* farm."

"The Gottwald estate's farm," said Doctor Pond.

"That a man?"

"You know it isn't."

"Well, I'm a man. As far as men go, this here is my farm more'n it's anybody else's. I'm the only man who ever cared about it, ever did anything about it." He turned earnestly to Paul. "You know the will says you got to keep it just like it is?"

"I plan to."

"And keep me on," said Mr. Haycox.

"Well, I don't know for sure," said Paul. This was a complication he hadn't foreseen. He planned to do the work himself. That was the point of the undertaking.

"That *isn't* in the will," said Doctor Pond, pleased to have found something that shocked respect into Mr. Haycox.

"All the same, you got to keep me on," said Mr. Haycox. "This is what I do." He gestured at the yard and buildings, all neat. "This is what I've done."

"Gottwald bought this place from Mr. Haycox's father," Doctor Pond explained. "There was some sort of informal agreement, I think, that Mr. Haycox could have the job of caretaker for his lifetime."

"Informal, hell!" said Mr. Haycox. "He *promised*, Gottwald did. This here's been our family's for more'n a hundred years—lots more. And I'm the last of the line, and Gottwald promised, by God, he promised it'd be the same as mine till it came time for me to go."

"Well, the time has come," said Doctor Pond.

"Dead—Gottwald meant when I was dead. I got twice as many years behind me as you do, sonny boy, and twice as many ahead of me." He moved closer to Doctor Pond, and squinted at him. "I've moved so many big piles of shit in my life, figure I could throw a little dab like you clean over the barn."

Doctor Pond's eyes widened, and he backed away. "We'll see about that," he said faintly.

"Look," said Paul hastily, "I'm sure we can work this out. Soon as I close the deal, Mr. Haycox, you'll be working for me."

"Things going to be *just* like they were?"

"My wife and I'll be coming out from time to time." Now didn't seem to be the time to tell him or anyone that he and Anita would be permanent residents.

Haycox didn't care for this much. "When?"

"We'll give you plenty of notice."

He nodded grimly. Then, unexpectedly and charmingly, Mr. Haycox smiled. "Wonder if I went and offended that there Doctor of Realty?" Pond had fled. "Well, I'll be getting back to work. Long as this here is going to be your farm, you might's well fix the pump. Needs a new packing."

"Afraid I don't know how," said Paul.

"Maybe," said Mr. Haycox walking away, "maybe if you'd of gone to college another ten or twenty years, somebody would of gotten around to showing you how, *Doctor*."

16

ANITA SEEMINGLY MISTOOK Paul's quite excitement for daydreams of happy hours to come at the Meadows, which were less than two weeks away.

She didn't know that he was learning to be a farmer and laying the groundwork for teaching her to be a farmer's wife.

It was a hot Saturday, and on the pretext of buying himself a fielder's mitt, Paul went to his farm—to his and Mr. Haycox's farm. There Mr. Haycox condescendingly and impatiently imparted half-truths about running the place, and gave Paul a vague confidence that he could get the hang of it after a while.

That evening at suppertime, Paul, satisfyingly pooped after having trailed Mr. Haycox for hours, asked his wife if she knew what day the coming Wednesday was.

She looked up from a list of things she was to pack for her trip to the Mainland and, more important, for Paul's trip to the Meadows. "Can't imagine. Have you got nice-looking tennis shoes for the trip?"

"They'll do. For your information, next Wednesday is—"

"Shepherd is taking twelve pairs of socks—all green. He's a captain, too, you know."

"I know."

"What do you make of that? It's kind of a surprise: the first time you get to be captain, he does, too."

"Maybe he sent a coupon to the Rosicrucians. How on earth do you know how many pairs of socks he's taking?"

"Well, he hasn't got a wife to help him plan, so he came over this afternoon to get my help. So I made a list of things he ought to take. Men are so helpless."

"They muddle through. Did he have anything interesting to say?"

She laid down the list and looked at him reproachfully. "Only about the police report about your pistol, and another one about the underworld people you were with that awful night in Homestead." She wadded her napkin and threw it down petulantly. "Paul—why don't you tell me these things? Why do I always have to find out from someone else?"

"Underworld!" snorted Paul. "Oh, for heaven's sake."

"Shepherd says Lasher and Finnerty are being watched as potential saboteurs."

"Everybody's being watched! Why do you listen to that old woman of a man!"

"Why don't *you* tell me what's going on?"

"Because those things were trivial. Because I was afraid you wouldn't see them that way and get all upset—the way you're getting upset. It's all fixed. Kroner fixed it."

"Shepherd said you could get ten years for the pistol business alone."

"Next time he's over, ask him if he has any idea how much time I'd get if I mashed up his long nose for him."

Paul's muscles were tight from the unaccustomed rigors of the afternoon, and animal smells had communicated to him a feel of primitive strength. The notion of pushing Shep-

herd's face in—a bizarre sport in a lifetime of pacifistic no-
tions—came as an unexpected complement to the day.
"Well, to hell with the captain of the Green Team, I say.
Again I'll ask, what day is the coming Wednesday?"

"I'm sure I don't know."

"Our engagement anniversary."

It was an anniversary with disquieting connotations for
both of them—an anniversary that neither had ever mentioned in their years of marriage. It was the date on which
Anita had announced to Paul that she was with child, his
child, and on which he had responded by offering her his
name, etc. Now, with the event softened by years of more or
less adequate marriage, Paul thought that they might senti-
mentally make it something that it was not. The anniversary,
more to the point, fell at an ideal time for the beginning of
his re-education program for Anita.

"And I have a special evening planned," he said; "not
like any evening we've ever had together, darling."

"Funny, I'd forgotten the date completely. Really?
Next Wednesday?" She gave him an odd, rebuking smile, as
though the story of their engagement had got twisted in her
mind—as though she thought *he* had brought about the event
by a now insignificant deception. "Well, that's sweet," she
said. "Kind of cute of you to remember. But, with the Meadows so close—" She was of such a methodical nature that
when something of importance was in the offing, other aspects of life could have no importance at all. To her it seemed
almost indecent to give attention to anything but the crucial
matter of the Meadows.

"To hell with the Meadows."

"You don't mean that."

"I mean we're still going out next Wednesday."

"Well, I hope you know what you're doing. You're the
captain."

"I'm the captain."

17

EDGAR R. B. HAGSTROHM, thirty-seven, R&R— 131313, Undercoater First Class, 22nd Surface Preserving Battalion, 58th Maintenance Regiment, 110th Building and Grounds Division, Reconstruction and Reclamation Corps, had been named after his father's favorite author, the creator of Tarzan—Tarzan, who, far away from the soot and biting winter of the Hagstrohms' home town, Chicago, made friends with lions and elephants and apes, and swung through trees on vines, and was built like a brick outhouse with square wheels and Venetian blinds, and took what he wanted of civilization's beautiful women in tree houses, and left the rest of civilization alone. E. R. B. Hagstrohm liked Tarzan as much as his father had, and hated being a little man and being in Chicago ten times as much.

And Edgar was reading about Tarzan in the bedroom when his fat wife, Wanda, called to him from her station before the picture window in the front room of their prefabricated home in Proteus Park, Chicago, a postwar development of three thousand dream houses for three thousand families with presumably identical dreams. "Gosh, here he comes, Edgar!"

"All right, all right, all right," said Edgar. "So he's coming! So what am I supposed to do, holler bloody murder, kiss his feet, and faint?" He took his time about getting off the bed, and he didn't smooth out the dent he'd made in the bedding. He laid his book open on the bedside table, so the visitors would see that he was a reader, and started for the living room. "What's he look like, Wan?"

"You gotta see, Ed—like a Chinese bird cage or something, all gold and fancy."

The Shah of Bratpuhr had asked his guide, Doctor Ewing J. Halyard, if he might see the home of a typical *Takaru*, freely translated, from one culture to another, as "average man." The request had been made as they were passing through Chicago from Carlsbad Caverns, and Halyard had stopped off at the local personnel office for the name of a representative American in the neighborhood.

The personnel machines had considered the problem and ejected the card of Edgar R. B. Hagstrohm, who was statistically average in every respect save for the number of his initials: his age (36), his height (5'7"), his weight (148 lbs.), his years of marriage (11), his I.Q. (83), the number of his children (2: 1 m., 9; 1 f., 6), the number of his bedrooms (2), his car (3 yr. old Chev. 2 dr. sed.), his education (h.s. grad, 117th in class of 233; maj. in business practice; 2nd string f'ball, b'k'tb'l; soc. comm., sen'r play; no coll.) his vocation (R&R), his avocations (spec'r sports, TV, softb'l, f'sh'g), and his war record (5 yrs., 3 ov'sea; T-4 radioman; 157th Inf. Div.; battle stars: Hjoring, Elbesan, Kabul, Kaifen, Ust Kyakhta; wounded 4 times; P'ple H't, 3 cl.; Silv. Star; Br'ze Star, 2 cl.; G'd Cond. Med.).

And the machines could have made an educated guess that, since Hagstrohm had gone that far in being average, he had probably been arrested once, had had sexual experience with five girls before marrying Wanda (only moderately satisfying), and had had two extramarital adventures since (one fleeting and foolish, the other rather long and disturbing), and that he would die at the age of 76.2 of a heart attack.

What the machines couldn't guess was that Edgar's second extramarital affair, the deep one, was with a widow named Marion Frascati, that it was still going on, and that Marion's deceased husband had been Lou Frascati, a secondcoater first class, Edgar's best friend. To their own profound shock, Edgar and Marion had found themselves in each other's arms a scant month after good old Lou's death. And again, and again, and again—and they'd tried to bring it to an end, honest-to-God they had. But it was like a bright, fat cherry on the gray mush of their lives. And they thought, wistfully, weakly, that maybe it wouldn't really matter as long as no one was hurt—the kids; sweet, loyal Wanda. And that Lou wouldn't have wanted anything more, now that he had another variety of bliss, than that good old Edgar and good old Marion make the most of life while they had the use of their flesh.

But they hadn't believed it. And the kids noticed something screwy was going on, and Wanda'd cried a couple of times lately and refused to tell him why, and probably Lou, wherever he was. . . . Anyway, Edgar was going to go on seeing Marion, but he was going to tell Wanda, God bless her and God help her—tell her, and— Who was banging on the Hagstrohm door but the goddam Shah of Bratpuhr, for chrissakes.

"Come in, come in," said Edgar, and he added under his breath, "your majesty, your highness, emperor of the universe and all the ships at sea, you nosy son-of-a-bitch."

When Halyard had phoned him about the visit, Hagstrohm had made a point of not being impressed by the Shah's title, or by Halyard's rank. It was rare that he got the opportunity to show what he thought of rank—that a man was a man for all that. He was going to behave perfectly naturally, just as he would if the callers had been fellow Reeks and Wrecks. Wanda had taken a different view, and had started frantically to clean the place from top to bottom, and to make lemonade and send Edgar, Jr., out for little cookies, but big Edgar had put a stop to all that. He put the kids out, and that was the only cleaning up that was to be done.

The door opened, and in came the Shah, followed by

Khashdrahr, Halyard, and Doctor Ned Dodge, the manager of Proteus Park.

"Aha!" said the Shah, gingerly touching the enameled steel wall of the living room. "Mmmmm."

Edgar held out his hand, and the parade brushed past it, heedless. "Well, kiss mine," he muttered.

"Eh?" said Doctor Dodge.

"You heard me."

"You're not in a saloon now, Hagstrohm," whispered Dodge. "Watch yourself; this is international relations."

"All right if I go to a saloon?"

"What's eating you, anyway?"

"The guy walks into my house and won't even shake my hand."

"It's not the custom in his country."

"Is it in yours?"

Dodge turned his back and grinned hospitably at the Shah. "Two bedrooms, living room with dining alcove, bath, and kitchen," he said. "This is the M-17 house. Radiant heating in the floor. The furniture was designed after an exhaustive national survey of furniture likes and dislikes. The house, the furniture, and the lot are sold as a package. Simplified planning and production all the way round."

"*Lakki-ti, Takaru?*" piped the Shah, looking at Edgar closely for the first time.

"What's he say?"

"He wants to know if you like it here," said Khashdrahr.

"Sure—I guess. It's all right. I suppose. Yeah."

"It's nice," said Wanda.

"Now, if you'll follow me into the kitchen," said Doctor Dodge, leaving Wanda and Edgar behind, "you'll see the radar range. Cooks by high frequency, and cooks the inside of whatever's being cooked as fast as the outside. Cooks anything in a matter of seconds, with perfect control. Make bread without a crust, if you want to."

"What is the matter with crust on bread?" asked Khashdrahr politely.

"And this is the ultrasonic dishwasher and clotheswasher," said Dodge. "High-frequency sound passing through the water strips dirt and grease off anything in a matter of seconds. Dip in, take out, bingo!"

"And then what does the woman do?" asked Khashdrahr.

"Then she puts the clothes or dishes in this drier, which dries them out in a matter of seconds, and—here's a nifty trick, I think—gives the clothes a spanking-clean outdoors odor, like they were dried in the sun, see, with this little ozone lamp in here."

"And then what?" asked Khashdrahr.

"She feeds the clothes through this ironer, which can do what was an hour's ironing before the war in three minutes. Bing!"

"And then what does she do?" asked Khashdrahr.

"And then she's done."

"And then what?"

Doctor Dodge reddened perceptibly. "Is this a joke?"

"No," said Khashdrahr. "The Shah would like to know what it is that the woman *Takaru*—"

"What's a *Takaru*?" said Wanda suspiciously.

"Citizen," said Halyard.

"Yes," said Khashdrahr, smiling at her oddly, "citizen. The Shah would like to know why she has to do everything so quickly—this in a matter of seconds, that in a matter of seconds. What is it she is in such a hurry to get at? What is it she has to do, that she mustn't waste any time on these things?"

"Live!" said Doctor Dodge expansively. "Live! Get a little fun out of life." He laughed, and clapped Khashdrahr on the back, as though to jar him into feeling some of the jollity in this average American man's home.

The effect on Khashdrahr and the Shah was a poor one.

"I see," said the interpreter coldly. He turned to Wanda. "And how is it you live and get so much fun out of life?"

Wanda blushed and looked down at the floor, and worried the carpet edge with her toe. "Oh, television," she murmured. "Watch that a lot, don't we, Ed? And I spend a lot of time with the kids, little Delores and young Edgar, Jr. You know. Things."

"Where are the children now?" asked Khashdrahr.

"Over at the neighbors' place, the Glocks, watching television, I expect."

"Would you like to see the ultrasonic washer work?" said Doctor Dodge. "Right before your eyes, bing! Takes off egg, lipstick, bloodstains—"

"The transducer's shot again," said Edgar, "so the washer's out of commission. Wanda's been doing the washing in a tub for a month now, waiting for a new transducer."

"Oh, I don't mind," said Wanda. "Really, I like doin' 'em that way. It's kind of a relief. A body needs a change. I don't mind. Gives me something to do."

Halyard ended the silence that followed her statement with a brisk suggestion that they leave these good people alone and have a look at the central recreation pavilion down the street.

"If we hurry," said Doctor Dodge, "we'll probably catch the leathercraft class still in session."

The Shah patted the radar stove, the laundry console, and peered for a moment at the television screen, which showed five persons seated around a conference table, arguing earnestly. *"Brahouna!"* he chuckled.

Khashdrahr nodded. *"Brahouna! Live!"*

As the party left, Halyard was explaining that the house and contents and car were all paid for by regular deductions from Edgar's R&RC pay check, along with premiums on his combination health, life, and old age security insurance, and that the furnishings and equipment were replaced from time to time with newer models as Edgar—or the payroll machines, rather—completed payments on the old ones. "He has a *complete* security package," said Halyard. "His standard of living is constantly rising, and he and the country at large are protected from the old economic ups and downs by the orderly, predictable consumer habits the payroll machines give him. Used to be he'd buy on impulse, illogically, and industry would go nutty trying to figure out what he was going to buy next. Why, I remember when I was a little boy, we had a crazy neighbor who blew all his money on an electric organ, while he still had an old-fashioned icebox and kerosene stove in his kitchen!"

Edgar closed the door and leaned against it, against the door of his M-17 castle.

Wanda sank to the couch. "The place looked nice, I think," she said. She said it whenever a visitor—Amy Glock, Gladys Pelrine, the Shah of Bratpuhr, anybody—left.

"Yep," said Edgar. And he felt evil and damned as he looked at Wanda, good, good soul, who'd never done anything to offend him, whose love for him was as big as all outdoors. He fingered the three ten-dollar bills in his pocket, his take-home pay—cigarette money, recreation money, small luxury money the machines let him have. This tiny atom of the economy under his control he was going to spend, not on himself or Wanda or the kids, but on Marion. Edgar's troubled heart had gone out to the crazy man in Halyard's story, the guy who'd bought himself an electric organ. Expensive, impractical, strictly personal—above and beyond the goddamned package.

But deceit was another thing. "Wanda," said Edgar, "I'm no good."

She knew what he was talking about, all right. She wasn't in the least surprised. "Yes, you are, Edgar," she said lamely. "You're a fine man. I understand."

"About Marion?"

"Yes. She's very beautiful and charming. And I'm not

exactly a girl any more, and I expect I'm pretty dull." She started to cry, and, good soul that she was, she tried to keep him from seeing it. She hurried into the kitchen, took four suppers from the deep freeze, and thrust them into the radar range. "Call the children, will you please, Edgar?" she said in a small, high voice. "Supper will be ready in twenty-eight seconds."

Edgar shouted the children's names into the twilight, and returned to Wanda. "Listen, Wan—it isn't you. The Lord knows it isn't your fault." He hugged her from behind, and she twisted away and pretended to adjust dials on the range, though there was no adjusting to be done. Clockwork was doing everything.

Chimes rang, the clockwork clicked, and the range's humming stopped. "Call the children before everything gets cold," she said.

"They're coming." Edgar tried to hug her again, and she let him this time. "Listen," he said passionately, "it's the world, Wan—me and the world. I'm no good to anybody, not in *this* world. Nothing but a Reek and Wreck, and that's all my kids'll be, and a guy's got to have kicks or he doesn't want to live—and the only kicks left for a dumb bastard like me are the bad ones. I'm no good, Wan, no good!"

"It's me that's no good to anybody," said Wanda wearily. "Nobody needs me. You or even little old Delores could run the house and all, it's so easy. And now I'm too fat for anybody but the kids to love me. My mother got fat, and my grandmother got fat, and guess it's in the blood; but somebody needed them, they were still some good. But you don't need me, Ed, and you can't help it if you don't love me any more. Just the way men are, and you can't help it if you're the way God made you." She looked at him lovingly, pityingly. "Poor man."

Delores and Edgar, Jr., bustled in, and Edgar and Wanda composed themselves and told their children all about the Shah.

The subject was soon exhausted, and at dinner only the children spoke and touched their food.

"Somebody sick?" said Edgar, Jr.

"Your mother isn't well. She has a headache," said Edgar.

"Yeah? That's too bad, Mom."

"Just a little thing," said Wanda. "It'll pass."

"How about you, Pop?" said Edgar, Jr. "You well enough to take in the basketball game at the pavilion tonight?"

Edgar kept his eyes on his plate. "Like to," he mumbled. "Promised Joe I'd go bowling with him tonight."

"Joe Prince?"

"Yeah, Joe Prince."

"Why, Daddy," said Delores, "we saw Mr. Prince over to the Glocks', and he said he was going to the basketball game."

"He did not!" said Edgar, Jr., fiercely. "Just be quiet. You don't know what you're talking about. He didn't say that at all."

"He did, too!" said Delores stubbornly. "He said—"

"Delores, honey," said Wanda, "I'm sure you misunderstood Mr. Prince."

"Yes," said Edgar, Jr., "I remember now he said he was going bowling with Pop. Sis got it all wrong, Mom." His hands were trembling, and, clumsily, he knocked over his milk glass. Both he and his father jumped to their feet to catch it before it toppled all the way. Young Edgar caught it, and when his eyes met old Edgar's they were full of hate. "Guess I'm too tired to go to the ball game after all," he said. "Guess I'll stay home and watch television with Mom."

"Don't miss any good times on my account," said Wanda. "I get along just fine by myself."

There was a series of sharp taps on the picture window, and the Hagstrohms looked up to see the Shah of Bratpuhr rattling his ringed fingers against the glass. He had just returned from the pavilion to the limousine, which had been left in front of the Hagstrohm's M-17 home.

"*Brahouna!*" cried the Shah cheerfully. He waved. "*Brahouna, Takaru.*"

" 'Live!' " translated Krashdrahr.

18

WHEN WEDNESDAY CAME, Paul stopped by his farm early in the morning and gave Mr. Haycox his instructions. Mr. Haycox made it clear that he wasn't a parlor maid.

Reluctantly, Paul gave Mr. Haycox to understand that he could do the job or clear out, and that the job had better be well done. It was that important to Paul that everything be perfect for the delicate transformation of Anita.

"You think you can just go around buying anybody to do anything you damn please," said Mr. Haycox. "Well, you're mistaken this time, Doctor. You can take your doctor's degree, and—"

"I don't want to fire you."

"Then don't!"

"For the last time, as a favor to me—"

"Why didn't you say so in the first place?"

"Say what?"

" 'As a favor.' "

"All right; as a favor—"

"As a favor, just this once," said Mr. Haycox. "I'm no parlor maid, but I try to be a good friend."

"Thanks."

"Nothing at all. Don't mention it."

During the day, Anita called Paul to ask what she was to wear.

"Old clothes."

"A barn dance?"

"Not quite, but close. Dress as though it were."

"Paul, with the Meadows so close and all, do you think we should be going out and tearing around?"

"The Meadows isn't a funeral."

"It could be, Paul."

"Just for tonight, let's forget the Meadows. Tonight it's going to be just Paul and Anita, and to hell with everybody else."

"That's very easy to say, Paul. It's a sweet idea and everything, but—"

"But what?" he asked irritably.

"Well, I don't know; I don't want to nag, but it does seem to me that you're being awfully slap-happy about the Meadows, about the Blue Team."

"What should I be doing?"

"Shouldn't you be training or something? I mean, shouldn't you be getting lots of sleep and eating the right foods and jogging around a little after work? And cutting down on cigarettes, maybe?"

"What?"

"You've got to be in shape if the Blue Team's going to win."

Paul laughed.

"Now listen, Paul, you needn't laugh. Shepherd says he's seen careers made and broken by how men made out as team captains at the Meadows. Shepherd's given up smoking completely."

"You can tell him I've taken up hashish to speed up my reaction time. His fast ball will look like a toy balloon blowing over home plate. We *are* going out tonight."

"All right," she said gloomily. "All right."

"I love you, Anita.

"I love *you*, Paul."

And she was ready when he got home, not as Ilium's Lady of the Manor but as a trim, kittenish girl in denim trousers rolled above her knees. She wore one of Paul's shirts, with its tails knotted below her breasts, white sneakers, and a red bandana about her neck.

"Is this right?"

"Perfect."

"Paul—I don't understand what's going on. I called up the Country Club, and they don't know about any barn dance. And neither do the clubs in Albany, Troy, or Schenectady." Anita, Paul knew, hated surprises, couldn't bear not to be on top of every situation.

"This is a private one," said Paul. "Just for the two of us. You'll see when the time comes."

"I want to know now."

"Where are our anniversary martinis?" The table where the pitcher and glasses awaited him every night was bare.

"You're on the wagon until after the Meadows."

"Don't be ridiculous! Everybody is going to be drinking for two weeks up there."

"Not the captains. Shepherd says *they* can't afford to drink."

"That shows how much he knows. The drinks are on the house."

Paul mixed martinis, drank more than his usual ration, and changed into a suit of stiff, crackling denim overalls he'd bought in Homestead that afternoon. He was sorry to see that Anita was getting no pleasure from the suspense he'd built up. Instead of happy anticipation, she showed signs of suspicion.

"Ready?" he said brightly.

"Yes—I suppose."

They walked in silence to the garage. With a grand gesture, Paul held the car door open.

"Oh, Paul, *not* the old car."

"There's a reason."

"There couldn't be a reason good enough to get me in that thing."

"Please, Anita—you'll see soon enough why we've got to take this one."

She got in and sat on the edge of the seat, trying to come in contact with the car as little as possible. "Honestly! I mean really!"

They rode like strangers. On the long grade by the golf course, however, she unbent a trifle. In the beams of the headlights was a pale and hairy man in green shorts, green socks, and a green shirt with the word "Captain" written across it. The man was jogging along the shoulder of the road, now and then breaking his pace to pirouette and shadowbox, then picking up his jogging again.

Paul blasted Shepherd with his automobile horn, and was delighted to see him bound across the ditch to get out of his way.

Anita rolled down her window and cheered.

The captain of the Green Team waved, his face twisted by exertion.

Paul pressed the throttle to the floor, laying down a cloud of burned oil and carbon monoxide.

"That man's got a lot of get up and go," said Anita.

"He fills me full of lie down and die," said Paul.

They were passing the battlements of the Ilium Works now, and one of the guards, recognizing Paul's car from his pillbox, waggled his fifty-caliber machine gun in friendly fashion.

Anita, who had been getting more and more restless, made as though to grab the wheel. "Paul! Where are you going? Are you crazy?"

PLAYER PIANO

He brushed her hand away, smiled, and kept on going across the bridge into Homestead.

The bridge was blocked again by Reeks and Wrecks who were painting yellow lines to mark traffic lanes. Paul looked at his watch. They had ten more minutes until time for, as the expression went, knocking off work. Paul wondered if Bud Calhoun had thought up this project. Like most of the R&R projects, it was, to Paul at least, ironic. The four-lane bridge had, before the war, been jammed with the cars of workers going to and from the Ilium Works. Four lanes had been nothing like enough, and a driver stayed within his lane or got the side of his car ground off. Now, at any time of day, a driver could swerve from one side of the bridge to the other with perhaps one chance in ten thousand of hitting another vehicle.

Paul came to a stop. Three men were painting, twelve were directing traffic, and another twelve were resting. Slowly, they opened a lane.

"Hey, Mac, your headlamp's busted."

"Thanks," said Paul.

Anita slid across the seat to get close to him, and he saw that she was scared stiff. "Paul—this is awful. Take me home."

Paul smiled patiently and drove into Homestead. The hydrant in front of the saloon by the end of the bridge was going again, and he had to park down the block. The same dirty boy was making paper boats for the amusement of the crowd. Leaning against a building and smoking nervously was a seedy old man who looked familiar to Paul. Then Paul realized that the man was Luke Lubbock, the indefatigable joiner, who was lost in the limbo of mufti, waiting for the next parade or meeting to start. With mixed emotions he looked around for Lasher and Finnerty, but saw no sign of them. Very probably they were in the saloon's dark, rearmost booth, agreeing on everything.

"Paul—is this your idea of a joke? Take me home, *please*."

"Nobody's going to hurt you. These people are just your fellow Americans."

"Just because they were born in the same part of the world as I was, that doesn't mean I have to come down here and wallow with them."

Paul had expected this reaction, and remained patient in the face of it. Of all the people on the north side of the river, Anita was the only one whose contempt for those in Homestead was laced with active hatred. She was also the only wife on the north side who had never been to college at all. The usual attitude of the Country Club set toward Homesteaders was contempt, all right, but it had an affectionate and amused undertone, the same sort of sentiment felt by most for creatures of the woods and fields. Anita hated Homesteaders.

If Paul were ever moved to be extremely cruel to her, the cruelest thing he could do, he knew, would be to point out to her why she hated as she did: if he hadn't married her, this was where she'd be, what she'd be.

"We're not getting out," said Paul. "We'll just sit here a few minutes and watch. Then we'll move on."

"Watch what?"

"Whatever there is to see. The line painters, the man running the hydrant, the people watching him, the little boy making boats, the old men in the saloon. Just keep looking around. There's plenty to see."

She didn't look around, but slouched down in the seat and stared at her hands.

Paul had an idea what she was thinking—that for some reason she couldn't understand, he was doing this to humiliate her, to recall her humble origins. Had that been what he wanted to do, he would have been completely successful, because her virulent hate had decayed. She'd fallen silent and tried to make herself small.

"You know why I brought you here?"

Her voice was a whisper. "No. But I want to go home, Paul. Please?"

"Anita—I brought us here because I think it's high time we got a completely new perspective, not on just our relationship to ourselves, but on our relationship to society as a whole." He didn't like the sound of the words as they came out, sententious and inflated. Their impact on Anita was nothing.

He tried again: "In order to get what we've got, Anita, we have, in effect, traded these people out of what was the most important thing on earth to them—the feeling of being needed and useful, the foundation of self-respect." That wasn't much good either. He wasn't getting through to Anita yet. She still seemed certain that she was somehow being punished by him.

He tried once more: "Darling, when I see what we've got, and then see what these people have got, I feel like a horse's ass."

A glimmering of understanding crossed Anita's face. Guardedly, she cheered up a little. "Then you're not mad at me?"

"Lord, no. Why should I be mad at you?"

"I don't know. I thought maybe you thought I nagged too much—or maybe you thought something was going on between Shepherd and me."

This last—this suggestion that he would ever worry about Shepherd—threw Paul completely off the orderly course of re-educating Anita. The notion that he might be jealous of the captain of the Green Team was so ludicrous, showed so poor an understanding, that it commanded his full attention. "I'll be jealous of Shepherd when you're jealous of Katharine Finch," he laughed.

This, to his surprise, Anita chose to take seriously. "You don't mean that!"

"Mean what?"

"That I should be jealous of Katharine Finch. That dumpy little—"

"Wait a minute!" The conversation was really afield now. "I just meant there was about as much chance of there being something between Katharine and me as there was of there being something between you and Shepherd."

She was still on the defensive, and apparently hadn't grasped the negative sense of his parallel. She came back at him aggressively. "Well, Shepherd is certainly a more attractive man than Katharine is a woman."

"I'm not arguing that," said Paul desperately. "I don't want to argue that at all. There isn't anything between Katharine and me, and there isn't anything between you and Shepherd. I was simply pointing out how absurd it would be for either one of us to suspect the other."

"You don't think I'm attractive?"

"I think you're devastatingly attractive. You know that." His voice had gotten loud, and as he glanced out at the street scene he saw that he and Anita, the would-be observers, were being observed. A paper boat shot the rapids to the storm sewer unnoticed. "I didn't bring us here to accuse each other of adultery," he whispered hoarsely.

"Then why did you?"

"I told you: so we could both get the feel of the world as a whole, not just our side of the river. So we could see what our way of life has done to the lives of others."

Anita was on top of the situation now, having successfully attacked and confused Paul, and having found that she wasn't being baited or punished. "They all look perfectly well fed to me."

"But they've had the spiritual stuffing knocked out of them by people like my father, like Kroner and Baer and Shepherd, like us."

"They couldn't have been too well stuffed in the first place, or they wouldn't be here."

Paul was mad, and the delicate mechanism that kept

him from hurting her stripped its gears. "Here, but for the grace of God, go you!"

"Paul!" She burst into tears. "That's not fair," she said brokenly. "Not at all fair. I don't know why you had to say that."

"It isn't fair for you to cry."

"You're cruel, that's what you are—just plain cruel. If you wanted to hurt me, congratulate yourself. You certainly did." She blew her nose. "I must have had something these people don't, or you wouldn't have married me."

"Oligomenorrhea," he said.

She blinked. "What's that?"

"Oligomenorrhea—that's what you had that these others don't. Means delayed menstrual period."

"How on earth did you ever learn a word like that?"

"I looked it up a month after we were married, and it etched itself on the inside of my skull."

"Oh." She turned crimson. "You've said enough, quite enough," she said bitterly. "If you won't drive me home, I'll walk."

Paul started the car, abused the gears with savage satisfaction, and drove back across the bridge, toward the north side of the river.

When they'd reached the mid-point of the bridge, he was still warmed and excited by the sudden fight with Anita. By the time they were under the guns of the Ilium Works, rationality and remorse were setting in.

The fight had been a complete surprise. Never had they gone at it so poisonously. More surprising, Paul had been the vicious one, and Anita had been little more than a victim. Confusedly he tried to remember the events that had led up to the fight. His memory was no help.

And how completely fruitless and destructive the fight had been! In the heat of a bad instant he had said what he knew would hurt her most, would, by extension, make her hate him most. And he hadn't wanted to do that. God knows he hadn't. And here he was with his cheery and careful plans for starting a new life with her shot to hell.

They were passing the golf course now. In minutes they'd be home.

"Anita—"

By way of an answer, she turned on the car radio and impatiently twiddled the dials, waiting for the volume to come up, presumably to drown him out. The radio hadn't worked for years.

"Anita—listen. I love you more than anybody on earth. Good God but I'm sorry about what we said to each other."

"I didn't say anything to you like what you said to me."

"I could cut my tongue out for having said those things."

"Don't use any of our good kitchen knives."

"It was a freak."

"So am I, apparently. You passed our driveway."

"I meant to. I have a surprise for you. Then you'll see how much I really love you—how insignificant that stupid fight was."

"I've had quite enough surprises tonight, thank you. Turn around, please. I'm worn out."

"This surprise cost eight thousand, Anita. Still want to turn around?"

"Think I can be bought, do you?" she said angrily, but her expression was softening, answering her own question. "What on earth could it be? Really? Eight thousand dollars?"

Paul relaxed, settling back in his seat to enjoy the ride. "You don't belong in Homestead, sweetheart."

"Oh, hell—maybe I do."

"No, no. You've got something the tests and machines will never be able to measure: you're artistic. That's one of the tragedies of our times, that no machine has ever been built that can recognize that quality, appreciate it, foster it, sympathize with it."

"It is," said Anita sadly. "It is, it is."

"I love you, Anita."

"I love *you*, Paul."

"Look! A deer!" Paul flicked on his bright lights to illuminate the animal, and recognized the captain of the Green Team, still jogging, but now in an advanced state of exhaustion. Shepherd's legs flailed about weakly and disjointedly, and his feet struck the pavement with loud, limp slaps. There was no recognition in his eyes this time, and he floundered on heedlessly.

"With every step he hammers another nail into my coffin," said Paul, lighting a fresh cigarette from the one he had just finished.

Ten minutes later he stopped the car, went around to Anita's side, and affectionately offered his arm. "The latchstring is out, darling, for a whole new and happier life for the two of us."

"What does that mean?"

"You'll see." He led her to the front door of the low little house through a dark, fragrant tunnel roofed and walled by lilacs. He took her hand and placed it on the latchstring. "Pull."

She tugged gingerly. The latch inside clattered free, and the door swung open. "Oh! Ohhhh—Paul!"

"Ours. This belongs to Paul and Anita."

She walked in slowly, her head back, her nostrils wide. "I feel like crying, it's so darling."

Hastily, Paul checked the preparations for the tricky hours ahead, and was delighted. Mr. Haycox, probably in an orgy of masochism, had scrubbed every surface. Gone were the soot and dust, leaving only the clean, soft, glowing patina of age over everything—the pewter on the mantel, the cherry case of the grandfather clock, the black ironware on the hearth, the walnut stock and silver inlays of the long rifle on the wall, the tin potbellies of the kerosene lamps, the warm, worn maple of the chairs. . . . And on a table in the center of the room, looking archaic, too, in the soft light, were two glasses, a pitcher, a bottle of gin, a bottle of vermouth, and a bucket of ice. And beside these were two glasses of whole, fresh milk from the farm, fresh hard-boiled eggs from the farm, fresh peas from the farm, and fresh fried chicken from the farm.

As Paul mixed the drinks, Anita went about the room sighing happily, touching everything lovingly. "Is it really ours?"

"As of yesterday. I signed the final papers. Do you really feel at home here?"

She dropped into a chair before the fireplace and took the glass he handed her. "Can't you tell? Don't I radiate how I feel?" She laughed quietly. "He wants to know if I like it. It's priceless, you brilliant darling, and you got it for eight thousand dollars! Aren't you smart!"

"Happy anniversary, Anita."

"I want a stronger word than happy."

"Ecstatic anniversary, Anita."

"Ecstatic anniversary to you, Paul. I love you. Lord, how I love you!"

"I love *you*." He had never loved her so much.

"Do you realize, darling, that that grandfather clock alone is worth almost a thousand dollars?"

Paul felt terribly clever. It was fantastic how well things were turning out. Anita's contentment with the place was genuine, and the process of weaning her from one house to another, from one way of life to another, seemed, in a miraculous few minutes, to have been almost completed. "This *is* your kind of surroundings, isn't it."

"You know it is."

"Did you know the clock had wooden works? Think of it? Every part whittled out of wood."

"Don't worry about it. That's easily remedied."

"Hmm?"

"We can get an electric movement put in."

"But the whole charm—"

She was in a transport of creativity now, and didn't hear him. "You see—with the pendulum gone, an electrostatic dust precipitator would fit right in the lower part of the case."

"Oh."

"And you know where I'd put it?"

He looked around the room and saw no spot for it other than where it was. "That niche there seems ideal."

"In the front hall! Can't you just see it there?"

"There is no front hall," he said in puzzlement. The front door opened right into the living room.

"*Our* front hall, silly."

"But, Anita—"

"And that spice cabinet on the wall—wouldn't it be darling with some of the drawers sticking out, and with philodendron growing from them? I know just the spot in the guest room."

"Swell."

"And these priceless rafters, Paul! This means we can have rough-hewn beams in our living room, too. Not just in the kitchen, but the living room, too! And I'll eat your classification card if that dry-sink won't take our television set."

"I was looking forward to eating it myself," said Paul quietly.

"And these wide-board floors: you can imagine what they'll do for the rumpus room."

"What did the rumpus room ever do for me?" said Paul grimly.

"What did you say?"

"I said, what did the rumpus room ever do for me?"

"Oh. I see." She laughed perfunctorily and, her eyes bright, she searched for more plunder.

"Anita—"

"Yes? Oh! What a delightful Cape Cod lighter."

"Listen to me for just a minute."

"Certainly, darling."

"I bought this place for us to live in."

"You mean just the way it is?"

"Exactly. It can't be changed."

"You mean we can't take any of these things out?"

"No. But we can move ourselves in."

"This is another one of your jokes. Don't tease me, darling. I'm having such a good time."

"I'm not teasing! This is the life I want. This is where I want to live it."

"It's so dark, I can't see by your face whether you're serious or not. Turn on the lights."

"No lights."

"No electricity?"

"Only what's in your hair."

"How do they run the furnace?"

"No furnace."

"And the stove?"

"Firewood. And the refrigerator is a cold spring."

"How perfectly hideous!"

"I'm serious, Anita. I want us to live here."

"We'd die in six months."

"The Haycox family lived here for generations."

"You *are* playful tonight, aren't you? Just so straight-faced and everything, keeping your joke alive. Come here and kiss me, you sweet clown."

"We're going to spend the night here, and tomorrow I'm going to do the chores. Will you give it a try, anyway?"

"And I'll be a good old fat farm Mama, and get break-fast on the wood stove—coffee, home-grown eggs and cream, home-baked biscuits drowned in homemade butter and jam."

"Would you?"

"I'd drown in butter and jam first."

"You could learn to love this life."

"I couldn't, and you know it."

His temper was rising again, in response to bitter disap-

pointment, as it had done an hour before in Homestead. And
again he was looking for something short of a slap in her face
that would shock humility into her. The sentence that came
out had been ready for a long time. He spoke it now, not
because now was the right time, but because it packed a
punch.

"It doesn't matter what you think," he said evenly.
"I've made up my mind to quit my job and live here. Do you
understand? I'm going to quit."

She folded her arms across her chest, as though fighting
a chill, and rocked in silence for a few moments. "I thought
maybe that was coming," she said at last. "I thought maybe
that was what you were up to. I'd hoped it wasn't, Paul. I'd
prayed it wasn't. But—well, here we are, and you've said it."
She lit a cigarette, smoked it in shallow, tasteless puffs, and
blew the smoke through her nose. "Shepherd said you
would."

"He said I was about to quit?"

"No. He said you were a quitter." She sighed heavily.
"He knows you better than I do, apparently."

"God knows it'd be easy enough to stick with the system, and keep going right on up. It's getting out that takes
nerve."

"But why quit, if it's so easy to stick with it?"

"Didn't you hear anything I said in Homestead? That's
why I took you there, so you'd get the feel of things."

"That silly business about Katharine Finch and Shepherd?"

"No, no—God no. About how people like us have
taken all the self-respect from all the others."

"You said you felt like a horse's ass. I remember that."

"Don't you, sometimes?"

"What an idea!"

"Your conscience, dammit—doesn't it ever bother
you?"

"Why should it? I've never done anything dishonest."

183

"Let me put it another way: do you agree things are a mess?"

"Between us?"

"Everywhere! The world!" She could be appallingly nearsighted. Whenever possible, she liked to reduce any generalization to terms of herself and persons she knew intimately. "Homestead, for instance."

"What else could we possibly give the people that they haven't got?"

"There! You made my point for me. You said, what else could *we* give *them*, as though everything in the world were ours to give or withhold."

"Somebody's got to take responsibility, and that's just the way it is when somebody does."

"That's just it: things haven't always been that way. It's new, and it's people like us who've brought it about. Hell, everybody used to have some personal skill or willingness to work or something he could trade for what he wanted. Now that the machines have taken over, it's quite somebody who has anything to offer. All most people can do is hope to be given something."

"If someone has brains," said Anita firmly, "he can still get to the top. That's the American way, Paul, and it hasn't changed." She looked at him appraisingly. "Brains and nerve, Paul."

"And blinders." The punch was gone from his voice, and he felt drugged, a drowsiness from a little too much to drink, from scrambling over a series of emotional peaks and pits, from utter frustration.

Anita caught the strap of his overalls and pulled him down to kiss him. Paul yielded stiffly.

"Ohhhhhhh," she chided, "you're *such* a little boy sometimes." She pulled him down again, this time making sure he kissed her on the lips. "You stop worrying, now, you hear?" she whispered in his ear.

"Descent into the Maelstrom," he thought wearily, and

closed his eyes, and gave himself over to the one sequence of events that had never failed to provide a beginning, a middle, and a satisfactory end.

"I love you, Paul," she murmured. "I don't want my little boy to worry. You're not going to quit, sweetheart. You're just awfully tired."

"Mmmm."

"Promise not to think any more about it?"

"Mmmm."

"And, we *are* going to Pittsburgh, aren't we?"

"Mmmm."

"And what team is going to win at the Meadows?"

"Mmmm."

"Paul—"

"Hmmm?"

"What team is going to win?"

"Blue," he whispered sleepily. "Blue, by God, Blue."

"That's my boy. Your father would be awfully proud."

"Yup."

He carried her across the wide-board floor into the pine-wainscoted bedroom and laid her down on a patchwork quilt on a bird's-eye maple bed. There, Mr. Haycox had told him, six independent people had died, and fourteen had been born.

19

Doctor Paul Proteus, for want of a blow severe enough to knock him off the course dictated by the circumstances of his birth and training, arrived uneventfully at the day when it was time for men whose development was not yet complete to go to the Meadows.

The crisis was coming, he knew, when he would have to quit or turn informer, but its approach was unreal, and, lacking a decisive plan for meeting it, he forced a false tranquillity on himself—a vague notion that everything would come out all right in the end, the way it always had for him.

The big passenger plane, after an hour in the air, circled over the shore, where the pine forest met the waters at the source of the St. Lawrence. The plane dropped lower, and the landing strip in the forest could be seen, and then the cluster of log lodges and dining hall and shuffleboard courts and tennis courts and badminton courts and softball diamonds and swings and slides and bingo pavilion of the Mainland, the camp for women and children. And jutting into the river was a long dock and three white yachts, the port of embarkation for men going to the island called the Meadows.

"I guess this is just about goodbye," said Paul to Anita, as the plane came to a stop.

"You look wonderful," said Anita, straightening his blue captain's shirt for him. "And what team is going to win?"

"Blue," said Paul. *"Gott mit uns."*

"Now, I'm going to be working on Mom here, while—"

"Ladies over here!" boomed the public address system.

"Men will assemble over on the dock. Leave your luggage where it is. It will be in your cabins when you arrive."

"Goodbye, darling," said Anita.

"Goodbye, Anita."

"I love you, Paul."

"I love *you*, Anita."

"Come on," said Shepherd, who had arrived on the same plane. "Let's get going. I'm anxious to see just how hot this Blue Team is."

"Blue Team, eh?" said Baer. "Worried about the Blue Team, are you, eh? Eh? White. White's the one to look out for, boy." He stretched out his white shirt for them to admire. "See? See? That's the shirt to look out for. See? Aha, aha—"

"Where's Doctor Kroner?" said Shepherd.

"Went up yesterday," said Paul. "He's among the official greeters, so he's already on the island." He waved once more to Anita, who was going down a gravel path toward the Mainland's buildings with a dozen other women, Katharine Finch and Mom Kroner among them, and a handful of children. All day, planes would be bringing more.

Anita sidled up to Mom and took her fat arm.

Concealed loudspeakers in the virgin forest burst into song:

> "To you, beautiful lady, I raise my eyes;
> My heart, beautiful lady, to your heart sighs.
> Come, come, beautiful lady, to Paradise . . ."

The song died in a clatter in the loudspeaker, a cough, and then a command: "Men with classification numbers from zero to one hundred will please board the *Queen of the Meadows*; those with numbers from one hundred to two hundred and fifty will board the *Meadow Lark*; those with numbers above two hundred and fifty will get on the *Spirit of the Meadows*."

Paul, Shepherd, Baer, and the rest of the contingent from the Albany-Troy-Schenectady-Ilium area walked out onto the dock where earlier arrivals were waiting. All put on dark glasses, which they would wear during the next two weeks to protect their eyes from the unrelenting glare of the summer sun on the river, and on the whitewashed buildings, white gravel paths, white beach, and white cement courts of the Meadows.

"Green's going to win!" shouted Shepherd.

"You tell 'em, Cap!"

Everyone shouted and sang, the marine engines burbled and roared, and the three yachts shot toward the island in V-formation.

Squinting through spray, Paul watched the Meadows come closer and closer, hot, bleached, and sanitary. The white serpent stretching the island's length could now be seen as a row of white cubes, the insulated cement-block structures called, in Meadows parlance dating back to more primitive facilities, tents. The amphitheater on the island's northernmost tip looked like a dinner plate, and the sports area around it was a geometric patchwork of every imaginable kind of court. Whitewashed rocks everywhere framed the paths and gar—

The air quaked with a sharp, painful crash. And another. Another. *"Blam!"*

Rockets from the island were exploding overhead. In another minute the three yachts were rumbling and fuming into their slips, and the band was playing "The Star-Spangled Banner."

> "And the rockets red glare,
> The bombs bursting in air . . ."

The bandmaster held up his baton, and the bandsmen paused significantly.

"Vuuuuzzzzzzip!" went a rocket. *"Kablooooom!"*

"Gave proof through the night,
That our flag was still there . . ."

After the anthem came a cheery kaleidoscope of "Pack
Up Your Troubles," "I Want a Girl," "Take Me Out to the
Ball Game," "Working on the Railroad."

The new arrivals scrambled over the decks to catch the
hands extended from the wharf by a rank of older men, most
of whom were fat, gray, and balding. These were the Grand
Old Men—the district managers, the regional managers, the
associate vice-presidents and assistant vice-presidents
and vice-presidents of the Eastern and Middle-Western divisions.

"Welcome aboard!" was the greeting, and always had
been. "Welcome aboard!"

Paul saw that Kroner was reserving his big hand and
welcome for him, and he picked his way across the deck until
he reached the hand, took it, and stepped to the wharf.

"Good to have you aboard, Paul."

"Thank you, sir. It's good to be aboard." A number of
the other older men paused in their greetings to look in
friendly fashion at the bright young son of their departed
wartime leader.

"Report to the Ad Building for registration, then check
into your tents to make sure your luggage is there," said the
public address system. "Get to know your tentmate, then
lunch."

With the band leading them, the new arrivals swung
along the gravel walk to the Administration Building.

Across the building's entrance was a banner declaring:
"The Blue Team Welcomes You to the Meadows."

There were cries of good-natured outrage, and human
pyramids were built in a twinkling, with the top men clawing
down the infuriating message.

A young member of the Blue Team slapped Paul on the
back. "What an idea, Cap'n!" he crowed. "Boy, that really

showed 'em who's got the wide-awake outfit. And we'll go on showing these guys, too."

"Yep," said Paul, "you bet. That's the spirit." Apparently this was the youngster's first visit to the Meadows. In this state of nature he didn't know that the banner was the work of a special committee whose sole mission was to stir up team rivalry. There would be more such goads at every turn.

Inside the door was a green placard: "Abandon All Hope, Ye Who Don't Wear Green Shirts!"

Shepherd whooped delightedly, brandished the placard overhead, and in the next second was thrown to the floor by a wave of Blues, Whites, and Reds.

"No rough-housing indoors!" said the loudspeaker sharply. "You know the rules. No roughhousing indoors. Save your ginger for the playing field. After registration, report to your tents, get to know your buddies, and be back for lunch in fifteen minutes."

Paul arrived at his tent ahead of his as yet unknown buddy. The two of them, according to the foreword in the *Song Book*, would develop a sort of common-law brotherhood as a result of their having shared so much beauty, excitement, and deep emotion together.

The chill of the air-conditioned room made him feel dizzy. Coming out of this flicker of vertigo, Paul's eyes focused on a dinner-plate-size badge on the pillow of his bunk. "Dr. Paul Proteus, Wks. Mgr., Ilium, N. Y.," it said. And, below this, "Call Me Paul or Pay Me $5." The second part of the legend was on every badge. The only man who was not to be called by his first name at the Meadows was the Old Man himself, the successor of Paul's father, Doctor Francis Eldgrin Gelhorne. He, National Industrial, Commercial, Communications, Foodstuffs, and Resource Director, was damn well Doctor Gelhorne, sir, at any hour of the night or day, and anywhere he went.

And then Paul saw the badge on his buddy's pillow:

"Dr. Frederick Garth, Wks. Mgr., Buffalo, N. Y. Call Me Fred or Pay Me $5."

Paul sat down on the edge of his bed and struggled against the uneasy perplexity the sight of Garth's badge had precipitated. He had known many men, Shepherd for instance, who were forever seeing omens and worrying about them—omens in a superior's handshake, in the misspelling of a name in an official document, in the seating arrangement of a banquet table, in a superior's asking for or offering a cigarette, in the tone of . . . Paul's career, until recent weeks, had been graceful and easy all the way, and he'd found omen analysis dull, profitless. For him the omens were all good—or had been until now. Now, he, too, was growing aware of possibly malevolent spooks, revealing themselves in oblique ways.

Was it chance or ignorance or some subtle plot that had put him in the same cell with Garth, the other candidate for Pittsburgh? And why had Shepherd been made a captain, when the honor was reserved for those who were going high and far indeed? And why. . . . Manfully, Paul turned his thoughts into other channels, superficially, at least, and managed to laugh like a man who didn't give a damn about the system any more.

His buddy walked in, gray at the temples, tired, pale, and kind. Fred Garth wanted desperately to be liked by everyone, and had achieved a sort of social limbo, affecting no one very much one way or the other. He had risen because of this quality rather than in spite of it. Time and time again two powerful personalities, backed by impressive factions, had aspired for the same job. And the top brass, fearing a split if they chose one faction's man over the other, had named Garth as an inoffensive compromise candidate. There was a feeling, general enough not to be branded sour grapes, that Garth was all but over his head in the big assignments compromise politics had handed him. Now, though he was only in his early fifties, he seemed terribly old—willing, good-hearted, but apologetically weak, used up.

"Doctor Proteus! I mean Paul." Garth shook his head, laughed as though he'd done a comical thing, and offered a five-dollar bill to Paul.

"Forget it, Doctor Garth," said Paul, and handed it back to him. "I mean Fred. How are you?"

"Fine, fine. Can't complain. How's the wife and children?"

"All fine, fine, thanks."

Garth blushed. "Oh say, I'm sorry."

"About what?"

"I mean, that was silly of me, asking about your children when you haven't got any."

"Silly of me not to have any."

"Maybe, maybe. It's a trial, though, watching your kids grow up, wondering if they've got what it takes, seeing 'em just about killing themselves before the General Classification Tests, then waiting for the grades—" The sentence ended in a sigh. "I've just gone through that GCT business with my oldest, Brud, and I've got to live through the whole nightmare twice more still, with Alice and little Ewing."

"How'd Brud make out?"

"Hmmm? Oh—how'd he make out? His heart's in the right place. He wants to do well, and he boned up harder for the tests than any kid in the neighborhood. He does the best he can."

"Oh—I see."

"Well, he's going to get another crack at the tests—different ones, of course. He was under the weather when he took them the first time—tail end of some virus business. He didn't miss by much, and the Appeal Board made a special ruling. He gets his second chance tomorrow, and we'll have the grades around suppertime."

"He'll make it this time," said Paul.

Garth shook his head. "You'd think they'd give a kid something for trying, wouldn't you? God, you oughta see the little guy plugging away."

"Nice day," said Paul, changing the distressing subject.

Garth looked out of the window abstractedly. "It is, isn't it. God smiles on the Meadows."

"Probably did before we occupied it."

"I didn't make that up."

"Make what up?"

"About God smiling. That's from Doctor Gelhorne, of course. Remember? He said that last year on the closing day."

"Yep." Doctor Gelhorne said so many memorable things, it was hard for a person to stow them all away in his treasure house of souvenirs.

"Lunch!" said the loudspeakers. "Lunch! Remember the rule: get to know somebody new at each meal. Have your buddy on one side, but a stranger on the other. Lunch! Lunch!" Irrelevantly, the speakers blared "Oh How I Hate to Get Up in the Morning." Paul and Garth and five hundred other pairs walked across the parade ground to the dining hall.

As the crowd bore Paul and his buddy through the swinging screen doors, Kroner caught his arm and drew him to one side. Garth, like the good buddy he wanted to be, stepped out of line and waited.

"Tomorrow night," said Kroner. "The big meeting is tomorrow night—after the keynote play and bonfire."

"Fine."

"I told you the Old Man himself is coming. It's going to be that important. *You're* going to be that important. I don't quite know what's up, but I've a hunch it's going to be the biggest thing in your career."

"Gosh."

"Don't worry. With the blood you've got in your veins,

you've got more than what it'll take to do the job—whatever it is."

"Thanks."

Paul got back in line with Garth. "He certainly likes you, doesn't he?" said Garth.

"Old friend of my father's. Said it was good to have me aboard."

"Oh." Garth looked a little embarrassed. Paul's bald lie had pointed up for the first time their competitive situation. He let the lie pass. Shepherd would have hounded Paul, and, more subtly, Kroner, until he'd learned every word that had passed between them.

Paul felt real warmth for Garth. "Come on, buddy, let's find a couple of strangers."

"It's going to be tough. We've been around a long time, Paul."

"Look for some apple-cheeked youngster fresh out of school."

"There's one."

"Berringer!" said Paul, amazed. When the machines had made a list of Ilium men eligible for the Meadows, Berringer's card had stayed in its slot. He was the last man in the whole Works who deserved an invitation. Yet, here he was.

Berringer seemed to know what was going through Paul's head, and he returned Paul's gaze with an insolent smile.

Baer stepped between them. "Forgot, forgot—supposed to tell you," he said. "Berringer, about Berringer. Kroner said to tell you, and I forgot, forgot."

"How the hell did he get up here?"

"Kroner brought him up. Last minute thing, see? Hmm? Kroner thought it'd break his father's heart if the boy wasn't asked, and after what happened to Checker Charley and all."

"There goes the merit system," said Paul.

Baer nodded. "Yep—there it goes, there it goes, all

right." He shrugged and raised his eyebrows quizzically. "Zip zip, out the window."

Paul reflected that Baer was possibly the most just, reasonable, and candid person he'd ever known—remarkably machine-like in that the only problems he interested himself in were those brought to him, and in that he went to work on all problems with equal energy and interest, insensitive to quality and scale.

Paul glanced once more at Berringer, saw his luncheon companion was Shepherd and that his shirt was green, and forgot about him.

He and Garth finally found a pair of very young strangers with two empty seats between them, and sat down.

The redheaded youngster next to Paul looked at his badge. "Oh, Doctor Proteus. I've heard of you. How are you, sir?"

"Paul, not Doctor. Fine, how are you—" he studied his companion's badge—"Doctor Edmund L. Harrison, of the Ithaca Works?"

"Get to know the man next to you," said the loudspeaker. "Don't talk to anyone you know."

"Married?" said Paul.

"That's what you're here for, to get to know new people, to broaden your horizons," said the loudspeaker.

"Nossir, I'm en—"

"The more contacts you make here at the Meadows," said the loudspeaker, "the more smoothly industry will function, co-operationwise."

"I'm engaged," said Doctor Harrison.

"An Ithaca girl?"

"Two seats right over here, gentlemen—over in the corner. Right over there. Let's get our seats quickly, because there's a full program, and everybody wants to get down to knowing everybody else," said the loudspeaker.

"Nossir," said Doctor Harrison. "Atlanta." He looked at Paul's badge again. "Aren't you the son of—"

"Now that we're all seated and getting to know one another, how about a little song to pull us all together?" said the loudspeaker.

"Yes, he was my father," said Paul.

"Turn to page twenty-eight of the *Song Book,*" said the loudspeaker. "Twenty-eight, twenty-eight!"

"He was quite a man," said Harrison.

"Yes," said Paul.

" 'Wait Till the Sun Shines, Nellie!' " shouted the loudspeaker. "Find it? Twenty-eight! All right, now, let's go!"

The band at the far end of the hall, amplified to the din of an elephant charge, smashed and hewed at the tune as though in a holy war against silence. It was impossible even to be cordial to oneself in the midst of the uproar. Paul's stomach knotted and his tastebuds went dead, and the delicious, expensive food went down his gullet like boiled horsemeat and hominy grits.

"Paul, Paul, Paul, oh Paul!" shouted Baer from across the table. "Paul!"

"What?"

"That's you—you they're calling for; they're calling for you!"

"Don't tell me the captain of the Blue Team is such a coward he ran out at the last minute," the loudspeaker was saying sarcastically. "Come on! Where's that Blue captain?"

Paul stood, and held up his hand. "Here," he said in a voice inaudible even to himself.

Cheers and boos greeted him, in a proportion of one to three. He was pelted by wadded paper napkins and maraschino cherries from the tops of salads.

"Well," said the loudspeaker tauntingly, "let's hear your song."

Hands gripped Paul and hoisted him into the air, and he was borne down the aisle toward the bandstand by a flying wedge of blue-shirted men. They dumped him on the band-

stand and formed a cordon about him. The master of ceremonies, a fat, red old man with breasts like a woman's sticking through his wet T-shirt, thrust a *Song Book* into his hands.
The band blasted out the fight song of the Blue Team.

"Oh you Blue Team, you tried and true team," said
Paul. His voice came back at him, strange and frightening,
amplified electronically to fierce defiance and determination.
"There are no teams as good as you!"

At this point he was completely drowned out by the
stamping of feet, whistles, catcalls, and the clank of spoons on
glasses. The master of ceremonies, delighted with the high
spirits he was evoking, handed Paul a blue banner to wave.
No sooner were Paul's hands on the staff than he saw the
ranks of his protectors split wide open. Berringer, his head
lowered, his thick legs driving, charged him.

In the scuffle, Paul swung at the informality-maddened
Berringer, missed, and was knocked, *hors de combat*, off the
bandstand and halfway through the kitchen doors.

"Please! Please!" the loudspeaker was pleading. "There
are very few rules at the Meadows, but the few that there are
must be observed! Get back to your seat, now, you in the
green shirt. There's to be no rough stuff indoors. Do you
understand?"

Laughter was general.

"One more outburst like this one, and you'll be asked
to leave the island!"

Kind hands picked up Paul, and he found himself looking into the grave, dull face of Luke Lubbock, the perennial
joiner, who wore a busboy's uniform. One of the cooks, who
had been watching with disdain, turned away quickly when
Paul looked at him, and disappeared into the big meat locker.

As Paul's teammates carried him back to his seat, he
realized fleetingly, as a fragment of a nightmare, that the cook
had been Alfy, the master of silent television.

"Now, now," said the loudspeaker. "No more rough

stuff, or we'll have to call off the rest of the fun. Now, where's the captain of the White Team?"

When the fun was over, Paul and Doctor Harrison of Ithaca walked out together.

"You have ten minutes of free time until the memorial service," said the loudspeaker. "Ten minutes to make new contacts before the memorial service."

"Nice meeting you, sir," said Doctor Harrison.

"I enj—"

"My wild Irish rose," howled the loudspeaker, "the sweetest flow'r that grows—" The refrain ended in a clatter. "Your attention, please. The Program Committee has just informed me that we're running seven minutes behind schedule, so would you please form up at the Oak right away, please. The memorial service will take place right away."

A reverent hush settled like smog over the perspiring crowd that had dispersed over the shuffleboard courts and around the ping-pong tables near the dining hall. Now they began to form about the Oak, the official symbol for the entire national organization. Its image was on every letter-head, and, stitched in a rectangle of white silk, its image snapped in the breeze, just below the American Flag on the parade-ground mast.

The youngsters imitated the oldsters' uniform stances of piety: eyes fixed on the lower branches of the magnificent old tree, hands folded before their genitals.

"White's going to win!" cried a short, thin youngster with big teeth.

The older men looked at him with sadness, with melancholy rebuke. Now was not the time for such horseplay. Now was almost the only time that was not the time. The youngster's outburst of infinite bad taste would poison his next two weeks, and probably his career. He had in an instant become "the boy who yelled at memorial service." That described him, and nobody would care to investigate him any further. Now, if he turned out to be a spectacular athlete

. . . No. His flaccid physique and pale skin indicated that this avenue to forgiveness was closed to him.

Paul looked at him sympathetically, and recalled similar bad starts from the past. The man would be terribly lonely, turn to a career of surly drinking, and never be invited again.

The only sounds now were the rustling of leaves and the fluttering of the flags, and now and then the clatter of dishes and silverware from the dining hall.

A harried-looking photographer ran in front of the group, dropped to one knee, fired a flashbulb, and ran away again.

"Vuuuuzzzzzzip!" went a rocket. *"Kabloooom!"* A parachuted American Flag was flung from the bomb to drift lazily to the river.

Kroner detached himself from the crowd and walked soberly to the thick tree trunk. He turned and looked down at his hands thoughtfully. His first words were so soft, so choked with emotion, that few heard them. He inhaled deeply, threw back his shoulders, raised his eyes, and gathered strength to say them again.

In the brief moment before Kroner spoke again, Paul looked about himself. His eyes met those of Shepherd and Berringer, and what passed between them was tender and sweet. The crowd had miraculously become a sort of homogenized pudding. It was impossible to tell where one ego left off and the next began.

"It is our custom," said Kroner; "it is the custom here at the Meadows—our custom, our Meadows—to meet here under our tree, our symbol of strong roots, trunk, and branches, our symbol of courage, integrity, perseverance, beauty. It is our custom to meet here to remember our departed friends and co-workers."

And now he forgot the crowd, and talked to the fat cumulus clouds scudding over the blue sky. "Since last we met, Doctor Ernest S. Bassett has left our world for his reward in a better one. Ernie, as you all know, was—"

199

The photographer ran out, flashed a bulb in Kroner's face, and disappeared again.

"Ernie was manager of the Philadelphia Works for five years, of the Pittsburgh Works for seven. He was my friend; he was *our* friend: a great American, a great engineer, a great manager, a great pioneer at the head of the procession of civilization, opening new, undreamed-of doors to better things, for better living, for more people, at less cost."

Now and then brokenly, Kroner told of Ernie Bassett as a young engineer, and he traced his career from works to works.

"He gave himself unstintingly engineeringwise, managershipwise, personalitywise, Americanwise, and—" Kroner paused to look impressively from face to face. Again he talked to the clouds—"heartwise."

A man stepped from the crowd to hand Kroner a long white box. Kroner opened it slowly and studied it thoughtfully before showing its contents to anyone else. At last he reached in and unfurled a blue and white pennant, the Armed Forces "E" that Bassett had won during the war as manager of the Philadelphia Works.

A muted bugle played taps.

Kroner knelt at the foot of the tree and placed Ernie Bassett's pennant there.

The photographer dashed up, got the picture, and dashed away.

"Vuuuuzzzzzip! Kablooom!"

A male choir, concealed in the shrubbery, sang ever so softly—to the tune of "Love's Sweet Song":

"Fellows at the Meadows,
 Lift your tankards high;
 Toast our living symbol, reaching toward the sky.
 Grown from but an acorn,
 Giant now you are;
 May you ne'er stop growing;

Rise to the stars!
Proud sy-him-bol a-hov
Ourrrrrrrrs."

"A minute of silence in unspoken prayer for departed friends," said the loudspeaker.

All through the minute of silence, Paul was aware of a snuffling in the background. Someone's dam of reserve had broken under the impact of the ceremony—someone who must have been awfully close to Bassett. There were tears standing in many eyes, and here and there teeth were sunk in unstable lips, but nowhere could Paul see the sobber. Suddenly he spotted him, not in the crowd, but in the dining hall. Luke Lubbock, a pile of dirty dishes in his arms, had been completely carried away. Big, honest tears for the manager of the Pittsburgh Works flooded his cheeks. Rather roughly, the headwaiter hustled him away from the screen door.

"Vuuuuzzzzzzip! Kablooooom!"

The band exploded into "The Stars and Stripes Forever," and Kroner was half led from the tree by other oldsters who had known Bassett well. The crowd dispersed.

Paul looked longingly at the doors of the saloon, which was located in a separate white building. He tested the doors to make sure they were really locked, and of course they were. The saloon never opened until the cocktail hour, after the games.

"Your attention!" said the loudspeaker. "Your attention, please. The program for the rest of the day:

"In ten minutes the teams will meet at their captains' tents for assignments to various sports. Formal competition will not begin until tomorrow morning. After assignment, relax, get to know your buddy, don't hang around with the same old crowd.

"Cocktails at five-thirty. Supper at six-thirty. Now—attention to this change: the keynote play and bonfire will *not*

take place tonight. Will *not*. They will take place tomorrow
night, and there will be a group sing tonight in the amphitheater instead. Taps at midnight.

"Team captains, team captains—will you please report
to your tents."

Without much hope, Paul rattled the saloon doors,
thinking he might be able to talk a floor sweeper inside into
getting him a little something.

"I've just been informed," said the loudspeaker, "I've
just been informed that the captain of the Blue Team is not in
his tent. Doctor Paul Proteus; Doctor Paul . . ."

20

THE SHAH OF BRATPUHR'S golden turban hung unfurled
like a roller towel in heaven from the hat rack in Miami
Beach.

"Puka pala koko, puku ebo koko, nibo aki koko," said the
Shah.

"What's the foreign gentleman after?" asked Homer
Bigley, proprietor of the barber shop.

"He wants a little off the sides, a little off the back, and
leave the top alone," mumbled Khashdrahr Miasma, under a
steaming towel in the barber chair next to the Shah's.

Doctor Ewing J. Halyard was giving himself a ragged
manicure with his teeth in one of the waiting chairs, while
his charges received their first American haircuts. He smiled
and nodded at whatever was being said, but heard nothing

save the soft crackle of the letter in his breast pocket as he shifted nervously in a search for comfort no chair could give him. The letter, from the personnel officer of the State Department, had pursued him from New York to Utica to Niagara Falls to Camp Drum to Indianapolis to St. Louis to Fort Riley to Houston to Hollywood to the Grand Canyon to Carlsbad Caverns to Hanford to Chicago to Miami Beach, where he roosted long enough for the letter to catch him— catch him like a javelin, quivering squarely between the shoulder-blades of his spirit. He was lobster-red from a day on the sand, but beneath this stinging veneer of fine health and spirits he was cold and dead-white with fear. "My dear Mr. Halyard," it had begun. "My dear *Mr.* . . ."

While Halyard brooded, Homer Bigley, with the reflexes born of a life of barbering, selected his scissors, clicked them in air about the sacred head, and, as though his right hand were serviced by the same nerve as his diaphragm and voicebox, he began to cut hair and talk—talked to the uncomprehending Shah after the fashion of an extroverted embalmer chatting with a corpse.

"Yessir, picked a nice time to come. They call this the off-season, but I say it's the nicest time of year. Cheapest time, too. But that isn't what I meant. It's fifteen degrees cooler right here and now than it is in New York City, and I'll bet not one person in fifty up north knows that. Just because the fact hasn't been promoted. Everything's promotion. Ever stop to think about that? Everything you think you think because somebody promoted the ideas. Education— nothing but promotion.

"Good promotion and bad promotion. Barbers, now, they get a lot of bad promotion on account of cartoons and television comedians, you know? Can't pick up a magazine or turn on the television without you see a joke about a barber cutting somebody. And sure, maybe that's good for a little snicker, maybe, and God knows the world can use a few snickers, but I don't think it's right to hurt somebody to give somebody else a snicker. I mean that it all kind of cancels out, and nobody's ahead. And I just wonder if any of those comedians or cartoon people ever stop to think about the thousands of barbers who go from one year to the next without they ever cut a customer, and still these people go around telling everybody that barbers are slashing so many arteries and veins you wonder how the sewers can handle it all. But seems like nobody ever thinks about what's maybe sacred to somebody, any more.

"Matter of fact, of course, used to be barbers did *bleed* people, of course, and got paid for it, too. One of the oldest professions on earth, if you stop to think about it, but nobody does. Used to be sort of doctors, bleeding people and setting their bones and all, and then the doctors got sore and took over all that stuff and left the barbers haircutting and shaving. Very interesting history. But my father used to say, before he died, of course, that the barbers would be here long after the last doctor's laid away, and there was a lot in what he said. He was worth listening to.

"Nowadays, by golly, it takes more time and skill to cut hair'n to do what the doctors do. If you had syphilis or the clap or scarlet fever or yellow fever or pneumonia or cancer or something, why, hell, I could cure you while I was drawing the water for a shampoo. Take a little old needle, puncho! squirto! miracle! and give you a clean bill of health along with your change. Any barber could do what a doctor does nowadays. But I'll give you fifty dollars if you can show me a doctor who can cut hair.

"Now, they say barbering isn't a profession, but you take the other professions that got so big for their breeches since the Middle Ages and look down on barbering. You take medicine, you take the law. Machinery!

"Doctor doesn't use his head and education to figure out what's the matter with you. Machines go over you—measure this, measure that. Then he picks out the right miracle stuff, and the only reason he does is on account of the machines tell him that's what to do. And the lawyers! Of course, I say it's a pretty good thing what happened to them, because it was a bad thing for them, which couldn't help to be a good thing for everybody else. I didn't say that. My father said it. Those are his words. But the law's the law now, and not a contest between a lot of men paid to grin and lie and yell and finagle for whatever somebody wanted them to grin and lie and yell and finagle about. By golly, the lie detectors know who's lying and who's telling the truth, and those old card machines know how the law runs on whatever the case is about, and they can find out a helluva sight quicker'n you can say habeas corpus what judges did about cases like that before. And that settles it. No more of this fast footwork. Hell, if I had a lie detector and card machines and all, I could run a law business here and fix you up with a divorce or a million dollar damage suit or whatever you needed whatsoever while you were sticking your feet and a dime into that shoeshine machine.

"Used to be sort of high and mighty, sort of priests, those doctors and lawyers and all, but they're beginning to look more and more like mechanics. Dentists are holding up pretty good, though. They're the exception that proves the rule, I say. And barbering—one of the oldest professions on earth, incidentally—has held up better than all the rest. Machines separated the men from the boys, you might say.

"The men from the boys—that's what they used to say in the Army, Sergeant Elm Wheeler would. Memphis boy. 'Here we go, boys,' he'd say. 'Here's where we separate the men from the boys.' And off we'd go for the next hill, and the medics'd follow and separate the dead from the wounded. And then Wheeler'd say, 'Here we go, here's where we separate the men from the boys.' And that went on till we got separated from our battalion and Wheeler got his head separated from his shoulders.

"But you know, terrible as that mess was—not just Wheeler, but the whole war—it brought out the greatness in the American people. There's something about war that brings out greatness. I hate to say that, but it's true. Of course, maybe that's because you can get great so quick in a war. Just one damn fool thing for a couple of seconds, and you're great. I could be the greatest barber in the world, and maybe I am, but I'd have to prove it with a lifetime of great haircutting, and then nobody'd notice. That's just the way peacetime things are, you know?

"But Elm Wheeler, you couldn't help but notice him when he went hog-wild after he got a letter from his wife saying she'd had a baby, and he hadn't seen her for two years. Why, he read that and ran up to a machine-gun nest and shot and hand-grenaded everybody in it something awful, then he ran up to another one and mashed up all the people there with his rifle butt, and then, after he'd busted that, he started after a mortar emplacement with a rock in each hand, and they got him with a shell fragment. You could of paid a surgeon a thousand dollars, and he couldn't of done a nicer job. Well, Elm Wheeler got the Congressional Medal for that, and they laid it in his coffin with him. Just laid it there. Couldn't hang it around his neck, and if they'd put it on his chest, I expect they'd of had to use solder, he was so full of lead and scrap iron.

"But *he* was great, and nobody'd argue about that, but do you think he could of been great today, in this modern day and age? Wheeler? Elm Wheeler? You know what he would be today? A Reek and Wreck, that's all. The war made him, and this life would of killed him.

"And another nice thing about war—not that anything about war is nice, I guess—is that while it's going on and you're in it, you never worry about doing the right thing. See? Up there, fighting and all, you couldn't be righter. You could of been a heller at home and made a lot of people unhappy and all, and been a dumb, mean bastard, but you're king over there—king to everybody, and especially to yourself. This above all, be true to yourself, and you can't be false to anybody else, and that's it—in a hole, being shot at and shooting back.

"These kids in the Army now, that's just a place to keep 'em off the streets and out of trouble, because there isn't anything else to do with them. And the only chance they'll ever get to be anybody is if there's a war. That's the only chance in the world they got of showing anybody they lived and died, and for something, by God.

"Used to be there was a lot of damn fool things a dumb bastard could do to be great, but the machines fixed that. You know, used to be you could go to sea on a big clipper ship or a fishing ship and be a big hero in a storm. Or maybe you could be a pioneer and go out west and lead the people and make trails and chase away Indians and all that. Or you could be a cowboy, or all kinds of dangerous things, and *still* be a dumb bastard.

"Now the machines take all the dangerous jobs, and the dumb bastards just get tucked away in big bunches of prefabs that look like the end of a game of Monopoly, or in barracks, and there's nothing for them to do but set there and kind of hope for a big fire where maybe they can run into a burning building in front of everybody and run out with a baby in their arms. Or maybe hope—though they don't say so out loud because the last one was so terrible—for another war. Course, there isn't going to be another one.

"And, oh, I guess machines have made things a lot better. I'd be a fool to say they haven't, though there's plenty who say they haven't, and I can see what they mean, all right. It does seem like the machines took all the good jobs, where a man could be true to hisself and false to nobody else, and left all the silly ones. And I guess I'm just about the end of a race, standing here on my own two feet.

"And I'm lucky barbering held out as long as it did— long enough to take care of me. And I'm glad I don't have any kids. That way it comes out even, and I don't have to think about this shop not being here for them, about nothing being for them but the Army or the Reeks and Wrecks, probably—unless an engineer or manager or research man or bureaucrat got at my wife, and the kids had their brains instead of mine. But Clara'd let one of those jerks at her just about as quick as you could stuff a pound of oleomargarine up a cat's ass with a hot awl.

"Anyway, I hope they keep those barber machines out of Miami Beach for another two years, and then I'll be ready to retire and the hell with them. They had the man who invented the damn things on television the other night, and turns out he's a barber hisself. Said he kept worrying and worrying about somebody was going to invent a haircutting machine that'd put him out of business. And he'd have nightmares about it, and when he'd wake up from them, he'd tell hisself all the reasons why they couldn't ever make a machine that'd do the job—you know, all the complicated motions a barber goes through. And then, in his next nightmare, he'd dream of a machine that did one of the jobs, like combing, and he'd see how it worked clear as a bell. And it was just a vicious circle. He'd dream. Then he'd tell hisself something the machine couldn't do. Then he'd dream of a machine, and he'd see just how a machine *could* do what he'd said it couldn't do. And on and on, until he'd dreamed up a whole machine that cut hair like nobody's business. And he sold his plans for a hundred thousand bucks and royalties, and I don't guess he has to worry about anything any more.

"Ever stop to think what a funny thing the human mind is? And there you are, sir, how's that look to you?"

"Sumklish," said the Shah, and he took a long drink from the flask Khashdrahr handed him. He studied himself soberly in the mirror Bigley held up for him. *"Nibo bakula ni provo,"* he said at last.

"He likes it?" asked Bigley.

"He says it's nothing a turban won't cover," said Khashdrahr, whose haircut was also over. He called to Halyard. "Your turn, Doctor."

"Hmmm?" said Halyard absently, looking up from the letter. "Oh—no haircut for me. Think we ought to go back to the hotel for a rest, eh?" He glanced at the letter once more:

My dear Mr. Halyard:

We have just completed an audit of the personnel cards for our Department, checking the information coded on them against the facts.

During this audit, it was discovered that you failed to meet the physical-education requirements for a bachelor's degree from Cornell University, and that the degree was awarded you through a clerical oversight of this deficiency. I regret to inform you that you are, therefore, technically without a bachelor's degree, and, hence, technically ineligible for the M.A. and Ph.D. degrees which also appear on your record.

Since there are, as you know, severe penalties for willfully coding false information on personnel cards, we are obliged to advise you that you are officially without a college degree of any sort, and that you are transferred from staff to probationary status for a period of eight weeks, in which time you will return to Cornell and make up this deficiency.

Perhaps you can work this small chore into your itinerary, and give the Shah an opportunity to see a representative American institution of higher learning.

I have been in touch with Cornell about this mix-up, and they assure me that they will arrange for you to take the physical-education tests whenever you like. You will not have to take the course, but only the final examinations. These tests, I understand, are quite simple: swim six lengths of the swimming pool, do twenty pushups, fifteen chinnings, climb a rope, stand on your . . .

21

THE MOON WAS full over the Thousand Islands, and, on one of them at least, there were a thousand eyes to see it. The cream of the East and Middle West, engineeringwise and managerwise, was met in the amphitheater of the Meadows. It was the second night, the night of the keynote play and the bonfire. The stage in the center of the circling stone seats was hidden beneath a pair of steel quarter-spheres, which would presently open like the shells of a steamed quahog.

Kroner sat down next to Paul and laid his hand on Paul's knee. "Nice night, boy."

"Yessir."

"Think we've got a good team this year, Paul."

"Yessir. They look good." After one day of competition, the Blue Team did look good, good despite the large proportion of top—hence tired and old—executives in its ranks. That afternoon the Blues had knocked the captain of the Greens, Shepherd, out of the box after three innings. Shepherd, in his determination to win and his horror of losing, had blown up completely.

Paul, by contrast, had played heads-up ball all the way, effortlessly, laughingly, wholly out of character. In analyzing the magical quality of the afternoon during the cocktail hour, Paul realized what had happened: for the first time since he'd made up his mind to quit, he really hadn't given a damn about the system, about the Meadows, about intramural politics. He'd tried not to give a damn before, but he hadn't had much luck. Now, suddenly, as of the afternoon, he was his own man.

Paul was half tight, and pleased with himself. Everything was going to be just fine.

"The Old Man wants to start the meeting shortly after his plane lands," said Kroner, "so we'll have to leave whatever's going on."

"O.K.," said Paul. "Swell." Swell night, tangy air, and a drowsy sort of harmlessness over everything. Maybe he'd give notice tonight, if he felt like it. No hurry. "Fine."

"Everybody in their seats, please," said the loudspeaker. "Will everybody take their seats. The Program Committee has just informed me that we are eight minutes behind time, so will everybody take their seats."

Everybody did. The band, wearing summer tuxedos, struck up a medley of Meadows favorites. The music faded. The quarter-spheres opened a trifle at the top, freeing a beam of light that shot through cigarette smoke to the deep-blue heavens. The music stopped, machinery underground grumbled, and the quarter-spheres sank into the earth, revealing:

An old man, with a white beard reaching to his waist, wearing a long white robe and golden sandals and a blue conical hat speckled with golden stars, sits atop an extraordinarily tall stepladder. He looks wise, just, and tired by responsibility. In one hand he holds a large dust cloth. Beside the ladder, and of the same height, is a slender pole. Another just like it stands across the stage. Between the two poles is a loop of wire, passing, like a clothesline, over pulleys fixed to the poles. Hanging from the wire are a series of metallic stars about two feet across. They are coated with fluorescent paint, so that a beam of invisible infrared light, playing on one star, then another, makes them come alive with dazzling color.

The old man, oblivious to the audience, contemplates the stars strung out before him, unhooks the star nearest to him, studies its surface, polishes a tarnished spot on it, shakes his head sadly, and lets the star fall. He looks down at the fallen star with regret, then at those still on the wire, then at the audience. He speaks.

OLD MAN. I am the Sky Manager. It is I who keep night skies shining brightly; I who, when a star's glory is tarnished beyond restoration, must take it from the firmament. Every hundred years I climb my ladder to keep the heavens bright. And now my time has come again.

(He pulls on the wire, bringing another star within reach. He removes the star and examines it.)

And this is a strange star to be shining in the modern heavens. And yet, a hundred years ago, when I last kept my vigil, it was proud and new, and only a few meteors, destroying themselves in a brilliant instant, shone more brightly than this. *(He holds up the star, and the infrared light makes it glow brightly, bringing out the lettering which says, "Labor Unionism." He dusts it desultorily, shrugs, and lets it drop.)* In brave company. *(Looks down at scrap heap.)* With stars named Rugged Individualism, Socialism, Free Enterprise, Communism, Fascism, and—*(Leaves sentence unfinished, and sighs.)*

It is not an easy job, not always a pleasant one. But One far wiser than I, infinitely good, has decreed that it must be done *(sighs)*, and be done dispassionately.

(He pulls on wire, and brings in another star, the biggest of all. The infrared light hits it, and it lights up brilliantly, and on it is the image of the Oak, the symbol of the organization.)

Alas, a young beauty. But already there are those who hate the sight of it, who clamor for it to be torn from the heavens. *(He dabs at it with his dust cloth, shrugs, and holds the star at arm's length, preparatory to dropping it.)* Enter a clean-cut, handsome young engineer from audience.

YOUNG ENG. *(Shakes foot of ladder.)* No! No, Sky Manager, no!

OLD MAN. *(Looks down curiously.)* What is this? A mere stripling challenges the caretaker of the heavens? *Enter unkempt young radical through trap door in stage.*

RADICAL. *(Sneeringly)* Take it down.

YOUNG ENG.   There's never been a more brilliant, beautiful star!

RADICAL.   There's never been a bloodier, blacker one!

OLD MAN.   *(Looks perplexedly from the two men to the star and back.)* Hmmmm. Are you prepared to appeal the fate of this star with reason rather than emotion? My duties require that I be the sworn enemy of emotion.

YOUNG ENG.   I am!

RADICAL.   I, too. *(Smiles.)* And I promise to take very little of your time.

CLOSE QUARTER-SPHERES.

OPEN QUARTER-SPHERES.

A tall judge's rostrum now surrounds the old man's ladder. The old man wears a judge's wig and robes. The radical and the young engineer are similarly robed and wigged after the fashion of English barristers.

OFFSTAGE

VOICE.   Oyez, oyez, oyez! The Court of Celestial Relations is now in session!

OLD MAN.   *(Bangs with gavel.)* Order in the court. The prosecution will proceed.

RADICAL.   *(Offensively ingratiating.)* Your honor, ladies and gentlemen of the jury, the prosecution will show that the star in question is as tarnished—nay, black!—as any ever hung in the heavens. I will call but one witness, but that witness in effect is a million witnesses, each of whom could tell the same sordid tale, tell the unvarnished truth in the same simple words from the heart. I'd like to call John Averageman to the stand.

OFFSTAGE

VOICE.   John Averageman, John Averageman. Take the stand, please. *Enter John Averageman through trap door in stage floor.*

   (He is slightly pudgy, shy, middle-aged, endearing. His clothes are cheap, verging on being comical. He is in awe of the court, and has perhaps had a couple of drinks to bolster his nerve.)

213

RADICAL. *(Touches John's arm.)* I'm looking out for you, John. Take your time about answering. Don't let them rattle you. Let me do the thinking, and you'll be all right.

OFFSTAGE

VOICE. Do you solemnly swear to tell the truth, the whole truth, and nothing but the truth, so help you God?

JOHN. *(Looks questioningly at radical.)* Do I?

RADICAL. You do.

RADICAL. John, suppose you tell the court what you did before the war, before this new star arose to spoil, to besmirch the heavens.

JOHN. I was a machinist in the Averagetown Works of the Averagetown Manufacturing Company.

RADICAL. And now?

JOHN. I'm in the Reconstruction and Reclamation Corps, sir. Shovelman First Class.

RADICAL. Suppose, for the edification of the court, you tell us what you made before the star arose, and what you make now.

JOHN. *(Stares upward, remembering and computing with difficulty.)* Well, sir, when the defense work and all got going before the war, seems to me I could make better'n a hundred a week with overtime. Best week I ever had, I guess, was about a hundred and forty-five dollars. Now I get thirty a week.

RADICAL. Uh-huh. In other words, as that star went up, your income dropped. To be exact, John, your income dropped about eighty per cent.

YOUNG ENG. *(Jumps to feet impulsively, likably.)* Your honor, I—

OLD MAN. Wait until the cross-examination.

YOUNG ENG. Yessir. Sorry, sir.

RADICAL. I think we've made it amply clear that the American standard of living has tumbled eighty per cent. *(His features assume an annoyingly pious expression.)* But enough of merely materialistic considerations. What has the ascent of this star meant to John Averageman in terms of his spirit? John, tell the court what you told me. Remember? About the engineers and managers—

214

JOHN.   Yessir. *(Looks hesitantly at young engineer.)* No offense, sir—

RADICAL.   *(Prodding.)* The truth can never be spoken without someone getting hurt, John. Go right ahead.

JOHN.   Well, sir, it hurts a man a lot to be forgotten. You know—to have the fellers in charge, the engineers and managers, just sort of look right through him like they don't see him. A guy likes to know somebody thinks enough of him to look out for him.

YOUNG ENG.   *(Urgently)* Your honor!

OLD MAN.   *(Severely)* I will not tolerate any further interruptions from you. The issues are far graver than I thought. *(To radical)* Please proceed.

RADICAL.   Go ahead, John.

JOHN.   Well, sir, that's just about it. Kind of summing up, seems like these days the engineers and managers and the like are everything, and the average man is just nothing any more.

RADICAL.   *(Pretends to be overcome by the tragedy of John's testimony. After seemingly searching for words and struggling with emotion for thirty seconds, he at last speaks, choked up and angry.)* Star of wonder, star of might; star of wondrous beauty bright. Take it down. *(Shakes fist.)* Take it down! *(Gestures at John.)* We've heard the voice of the people— the people, yes. "Take it down!" they say.

Who is it that says, "Leave it up?" Who? Not John, not the people. Who? *(Dramatically, he produces a pamphlet from his breast pocket.)* Your honor, ladies and gentlemen of the jury *(reads from pamphlet)*, at the start of the war, the average income for engineers and managers in this great land of ours was $8,449.27. Now, on this poisoned night, as the black star reaches its zenith, eighty per cent of John Averageman's pay check has been wrenched from him. And what is the average pay check for engineers and managers, you ask? *(Reads from the pamphlet again, with bitter emphasis on every syllable.)* Fifty-seven thousand eight hundred and ninety-six dollars and forty-one cents!

(Explosively.) Your witness!

(Radical slinks over to the far post and leans against it to watch contemptuously.)

YOUNG ENG. *(Softly, kindly)* John.

JOHN. *(Suspiciously, hostilely)* Yessir?

YOUNG ENG. John, tell me—when you had this large income, before the star arose, did you by any chance have a twenty-eight-inch television set?

JOHN. *(Puzzled)* No, sir.

YOUNG ENG. Or a laundry console or a radar stove or an electronic dust precipitator?

JOHN. No, sir, I didn't. Them things were for the rich folks.

YOUNG ENG. And tell me, John, when you had all that money, did you have a social insurance package that paid *all* of your medical bills, all of your dentist bills, and provided for food, housing, clothes, and pocket money in your old age?

JOHN. No, sir. There wasn't no such thing then, in those days.

YOUNG ENG. But you have them now, now that the *(sarcastically)* black star has risen, haven't you?

JOHN. Yessir, that's right, I do. But—

YOUNG ENG. John, you've heard of Julius Caesar? Good, you have. John, do you suppose that Caesar, with all his power and wealth, with the world at his feet, do you suppose he had what you, Mr. Averageman, have today?

JOHN. *(Surprised)* Come to think of it, he didn't. Huh! What do you know?

RADICAL. *(Furiously)* I object! What has Caesar got to do with it?

YOUNG ENG. Your honor, the point I was trying to make was that John, here, since the star in question has risen, has become far richer than the wildest dreams of Caesar or Napoleon or Henry VIII! Or *any* emperor in history! Thirty dollars, John—yes, that is how much money you make. But, not with all his gold and armies could Charlemagne have gotten one single electric lamp or vacuum tube! He would have given anything to get the security and health package you have, John. But could he get it? No!

JOHN.   Well, for heaven's sakes! But—

YOUNG ENG.   *(Anticipates John's objection.)* But the engineers and managers have forgotten Mr. Averageman?

JOHN.   Yessir, that's what I was going to say.

YOUNG ENG.   John, do you know that no manager or engineer would have a job if it weren't for you? How could we forget you for even a minute, when every minute of our lives is spent trying to give *you* what you want! Do you know who my boss is, John?

JOHN.   Don't believe I ever met the gentleman.

YOUNG ENG.   *(Smiling)* Oh, I think maybe you have. He's you, John! If I can't give you what you want, I'm through. We're all through, and down comes the star.

JOHN.   *(Blushing)* Gosh, I never looked at it quite that way before, sir. *(Laughs modestly.)* But I guess that's right, isn't it? What do you know about that? But—

YOUNG ENG.   But I make too much money? Fifty-seven thousand dollars? Is that what worries you?

JOHN.   Yessir, that's a lot of money.

YOUNG ENG.   John, before the star arose, the payroll for producing what I produce for you, for my boss, Mr. Averageman, ran to more than fifty-seven thousand dollars a week. Not a year, mind you, but a week! It looks to me, John, like you, the consumer, are the big winner, not me.

JOHN.   *(Whistles low, under his breath.)* Is that a fact! *(Points suddenly at radical, who is very restive.)* But, he said—

YOUNG ENG.   We've answered everything he's said, John. And I'd like to add one little thought. He'd like to take advantage of your good nature. He wants power, and he doesn't care about anything else. He'd like to make you swallow his half-truths, John, and get you to help him pull down the star, and put himself in power, and the whole world back in the Dark Ages!

JOHN.   *(Glowering.)* Oh, he would, would he?

   (Radical looks worried, then frightened and chagrined, and suddenly makes dash for trap door in stage. John is right after him, and trap door closes. Stage lights fade, and blue feature spot comes up on young engineer, who moves directly to center of

stage. Band starts "Battle Hymn of the Republic" softly, almost imperceptibly.)

YOUNG ENG. *(Reflectively, soberly, conversationally)* Yes, there are those who've clamored so loudly against our star that some have been convinced it is tarnished. And if that star were to come down, it would be partly our fault. Yes, ours! Every minute of the day we should be pointing out how beautiful it is, and why it is beautiful. We hold our peace too much.

(Points at star. Infrared beam hits it, making it glow beautifully.) Under it, we've become rich beyond the wildest dreams of the past! Civilization has reached the dizziest heights of all time!

(Music swells a little in volume.)

Thirty-one point seven times as many television sets as all the rest of the world put together!

(Music gets louder still.)

Ninety-three per cent of all the world's electrostatic dust precipitators! Seventy-seven per cent of all the world's automobiles! Ninety-eight per cent of its helicopters! Eighty-one point nine per cent of its refrigerators!

(Music gets louder still.)

Seventy-one point three per cent of the world's generating capacity!

Eighty-five per cent of its industrial control vacuum tubes!

Sixty-nine per cent of its fractional horsepower motors!

Ninety-eight point three per cent of . . .

(Music crescendos, drowning him out.)

(Fade feature spot. Launch rockets from shore.)

CLOSE QUARTER-SPHERES.

OPEN QUARTER-SPHERES.

The young engineer is gone, and so are the trappings of the court. The old man is at the top of his ladder, alone with his stars, as he was at the beginning.

He holds out the star bearing the image of the Oak,

smiles, hooks it onto the wire, and sends it out, where it glows in infrared.

OLD MAN.   Yes, out it goes again, brighter than all the rest. *(He reaches under his robe, and comes out with a powerful flashlight, whose beam he aims directly upward.)* And when I come back to examine the stars for stains in another century, will it gleam as it does now? Or? *(Looks meaningfully at the foot of the ladder.)* Well, what determines whether it will be tarnished or not? *(Looks at the audience.)* It depends on—*(Suddenly brings down the flashlight, so its beam strikes face after face after face in the audience.)* You! And You! And You! etc.
(Fire rockets. Hit "Stars and Stripes Forever" hard.)

CLOSE QUARTER-SPHERES.
(Turn on amphitheater floodlights.)

Kroner's hand crashed down on Paul's knee. "Phwew! The best keynoter yet! Paul—the story, the whole story in a nutshell!"

"You'll be interested in knowing—" said the loudspeaker over the applause. "Here's an announcement of interest: In the past, the keynote plays have been written by professional writers under our supervision. This play you've just seen was written, believe it or not, by an engineer and manager within the organization! Bill Holdermann, stand up! Stand up! Stand up, Bill!"

The audience went wild.

"I knew it!" shouted Kroner. "It was real! It went right to the heart. It had to be somebody inside!"

Holdermann, a shaggy, worn-out nobody from the Indianapolis Works, stood a few rows ahead of Paul, red, smiling, and with tears in his eyes. At the sunset of life, he had arrived. Perhaps a muffled wisp of the applause reached the ears of his wife, the woman who had had faith in him when no one else had, across the water, on the Mainland.

"Bonfire in five minutes," said the loudspeaker. "Five minutes to make new contacts, then the bonfire."

Shepherd struggled through the crowd and took Kroner's attention away from Paul. " 'Not with all his gold and armies,' " Shepherd quoted from the play. " 'Not with all his gold and armies could Charlemagne have gotten one single electric lamp or vacuum tube!' " He shook his head wonderingly, admiringly. "Don't tell me art is dying."

"Art who?" said Paul under his breath, and he walked away from them, into the twilight at the fringe of the ring of floodlights. The rest of the crowd drifted, tightly packed, toward the shore, where Luke Lubbock, Alfy, and others of the service staff were pouring kerosene on a hillock of pine fagots.

The play was virtually the same play that had begun every Meadows session, even before the war, when the island had belonged to a steel company. Twenty years ago, Paul's father had brought him up here, and the play's message had been the same: that the common man wasn't nearly as grateful as he should be for what the engineers and managers had given him, and that the radicals were the cause of the ingratitude.

When Paul had first seen the allegory, as a teen-ager, he'd been moved deeply. He had been struck full force by its sublime clarity and simplicity. It *was* a story in a nutshell, and the heroic struggle against ingratitude was made so vivid for his young mind that he'd worshipped his father for a little while as a fighter, a latter-day Richard the Lionhearted.

"Well," his father had said after that first play, years ago, "what are you thinking, Paul?"

"I had no idea—no idea that's what was going on."

"That's the story," his father had said sadly. "The whole story. That's the way it is."

"Yessir." Their eyes had met, and an inexpressibly sweet sense of eternal tragedy had passed between them, between their generations—a legacy of *Weltschmerz* as old as humanity.

Now, Paul stood by himself on a dark walk, bewildered by the picture of, as Kroner put it, the men at the head of the procession of civilization, the openers of doors to un-dreamed-of new worlds. This silly playlet seemed to satisfy them completely as a picture of what they were doing, why they were doing it, and who was against them, and why some people were against them. It was a beautifully simple picture these procession leaders had. It was as though a navigator, in order to free his mind of worries, had erased all the reefs from his maps.

Suddenly, light flashed in Paul's eyes, but less dazzling light than the Sky Manager's. He faced his own image in a mirror framed by fluorescent lamps. Over the mirror was the legend, THE BEST MAN IN THE WORLD FOR THE BEST JOB IN THE WORLD. The island was covered with such booby traps. The lamps about this mirror were old ones, and they gave off a wavering light tinged with greens and purples. They gave his skin the quality of corroded copper, and his lips and eye rims were lavender. He discovered that there was nothing disquiet-ing about seeing himself dead. An awakening conscience, un-accompanied by new wisdom, made his life so damned lonely, he decided he wouldn't much mind being dead. And the good offices of the cocktail hour were wearing away.

A drone in the sky to the east distracted him—probably the amphibian bearing the priceless two hundred and fifty pounds of Doctor Francis Eldgrin Gelhorne, and his know-how.

Paul took a step down the path, which turned off the lights, and headed back toward the bonfire, which was send-ing sparks and flames up hundreds of feet and turning the faces about it to a sweaty pink.

A professional actor, painted bronze, wearing an eagle-feather war bonnet and a beaded G-string, held up his hand and tilted his head back proudly. The crowd fell silent. "How!" He looked earnestly from face to face. "How! Many moons ago, my people made their home on this island."

The amphibian was circling the island now, coming lower.

"It's the Old Man all right," whispered Kroner to Paul. "Wouldn't look good to walk out on the ceremony, though. We'll have to stick it out."

"My people were brave people," said the Indian. "My people were proud and honest people. My people worked hard, played hard, fought hard, until it was time to go to the Happy Hunting Ground."

The same actor had been hired to play the Indian for years, ever since Paul had been coming to the Meadows. He'd been hired originally for his deep voice and beautiful muscles. Now, Paul noticed, his belly cast a shadow over his G-string, his left calf had developed a varicose vein, and war paint failed to hide the gray bags under his eyes. He had become such a regular at the Meadows, such a vital symbol— surpassed in that function only by Doctor Gelhorne and the Oak—that he was a man apart from the other hired help, on a first-name footing with the brass, and with the drinking privileges of a regular guest.

"Now our braves are gone, our strong young men— gone from this island, which belonged to my people, lo, these many moons ago," said the Indian. "Now other young men come. But the spirit of my people lives on, the Spirit of the Meadows. It is everywhere: in the wind through the pines, in the lapping of the great blue water, in the whir of an eagle wing, in the growl of summer thunder. No man can call this island his, no man can be happy here, who does not harken to the Spirit, who does not take the Oath of the Spirit."

There was the clattering of the switch in the loud-speaker again. "Young braves at the Meadows for the first step forward," said a pontifical voice, not that of the usual drover.

"Raise your right hands," said the Indian. "Repeat after me the Oath of the Spirit of the Meadows. I solemnly swear by the voice in the pines—"

"By the voice in the pines," said the neophytes.

"By the lapping of the great blue water, by the whir of the eagle wing—"

The Old Man's plane had skated across the water to the shore on the other side of the island and was roaring its engines as it inched up a ramp onto land.

"By the growl of the summer thunder," said the Indian.

"By the growl of the summer thunder."

"I will uphold the Spirit of the Meadows," said the Indian. "I will obey the wise commands of my chiefs, for the good of the people. I will work and fight fearlessly, tirelessly for a better world. I will never say the job is done. I will uphold the honor of my profession and what I represent at all times. I will seek out enemies of the people, enemies of a better world for all children, relentlessly."

"Relentlessly!" said someone in the crowd near Paul, passionately. He turned to see that Luke Lubbock, again swept into the mainstream of pomp and circumstance, held his hand high and swore to everything that came along. In Luke's left hand was a fire extinguisher, apparently for use in case the blaze spread.

When the oath was done, the Indian looked and saw it was good. "The Spirit of the Meadows is pleased," he said. "The Meadows belong to these stout-hearted braves, and it shall be a proud, happy place as it was, lo, these many moons ago."

A smoke bomb concealed before him screened him for a startling instant, and he was gone.

"The saloon is open," said the loudspeaker. "The saloon is open, and will be open until midnight."

Paul found himself walking beside the pleasant youngster he'd met at lunch, Doctor Edmund Harrison of the Ithaca Works. Shepherd and Berringer were right behind, flattering the life out of Kroner.

"Well, how'd you like it, Ed?" said Paul.

Harrison looked at him searchingly, started to smile,

and seemed to think it inadvisable. "Very well done," he said carefully. "Very professional."

"Jesus Christ," Berringer was saying, "I mean, Christ, boy, that was a show. You know, it's entertainment, and still you learn something, too. Christ! When you do both, that's art, boy. Christ, and that wasn't cheap to put on, either, I'll bet."

Ed Harrison of Ithaca stopped and picked up a bit of stone from the side of the path. "I'll be damned," he said. "An arrowhead!"

"A nice one, too," said Paul, admiring the relic.

"So there really *were* Indians on this island," said Harrison.

"For chrissakes, you crazy bastard," said Berringer. "You deaf, dumb, and blind? Whaddya think they been trying to tell you for the past half-hour?"

22

THE MEETING OF Doctors Paul Proteus, Anthony Kroner, Lou MacCleary, Executive Manager of National Industrial Security, and Francis Eldgrin Gelhorne, National Industrial, Commercial, Communications, Foodstuffs, and Resources Director, was to take place at the Meadows in the so-called Council House. The Council House was a frame building, away from the rest, that had been built in the old, wilder days as a lazaretto for surly drunks. Drinking at the Meadows had become more careful since the war—more mature, Kroner said—so the pesthouse fell into disuse and was finally converted into a meeting place for top-policy brass.

All save Doctor Gelhorne were now seated around a long meeting table, looking thoughtfully at the empty chair Gelhorne would be filling any minute. It was a time for silence. The mixing, the making of new contacts, the packing up of troubles in old kit bags went on noisily across the island, in the saloon. Here in the Council House there was no joy, only the summer-cottage aroma of mildew and incipient dry rot, and a grave awareness on the part of each of the three men that the world was their apple.

The shouts and songs that floated over the greensward from the saloon, Paul noted, had a piping quality. There wasn't the inimitable hoarseness of an honest-to-God drunk in the lot. It was unthinkable that there was a man in the saloon without a glass in his hand, but it was also unlikely that many men would have their glasses filled more than twice. They didn't drink at the Meadows now the way they used to in the old days when Finnerty and Shepherd and Paul had joined the organization. It used to be that they'd come up to the Meadows to relax and really tie one on as a relief from the terribly hard work of war production. Now the point seemed to be to pretend drunkenness, but to stay sober and discard only those inhibitions and motor skills one could safely do without.

Paul supposed there would be a couple of men who wouldn't realize what was going on, who would earnestly try to get as drunk as everyone else seemed. They would be frightfully alone and lost when the party broke up. And there would be one or two lonely drunks with nothing to lose anyway, men who had fallen into disfavor one way or another, who knew they had received their last invitation. And what the hell, the liquor was free. *De mortuis nil nisi bonum.*

There was a voice on the porch of the Council House. Doctor Gelhorne was on the other side of the door, pausing a moment for some last word with the world outside. "Look at those youngsters over there," Paul heard the Old Man say, "and tell me God isn't in his heaven."

As the doorknob turned, Paul continued to contemplate trivia, to atomize the fixtures and conventions of the only way of life he'd ever known, an easy, comfortable life, with simple answers for every doubt. That he was quitting that life, that now was perhaps the time he would do it—the grand idea over-shadowing all the little ones—rarely occupied his consciousness. It showed itself mainly in a sensation of being disembodied, or now and then of standing in a chilling wind. Maybe the right time to quit would come now, or a few months from now. There was no need to hurry, no need at all.

The door opened.

The three waiting men stood.

In came Doctor Francis Eldgrin Gelhorne, National Industrial, Commercial, Communications, Foodstuffs, and Resources Director. His spherical bulk was enclosed in a double-breasted, dark-blue suit. His single concession to the Meadows' tradition of informality was an unbuttoned collar and the sliding of his necktie knot a fraction of an inch below where it should have been. Though he was seventy, his hair was as thick and black as a twenty-year-old Mexican's. His fatness was turned into something impressive rather than comical by his perpetual I-smell-excrement expression.

He seemed to be the end of a race, as, Paul reflected, so many leaders seemed to be. It was hard to believe that when Gelhorne was gone there would ever be another man as wonderfully old, shrewd, and unafraid as he.

He cleared his throat. "We're here because somebody wants to kill us, wreck the plants, and take over the country. That plain enough for you?"

Everyone nodded.

"The Ghost Shirt Society," said Doctor Lou MacCleary, Executive Manager of National Industrial Security.

"The Ghost Shirt Society," said Director Gelhorne acidly. "Give a name to something, and you think you've got it. But you haven't got it. All you've got's the name. That's why we're here. All we've got is the name."

"Yessir," said Lou. "The Ghost Shirt Society. And we think the headquarters is in Ilium."

"We think," said Doctor Gelhorne. "We don't know anything."

"Yessir," said Lou.

Gelhorne fidgeted for a moment and looked about the room. His eyes fell on Paul. "How are you, Doctor Proteus?"

"Fine, thank you, sir."

"Uh-huh. Good. That's good." He turned to Lou MacCleary. "Let's see that report of yours that tells everything we don't know about the Ghost Shirt Society."

MacCleary gave him a thick typewritten manuscript.

Gelhorne, his lips moving, leafed through it, frowning. No one spoke or smiled or looked at anyone else.

Paul considered the notion of Doctor Gelhorne's being the last of a race, and decided it was true. He had got to the top through a disorderly route that the personnel machines would never tolerate. Had machines been watching things when Gelhorne started his climb to the top, his classification card would have come flying out of the card files like an old Wheaties box top.

He had no college degree of any kind, other than bouquets of honorary doctorates that had come to him in his late fifties and sixties.

He'd had nothing to do with industry, in fact, until he was thirty. Before that, he'd pulled a mail-order taxidermy business out of bankruptcy, sold his interest in it, and bought a trailer truck. He'd built his fleet to five trucks when he received a hot market tip, sold his business, invested the proceeds, and tripled his wealth. With this bonanza, he'd bought the largest, yet failing, ice-cream plant in Indianapolis, and put the business in the black inside of a year by building ice-cream routes servicing Indianapolis manufacturing plants during the lunch hour. In another year, he had his trucks carrying sandwiches and coffee along with ice cream. In another year, he was running plant cafeterias all over town, and the ice-cream business had become a minor division of Gelhorne Enterprises.

He'd found that many of the manufacturing firms were owned by third- or fourth-generation heirs who, by some seeming law of decay, didn't have the nerve or interest the plants' founders had had. Gelhorne, half playfully at first, had offered these heirs advice, and found them amazingly eager to surrender responsibility. He'd bought in, watched and learned, and, discovering nerve was as valuable as special knowledge, he'd become manager and part owner of a dozen small plants.

When war became certain and the largest corporations were looking about for new manufacturing facilities, Gelhorne had delivered his prosperous community of plants to General Steel, and become an officer of that corporation. The rule-of-thumb familiarity he had with many different industries, as represented by the plants he'd taken over, had been broader than that of any executives General Steel had developed within its own organization, and Gelhorne was soon spending all his time at the side of the corporation's war-rattled president.

There he'd come to the attention of Paul's father in Washington, and Paul's father had made Gelhorne his general executive manager when the whole economy had been made one flesh. When Paul's father died, Gelhorne had taken over.

It could never happen again. The machines would never stand for it.

Paul remembered a week end long ago, when he had been a tall, skinny, polite, and easily embarrassed youth, and Gelhorne had paid a call. Gelhorne had suddenly reached out and caught Paul by the arm as Paul passed his chair. "Paul, boy."

"Yessir?"

"Paul, your father tells me you're real smart."

Paul had nodded uncomfortably.

"That's good, Paul, but that isn't enough."

"No, sir."

"Don't be bluffed."

"No, sir, I won't."

"Everybody's shaking in his boots, so don't be bluffed."

"No, sir."

"Nobody's so damn well educated that you can't learn ninety per cent of what he knows in six weeks. The other ten per cent is decoration."

"Yes, sir."

"Show me a specialist, and I'll show you a man who's so scared he's dug a hole for himself to hide in."

"Yes, sir."

"Almost nobody's competent, Paul. It's enough to make you cry to see how bad most people are at their jobs. If you can do a half-assed job of anything, you're a one-eyed man in the kingdom of the blind."

"Yes, sir."

"Want to be rich, Paul?"

"Yes, sir—I guess so. Yes, sir."

"All right. I got rich, and I told you ninety per cent of what I know about it. The rest is decoration. All right?"

"Yes, sir."

Now, after many years, Paul and Doctor Francis Eldgrin Gelhorne were looking at each other over the long table in the Council House at the Meadows. They weren't close friends, and there was none of Kroner's aromatic paternalism about Gelhorne. This was business.

"There's nothing new about the Society in this report," said Gelhorne.

"Only the part about Finnerty," said Lou MacCleary. "It's been slow going."

"It certainly has," said Doctor Gelhorne. "Well, Doctor Proteus and Doctor Kroner, the point is that this Ghost Shirt nonsense might turn out to be something pretty big. And Lou, here, hasn't been able to get an agent into it to find out what they're up to or who's running it."

"This bunch is smart," said Lou. "They're being pretty selective about who gets in."

"But we think we know how to get a man into it," said Gelhorne. "We think they'd be very tempted by a discontented manager and engineer. We think they've already recruited at least one."

"Finnerty," said Kroner heavily. "He finally registered with the police, incidentally."

"Oh?" said MacCleary. "What did he say he was doing with his time?"

"Says he's getting out Braille editions of pornography."

"He's being pretty cute now," said Gelhorne, "but I think we'll fix his wagon all right. But that's a side issue. The point we're getting at, Paul, is that I think they'll take you into the Ghost Shirt Society under the right conditions."

"Conditions, sir?"

"If we fire you. As of now, as far as anyone outside this room knows, you're through. The rumor's already circulating at the saloon, isn't it, Lou?"

"Yes, sir. I let it slip in front of Shepherd at dinner."

"Good boy," said Gelhorne. "He'll be taking over Ilium, by the way."

"Sir, about Pittsburgh—" said Kroner worriedly. "I promised Paul that he was slated for that job when he was finished with the investigation."

"That's right. In the meanwhile, Garth will run the works there." Gelhorne stood briskly. "All right, Paul? Everything clear? You're to get off the island tonight and back to Ilium." He smiled. "It's really a break for you, Paul. It gives you a chance to clear up your record."

"Record, sir?" Things were happening so quickly now that Paul could only seize upon a word and repeat it as a question in order to keep in the conversation.

"That business of letting Finnerty go through the plant unescorted, and the pistol affair."

"The pistol affair," said Paul. "Can I tell my wife?"

"I'm afraid not," said Lou. "The plan is that nobody outside this room is to know."

"It'll be hard, I know," said Gelhorne sympathetically. "But just now I'm remembering a young boy who told me he didn't want to be an engineer when he grew up, he wanted to be a soldier. You know who that boy was, Paul?"

"Me?" said Paul bleakly.

"You. Well, now you're in the front lines, and we're proud of you."

"Your father would be proud of you, Paul," said Kroner.

"I guess he would. He really would be, wouldn't he," said Paul. Gratefully he was welcoming the blind, invigorating heat of anger. "Sir, Doctor Gelhorne, may I say one more thing before you leave?"

Kroner was holding the door open for the Old Man. "All right, by all means."

"I quit."

Gelhorne, Kroner, and MacCleary laughed. "Wonderful," said the Old Man. "That's the spirit. Keep that up, and you'll fool the hell out of them."

"I mean it! I'm sick of the whole childish, stupid, blind operation."

"Attaboy," said Kroner, smiling encouragingly.

"Give us two minutes to get to the saloon before you leave," said MacCleary. "Wouldn't do for us to be seen together now. And don't worry about packing. Your stuff is being packed right now, and it'll be down at the dock in time for the last boat."

He shut the door behind himself, Gelhorne, and Kroner.

Paul sank heavily back into his chair. "I quit, I quit, I quit," he said. "Do you hear me? I quit!"

"What a night," he heard Lou say on the porch.

"God smiles on the Meadows," said Doctor Gelhorne.

"Look!" said Kroner.

"The moon?" said Lou. "It *is* beautiful."

"The moon, yes—but look at the Oak."

"Oh—and the man," said Doctor Gelhorne. "What do you know about that!"

"A man, standing there alone with the Oak, with God and the Oak," said Kroner.

"Is the photographer around?" said Lou.

"Too late—he's going away now," said Kroner.

"Who was he?" said Doctor Gelhorne.

"We'll never know," said Lou.

"I don't want to know," said Kroner. "I want to remember this scene and think of him as a little bit of all of us."

"You're talking poetry," said the Old Man. "That's good, that's good."

Paul, alone inside, exhaled a puff of smoke with too much force, and coughed.

The men on the porch whispered something.

"Well, gentlemen," said Doctor Gelhorne, "shall we go?"

23

IF DOCTOR PAUL PROTEUS, former manager of the Ilium Works, hadn't found reality disquieting at all points, he wouldn't have shown himself in the saloon before boarding the last boat for the Mainland. As he made his way along the gravel path toward the noise and light of the saloon, however, the field of his consciousness narrowed down to a pinprick, and filling the field was a twinkling shot-glass.

The crowd fell silent as he entered, and then exploded into even greater excesses of happy noise. Quickly as Paul glanced about the room, he didn't catch a single man looking at him, nor, in the blurred vision of excitement, did he recognize a single face among these old friends.

"Bourbon and water," he said to the bartender.

"Sorry, sir."

"Sorry about what?"

"I can't serve you."

"Why not?"

"I've been told you're no longer a guest at the Meadows, sir." There was a prim satisfaction in the bartender's voice.

A number of people observed the incident, Kroner among them, but no one made a move to change the bartender's ruling.

It was a crude moment, and in its fetid atmosphere Paul made an ultimately crude suggestion to the bartender, and turned to leave with dignity.

What he still had to learn was that without rank, without guest privileges, he lived on a primitive level of social justice. He wasn't prepared when the bartender vaulted the bar and spun him around.

"Nobody says that to me, sonny Jim," said the bartender.

"Who the hell do you think you are?" said Paul.

"I'm no goddamn saboteur," said the bartender hotly. Everyone heard it, the ugliest word in the language, one that permitted no muttering withdrawal, no shaking of hands and forgetting it. Son-of-a-bitch could be softened with a smile, but not saboteur.

Somehow the idea of a wrecker of machines had become the smallest part of the word, like the crown of an iceberg. The greatest part of its mass, the part that called forth such poisonous emotions, was undefined: an amalgam of perversions, filth, disease, a galaxy of traits, any one of which would make a man a despicable outcast. The saboteur wasn't a wrecker of machines but an image every man prided himself on being unlike. The saboteur was the man who, if dead, would no longer make the world a trying place to live in.

"You want me to say it again?" said the bartender. "Saboteur. You're a stinking saboteur."

It was an electrifying situation, an elemental situation. Here one big man had offered the ultimate insult to another big man. No one looked as though he were willing to bring the drama to an end, or as though he thought he could. It was like seeing a man caught in a threshing machine, beyond saving. As long as God had precipitated the tragedy, the onlookers might as well watch and learn what a threshing machine would do to a man once it caught him.

Paul hadn't hit anyone since his sophomore year in high school. He had none of what bayonet instructors hoped to instill in their pupils, the will to close with the enemy. It was an unpromising sort of will, he thought. Still, obedient to some system of involuntary nerves and glands, his hands tightened into fists, and his feet spaced themselves to form a solid bipod from which to swing.

Just as there is no encore for the *1812 Overture* save "The Stars and Stripes Forever," so Paul had no choice of rejoinders. "Saboteur yourself," he said evenly, and swung at the bartender's nose.

Absurdly, the bartender collapsed, snuffling and snorting. Paul walked out into the night, like Wild Bill Hickock, like Dan'l Boone, like the bargeman on the book jacket, like— He was suddenly spun around again. For a split second, he saw the bartender's red nose, white face, white apron, and white fist. A brilliant flash illuminated the inside of his skull, and then midnight.

"Doctor Proteus—Paul."

Paul opened his eyes to find himself staring up at the Big Dipper. A cool breeze played across his aching head, and he couldn't see where the voice was coming from. Someone had stretched him out on the cement bench that ran the length of the dock, to be loaded with the band and the outgoing mail aboard the last boat for the Mainland.

"Doctor Proteus—"

Paul sat up. His lower lip was shredded and puffed, and his mouth tasted of blood.

"Paul, sir—"

The voice seemed to be coming from behind the spiraea hedge at the foot of the dock. "Who's that?"

Young Doctor Edmund Harrison emerged from the shrubbery furtively, a highball in his hand. "I thought you might want this."

"That's real Christian of you, Doctor Harrison. Guess I'm well enough to sit up and take nourishment now."

"Wish *I*'d thought of it. It was Kroner's idea."

"Oh? Any message?"

"Yes—but I don't think you'll want it. I wouldn't, if I were in your spot."

"Go ahead."

"He says to tell you it's always darkest before the dawn, and every cloud has a silver lining."

"Um."

"But you ought to see the bartender," said Harrison brightly.

"Aaaaaah. Tell me all."

"He's got a nosebleed that won't stop because he can't stop sneezing. Looks like a vicious circle that with luck could last for years."

"Wonderful." Paul felt better. "Look, you'd better beat it before your luck runs out and somebody sees you with me."

"Mind telling me what on earth you did?"

"It's a long, sordid story."

"I guess. Boy! one day you're king, the next day you're out on your tail. What're you going to do?"

Talking softly there in the dark, Paul began to appreciate what a remarkable young man he'd picked to sit down beside the first day—this Ed Harrison. Harrison had apparently taken a liking to Paul, and now, with no personal reasons for turning against Paul, he was sticking with him as a friend. This was integrity, all right, and a rare variety, because it often amounted, as it might amount now, to career suicide.

"What am I going to do? Farm, maybe. I've got a nice little farm."

"Farm, eh?" Harrison clucked his tongue reflectively. "Farm. Sounds wonderful. I've thought of that: up in the morning with the sun; working out there with your hands in the earth, just you and nature. If I had the money, sometimes I think maybe I'd throw this—"

"You want a piece of advice from a tired old man?"

"Depends on which tired old man. You?"

"Me. Don't put one foot in your job and the other in your dreams, Ed. Go ahead and quit, or resign yourself to this life. It's just too much of a temptation for fate to split you right up the middle before you've made up your mind which way to go."

"That's what happened to you?"

"Something like that." He handed Harrison the empty glass. "Thanks, better beat it. Tell Doctor Kroner it never rains but what it pours."

The cabin cruiser, *Spirit of the Meadows*, grumbled into her slip, and Paul climbed aboard. A few minutes later the band got on with their instruments, and a last call was put out over the loudspeakers. The lights in the saloon blinked off, and knots of remarkably sobered roisterers crossed the parade ground to their tents.

The rattle of the switch, the scratch of a needle, and the loudspeakers sang for the last time that night:

"Fare thee well, for I must leave you,
  Please don't let this parting grieve you;
  Fare thee well, the time has come for us to
    say goodbye.
  Adieu, adieu, kind friends, adieu,
    yes, adieu! . . ."

And Paul waved wanly, apathetically. This was goodbye to his life so far, to the whole of his father's life. He hadn't had the satisfaction of telling someone he'd quit, of being believed; but he'd quit. Goodbye. None of this had anything to do with him any more. Better to be nothing than a blind doorman at the head of civilization's parade.

And as Paul said these things to himself, a wave of sadness washed over them as though they'd been written in sand. He was understanding now that no man could live without roots—roots in a patch of desert, a red clay field, a mountain slope, a rocky coast, a city street. In black loam, in mud or sand or rock or asphalt or carpet, every man had his roots down deep—in *home*. A lump grew in his throat, and he couldn't do anything about it. Doctor Paul Proteus was saying goodbye forever to home.

"So long," he said. And then, in spite of himself, "So long, gang."

A laggard group, genuinely inebriated, was being coaxed out of the saloon. They were singing an effusively sentimental rendition of "Toast the Oak." They draped their arms over each other's shoulders; and made clumsily for the great tree. Their voices came clearly to Paul over the flat, green lawns:

"Grown from but an acorn,
  Giant now you are;

> May you ne'er stop growing;
> Rise to the stars!
> Proud sy-him-bol a-hov
> Ourrrrrrrrrs."

There was a reverent pause, broken by an exclamation. "Jesus!" It was Berringer's voice, Berringer's word.

" 'Smatter?"

"Look at the tree—around the bottom!"

"Holy smokes!"

"Somebody's stripped the bark off clear around," said Berringer hollowly.

"Who?"

"Who do you think?" said Berringer. "That stinking saboteur. Where is he?"

The *Spirit of the Meadows* gunned her engines and backed into open water.

"Hey," cried a lonely, frightened voice in the night. "Hey—somebody's killed the Oak."

"Killed the Oak," echoed the shore.

The loudspeakers clattered on again, and a chilling war whoop filled the air. "Beware the Ghost Shirt!" shrieked a terrible voice.

"Ghost Shirt," said the shore, and all was deathly still.

24

Eₙ ʀᴏᴜᴛᴇ ʙʏ air from Miami Beach to Ithaca, New York, home of Cornell University, the Shah of Bratpuhr caught a nasty cold. When seven *prakhouls* (that quantity of fluid that can be contained in the skin of an adult male Bratpuhrian marmot) of *Sumklish* improved the Shah's spirits but did nothing for his respiratory system, it was decided that the plane should land in Harrisburg, Pennsylvania, in order that the Shah might rest and try the magic of American medicine.

With seven *prakhouls* of *Sumklish* under his belt, the Shah called cheery messages to pretty female *Takarus* on his way to the doctor's office.

"Pitty fit-fit, sibi Takaru? Niki fit-fit. Akka sahn nibo fit-fit, simi Takaru?"

Khashdrahr, who was without the benefit of *Sumklish*, was livid with embarrassment. "Shah says it is a nice day," he explained unhappily.

"Fit-fit, pu sibi bonanza?" called the Shah to a small blonde who had her hands in a streetcorner manicure machine.

She blushed, and jerked her hands from the machine and stalked away, leaving the machine to buff away at nothingness. A street urchin stuck his grubby hands in for the remainder of the operation, and drew them out with gleaming, red-enameled nails.

"I'm glad he likes the weather," said Halyard glumly. For many weeks now, they'd traveled without the subject's coming up once, and Halyard had hopefully told himself that the Shah really was different from his other guests in this respect, different from the French and Bolivians and Czechs and Japanese and Panamanians and Yaps and. . . . But, no. The Shah, too, was now getting curious about American-type women. Halyard, at a frightful price in dignity, was once more going to have to perform the role of utterly perfect host—or pimp.

"Fit-fit?" called the Shah, as they pulled up to a stoplight.

"Look," said Halyard reproachfully to Khashdrahr, "tell him he just can't walk up to any American girl at all and ask her to sleep with him. I'll see what I can do, but it won't be easy."

Khashdrahr told the Shah, who waved him away. Before anyone could stop him, the Shah was out on the sidewalk, confidently confronting a startlingly beautiful, dark-skinned brunette. *"Fit-fit, sibi Takaru?"*

"Please," said Halyard to her, "please excuse my friend. He's a bit under the weather."

She took the Shah's arm, and together they climbed back into the limousine.

"I'm afraid there's been a terrible misunderstanding, young lady," said Halyard. "I hardly know how to put it. I, ah, he, that is— What I mean to say, rather, is he wasn't offering you a ride."

"He was asking for something, wasn't he?"

"Yes."

"There's been no misunderstanding."

"Fit-fit," said the Shah.

"Quite so," said Halyard.

Khashdrahr began looking out of the window with fresh interest, wildness, in fact, and Halyard had difficulty holding himself in check.

"Here we are," said the driver. "Here's Doctor Pepkowitz's office."

"Yes, well, you wait in the car, young lady," said Halyard, "while the Shah goes in here for a cold treatment."

The Shah was grinning, and inhaling and exhaling rapidly.

"His sniffles are gone," said Khashdrahr wonderingly.

"Drive on," said Halyard. He had seen a similar miracle cure of an Ecuadorian brigadier's hives.

The girl seemed restless and unhappy, and utterly out of character, Halyard thought. She smiled constantly, unconvincingly, and was apparently anxious to get the whole thing over with. Halyard still couldn't believe that she knew what the whole thing was.

"Where are we going now?" she said, grimly cheerful. "A hotel, I suppose."

"Yes," said Halyard unevenly.

"Good." She patted the Shah on his shoulder, and burst into tears.

The Shah was distressed and tried clumsily to comfort her. *"Oh, nibo souri, sibi Takaru. Akka sahn souri? Ohhh. Tipi Takaru. Ahhhh."*

"There, now," said Halyard. "See here."

"I don't do this every day," she said, blowing her nose. "Please excuse me. I'll try to be better."

"Certainly. We understand," said Halyard. "The whole thing has been a terrible mistake. Where would you like us to leave you off?"

"Oh, no—I'm going through with it," she said gloomily.

"Please—" said Halyard. "Perhaps it would be better for all concerned if—"

"If I lost my husband? Better if he shot himself or starved?"

"Certainly not! But why would those terrible things happen if you refused to— That is—"

"It's a long story." She dried her eyes. "My husband, Ed, is a writer."

"What's his classification number?" said Halyard.

"That's just it. He hasn't one."

"Then how can you call him a writer?" said Halyard.

"Because he writes," she said.

"My dear girl," said Halyard paternally, "on that basis, we're all writers."

"Two days ago he had a number—W-441."

"Fiction novice," Halyard explained to Khashdrahr.

"Yes," she said, "and he was to have it until he'd completed his novel. After that, he was supposed to get either a W-440—"

"Fiction journeyman," said Halyard.

"Or a W-255."

"Public relations," said Halyard.

"Please, what are public relations?" said Khashdrahr.

"That profession," said Halyard, quoting by memory from the *Manual*, "that profession specializing in the cultivation, by applied psychology in mass communication media, of favorable public opinion with regard to controversial issues and institutions, without being offensive to anyone of importance, and with the continued stability of the economy and society its primary goal."

"Oh well, never mind," said Khashdrahr. "Please go on with your story, *sibi Takaru*."

"Two months ago he submitted his finished manuscript to the National Council of Arts and Letters for criticism and assignment to one of the book clubs."

"There are twelve of them," Halyard interrupted. "Each one selects books for a specific type of reader."

"There are twelve types of readers?" said Khashdrahr.

"There is now talk of a thirteenth and fourteenth," said Halyard. "The line has to be drawn somewhere, of course, because of the economics of the thing. In order to be self-supporting, a book club has to have at least a half-million members, or it isn't worth setting up the machinery—the electronic billers, the electronic addressers, the electronic wrappers, the electronic presses, and the electronic dividend computers."

"And the electronic writers," said the girl bitterly.

"That'll come, that'll come," said Halyard. "But Lord knows getting manuscripts isn't any trick. *That's* hardly the problem. Machinery's the thing. One of the smaller clubs, for instance, covers four city blocks. DSM."

"DSM?" said Khashdrahr.

"Excuse me. Dog Story of the Month."

Khashdrahr and the Shah shook their heads slowly and made clucking sounds. "Four city blocks," echoed Khashdrahr hollowly.

"Well, a fully automatic setup like that makes culture very cheap. Book costs less than seven packs of chewing gum. And there are picture clubs, too—pictures for your walls at amazingly cheap prices. Matter of fact, culture's so cheap, a man figured he could insulate his house cheaper with books and prints than he could with rockwool. Don't think it's true, but it's a cute story with a good point."

"And painters are well supported under this club system?" asked Khashdrahr.

"Supported—I guess!" said Halyard. "It's the Golden Age of Art, with millions of dollars a year poured into reproductions of Rembrandts, Whistlers, Goyas, Renoirs, El Grecos, Dégas, da Vincis, Michelangelos . . ."

"These club members, they get just any book, any picture?" asked Khashdrahr.

"I should say not! A lot of research goes into what's run off, believe me. Surveys of public reading tastes, readability and appeal tests on books being considered. Heavens, running off an unpopular book would put a club out of business like that!" He snapped his fingers ominously. "The way they keep culture so cheap is by knowing in advance what and how much of it people want. They get it right, right down to the color of the jacket. Gutenberg would be amazed."

"Gutenberg?" said Khashdrahr.

"Sure—the man who invented movable type. First man to mass-produce Bibles."

"*Alla sutta takki?*" said the Shah.

"Eh?" said Halyard.

"Shah wants to know if he made a survey first."

"Anyway," said the girl, "my husband's book was rejected by the Council."

"Badly written," said Halyard primly. "The standards are high."

"Beautifully written," she said patiently. "But it was twenty-seven pages longer than the maximum length; its readability quotient was 26.3, and—"

"No club will touch anything with an R.Q. above 17," explained Halyard.

"And," the girl continued, "it had an antimachine theme."

Halyard's eyebrows arched high. "Well! I should hope they wouldn't print it! What on earth does he think he's doing? Good lord, you're lucky if he isn't behind bars, inciting to advocate the commission of sabotage like that. He didn't really think somebody'd print it, did he?"

"He didn't care. He had to write it, so he wrote it."

"Why doesn't he write about clipper ships, or something like that? This book about the old days on the Erie Canal—the man who wrote that is cleaning up. Big demand for that bare-chested stuff."

She shrugged helplessly. "Because he never got mad at clipper ships or the Erie Canal, I guess."

"He sounds very maladjusted," said Halyard distastefully. "If you ask me, my dear, he needs the help of a competent psychiatrist. They do wonderful things in psychiatry these days. Take perfectly hopeless cases, and turn them into grade A citizens. Doesn't he believe in psychiatry?"

"Yes, indeed. He watched his brother find peace of mind through psychiatry. That's why he won't have anything to do with it."

"I don't follow. Isn't his brother happy?"

"Utterly and always happy. And my husband says somebody's just *got* to be maladjusted; that somebody's got to be uncomfortable enough to wonder where people are, where they're going, and why they're going there. That was the trouble with his book. It raised those questions, and was rejected. So he was ordered into public-relations duty."

"So the story has a happy ending after all," said Halyard.

"Hardly. He refused."

"Lordy!"

"Yes. He was notified that, unless he reported for public-relations duty by yesterday, his subsistence, his housing permit, his health and security package, *everything*, would be revoked. So today, when you came along, I was wandering around town, wondering what on earth a girl could do these days to make a few dollars. There aren't many things."

"This husband of yours, he'd rather have his wife a—Rather, have her—" Halyard cleared his throat "—than go into public relations?"

"I'm proud to say," said the girl, "that he's one of the few men on earth with a little self-respect left."

Khashdrahr translated this last bit, and the Shah shook his head sadly. The Shah removed a ruby ring and pressed it into her hand. *"Ti, sibi Takaru. Dibo. Brahous brahouna, houna saki. Ippi goura Brahouna ta tippo a mismit."* He opened the limousine door for her.

"What did the gentleman say?" she asked.

"He said to take the ring, pretty little citizen," said Khashdrahr tenderly. "He said goodbye and good luck, and that some of the greatest prophets were crazy as bedbugs."

"Thank you, sir," she said, climbing out and starting to cry again. "God bless you."

The limousine pulled away from her. The Shah waved wistfully. *"Dibo, sibi Takaru,"* he said, and was seized by a violent sneezing fit. He blew his nose. *"Sumklish!"*

Khashdrahr handed him the sacred flask.

25

WHEN THE SPIRIT OF THE MEADOWS churned up to the dock at the Mainland, the public address system, turned low, was murmuring "Good Night, Sweetheart," a sweet wraith of music a whisper above the voice in the pines, the lapping of the great blue water, the whir of the eagle wing.

No lights shone from the women's and children's lodges. In the Central Administration Building was a single square of light, silhouetting a sleeping clerk.

As Paul made for it, to ask the clerk where he might find Anita, lights flashed in his night-accustomed eyes. When his pupils had adjusted themselves to the glare, he found himself staring at his reflection in a mirror again, under the legend, THE BEST WIFE FOR THE BEST MAN FOR THE BEST JOB IN THE WORLD.

He hurried past the mirror, wondering how many times Anita had contemplated her reflection and the legend here, wondering how she would take the news that her Best Man had become merely a man, with no job at all.

He woke up the clerk, who called the matron in charge of the lodge where Anita slept.

"What's matter with the party over there?" said the clerk sleepily, waiting for the matron to answer. "You're about the tenth guy to come over here tonight. Usually they don't start coming until about the fourth day. Now, what's the matter with the matron, anyway? The phone's right by her bunk." He glanced at the clock. "You know what time it is? You haven't got time to make a nickel. The last boat back for the island leaves in three minutes."

"Keep ringing. I'm not going back."

"If you're going to spend the night, don't tell me about it. There're about twenty-seven rules against it."

Paul handed him a ten-dollar bill. "Keep ringing."

"For that, you can be invisible for a week. Whaddya like? Blondes, brunettes, redheads? Aha! She answered. Where the hell you been?" he asked the matron. "You got a Mrs. Paul Proteus there?" He nodded. "Uh-huh, uh-huh. O.K. Leave a note on her bunk, will you." He turned to Paul. "She's out, Doctor."

"Out?"

"Walking in the moonlight, probably. Matron says she's a great walker."

If Anita was a great walker, it was news to Paul. He'd seen her drive a car to the house across the street from theirs, and she denied all the tenets of physical culture by remaining young and graceful while eating like a farmhand and conserving her strength like a princess. Bound feet and six-inch fingernails wouldn't have restricted her activities in the least.

Paul sat down on a wicker chair in the cool blue shadows of the Administration Building's porch and rested his feet on the peeling bark of the log railing to wait.

Now the lights along the walks blinked on and off, a silent signal, warning that the last boat was about to leave for the island.

There was laughing, and quick crunching in the gravel, and a couple ran from the woods toward the dock. Their insistence on keeping their arms about each other's waists made their progress as graceless as a sack race. This annoyed Paul as a critic. It was painful to watch a clumsily conducted mating rite, knowing, from long experience with the skilled Anita, how much like a dance it could be when done properly.

There—she was making him slow down now, and their gait through the trees, against the moon, was more orderly.

Paul had been sure that the farewell kiss would be an ungainly business, but, all credit to her, they stopped, and took the time and stances to do it right. Good.

Paul watched them with increasing identification with the man. Paul had always been a petty thief of others' high moments, and his hunger for this particular sort of moment was acute. With his old life gone, and his new one, whatever it was to be, not yet begun, he was voracious for love— Anita's love, vividly imagined love, vicarious love—any love, whatever was immediately available.

Now she was coming back, slowly, thoughtfully, content. Wonderful.

The lights on the booby-trap mirror flashed on. The woman smoothed her slacks over her hips and tucked in a wisp of hair. She lingered before her image a long time, turning this way and that, seemingly pleased, as well she might be, by the shape of her breasts ingenuously hidden under tight green cotton, with the word "Captain" undulating uphill, downdale.

"Anita!"

She jumped, and quickly folded her arms across her bosom in a protective gesture. Slowly her arms went to her sides again, and she stood erect, a woman with nothing to hide, least of all Shepherd's shirt. "Hello, Paul." She walked over to the porch where he sat, stately, cold, and sat down beside him. "Well?"

When he said nothing, her poise began to fail and she plucked nervously at the bark on the log railing, pulling off little strips and throwing them out into the summer night. "Go ahead," she said at last.

"*Me* go ahead?" said Paul.

"Don't you think an explanation is in order?"

"Decidedly."

"You *did* get fired, didn't you?"

"Yes, but not for breaking a Commandment."

"Is wearing another man's shirt adultery in your book?" Underneath, she was plainly rattled.

Paul was delighted. He was sure now that he could bluff her into coming away with him. It was inconceivable that she was using the boring, sententious, contentious Shepherd for anything but a hollow threat to him, but this semblance of wrongdoing could now be turned to advantage. "Wouldn't you say the shirt was symptomatic, coupled with fornication in the underbrush?" he said.

"If you mean do I love him, the answer is yes."

Paul laughed quietly.

"I'm glad you're taking it so well," she said primly. "I guess it proves what I thought all along."

"Which was—?"

Unexpectedly she burst into tears. "That I wasn't any damn use to you at all! Finnerty was right," she sobbed. "All you need is something stainless steel, shaped like a woman, covered with sponge rubber, and heated to body temperature."

It was Paul's turn to be startled. "Anita—darling, listen."

"And you'd lend it to anybody, if you didn't need it just then."

"Hell's bells, I—"

"I'm sick of being treated like a machine! You go around talking about what engineers and managers do to all the other poor, dumb people. Just look what an engineer and manager did to me!"

"For heaven's sakes, sweetheart, I—"

"You talk about how wrong it is for smart people to lord it over people who aren't so smart, and then go around our house showing off your great big I.Q. like it was on a sandwich sign. All right, so I'm dumb."

"No you aren't, Angel. Listen, I—"

"Saboteur!"

Paul fell back in his seat and shook his head, as though groggily trying to avoid a clubbing. "For the love of God, listen, will you?" he begged.

"Go on." She was magnificently on top of the situation again.

"Darling, what you say may be true. I don't know. But please, sweetheart, wife, I need you now like I never needed anybody in all my life."

"Ten minutes ought to take care of that. At the outside," she added scornfully.

"For richer, for poorer, in sickness as in health," said Paul. "Remember that Anita? Do you remember?"

"You're still rich, and you're not sick." She looked at him with passing concern. "You're not sick, are you?"

"At heart."

"You'll get used to it. I did."

"I'm sorry, Anita—I didn't know it had been that bad. I see now that it probably was."

"Next time I'll marry for love."

"Shepherd?"

"He needs me, respects me, believes in the things I believe in."

"I hope you'll be very happy," said Paul, standing.

Her lips trembled, and she burst into tears again. "Paul, Paul, Paul."

"Hmmmm?"

"I like you. Don't forget that ever."

"And I like *you*, Anita."

"Doctor Proteus," called the clerk through the window.

"Yes?"

"Doctor Kroner called and said you were to be driven over to the railroad station tonight. The jeep's on the other side of the building, waiting. We've got half an hour to make the 12:52."

"Coming."

"Kiss me," said Anita.

It was a stunning kiss, and, in its wake of lackadaisical-ness, Paul realized that she had had absolutely nothing to gain by the kiss, that she had done it out of, of all things, the goodness of her heart.

"Come with me, Anita," he whispered.

"I'm not as dumb as you think." She pushed him away firmly. "Goodbye."

26

DOCTOR PAUL PROTEUS, an unclassified human being, was put aboard the 12:52, where he shared an ancient coach, half cuspidor, half humidor, with sixty troops on furlough from Camp Drum.

"*Great Bend. The stop is Great Bend,*" said a tape record-ing through a loudspeaker over Paul's head. The engineer pressed a button in his cab as he pulled into each station, down came the steps, and out came the voice. "*Next station, Carthage. Next station, Carthage. Click.*"

"*'Board!*" bawled another loudspeaker on the outside of the car.

An old man, kissing his wife goodbye on the rotting planks of the Great Bend platform, looked apologetically at the urgent voice, as though to ask the man to wait just a second more for him to say one last word. "*'Board!*" Ma-chinery whirred, and the coach steps arose from the platform, nestled into one another, and disappeared into their niche.

"Coming! Coming!" cried the old man, and jogged unhappily toward the moving train as fast as his brittle legs would carry him. He caught the handrail, swung aboard, and stood panting in the vestibule. He fumbled for his ticket, dropped it into the mechanism on the door. The mechanism considered it, found everything in order, pulled back the door bolt, and let him into the frieze and cast-iron monument to tobacco.

He settled, winded, in the seat next to Paul's. "Son-of-a-bitch won't even wait a second for an old man," he said bitterly.

"It's a machine," said Paul. "All automatic."

"Don't mean he ain't a son-of-a-bitch."

Paul nodded appreciatively.

"Used to be conductor on this line."

"Oh?" The man had the florid, righteous look of a specialized bore, and Paul wasn't interested in listening to him.

"Yes, forty-one years," he said. "For-tee-wunnn years!"

"Huh!"

"For-tee-wunnnn. Two times twenty plus one. And I'd like to see one of them machines deliver a baby."

"Huh! You delivered a baby, eh?"

"Yep. Little boy. By coincidence I done it in the men's room." He chuckled richly. "For-tee-wunnnn years!"

"Huh."

"And I never seen the machine yet that'd watch out for a little girl three years old all the way from St. Louis to Poughkeepsie."

"Nope. Guess not," said Paul. He filed this remark away for his next meeting with Bud Calhoun. He could see the device now—sort of an Iron Maiden, without the spikes, of course, and electronic, of course, that would grasp a little girl firmly at St. Louis, and eject her into the arms of relatives at Poughkeepsie.

"For-tee-wunnnn years! With machines you get *quan*-titty, but you don't get *qual*-itty. Know what I mean?"

"Yup," said Paul.

"Carthage," said the tape recording. *"The stop is Carthage. Next station, Deer River."*

Paul settled back against the unyielding seat with a sigh of relaxation, and closed his eyes in a pretense of sleep.

"For-tee-wunnnn years! These machines never help an old lady down the steps."

In time the old conductor ran out of examples of man's superiority over machines and took to anticipating the tape recording's station calling, casually, contemptuously, as though any fool could do it. "Deer River. The stop is Deer River. Next station, Castorland."

"Deer River. The stop is Deer River," said the tape recording. *"Next station, Castorland."*

"Ha! What'd I tell you?"

Paul actually did drop off to sleep fitfully, and at last, at Constableville, he saw his companion slipping his ticket into the door slot and being let off. Paul checked his ticket to make sure it wasn't bent or torn, that it would unlock the door at Ilium. He'd heard tales of addled old ladies locked aboard cars for days for having misplaced their tickets, or for having missed their stops. Hardly a newspaper was printed that didn't have a human interest story about car clean-up crews from the Reeks and Wrecks liberating somebody.

The old displaced conductor disappeared into the Constableville night, and Paul wondered at what thorough believers in mechanization most Americans were, even when their lives had been badly damaged by mechanization. The conductor's plaint, like the lament of so many, wasn't that it was unjust to take jobs from men and give them to machines, but that the machines didn't do nearly as many human things as good designers could have made them do.

"Constableville. The stop is Constableville. Next station, Remsen."

A poker game was going on in the facing seats behind Paul, and a superannuated first sergeant, zebra-like under symbols for patience, individual bloodlettings, and separations from home, was telling tales of the last war—of the Last War.

"Jesus," he said, riffling through the deck absently, as though his mind were a thousand miles away, "there we was, and there they was. Imagine the men's room there's a hogback, with the bastards dug in deep on the reverse slope." The recruits looked at the men's room through narrowed, battle-wise eyes, and the sergeant shuffled the cards some more. "The night before, a lucky shot knocked out the generator."

"Holy cow!" said a recruit.

"You can say that again," said the sergeant. "Anyway—five-card stud, nothing wild—there we were with no juice, eighteen of us facing five hundred of them. The microwave sentinels, the proximity mines, the electric fence, the fire-control system, the remote-control machine gun nests—pfft! No juice, Queen, ace, ace, and dealer gets a deuce. Bet the first ace.

"Well, boys—a dime to me? Raise it a dime just to make things interesting. Well, boys, then the fun started. At seven hundred hours they tried a hundred-man patrol on us, to see what we had. And we had nothin'! And communications was cut to hell, so we couldn't call for nothin'. All our robot tanks'd been pulled out to support a push the 106th was makin', so we was really alone. Snafu. So, I sent Corporal Merganthaler back to battalion for help. —Two queens, no help, two aces, and dealer catches another lousy deuce. Bet the aces. So over they come, screamin' bloody murder, and us with nothing but our goddamn rifles and bayonets workin'. Looked like a tidal wave comin' over at us. —Aces check? Aw, hell, deuces'll try a dime. —Just then, up comes Merganthaler with a truck and generator he's moonlight-requisitioned from the 57th. We hooked her into our lines, cranked her up, and my God, I wish you could of seen it. The poor bastards fryin' on the electric fence, the proximity mines poppin' under 'em, the microwave sentinels openin' up with the remote-control machine-gun nests, and the fire-control system swiveling the guns and flamethrowers around as long as anything was quiverin' within a mile of the place. And that's how I got the Silver Star."

Paul shook his head slightly as he listened to the sergeant's absurd tale. That, then, was the war he had been so eager to get into at one time, the opportunity for basic, hot-tempered, hard-muscled heroism he regretted having missed. There had been plenty of death, plenty of pain, all right, and plenty of tooth-grinding stoicism and nerve. But men had been called upon chiefly to endure by the side of the machines, the terrible engines that fought with their own kind for the right to gorge themselves on men. Horatio on the bridge had become a radio-guided rocket with an atomic warhead and a proximity fuse. Roland and Oliver had become a pair of jet-driven computers hurtling toward each other far faster than the flight of a man's scream. The great tradition of the American rifleman survived only symbolically, in volleys fired into the skies over the dead in thousands of military cemeteries. Those in the graves, the front-line dead, were heirs to another American tradition as old as that of the rifleman, but once a peaceful tradition—that of the American tinker.

"Gosh! Sarge, how come you never went after a commission?"

"Me go back to college at my age? I'm not the school kind, sonny. Gettin' that B.S. was enough for me. Two more years and an M.A. for a pair of lousy gold bars? Naaaaaah! —And a queen, and no help, and a jack, and no help, and a five, and no help, and dealer gets a—what do you know? Three deuces. Looks like my lucky day, boys."

"Middleville. The stop is Middleville. Next station, Herkimer."

"Sarge, d'ya mind talkin' about your wound stripes?"

"Hmmm? No—guess not. This 'un's for a dose of Gamma rays at Kiukiang. This 'un's—lemme see—radioactive dust in the bronchial tubes at Afyon Karahisar. And this little bastard—uh—trenchfoot at Kransystav."

"Sarge, what was the best piece you ever had?"

"A little redheaded half-Swede, half-Egyptian in Farafangana," said the Sarge without hesitation.

"Boy! I hope that's where they send me."

That much of a fine old American military tradition, Paul supposed, would always be alive—send me where the tail is.

"Herkimer. The stop is Herkimer. Next station, Little Falls."

"Say, Sarge, is this train a local?"

"You might call it that. How's about a round of cold hands for the odd change?" said the sergeant.

"O.K. with me. Oops. Lousy trey. A queen for Charley. An eight for Lou. And, I'll be go to hell, the Sarge catches a bullet."

"Say, Sarge, hear Pfc. Elmo Hacketts is shipping out."

"Yep. Been asking for overseas ever since he joined the outfit. Pair of treys for Ed, nothing for Charley, jack for Lou, and dealer catches a— I'll be damned."

"Ace!"

"Little Falls. The stop is Little Falls. Next station, Johnsonville."

"Here we go around again, and— What you know about that?" said the sergeant. "Ed's got three treys. Yep—hate to see Hacketts go. With a coupla years seasoning, I could see him as a helluva fine guidon bearer. But, if he wants to throw all that over, that's his business. Nothing for Charley, and Lou gets my ace. Three treys got it so far."

"Where's Hacketts going? You know?"

"And no help, and help, and no help, and no help," said the sergeant. "Yeah, his orders came through today. Last time around, boys. No help, no help, no help, and—"

"Jesus!"

"Sorry about that third ace, Ed. Guess that one's mine too. Yeah, Hacketts gets his overseas duty all right. Shipping out for Tamanrasset tomorrow morning."

"Tamanrasset?"

"The Sahara Desert, you dumb bastard. Don't you know any geography?" He grinned wolfishly. "How about a little blackjack for laughs?"

Paul sighed for Hacketts, born into a spiritual desert, now being shipped to where the earth was sterile, too.

"Johnsonville . . . Ft.   Plain . . . Fonda . . . Ft. Johnson . . . Amsterdam . . . Schenectady . . . Cohoes . . . Watervliet . . . Albany . . . Rensselaer . . . Ilium, the stop is Ilium."

Bleary-eyed, Paul shuffled to the door, inserted his ticket, and stepped onto the Ilium station platform.

The door on the baggage compartment clattered open, a coffin slid onto a waiting freight elevator and was taken into the refrigerated bowels of the station.

No cabs had bothered to meet the unpromising train. Paul phoned the cab company, but no one answered. He looked helplessly at the automatic ticket vendor, the automatic nylon vendor, the automatic coffee vendor, the automatic gum vendor, the automatic book vendor, the automatic newspaper vendor, the automatic toothbrush vendor, the automatic Coke vendor, the automatic shoeshine machine, the automatic photo studio, and walked out into the deserted streets on the Homestead side of the river.

It was eight miles through Homestead, across the bridge, and up the other side of the river to home. Not home, Paul thought, but the house where his bed was.

He felt dull, mushy inside, with an outer glaze of bright heat—sleepy yet sleepless, assailed by thoughts yet thoughtless.

His footsteps echoed against Homestead's gray façades, and lifeless neon tubes, proclaiming one thing and another of no importance at this hour, were empty, cold glass for want of the magic of electrons in flight through inert gas.

"Lonesome?"

"Huh?"

A young woman, with bosoms like balloon spinnakers before the wind, looked down from a second-story window. "I said, are you lonesome?"

"Yes," said Paul simply.

"Come on up."

"Well," Paul heard himself saying, "all right, I will."

"The door next to the Automagic Market."

He climbed the long, dark stairway, each riser of which proclaimed Doctor Harry Friedmann to be a painless dentist, licensed under the National Security and Health Plan. "Why," asked Friedmann rhetorically, "settle for less than a D-006?"

The door on the hallway, next to Doctor Friedmann's, was open, the woman waiting.

"What's your name, honey?"

"Proteus."

"Any relation to the big cheese across the river?"

"My half-brother."

"You the black sheep, honey?"

"Yup."

"Screw your brother."

"Please," said Paul.

He awoke once during the remainder of the night with her, awoke from a dream in which he saw his father glowering at him from the foot of the bed.

She mumbled in her sleep.

As Paul dropped off once more, he murmured an automatic reply. "And I love *you*, Anita."

27

Doctor Paul Proteus had been his own man, alone in his own house for a week. He'd been expecting some sort of communication from Anita, but nothing came. There was nothing more, he realized wonderingly, to be said. She was still at the Mainland, probably. The Meadows session had another week to run. After that would come the muddle of her separating her effects from his—and divorce. He wondered on what grounds she would divorce him. Extreme mental cruelty amused him, and he supposed it was close enough to the truth. Any variation from any norm pained her terribly. She'd have to leave New York State, of course, since the only grounds for divorce there were adultery, and incitement to conspire to advocate sabotage. A case could be made for either, he supposed, but not with dignity.

Paul had gone to his farm once, and, in the manner of a man dedicating his life to God, he'd asked Mr. Haycox to put him to work, guiding the hand of Nature. The hand he grasped so fervently, he soon discovered, was coarse and sluggish, hot and wet and smelly. And the charming little cottage he'd taken as a symbol of the good life of a farmer was as irrelevant as a statue of Venus at the gate of a sewage-disposal plant. He hadn't gone back.

He'd been to the Works once. The machinery had been shut off during the Meadows session, and only the guards were on duty. Four of them, now officious and scornful, had telephoned to Kroner at the Meadows for instructions. Then they'd escorted him to what had been his desk, where he'd picked up a few personal effects. They'd made a list of what he'd taken, and questioned his claim to each item. Then they'd marched him back into the outside world, and shut the gates against him forever and ever.

Paul was in the kitchen now, before the laundry console, seated on a stool, watching television. It was late afternoon, and, for the unadorned hell of it, he was doing his own laundry.

"Urdle-urdle-urdle," went the console. *"Urdle-urdle-ur dull! Znick. Bazz-wap!"* Chimes sounded. *"Azzzzzzzzzz. Fromp!"* Up came the anticlimactic offering: three pairs of socks, three pairs of shorts, and the blue Meadow's T-shirts, which he was using for pajamas.

On the television screen, a middle-aged woman was counseling her teen-age son, whose hair and clothes were disordered and soiled.

"Fightin' don't help, Jimmy," she was saying sadly. "Lord knows nobody ever brought any more sunshine into the world by bloodyin' somebody's nose, or by havin' his own nose bloodied."

"I know—but he said my I.Q. was 59, Ma!" The boy was on the point of tears, he was so furious and hurt. "And he said Pop was a 53!"

"Now, now—that's just child's talk. Don't you pay it no mind, Jimmy."

"But it's true," said the boy brokenly. "Ma, it's true. I went down to the police station and looked it up! Fifty-nine, Ma! and poor Pop with a 53." He turned his back, and his voice was a bitter whisper: "And you with a 47, Ma. A 47."

She bit her lip and looked heartbroken, then, seeming to draw strength miraculously from somewhere above eye level, she gripped the kitchen table. "Jimmy, look at your mother."

He turned slowly.

"Jimmy, I.Q. isn't everything. Some of the unhappiest people in this world are the smartest ones."

Since the start of his week of idleness at home, Paul had learned that this, with variations, was the basic problem situation in afternoon dramas, with diseases and injuries of the optic nerve and locomotor apparatus close seconds. One program was an interminable exploration of the question: can a woman with a low I.Q. be happily married to a man with a high one? The answer seemed to be yes and no.

"Jimmy, boy, son—I.Q. won't get you happiness, and St. Peter don't give I.Q. tests before he lets you in those Pearly Gates. The wickedest people that ever lived was the smartest."

Jimmy looked suspicious, then surprised, then guardedly willing to be convinced. "You mean—a plain fellow like me, just another guy, folks like us, Ma, you mean we're as good as, as, as, well, Doctor Garson, the Works Manager?"

"Doctor Garson, with his 169 I.Q.? Doctor Garson, with his Ph.D., D.Sc., and his Ph. and D. I-don't-know-what-else? Him?"

"Yeah, Ma. Him."

"Him? Doctor Garson? Jimmy, son, boy—have you seen the bags under his eyes? Have you seen the lines in his face? He's carryin' the world around on his shoulders, Jimmy. That's what a high I.Q. got him, Doctor Garson. Do you know how old he is?"

"An awful old man, Ma."

"He's ten years younger than your Pa, Jimmy. *That's* what brains got him."

Pa came in at that moment, wearing the brassard of a Reconstruction and Reclamation Corps Asphalt Leveler, First Class. He was cheery, pink, in first-rate health. "Hi, there, folks," he said. "Everything hunky-dory in my little old home, eh?"

Jimmy exchanged glances with his mother, and smiled oddly. "Yessir, reckon it is. I mean, you're darn right it is!"

In came the organ music, the announcer, and the washless, rinseless wash powder, and Paul turned down the volume.

The door chimes were ringing, and Paul wondered

how long they'd been at it. He might have turned on the televiewer, to see if the bell ringer was worth opening the door for, but he was hungry for companionship—just about any kind—and he went to the door gladly, gratefully.

A policeman looked at him coldly. "Doctor Proteus?"

"Yes?"

"I'm from the police."

"So I see."

"You haven't registered."

"Oh." Paul smiled. "Oh—I've been meaning to do that." And he had meant to do it, too.

The policeman did not smile. "Then why haven't you?"

"I haven't found the time."

"You better start looking for it, hard, Doc."

Paul was annoyed by this rude young man, and he was inclined, as he had been inclined with the bartender at the Meadows, to put him in his place. But he thought better of it this time. "All right. I'll be down to register tomorrow morning."

"You'll be down to register in an hour, today, Doc." The honorific *Doc*, Paul was learning, could be spoken in such a way as to make a man wish to God he'd never come within ten miles of a university.

"Yes—all right, whatever you say."

"And your industrial identification card—you've failed to turn that in."

"Sorry. I'll do that."

"And your firearms and ammunition permit."

"I'll bring that."

"And your club membership card."

"I'll find it."

"And your airline pass."

"All right."

"And your executive security and health policy. You'll have to get a regular one."

"Whatever you say."

"I think that's all. If anything else comes up, I'll let you know."

"I'm sure you will."

The young policeman's expression softened suddenly, and he shook his head. "Lo! How the mighty are fallen, eh, Doc?"

"Lo! indeed," said Paul.

And an hour later Paul reported politely at the police station, with a shoebox full of revoked privileges.

While he waited for someone to notice him, he interested himself in the radiophoto machine behind glass in one corner, which was fashioning a portrait of a fugitive, and noting beside it a brief biography. The portrait emerged from a slit in the top of the machine bit by bit—first the hair, then the brows, on line with the word WANTED, and then, on line with the large, fey eyes, the name: Edgar Rice Burroughs Hagstrohm, R&R-131313. Hagstrohm's sordid tale emerged along with his nose: "Hagstrohm cut up his M-17 home in Chicago with a blow-torch, went naked to the home of Mrs. Marion Frascati, the widow of an old friend, and demanded that she come to the woods with him. Mrs. Frascati refused, and he disappeared into the bird sanctuary bordering the housing development. There he eluded police, and is believed to have made his escape dropping from a tree onto a passing freight—"

"You!" said the desk sergeant. "Proteus!"

Registration involved the filling out of a long, annoyingly complicated form that started with his name and highest classification number, investigated his reasons for having fallen from grace, asked for the names of his closest friends and relatives, and ended with an oath of allegiance to the United States of America. Paul signed the document in the presence of two witnesses, and watched a coding clerk translate it, on a keyboard, into terms the machines could understand. Out came a card, freshly nicked and punched.

"That's all," said the police sergeant. He dropped the card into a slot, and the card went racing through a system of switches and sidings, until it came to rest against a thick pile of similar cards.

"What does that mean?" said Paul.

The sergeant looked at the pile without interest. "Potential saboteurs."

"Wait a minute—what's going on here? Who says I am?"

"No reflection on you," said the sergeant patiently. "Nobody's said you are. It's all automatic. The machines do it."

"What right have they got to say that about me?"

"Oh, they know, they know," said the sergeant. "They've been around. They do that with anybody who's got more'n four years of college and no job." He studied Paul through narrowed lids. "And you'd be surprised, Doc, how right they are."

A detective walked in, perspiring and discouraged.

"Any break on the Freeman case, Sid?" said the sergeant, losing interest in Paul.

"Nah. All the good suspects came off clean as a whistle on the lie detector."

"Did you check the tubes?"

"Sure. We put in a whole new set, had the circuits checked. Same thing. Innocent, every damn one of 'em. Not that every damn one of 'em wouldn't of liked to of knocked him off." He shrugged. "Well, more leg work. We've got one lead: the sister says she saw a strange man around the back of Freeman's house a half-hour before he got it."

"Got a description?"

"Partial." He turned to the coding clerk. "Ready, Mac?"

"All set. Shoot."

"Medium height. Black shoes, blue suit. No tie. Wedding ring. Black hair, combed straight back. Clean-shaven. Warts on hands and back of neck. Slight limp."

The clerk, expressionless, punched keys as he talked.

"Dinga-dinga-dinga-ding!" went the machine, and out came a card.

"Herbert J. van Antwerp," said Mac. "Forty-nine fifty-six Collester Boulevard."

"Nice work," said the sergeant. He picked up a microphone. "Car 57, car 57—proceed to . . ."

As Paul walked into the bright sunlight of the street, a Black Maria, its siren silent, its tires humming the song of new rubber on hot tar, turned into the alleyway that ran behind the station house.

Paul peered curiously at it as it stopped by a barred door.

A policeman dismounted from the back of the shiny black vehicle and waved a riot gun at Paul. "All right, all right, no loitering there!"

Paul started to move on, lingering an instant longer for a glimpse of the prisoner, who sat deep in the wagon's dark interior, misty, futile, between two more men with riot guns.

"Go on, beat it!" shouted the policeman at Paul again.

Paul couldn't believe that the man would actually loose his terrible hail of buckshot on a loiterer, and so loitered a moment longer. His awe of the riot gun's yawning bore was tempered by his eagerness to see someone who had made a worse botch of getting along in society than he had.

The iron door of the station house clanged open, and three more armed policemen waited to receive the desperado. The prospect of his being at large in the alley for even a few seconds was so harrowing, seemingly, that the policeman who had been badgering Paul now gave his full attention to covering the eight or ten square feet the prisoner would cross in an instant. Paul saw his thumb release the safety catch by the trigger guard.

"All righty, no funny stuff, you hear?" said a nervous voice in the wagon. "Out you go!"

A moment later, Doctor Fred Garth, wearing a badly torn Blue Team shirt, unshaven, his eyes wide, emerged into the daylight, manacled and sneering.

Before Paul could believe in the senseless scene, his old tent- and teammate, his buddy, the man next in line for Pittsburgh, was inside.

Paul hurried around to the front, and back into the office where he'd filled out the papers and turned in his credentials.

The sergeant looked up at him superciliously. "Yes?"

"Doctor Garth—what's he doing here?" said Paul.

"Garth? We got no Garth here."

"I saw them bring him in the back door."

"Naah." The sergeant went back to his reading.

"Look—he's one of my best friends."

"Should of stuck with your dog and your mother," said the sergeant without looking up. "Beat it."

Bewildered, Paul wandered back to the street, left his old car parked in front of the station house, and walked up the hill to the main street of Homestead, to the saloon at the foot of the bridge.

The town hall clock struck four. It might have struck midnight or seven or one, for all the difference it made to Paul. He didn't have to be anywhere at any time any more— ever, he supposed. He made up his own reasons for going somewhere, or he went without reasons. Nobody had anything for him to do anywhere. The economy was no longer interested. His card was of interest now only to the police machines, who regarded him, the instant his card was introduced, with instinctive distrust.

The hydrant was going as usual, and Paul joined the crowd. He found himself soothed by the cool spray from the water. He waited with eagerness for the small boy to finish fashioning his paper boat, and enjoyed the craft's jolting prog-

ress toward certain destruction in the dark, gurgling unknown of the storm sewer.

"Interesting, Doc?"

Paul turned to find Alfy, the television shark, at his
elbow. "Well! Thought you were at the Meadows."

"Thought *you* were. How's the lip?"

"Healing. Tender."

"If it's any consolation, Doc, the bartender's still
sneezing."

"Good, wonderful. Did you get fired?"

"Didn't you know? Everybody got sacked, the whole
service staff, after that tree business." He laughed. "They're
doing their own cooking, making their own beds, raking the
horseshoe pits, and all, all by theirselves."

"Everybody?"

"Everybody below works manager."

"They're cleaning their own latrines, too?"

"The dumb bunnies, Doc, with I.Q.'s under 140."

"What a thing. Still play games, do they?"

"Yep. Last I heard, Blue was way out ahead."

"You don't mean it!"

"Yeah, they were so ashamed of you, they just about
killed theirselves to win."

"And Green?"

"Cellar."

"In spite of Shepherd?"

"You mean Jim Thorpe? Yeah, he entered everything,
and tried to make every point."

"So—"

"So nobody made any points. Last I heard, his team was
trying to convince him he had virus pneumonia and ought to
spend a couple of days in the infirmary. He's got something,
that's for sure." Alfy looked at his watch. "Say, there's some
chamber music on channel seven. Care to play?"

"Not with you."

"Just for the hell of it. No money. I'm just getting

checked out on chamber music. A whole new field. C'mon, Doc, we'll learn together. You watch the cello and bass, and I'll watch the viola and violin. O.K.? Then we'll compare notes and pool our knowledge."

"I'll buy you a beer. How's that?"

"That's good; that's very good."

In the bar's damp twilight, Paul saw a teen-ager looking at him hopefully from a booth. Before him, on the table top, were three rows of matches: three in the first row, five in the second, seven in the third.

"Hello," said the young man uneasily, hopefully. "Very interesting game here. The object of the game is to make the other guy take the last match. You can take as many or as few as you want from any given row at each turn."

"Well—" said Paul.

"Go ahead," said Alfy.

"For two dollars?" said the youngster nervously.

"All right, for two." Paul took a match from the longest row.

The youngster frowned and looked worried, and countered. Three moves later, Paul left him looking disconsolately at the last match. "Goddammit, Alfy," he said miserably, "look at that. I lost."

"This is your first day!" said Alfy sharply. "Don't get discouraged. All right, so you lost. So you're just starting out." Alfy clapped the boy on the shoulder. "Doc, this is my kid brother, Joe. He's just starting out. The Army and the Reeks and Wrecks are hot for his body, but I'm trying to set him up in business for hisself instead. We'll see how this match business works out, and if it doesn't, we'll think of something else."

"I used to play it in college," said Paul apologetically. "I've had a lot of experience."

"College!" said Joe, awed, and he smiled and seemed to feel better. "Jesus, no wonder." He sighed and sat back, depressed again. "But I don't know, Alfy—I'm about ready to throw in the towel. Let's face it, I haven't got the brains." He lined up the matches again, and picked at them, playing a game with himself. "I work at it, and I just don't seem to get any better at it."

"Sure you work!" said Alfy. "Everybody works at something. Getting out of bed's work! Getting food off your plate and into your mouth's work! But there's two kinds of work, kid, work and *hard* work. If you want to stand out, have something to sell, you got to do *hard* work. Pick out something impossible and do it, or be a bum the rest of your life. Sure, everybody worked in George Washington's time, but George Washington worked *hard*. Everybody worked in Shakespeare's time, but Shakespeare worked *hard*. I'm who I am because I work *hard*."

"O.K., O.K., O.K.," said Joe. "Me, Alfy, I haven't got the brains, the eye, the push. Maybe I better go down to the Army."

"You can change your name before you do, kid, and don't bother me again," said Alfy tensely. "Anybody by the name of Tucci stands on his own two feet. It's always been that way, and that's the way it's always going to be."

"O.K.," said Joe, coloring. "Awri. So I give it a try for a couple more days."

"O.K.!" said Alfy. "See that you do."

As Alfy hurried to the television set, Paul stayed at his side. "Listen, do you happen to know who Fred Garth is?"

"Garth?" He laughed. "I didn't at first, but I sure as hell do now. He's the one that ringbarked the oak."

"No!"

"Yep. And they never even thought of questioning him. *He* was on the committee that was supposed to do the questioning."

"How'd they catch him?"

"Gave hisself away. When the tree surgeon got there to patch up the tree, Garth tossed his tools in the drink."

"Alfy!" said the bartender. "You missed the first number."

Alfy pulled up a bar stool.

Paul sat down next to him and engaged the bartender in conversation. Their talk was disjointed, as Alfy kept the man busy twisting the television set's volume knob.

"Ever see Finnerty around?" said Paul.

"The piano player?"

"Yeah."

"What if I have?"

"I'd just like to see him, is all. A friend of mine."

"Lot's of people'd like to see Finnerty these days."

"Uh-huh. Where's he keep himself?"

The bartender looked at him appraisingly. "Nobody sees Finnerty these days."

"Oh? He's not living with Lasher any more?"

"Full of questions today, aren't you? Nobody sees Lasher these days."

"I see." Paul didn't. "They leave town?"

"Who knows? Come on, I haven't got all day. What'll it be?"

"Bourbon and water."

The bartender mixed the drink, set it before Paul, and turned his back.

Paul drank the health of his hostile or apathetic companions in the new life he'd chosen, coughed, smiled, smacked his lips judiciously, trying to determine what wasn't quite right about the drink, and fell senseless from the barstool.

28

"**F**ROM **B**LUE **C**AYUGA," piped the young voices in the autumn evening—

> "From hill and dell,
> Far rings the story of the glory of Cornell—"

Doctor Harold Roseberry, PE-002, laid two documents side by side on the naked, waxy expanse of the top of his rosewood desk. The desk, big enough for a helicopter to land on, was a gift from the Cornell alumni, and a silver plate on one corner said so. Justification of the lavish gift was inlaid in precious woods on the desk top: the football scores run up by the Big Red during the past five seasons. The why and wherefore of this object, at least, would leave no questions in the minds of future archæologists.

"From East and West the crashing echoes answering call," cried the young voices, and Doctor Roseberry found it extremely difficult to concentrate on the two documents before him: a memo from the dean of the School of Arts and Sciences, a quaint, antique man in a quaint, antique part of the university; and a five-year-old letter from a carping alumnus who objected to the deportment of the team when off the playing field. The memo from the dean said that a Mr. Ewing J. Halyard had arrived in town in order to show the university to the Shah of Bratpuhr, and, incidentally, to make up a seventeen-year-old credit deficiency in physical education. The memo asked that Doctor Roseberry assign one of his staff to the chore of giving Halyard the final physical-education tests the next morning.

> "Cornell victorious!
> The champions of all!"

came the voices.

Doctor Roseberry was inclined to react ironically to the last line of the song. "Certainly, victorious last year, four years afore that," he muttered in his pregnant solitude. But here was another year that might not look so hot inlaid in rosewood. "Tomorrow and tomorrow and tomorrow," he said wearily. Every coach in the Ivy League was out to knock him down to a PE-003 again, and two losses would do it. Yale and Penn were loaded. Yale had floated a bond to buy the whole Texas A&M backfield, and Penn had bought Breslaw from Wisconsin for $43,000.

Roseberry groaned. "How the hell long they think a man can play college football?" he wanted to know. Six years before, Cornell had bought him from Wabash College, and asked him to list his idea of a dream team. Then, by God they'd bought it for him.

"But what the hell they think they bought?" he asked himself. "Sumpin' made outa steel and *see*-ment? Supposed to last a lifetime, is it?" They hadn't bought him so much as a water boy since, and the average age of the Big Red was now close to thirty-one.

> "Far above Cayuga's waters,
> With its waves of blue,
> Stands our noble Alma Mater,
> Glorious to view—"

came the voices.

"Certainly it's glorious," said Doctor Roseberry. "Who the hell you figure paid for it?" In its first two years the football team had paid for itself. In the next three, it had paid for a new chemistry building, a heat and power laboratory, a new administration building for the Agricultural Engineering Department, and four new professorial chairs: the Philosophy of Creative Engineering, Creative Engineering History, Creative Public Relations for Engineers, and Creative Engineering and the Captive Consumer.

Roseberry, who wasn't expected to pay any attention to the academic side of the university, had nonetheless kept a careful accounting of all these improvements, glorious to view, that had been added since he and his football team had arrived far above Cayuga's waters. In anticipation of a poor season, he was roughing out in his mind a polemic letter to the alumni, in which the academic expenditures would figure prominently. He had the first line of the letter, following the salutation, "Sportsmen," already perfected, and enjoyed imagining it written out in capitals:

"IS THE FOOTBALL BUSINESS AT CORNELL GOING TO BE RUN ON A BUSINESS-LIKE BASIS, OR IS THE BIG RED GOING TO BE BLED WHITE?"

And then the next sentence sprang inspirationally to mind: "IN THE PAST FIVE YEARS, NOT ONE CENT HAS BEEN REINVESTED IN THE BUSINESS, NOT ONE CENT LAID ASIDE FOR DEPRECIATION!"

He saw now that the whole thing would have to be in caps. The situation called for a letter with real punch.

The telephone rang.

"Doctor Roseberry speakin'."

"This is Buck Young, Doc. Note here says you wanted me to call." The husky voice was tinged with uneasiness, just as Roseberry had hoped it would be. He could imagine that Buck had sat by the phone with the note in his hand for several minutes before he'd dialed. Now that Buck had gone this far, Roseberry told himself, he'd go the rest of the way too.

"Yeah, yeah," said Roseberry, smiling captivatingly. "Bucky boy, how are you?"

"Fine. What's on your mind?"

"Maybe I should ask what's on yours."

"Thermodynamics. Stress analysis. Fluid flow. Differential equations."

"Aaah," said Roseberry, "why'n't you loosen up and have a beer with me down at The Dutch? You hear the news I got, I think maybe you'll get something else on your mind."

> "Cheer, cheer, here we are again
> To cheer with all our might—"

sang the voices, and Doctor Roseberry waited impatiently for the racket to stop. If they had to have a football rally, he wished they'd hold it somewhere where it wouldn't bother him and his team. That was another thing: Cornell was so cheap, they quartered their athletes on the campus rather than setting up a separate establishment away from all the student racket. "Wait'll they shut up, Bucky boy, and I can hear myself think."

> "Cheer, cheer, here we are again,
> To cheer for the Red and White!"

Either Cornell was going to get progressive, or they could find themselves another coach, Roseberry told himself. Now, Tennessee—there *was* a progressive setup. *They* kept *their* team in Miami Beach, and no wonder Milankowitz went there for $35,000, after he turned down Chicago for $40,000. "O.K., Bucky, I can hear again. What about I meet you down at The Dutch for a couple of quick ones in fifteen minutes?"

The voice was faint, reluctant. "Just for half an hour."

Doctor Roseberry climbed into his black convertible in the team parking lot, and drove over to the Delta Upsilon fraternity house, on whose lawn he'd first spotted Buck Young playing interfraternity football. There, Young had done things for Delta Upsilon for nothing that any college in the country would have considered a steal at $50,000 a year.

That had been last fall, and D.U. had eked out the interfraternity football championship with 450 points to their opponents' six. Young had scored 390 of the points, and had thrown the passes for the other 54, the remaining touchdown being accounted for by a George Ward, whose name had somehow burned itself into Roseberry's memory along with all of the other statistics.

But Young had said firmly, when Roseberry had approached him, that he played football for fun, and that he wanted to be an engineer. A year ago, with the Big Red by far the biggest thing in the East, with the Yale and Penn alumni still to mobilize their economic resources, Roseberry could afford to be amused by Young's preference for a career in engineering. Now nothing was amusing, and Roseberry saw Young as his one chance to remain a PE-002 under the fouled-up Cornell football economics. He would sell a couple of supernatural linemen to Harvard, who would buy anything that was cheap, and use the proceeds to buy himself the services of Young at far below their value on the open market.

The Dutch, its paneling antiqued by the condensation from breaths of generations of adolescent alcoholics, was packed and noisy, and in almost every hand was the drink fashionable that season, benedictine and Pluto water, with a sprig of mint.

Doctor Roseberry was cheered and toasted by the children as he entered. He grinned, and colored becomingly, and inwardly demanded of himself and history, "What the hell these baby engineers got to do'th me, for chrissakes?" He pushed his way through the crowd, which claimed him for reasons not at all clear, to a dark corner booth, where Purdy and McCloud, the linemen whom he intended to sell to Harvard, were nursing the one beer a night apiece permitted during training. They were talking quietly, but darkly, and, as Doctor Roseberry approached, they looked up, but didn't smile.

"Evenin' boys," said Doctor Roseberry, sitting down on the small ledge not occupied by McCloud's backside, and keeping his eyes on the door through which Buck Young would be coming.

They nodded, and went on with their conversation. "No reason," said McCloud, "why a man can't play college ball till he's forty, if he takes good care of hisself." McCloud was thirty-six.

"Sure," said Purdy gravely, "a older man's got a certain matoority you don't find in the young ones." Purdy was thirty-seven.

"Look at Moskowitz," said McCloud.

"Yup. Forty-three, and still goin' strong. No reason why he shou'n't keep goin' until he's fifty. No reason why most men shou'n't."

"Bet I could go to the Reeks and Wrecks now and put together a Ivy League championship team out of guys past forty who're s'posed to be through."

"Planck," said Purdy. "Poznitsky."

"McCarren," said McCloud, "Mirro, Mellon. Ain't that right, Doc?" McCloud asked Roseberry the question casually.

"Yup, guess so. Hope so. Better. Kind of outfit I've got to work with."

"Um," said McCloud. He stared down into his beer, finished it off with a flourish, and looked plaintively at Roseberry. "O.K. if I have one more short one tonight?"

"Sure—why the hell not?" said Roseberry. "I'll even buy it."

McCloud and Purdy looked distressed at this, and both, on second thought, figured they'd better keep in good shape for the important Big Red season ahead.

Roseberry offered no reply to this clumsy gambit.

"Better not hit that stuff too hard," said a leering student, pointing to the two bottles of beer. "Not if Cornell's going to go on ruling the Ivy League, you better not, boys."

Purdy glowered at him, and the youngster retreated into the crowd. "One minute, they ask you should go out and bust both arms and legs so's they can say how tough Cornell is. Then the next minute, they want you should live like a goddam missionary," said Purdy bitterly.

"Like in the Army," said McCloud.

The subject reminded Doctor Roseberry of the letter and the memo he'd been reading in his office, and he patted his breast pocket to make sure he still had them.

"Like in the Army," said Purdy, "only no pension."

"Sure, give the best years of your life to some college, and what the hell they do when you're through? Toss you right into the Reeks and Wrecks. The hell with *you*, buddy."

"Look at Kisco," said Purdy.

"Died for dear old Rutgers, and his widow's got what?"

"Nuttin'! Nuttin' but a chenille *R* she can use as a bath mat, and a government pension."

"Shoulda saved his money!" said Doctor Roseberry impatiently. "He was makin' more'n the college president. How come he was so poor? Whose fault that?"

Purdy and McCloud looked down at their big hands and fidgeted. Both of them, in their prime, had made as much as the late Buddy Kisco, who had actually died for Rutgers. But both were likewise broke—forever broke, building flamboyant mansions in Cayuga Heights, buying new cars every six months, dressing expensively. . . .

"That's the thing," said McCloud plaintively. "A athalete has to keep up appearances. Sure, people think a athalete makes plenty, and he do on paper. But people never stop to think he's allus gotta keep up a expensive front."

Purdy leaned forward in excited agreement. "For who?" he demanded rhetorically. "For the athalete?"

"For Cornell!" said McCloud.

"Damn right!" said Purdy, leaning back, satisfied.

Buck Young, tall, massive, shy, appeared in the doorway

and looked around the room. Doctor Roseberry stood and waved, and left Purdy and McCloud to join him at the door.

"Bucky boy!"

"Doc." Buck seemed somewhat ashamed to be seen with the coach, and looked hopefully at a vacant booth. He was behaving as though he were keeping an appointment with a dope peddler, and, in a way, Doctor Roseberry reflected cheerfully, he was.

"Buck, I'm not going to waste any words, because there isn't much time. This offer won't be open many more days. Maybe it'll be off tomorrow. It's all up to the alumni," he lied.

"Uh-huh," said Buck.

"I'm prepared to offer you thirty thousand, Buck, six hundred a week, all year round, startin' tomorrow. What do you say?"

Young's Adam's apple bobbed. He cleared his throat. "Every week?" he asked faintly.

"That's how much we think of you, boy. Don't sell yourself short."

"And I could study, too? You'd give me time off for classes and study?"

Roseberry frowned. "Well—there's some pretty stiff rulings about that. You can't play college football, *and* go to school. They tried that once, and you know what a silly mess that was."

Buck ran his blunt fingers through his hair. "Golly, I dunno. That's a lot of money, but my family'd be awful surprised and disappointed. I mean—"

"I'm not askin' it for me, Buck! Think of your schoolmates. You want them to lose a game this year?"

"No," he murmured.

"Thirty-five grand, Buck."

"Jesus, I—"

"I have heard every word you've said," said a young redhead thickly. He wasn't drinking benedictine and Pluto

water, but sloshed instead a puddle of whisky and water on
the table as he sat down by Buck, facing Doctor Roseberry,
uninvited. Beneath his open-necked shirt the red of a Meadows T-shirt showed plainly. "Heard it all," he said, and he
laid his hand on Buck's shoulder gravely. "Here you are at a
crossroads, my boy. You're lucky. Not many crossroads left
for people. Nothing but one-way streets with cliffs on both
sides."

"Who the hell are you?" said Doctor Roseberry irritably.

"Doctor, *Doctor*, mind you, Edmond L. Harrison of the
Ithaca Works. Call me Ed, or pay me five dollars."

"Let's get away from this lush," said Doctor Roseberry.

Harrison banged on the table with his fist. "Hear me
out!" He appealed to Buck, whose exit he blocked. "The
eminent Doctor Roseberry represents one road, and I the
other. I am you, if you continue on your present course, five
years from now."

His eyes were half closed, and after the fashion of benign drunks he seemed on the verge of tears, so powerfully
was he compelled to love and help others. "If you are good,"
he said, "and if you are thoughtful, a fractured pelvis on the
gridiron will pain you less than a life of engineering and
management. In that life, believe me, the thoughtful, the
sensitive, those who can recognize the ridiculous, die a thousand deaths."

Doctor Roseberry leaned back and folded his hands
across his flat, hard belly. If he'd thought of it, he would have
hired a professional actor to do what Doctor Harrison was
doing for nothing. "How do you mean?" he asked helpfully.

"The best man I knew at the Meadows—"

"The *Meadows*?" said Buck in awe.

"The Meadows," said Harrison, "where the men at the
head of the procession of civilization demonstrate in private
that they are ten-year-olds at heart, that they haven't the
vaguest notion of what they're doing to the world."

"They're opening new doors at the head of the procession!" said Buck hotly, shocked by the blunt, near-sabotage talk, and now fighting it, like the good citizen he was. He'd learned the resounding phrase about opening doors in a freshman orientation program, at which a Doctor Kroner had been the impressive chief speaker.

"Slamming doors in everybody's face," said Harrison. "That's what they're doing."

"Keep your voice down," warned Doctor Roseberry.

"I don't care," said Harrison stridently, "not after what they did to the only grownup there. They gave Proteus the sack, that's what they did."

"Proteus has been dead for years," said Buck, sure Harrison was a fake.

"His son, his son, Paul," said Harrison. "So let me say, my boy, go out and make your money on the gridiron, with blood and sweat and sinew. There's honor and glory in that—a little, anyway—and you'll never hate yourself. But keep the hell away from the head of the procession, where you'll get it in the neck if you can't get a lump in your throat over the ups and downs of a bunch of factories." He attempted to rise, failed once, made it the next time. "And now, goodbye."

"Where are you going?" said Doctor Roseberry. "Stick around, stick around."

"Where? First to shut off that part of the Ithaca works for which I am responsible, and then to an island, perhaps, a cabin in the north woods, a shack in the Everglades."

"And do what?" said Buck, baffled.

"Do?" said Harrison. "*Do?* That's just it, my boy. All of the doors have been closed. There's nothing to do but to find a womb suitable for an adult, and crawl into it. One without machines would suit me particularly."

"What have you got against machines?" said Buck.

"They're slaves."

"Well, what the heck," said Buck. "I mean, they aren't people. They don't suffer. They don't mind working."

"No. But they compete with people."

"That's a pretty good thing, isn't it—considering what a sloppy job most people do of anything?"

"Anybody that competes with slaves becomes a slave," said Harrison thickly, and he left.

A dark man, dressed like a student, but much older-looking, set down his untouched benedictine and Pluto water on the bar, studied the faces of Roseberry and Young as though memorizing them, and followed Harrison out of the building.

"Let's go out in the lobby, where we can talk," said Roseberry, as a cycle of songs began.

"Cheer, cheer, here we are again," cried the young voices, and Young and Roseberry moved into the lobby.

"Well?" said Doctor Roseberry.

"I—"

"Doctor Roseberry, I believe?"

Roseberry looked up at the intruder, a sandy-mus-tached gentleman, in a violet shirt, matching boutonniere, and a gay waistcoat contrasting with his dark suit. "Yes?"

"My name is Halyard, E. J., of the State Department. And these gentlemen here are the Shah of Bratpuhr, and his interpreter, Khashdrahr Miasma. We were just leaving for the president's house, and I happened to spot you."

"Charmed," said Doctor Roseberry.

"Brahous brahouna, bouna saki," said the Shah, bowing slightly.

Halyard laughed nervously. "Guess we have a little business tomorrow morning, eh?"

"Oh," said Roseberry, *"you're* the one—the one for the phys. ed. finals."

"Yes, yes indeed. Haven't had a cigarette in two weeks. Will it take long?"

"No, I don't think so. Fifteen minutes ought to do the trick."

"Oh? That short a time, eh? Well, well." The tennis shoes and shorts he'd bought that afternoon wouldn't get much wear in that time.

"Oh, 'scuse me, gents," said Roseberry. "This here's Buck Young. Student just now."

"Lakki-ti Takaru?" the Shah asked Buck.

" 'Like it here?' " translated Khashdrahr.

"Yessir. Very much, sir, your highness."

"A lot different from my day," said Halyard. "By gosh, we had to get up every morning bright and early, climb the hill in all kinds of weather, and sit there and listen to some of the dullest lectures you ever heard of. And, of course, some poor fish would have to get up in front of us and talk every day of the week, and chances are he wasn't much of a speaker, and anyway no showman."

"Yes, the professional actors and the television circuits are a big improvement, sir," said Buck.

"And the exams!" said Halyard. "Pretty cute, you know, punching out the answers, and then finding out right off if you passed or flunked. Boy, believe me, we used to have to write our arms off, and then we'd have to wait weeks for a prof to grade the exams. And plenty of times they made bad mistakes on the grades."

"Yessir," said Buck politely.

"Well, I'll see one of your assistants tomorrow, eh?" said Halyard to Roseberry.

"I intend I should give you the tests personal," said Roseberry.

"Well! I guess *that's* an honor, with the season just beginning."

"Sure," said Roseberry. He reached into his breast pocket and produced the letter and the memo. He handed the letter to Halyard. "Here's something you should oughta read before you come."

"Fine, thanks." Halyard took it, supposing it was a list of the things he would have to do. He smiled warmly at Roseberry, who had given every indication that Halyard would be given an exceedingly simple and short series of tests. A mere fifteen minutes, he'd said. That would do it.

Halyard glanced at the letter, and couldn't imagine what it was all about at first. It was addressed to the president of Cornell, Doctor Albert Herpers, not to him. Moreover, the date on it indicated that it was five years old.

Dear Doctor Herpers: he read—

I had occasion to see the wearers of the Red and White after the Penn game in Philadelphia this Thanksgiving, and I must say I was ashamed to admit to anyone that I had ever come within fifty miles of Ithaca.

I was dining in the Club Cybernetics after the game, when the team, led by this new man, Doctor Roseberry, arrived en masse . . .

The letter went on to describe the bacchanal that followed, with particular emphasis on the crudities of Roseberry's behavior—

while, mind you, all were wearing what I, perhaps in my old-fashioned way, consider sacred, the C of the Big Red. . . .

In view of this, Doctor Herpers, I feel constrained to point out, as a loyal alumnus, that Doctor Roseberry, in his first year with the Big Red, is off to an extremely poor start. In the brief time of his incumbency, I have no doubt that the shockingly public moral turpitude of the team has made a worse name for what I was once proud to claim as my Alma Mater than a lifetime of gridiron victories can possibly offset. . . .

It is my fervent hope that Roseberry will be forced to resign forthwith, or, failing that, that outraged alumni sell him to some Grade C school forthwith.

To this end, I am sending copies of this letter to the Alumni Secretary, to each of the local alumni chapters, to the Trustees, and to the Secretary of Athletics in Washington, D. C.

Very truly yours,

Doctor Ewing J. Halyard

"Oh," said Halyard, his poise gone, suddenly looking ridiculous in the clothes that had been high fashion a moment before. "Saw this, did you?"

"Doctor Herpers thought I'd be interested."

A sickly grin framed Halyard's white teeth. "Long time ago, wasn't it, Doctor? Seems like a hundred years."

"Like yesterday."

"Ha ha. Lot of water under the dam since those days, eh?"

The Shah looked questioningly at Khashdrahr for an explanation of what made Halyard so gray suddenly. Khashdrahr shrugged.

"*Over* the dam," said Buck Young, filling the grim void in the conversation. "Or under the *bridge*."

"Yes. Quite so," said Halyard hollowly. "Well, best we should go. See you in the morning."

"Wouldn't miss it for the world."

Doctor Roseberry turned back to Buck Young, as Halyard, his face somber, shepherded the Shah and Khashdrahr into the Ithaca night. The Shah was sneezing violently.

"Well, kid," said Roseberry. "What say to thirty-five grand? Yes or no?"

"I—"

"Thirty-six."

"Yes," whispered Buck. "Hell yes."

When the two went back into The Dutch to drink to the deal, Purdy and McCloud were still talking gloomily in their dark corner.

"Sure," said Purdy, "Roseberry's a tough guy to work for, but thank God you ain't workin' for Harvard."

McCloud nodded. "Yeah, work there, and 'ey won't letch wear nothin' but dark-gray flannels in the winter, and seersucker in the summer."

They both shuddered, and furtively refilled their glasses from a half-case hidden under the table.

"Wit'out shoulders," said Purdy.

29

Doctor Paul Proteus, to all practical purposes Mr. Paul Proteus, dreamed of nothing but pleasant things under the benign drug, and spoke simultaneously, without reflection but truthfully, on whatever subject was brought to his attention. The talking he did, the answering of questions, went on as though it were being done by a person hired to represent him, while Paul personally gave his attention to entertaining phantasmagoria within the privacy of his closed eyelids.

"Did you really get fired, or was it a pretense?" said the voice.

"Pretense. Supposed to get into the Ghost Shirt Society and find out what they're up to. Only I quit, and they don't know that, yet." Paul chuckled.

And in his dream, Paul danced powerfully, gracefully, to the hectic rhythms of the *Building 58 Suite*.

"Furrazz-ow-ow-ow-ow-ow-ak! ting!" went lathe group three, and Paul leapt and spun among the machines, while, pink amid the gray machines in the building's center, Anita lay invitingly in a rainbow-colored nest of control wires. Her part in the dance called for her only to lie there motionless, while Paul approached and fled, approached and fled in frenzied, random action.

"Why are you quitting?"

"Sick of my job."

"Because what you were doing was morally bad?" suggested the voice.

"Because it wasn't getting anybody anywhere. Because it was getting everybody nowhere."

"Because it was evil?" insisted the voice.

"Because it was pointless," said Paul's representative, as Kroner joined the ballet, ponderously, earthbound, with a methodical marching to the voices of the punch presses in the basement: *"Aw-grumph! tonka-tonka. Aw-grumph! tonka-tonka . . ."*

Kroner looked lovingly at Paul, caught him as he bounded past, and carried him in a bearlike embrace toward Anita. Paul squirmed free in the nick of time, and off he went again, leaving Kroner in tears, urging Anita to follow him into the out-of-doors.

"Then you're against the organization now?"

"I'm *not with* them now."

Shepherd, clumsily but energetically, entered the growing tableau from the basement, choosing as his theme the hoarse voices of the welders: *"Vaaaaaaa-zuzip! Vaaaaaaa-zuzip!"* Shepherd marked time with one foot, watching Paul's gyrations, another rejection of Kroner, another effort to coax the dead-panned Anita from her nest amid the machines. Shepherd watched with puzzlement and disdain, shrugged, and walked straight to Kroner and Anita. The three settled in the nest of wires, and together followed Paul's movements with baffled, censorious eyes.

286

Suddenly, a window by which Paul was bounding flew open, and Finnerty's face was thrust into the opening.

"Paul!"

"Yes, Ed?"

"You're on our side now!"

The *Building 58 Suite* stopped abruptly, and a black curtain fell between Paul and the rest of the cast, save Finnerty.

"Hmmm?" said Paul.

"You're on our side," said Finnerty. "If you're not with them, you're with us!"

Paul's head was aching now, and his lips were dry. He opened his eyes and saw Finnerty's face, gross, caricatured by its closeness.

"With who? Whom?"

"The Ghost Shirt Society, Paul."

"Oh, them. What do they think, Ed?" he asked drowsily. He was on a mattress, he realized, in a chamber whose air was still and damp, dense with the feel of dead mass pressing down from above. "What they think, Ed?"

"That the world should be restored to the people."

"By all means," said Paul, trying to nod. His muscles were only faintly connected to his will, and his will, in turn, was a fuzzy, ineffectual thing. "People oughta get it back."

"You're going to help."

"Yup," murmured Paul. He was in a highly tolerant mood, full of admiration and well-wishing for anyone with convictions, and cheerfully *hors de combat* under the influence of the drug. Obviously, he couldn't be expected to do anything. And Finnerty began to fade again, and Paul danced once more in Building 58, danced God knows why, uncertain that there was an audience anywhere to appreciate his exertions.

"What do you think?" he heard Finnerty say.

"He'll do nicely," he heard another voice reply, and he recognized the voice as Lasher's.

"What's a ghost shirt?" murmured Paul between prickling lips.

"Toward the end of the nineteenth century," said Lasher, "a new religious movement swept the Indians in this country, Doctor."

"The Ghost Dance, Paul," said Finnerty.

"The white man had broken promise after promise to the Indians, killed off most of the game, taken most of the Indians' land, and handed the Indians bad beatings every time they'd offered any resistance," said Lasher.

"Poor Injuns," murmured Paul.

"This is serious," said Finnerty. "Listen to what he's telling you."

"With the game and land and ability to defend themselves gone," said Lasher, "the Indians found out that all the things they used to take pride in doing, all the things that had made them feel important, all the things that used to gain them prestige, all the ways in which they used to justify their existence—they found that all those things were going or gone. Great hunters had nothing to hunt. Great fighters did not come back from charging into repeating-arms fire. Great leaders could lead the people nowhere but into death in hopeless attack, or deeper into wastelands. Great religious leaders could no longer show that the old religious beliefs were the way to victory and plenty."

Paul, suggestible under the drug, was deeply disturbed by the plight of the redskins. "Golly."

"The world had changed radically for the Indians," said Lasher. "It had become a white man's world, and Indian ways in a white man's world were irrelevant. It was impossible to hold the old Indian values in the changed world. The only thing they could do in the changed world was to become second-rate white men or wards of the white men."

"Or they could make one last fight for the old values," said Finnerty with relish.

"And the Ghost Dance religion," said Lasher, "was that

last, desperate defense of the old values. Messiahs appeared, the way they're always ready to appear, to preach magic that would restore the game, the old values, the old reasons for being. There were new rituals and new songs that were supposed to get rid of the white men by magic. And some of the more warlike tribes that still had a little physical fight left in them added a flourish of their own—the Ghost Shirt."

"Oho," said Paul.

"They were going to ride into battle one last time," said Lasher, "in magic shirts that white men's bullets couldn't go through."

"Luke! Hey, Luke!" called Finnerty. "Stop the mimeo machine a second and come on over here."

Paul heard footsteps shuffling across the damp floor. He opened his eyes to see Luke Lubbock, his features sour with the tragic stoicism of a dispossessed redskin, standing by his bed, wearing a white shirt fringed in an imitation of a buckskin shirt, and decorated with thunderbirds and stylized buffalo worked into the fabric with brightly insulated bits of wire.

"Ug," said Paul.

"Ug," said Luke, without hesitation, deep in his role.

"This isn't any joke, Paul," said Finnerty.

"Everything's a joke until the drug wears off," said Lasher.

"Does Luke think *he's* bulletproof?" said Paul.

"It's the symbolism of the thing!" said Finnerty. "Don't you get it yet?"

"I expect," said Paul amiably, dreamily. "Sure. You bet. I guess."

"What *is* the symbolism?" asked Finnerty.

"Luke Lubbock wants his buffaloes back."

"Paul—come on, snap out of it!" said Finnerty.

"Okey dokey."

"Don't you see, Doctor?" said Lasher. "The machines are to practically everybody what the white men were to the

Indians. People are finding that, because of the way the machines are changing the world, more and more of their old values don't apply any more. People have no choice but to become second-rate machines themselves, or wards of the machines."

"God help us," said Paul. "But, I dunno, this Ghost Shirt thing—it's kind of childish, isn't it? Dressing up like that, and—"

"Childish—like Hitler's Brown Shirts, like Mussolini's Black Shirts. Childish like any uniform," said Lasher. "We don't deny it's childish. At the same time, we admit that we've got to be a little childish, anyway, to get the big following we need."

"Wait until he sits in on some meetings," said Finnerty. "They're like something out of *Alice in Wonderland*, Paul."

"All meetings are," said Lasher. "But, by some magic that's beyond my comprehension, meetings get things done. I could do with a little more dignity and maturity in our operations, because those are the things we're fighting for. But first of all we've got to fight, and fighting is necessarily undignified and immature."

"Fight?" said Paul.

"Fight," said Lasher. "And there's hope of putting up a good fight. This business of one set of values being replaced by force by another set of values has come up often enough in history—"

"Among the Indians and the Jews and a lot of other people who've been tyrannized by outsiders," said Finnerty.

"Yes, it's come up often enough for us to make a good guess as to what can happen this time," said Lasher. He paused. "What we can make happen."

"Beat it, Luke," said Finnerty.

"Yessir."

"Paul, are you listening?" said Finnerty.

"Yep. Interesting."

"All right," said Lasher, his voice low. "In the past, in a

situation like this, if Messiahs showed up with credible, dramatic messages of hope, they often set off powerful physical and spiritual revolutions in the face of terrific odds. If a Messiah shows up now with a good, solid, startling message, and if he keeps out of the hands of the police, he can set off a revolution—maybe one big enough to take the world away from the machines, Doctor, and give it back to the people."

"And you're just the boy to do it, too, Ed," said Paul.

"That's what I thought, too," said Lasher, "at first. Then I realized we could do much better starting off with a name that was already well known."

"Sitting Bull?" said Paul.

"Proteus," said Lasher.

"You don't have to do anything but keep out of sight," said Finnerty. "Everything will be done for you."

"*Is* being done," said Lasher.

"So you just rest now," said Finnerty gently. "Build up your strength."

"I—"

"You don't matter," said Finnerty. "You belong to History now."

A heavy door thumped shut, and Paul knew that he was alone again, and that History, somewhere on the other side of the door, would let him out only when it was good and ready to.

30

History, personified at this point in the life of Doctor Paul Proteus by Ed Finnerty and the Reverend James J. Lasher, let Paul out of his cell in an old Ilium air-raid shelter only in order for him to eliminate the wastes accrued in the process of his continued existence as an animal. Other signs of his being alive—outcries, protests, demands, profanity— were beneath History's notice until the proper time came, when the door swung open, and Ed Finnerty ushered Paul into his first meeting of the Ghost Shirt Society.

When Paul was led into the meeting chamber, another segment of the air-raid shelter system, everyone stood: Lasher, at the head of the table, Bud Calhoun, Katharine Finch, Luke Lubbock, Paul's tenant farmer Mr. Haycox, and a score of others, whose names Paul didn't know.

It wasn't a brilliant-looking aggregation of conspirators, on the whole, but a righteous and determined one. Paul supposed that Lasher and Finnerty had gathered the group on the basis of availability and trustworthiness rather than talent, starting, seemingly, with some of the more intelligent regulars at the saloon at the foot of the bridge. While the group was predominantly composed of Iliumites, Paul learned, every region of the country was represented.

Amid the mediocrity was a scattering of men who radiated a good deal of competence and, incidentally, prosperity, who seemed, like Paul, in the act of deserting a system that had treated them very well indeed.

As Paul studied these interesting exceptions, he looked at one of the seedier members adjacent, and was surprised by another familiar face—that of Professor Ludwig von Neumann, a slight, disorderly old man, who had taught political science at Union College in Schenectady until the Social Sciences Building had been torn down to make space for the new Heat and Power Laboratory. Paul and von Neumann had known each other slightly as members of the Ilium Historical Society, before the Historical Society Building had been torn down to make room for the new Ilium Atomic Reactor.

"Here he is," said Finnerty proudly.

Paul was given a polite round of applause. The expressions of the applauders were somewhat chilly, giving Paul to understand that he could never *really* be a full partner in their enterprise, since he had not been with them from the beginning.

The only exceptions to this snobbery were Katharine Finch, formerly Paul's secretary, and Bud Calhoun, both of whom seemed as amiable and unchanged as though they were lounging in Paul's outer office at the Works in the old days. Bud, Paul reflected, moved from situation to situation in the protective atmosphere of his imagination, while Katharine was similarly insulated by her adoration for Bud.

The formality of the meeting, the purposefulness in the faces, bluffed Paul into holding his peace for the moment. The chair on Lasher's left was pulled out for him, and Finnerty took the chair on Lasher's right.

As Paul sat down, he noted that only Luke Lubbock wore a ghost shirt, and he supposed that Luke couldn't accomplish anything without a uniform of some sort.

"Meeting of the Ghost Shirt Society will come to order," said Lasher.

Paul, with a trace of drug-inspired whimsey still in his bloodstream, had expected a show of fraternal-order nonsense, full of quasi-Indian talk. Instead, save for Luke Lubbock's shirt, the meeting belonged very much to the present, a sordid, realistic present, an angry present.

The Ghost Shirt Society, then, was simply a convenient

and dramatic title for a businesslike group, a title whose historical roots were of interest principally to Lasher and his disciple Finnerty, who entertained each other with elaborate commentaries on the insufferable status quo. For the rest, simple commentaries, special personal resentments, were reasons enough for joining anything that promised a change for the better. *Promised a change for the better, or,* Paul amended his thought after looking into some of the eyes, *promised some excitement for a change.*

What Bud Calhoun was doing here, Paul couldn't imagine, since Bud wasn't at all interested in political action and was without capacity for resentment. As Bud had said of himself, "All Ah want is time an' equipmen' to faht around with, and Ah'm happy as a pig in mud."

"We'll start with you, Z-II," said Lasher, looking at Katharine.

There were circles under Katharine's gentle, wondering eyes, and she looked startled when Lasher called on her, as though Lasher, the meeting, the underground chamber, had suddenly risen about her in her clean, girlish world. "Oh," she said, and rattled the papers on the table before her. "We now have seven hundred and fifty-eight ghost shirts on hand. Our quota for now was a thousand," she said wearily, "but Mrs. Fishbein—"

"No names!" cried several of the members.

"Sorry." She blushed, and referred to her papers. "Er, X-229 came down with cataracts and had to stop the design work. She'll be all right in about six weeks, and can get back to work. Also—there's a shortage of red wire."

"A-12!" said Lasher.

"Yessir," said a swarthy man, and Paul recognized him as one of the Works security guards out of uniform. A-12 wrote down the requisition for red wire, and grinned sheepishly at Paul.

"The shirts that *are* done are packaged, ready for delivery," said Katharine.

"Very good," said Lasher. "G-17, have you anything to report?"

Bud Calhoun smiled, and leaned back and rubbed his hands. "Comin' along jes' fine. Got two models ready fo' trial out at L-56's place some dark night."

"They'll make it through a works fence all right?" asked Lasher.

"Like a dose of salts," said Bud, "thout trippin' the alarm, neither."

"Who cares if the alarm's tripped or not?" said Finnerty. "The whole country's going to be in an uproar anyway."

"Just th'owed thet in," said Bud. "Also got an idea for a gimmick thet'd feed powah into the telephone system so it'd knock the guards flat on theah tails when they try to call for he'p." He chuckled merrily.

"Thought we were going to cut the phone wires."

"Could do thet, I s'pose," said Bud.

"What we want from you," said Lasher, "is a design for a good practical, cheap armored car for breaking through the works fences, something our people all over the country ought to be able to knock together in a hurry, with jalopies and sheet metal."

"Hell, we got thet," said Bud. "What Ah'm thinkin' of now, is how we can *really* fox 'em. See, if we wanted to, Ah figger we could fix a li'l ol—"

"Talk to me about it *after* the meeting," said Lasher.

Bud looked momentarily unhappy, and then began sketching on a pad before him. Paul saw that he had drawn an armored car, to which he was adding antennae, a radar dome, spikes, flails, and other instruments of terrible slaughter. His eyes met Paul's, and he nodded. "Very in'er'stin' problem," he whispered.

"All right," said Lasher. "Recruiting. D-71—got something for us?"

"He's in Pittsburgh," said Finnerty.

"That's right," said Lasher. "Forgot. Seeing what he can do with the Moose there."

Luke Lubbock cleared his throat several times, and riffled papers. "Sir, he asked me to give his report, sir."

"Go ahead."

"We got a man in every chapter of the Royal Parmesans. That's fifty-seven chapters."

"Good men?" said someone.

"You can count on D-71," said Lasher. "Anybody he or his boys recruit gets exactly the same treatment you did— the Mickey, then the questioning under sodium pentathol."

"O.K.," said the questioner. "Just wanted to make sure nobody was getting sloppy at this stage of the game."

"Relax," said Finnerty, very tough, out of the corner of his mouth.

"Him too?" said the questioner, pointing at Paul.

"Him especially," said Lasher. "We know things about Proteus he'd be surprised to know about himself."

"No names," said Paul.

Everybody laughed. It seemed to be a welcome bit of humor that broke the tension of the meeting.

"What's funny?" said Paul.

"You're *the* name," said Lasher.

"Now wait, just a minute—"

"What are you worried about? You don't have to do anything," said Finnerty. "What a break, Paul. Wouldn't *we* like to be able to serve the cause just sitting down here, keeping away from the cops—no responsibilities, no chances to take."

"It's pretty soft all right," said Paul, "but not quite soft enough. I'm walking out. Sorry."

"They'll kill you, Paul," said Finnerty.

"You'd kill him, if you were told to," said Lasher.

Finnerty nodded. "That's right, Paul, I would. I'd have to."

Paul sank back into his chair. He found that he wasn't

really shocked by the alternatives of life and death just presented to him. It was such a *clean-cut* proposition, unlike anything he'd ever encountered before. Here were honest-to-God black and white, not at all like the muddy pastels he'd had to choose from while in industry. Having it put like that, *Do as we say or get killed*, had the same liberating effect as the drug of a few hours ago had had. He couldn't make his own decisions for reasons anybody could understand.

So Paul leaned back in his chair and began to take a real interest in what was going on.

Luke Lubbock finished reading D-71's report on recruiting in the lodges across the country. The goal, to have at least two influential Ghost Shirt Society members in every major social organization in every major industrial city, was about sixty per cent realized.

"S-1—what have you got to say for yourself?" said Lasher.

"We're getting the word around about who the *Leader* is," said Finnerty. "Take a few days to see what sort of effect it has."

"Don't see how it could be anything but good," said Lasher.

"Recruiting should really go to town now," said Finnerty.

"What's the score on that television bug?" asked the Works security guard. "Wasn't you going after him personal?"

"Alfy Tucci?" said Finnerty.

"No names!"

"Kick that name around all you want," said Lasher glumly. "He isn't ours."

"That's right," said Finnerty. "He isn't anybody's, and never will be. He never joined anything, his father never joined anything, and his grandfather never joined anything, and if he ever has a son, *he'll* never join anything either."

"What's his reason?" asked Paul.

"Says it's all he can do to figure out what he represents without trying to represent a thousand other people besides," said Finnerty.

"Are there any conditions under which he'd join?" asked the man who'd been nervous about loose recruiting methods.

"One," said Finnerty. "When everybody looks and thinks exactly the way Alfy Tucci does."

Lasher smiled sadly. "The great American individual," he said. "Thinks he's the embodiment of liberal thought throughout the ages. Stands on his own two feet, by God, alone and motionless. He'd make a good lamp post, if he'd weather better and didn't have to eat. All right, where were we?"

"We got a date yet?" asked Mr. Haycox politely.

"We'll get a date two days before it happens, and no sooner!" said Lasher.

"Could I ask a question?" said Paul.

"Don't know why not. I haven't succeeded in heading anybody else off, yet."

"What, generally, is supposed to happen on *this date*?"

"A special meeting of every chapter of every big social organization in the country, outside of the engineers' and managers', will have been called. At the meetings, our people, big men in the organizations, will tell the members that all over the country men are marching through the streets on their way to wreck the automatic factories and give America back to the people. Then they'll put on their ghost shirts and lead whoever will follow, starting with a few more of our people planted around.

"This is the headquarters group here, but the movement is largely decentralized, with regional and local people responsible for their areas. We give them help on organization and recruiting and objectives and tactics, but, on the big day, the local people will be pretty much on their own. We'd like to have a bigger organization, a more centralized one. But that would lay us that much more open to the police. The way things stand now, the police don't know who we are and what we've got. On paper, we don't look like much. Actually, with our people placed right, we have a tremendous potential in fellow travelers."

"How many do you suppose will follow?" said Paul.

"As many people as are bored to death or sick of things the way they are," said Lasher.

"All of 'em," said Finnerty.

"And then what?" said Paul.

"And then we get back to basic values, basic virtues!" said Finnerty. "Men doing men's work, women doing women's work. People doing people's thinking."

"Which reminds me," said Lasher. "Who's going to do the job on EPICAC?"

"Last I heard D-71 say was, it's between the Moose and the Elks in Roswell who's goin' to do it," said Luke Lubbock.

"Put them both on it," said Lasher. "G-17, any bright ideas on how to knock off EPICAC?"

"Bes' idee," said Bud, " 'd be to put some kind of bomb in the coke machines. They got one in every chambah. That way, we'd git all of him, not just part." His hands were working in air, fashioning a booby trap for a coke machine. "See? Take a li'l ol' coke bottle, only fill her full of nitro. Then we run a li'l ol'—"

"All right. Make a sketch and give it to D-17, so he can get it to the right people."

"An' baloooooooowie!" said Bud, bringing his fist down on the table.

"Great," said Lasher. "Anybody else got anything on his mind?"

"What about the Army?" said Paul. "What if they're called out to—"

KURT VONNEGUT

"Both sides had better throw in the towel if somebody's crazy enough to give *them* real rifles and ammunition," said Lasher. "Fortunately, I think both sides know that."

"Where we stand now?" asked the nervous man.

"Not bad, not good," said Lasher. "We could put on a pretty good show now, if they forced our hand. But give us two more months, and we'll really have a surprise for them. All right, let's get this meeting over with, so we can all get to work. Transportation?"

On and on the reports went: transportation, communications, security, finance, procurement, tactics . . .

Paul felt as though he'd seen the surface scraped from a clean, straight rafter, and been shown the tunnels and flimsy membranes of a termite metropolis within.

"Public information?" said Lasher.

"We've mailed out warning letters to all the bureaucrats, engineers, and managers with classification numbers below one hundred," said Professor von Neumann. "Carbon copies to the news service, the radio network, and the television network."

"Damn good letter," said Finnerty.

"Rest of you like to hear it?" said von Neumann.

There were nods around the table.

"Countrymen," the professor read—

"Admittedly, we are all in this together. But—

"You, more than any of us, have spoken highly of progress recently, spoken highly of the good brought by great and continued material change.

"You, the engineers and managers and bureaucrats, almost alone among men of higher intelligence, have continued to believe that the condition of man improves in direct ratio to the energy and devices for using energy put at his disposal. You believed this through the three most horrible wars in history, a monumental demonstration of faith.

"That you continue to believe it now, in the most

300

mortifying peacetime in history, is at least disturbing, even to the slow-witted, and downright terrifying to the thoughtful.

"Man has survived Armageddon in order to enter the Eden of eternal peace, only to discover that everything he had looked forward to enjoying there, pride, dignity, self-respect, work worth doing, has been condemned as unfit for human consumption.

"Again, let me say we are all in this together, but the rest of us, for what we perceive as good, plain reasons, have changed our minds about the divine right of machines, efficiency, and organization, just as men of another age changed their minds about the divine right of kings, and about the divine rights of many other things.

"During the past three wars, the right of technology to increase in power and scope was unquestionably, in point of national survival, almost a divine right. Americans owe their lives to superior machines, techniques, organization, and managers and engineers. For these means of surviving the wars, the Ghost Shirt Society and I thank God. But we cannot win good lives for ourselves in peacetime by the same methods we used to win battles in wartime. The problems of peace are altogether more subtle.

"I deny that there is any natural or divine law requiring that machines, efficiency, and organization should forever increase in scope, power, and complexity, in peace as in war. I see the growth of these now, rather, as the result of a dangerous lack of law.

"The time has come to stop the lawlessness in that part of our culture which is your special responsibility.

"Without regard for the wishes of men, any machines or techniques or forms of organization that can economically replace men do replace men. Replacement is not necessarily bad, but to do it without regard for the wishes of men is lawlessness.

"Without regard for the changes in human life patterns that may result, new machines, new forms of organization, new ways of increasing efficiency, are constantly being introduced. To do this without regard for the effects on life patterns is lawlessness.

"I am dedicated, and the members of the Ghost Shirt Society are dedicated, to bringing this lawlessness to an end, to give the world back to the people. We are prepared to use force to end the lawlessness, if other means fail.

"I propose that men and women be returned to work as controllers of machines, and that the control of people by machines be curtailed. I propose, further, that the effects of changes in technology and organization on life patterns be taken into careful consideration, and that the changes be withheld or introduced on the basis of this consideration.

"These are radical proposals, extremely difficult to put into effect. But the need for their being put into effect is far greater than all of the difficulties, and infinitely greater than the need for our national holy trinity, Efficiency, Economy, and Quality.

"Men, by their nature, seemingly, cannot be happy unless engaged in enterprises that make them feel useful. They must, therefore, be returned to participation in such enterprises.

"I hold, and the members of the Ghost Shirt Society hold:

"That there must be virtue in imperfection, for Man is imperfect, and Man is a creation of God.

"That there must be virtue in frailty, for Man is frail, and Man is a creation of God.

"That there must be virtue in inefficiency, for Man is inefficient, and Man is a creation of God.

"That there must be virtue in brilliance followed by stupidity, for Man is alternately brilliant and stupid, and Man is a creation of God.

"You perhaps disagree with the antique and vain notion of Man's being a creation of God.

"But I find it a far more defensible belief than the one implicit in intemperate faith in lawless technological progress—namely, that man is on earth to create more durable and efficient images of himself, and, hence, to eliminate any justification at all for his own continued existence.

> "Faithfully yours,
> "Doctor Paul Proteus."

Professor von Neumann took off his glasses, rubbed his eyes, and stared at a paper clip before him, waiting for someone to say something.

"Yeah," said the transportation chairman tentatively. "Kinda long-haired, though, ain't it?"

"Sounded purty good," said the security chairman, "but shun't there be sumpin' in there 'bout— Well, I'm no good at words, but somebody else could fix it up. I don't know how to say it good, exactly."

"Go on, try," said Finnerty.

"Well, it just don't seem like nobody feels he's worth a crap to nobody no more, and it's a hell of a screwy thing, people gettin' buggered by things they made theirselves."

"That's in there," said Lasher.

Paul coughed politely. "Uh, you want me to sign it?"

Von Neumann looked surprised. "Heavens, they were signed and mailed out hours ago, while you were asleep."

"Thank you."

"You're welcome, Paul," said the professor absently.

"You don't expect that they'll really go along with us on the new controls, do you?" said the nervous man.

"Not for a minute," said Lasher. "But it will certainly get word around about us. When the big day comes, we want everybody to know that ours is a great, big bandwagon."

"Cops!" cried someone from far away in the network of chambers.

Gunfire boomed, echoed and crackled in the distance.

"The west exit!" commanded Lasher.

Papers were snatched from the table, stuffed into envelopes; lanterns were blown out. Paul felt himself swept along through the dark corridors by the fleeing crowd. Doors opened and shut, people stumbled and bumped into pillars and one another, but made no outcry.

Suddenly, Paul realized that the sound of the others' feet had stopped, and that he was following only the echoes of his own. Panting, stumbling in a nightmare of the policemen's echoing shouts and running footfalls, he blundered about the passages and chambers, coming again and again to barriers of dead rock. At last, as he turned away from one of these, he was dazzled by a flashlight beam.

"There's one, Joe. Get him!"

Paul charged past the flashlight, swinging both fists.

Something crashed against the side of his head, and he sprawled on the wet floor.

"Here's one that didn't get away, by God," he heard a voice say.

"Really socked him one, didn't you?"

"Don't pay to mess around with no stinking sabotoors, by God."

"Must be one of the small fry, eh?"

"Sure. Whadja expect? You think this was Proteus walking around in little circles all by hisself, like he don't know which way's up? Nossir, boy. Proteus is in the next county by now, lookin' out for his own sweet tail first, last, and always."

"Sabotagin' bastard."

"Yeah. O.K., you, on your feet and shag your tail."

"What happened?" mumbled Paul.

"Police. You just got brained for savin' Proteus' hide. Why'n't you wise up? He's nuts, guy. Hell, he's got it in his head *he's* gonna be king."

31

Paul's cellmate in the basement of police Headquarters was a small, elegant young Negro named Harold, who was in jail for petty sabotage. He had smashed a traffic safety education box—a tape-recording and loudspeaker arrangement—that had been fixed to a lamppost outside his bedroom window.

" 'Look out!' it say. 'Don't *you* go crossin' in the middle of the block!' " said Harold, mimicking the tape recording. "Fo' two years, ol' loudmouth and me done lived together. An' evah last time some'un come on pas', they hits 'at 'lectric eye, and ol' loudmouth, *he* just naturally *gotta* shoot off his big *ba-zoo*. 'Don' step out 'tween two parked cars,' he say. No matter who 'tis, no matter what tahm 'tis. Loudmouth, *he* don' care. Jus' gotta be sociable. 'Cayful, now! Don' you do this! Don' you do that!' Ol' mangy dog come bah at three in the mornin', and ol' loudmouth jus' gotta get his two cents wuth in. 'If you drahve,' he tells that ol' mangy dog, 'if you drahve, don' drink!' Then an' ol' drunk comes crawlin' along, and ol' gravelthroat tells *him* it's a city ohdnance ev'y bicycle jus' *gotta* have a *re*-flectah on the back."

"How long you in for?" said Paul.

"Fahve days. Judge said Ah could walk raht out. All Ah had to do was say Ah's sorry. Ah ain' goin' do that, 'cause," said Harold, "Ah *ain'* sorry."

Paul was glad that Harold was too bound up in his act of integrity to explore Paul's troubles. Not that it would have pained Paul to talk about them, but because they were extraordinarily difficult to describe. His own motivation was obscure, the cast was unwieldy, and, Paul realized, the denouement was still to come. Through all his adventures, he had been a derelict, tossed this way, then that. He had yet to lay a firm hand on the tiller.

The managers and engineers still believed he was their man; the Ghost Shirt Society was just as convinced that he belonged to them, and both had demonstrated that there was no middle ground for him.

When the police had identified Paul, they had been embarrassed by his I.Q., and his rank in the criminal hierarchy: the archcriminal, the would-be king of the saboteurs. There was no comparable rank in the Ilium police force, and the police had, out of humbleness and lifelong indoctrination, sent for inquisitors with adequate classification numbers and I.Q.'s.

Meanwhile, Paul and Harold passed the time of day.

"Ain' a *bit* sorry," said Harold. "Wha's 'at tap-tap-tappin'?"

The irregular tapping came from the other side of the sheet-metal wall that separated Paul's and Harold's barred cell from the totally enclosed tank for desperados next door.

Experimentally, Paul tapped on his side.

"Twenty-three—eight-fifteen," came the reply. Paul recognized the schoolboy's code: one for *A*, two for *B* . . . "Twenty-three—eight-fifteen" was "Who?"

Paul tapped out his name, and added his own query.

"Seven—one—eighteen—twenty—eight."

"Garth!" said Paul aloud, and he tapped out, "Chin up, boy." An exotic emotion welled up within him, and it took him a moment to understand it. For the first time in the whole of his orderly life he was sharing profound misfortune with another human being. Fate was making him feel a warmth for Garth, the colorless, the nervous, the enervated, that he had never felt for Anita, for Finnerty, for his parents, for anyone. "You fixed the tree?"

"You bet," tapped Garth.

"Why?"

"Boy flunked GCT again. He cracked up."

"Lord! Sorry," tapped Paul.

"Dead weight on world. Useless. Drag."

"Not so."

"But only God can make tree," tapped Garth.

"Blessed are fetishists. Inherited earth," tapped Paul.

"Rot, corrosion on our side."

"What next for you?" tapped Paul.

Garth tapped out the story of his being discovered as the criminal at the Meadows, of the furor, the threats, the actual tears shed over the wounded oak. He'd been locked up in the Council House, and guarded by dozens of angry, stalwart young engineers and managers. He'd been promised grimly that he would get the book thrown at him—years of prison, fines that would wipe him out.

When the police had arrived on the island to pick him up, they'd caught the hysteria of the brass and had treated Garth like one of the century's most terrible criminals.

"Only when we got back here and they booked me did they wake up," he tapped.

Paul, himself awed by Garth's crime, was puzzled by this twist. "How so?" he tapped.

"Ha!" tapped Garth. "What's my crime?"

Paul laughed wonderingly. "Treeslaughter?" he tapped.

"Attempted treeslaughter," tapped Garth. "Thing's still alive, though probably never have acorns again."

"Proteus!" called the cellblock loudspeaker. "Visitors. Stay where you are, Harold."

"Ain' going nowhere, 'cause Ah ain' sorry," said Harold. " 'Cayful, look out, now. Walk facin' the traffic.' "

The cell door buzzed and opened, and Paul walked to the green door of the visitors' room. The green door opened, whispered shut behind him, and he found himself face to face with Anita and Kroner.

Both were dressed funereally, as though not to compete for glamour with the corpse. Gravely, wordlessly, Anita handed him a carton containing a milkshake and a sheaf of funnypapers. She lifted her veil and pecked him on his cheek.

"Paul, my boy," rumbled Kroner. "It's been hard, hasn't it? How are you, my boy?"

Paul stepped back out of reach of the big, sapping, paternal hands. "Fine, thanks."

"Congratulations, Paul, darling," said Anita, her voice tiny.

"For what?"

"She knows, my boy," said Kroner. "She knows you're a secret agent."

"And I'm awfully proud of you."

"When do I get out?"

"Right away. Just as soon as we can transcribe what you found out about the Ghost Shirts, who they are, how they work," said Kroner.

"Home is all ready, Paul," said Anita. "I let the maid off, so we could have an old-fashioned American homecoming."

Paul could see her creating this old-fashioned atmosphere—putting a drop of Tabu on the filter of the electronic dust precipitator, setting the clockwork on the master control panel, which would thaw a steak dinner and load it into the radar stove at the proper moment, and turn on the television just as they crossed the threshold. Goaded by a primitive and insistent appetite, Paul gave her offer cautious consideration. He was pleased to find a higher order of human need asserting itself, a need that made him think, if not feel, that he didn't give a damn if he never slept with her again. She seemed to sense this, too, and, for want of any proclivities to interest Paul save sex, her smile of welcome and forgiveness became a thin and chilling thing indeed.

"Your bodyguards can eat later," said Kroner. He chuckled. "Say, that was quite a letter you wrote for the Ghost Shirts. Sounded wonderful, till you tried to make sense out of it."

"You couldn't?" said Paul.

Kroner shook his head. "Words."

"But it did one thing I'll bet you never expected," said Anita. "Can I tell him—about the new job?"

"Yes, Paul," said Kroner, "the Eastern Division needs a new manager of engineering."

"And *you're* the man, darling!" said Anita.

"Manager of engineering?" said Paul. "What about Baer?" Somehow Paul had expected the rest of the world to hold firm while his own life went spinning. And of that rest of the world nothing had seemed more firm than the union of Baer, the engineering genius, and Kroner, the rock of faith in technology. "He isn't dead, is he?"

"No," said Kroner sadly, "no, he's still alive—physically, that is." He placed a microphone on a table and moved up a chair, so that Paul might testify in comfort. "Well, who knows—maybe what happened is just as well. Poor Baer never was too stable, you know." He adjusted the microphone. "There. Now, you come over here, Paul, my boy."

"What about Baer?" insisted Paul.

"Oh," sighed Kroner, "he read that fool letter, cleaned out his desk drawers, and walked out. Sit right here, Paul."

The letter, then, had been *that* good, Paul thought, astonished at the upheaval it had caused in at least one man's life. But then he wondered if the letter hadn't won Baer's support by default of the opposition rather than by its being unanswerable. If someone with quicker wits than Kroner's had been at hand to argue against the letter, perhaps Baer would still have been on the job in Albany. "What was the official reaction to the letter?" asked Paul.

"Classified as top secret," said Kroner, "so anybody trying to circulate it will come under the National Security Act. So don't worry, my boy, it isn't going any farther."

"There *is* going to be an official reply, isn't there?" said Paul.

"That'd be playing right into their hands, wouldn't it—acknowledging publicly that this Ghost Shirt nonsense is

worth the notice of the system? That's exactly what they *want*
to have happen! Come on, now, sit down, and let's get this
over with, so you can get home and have a well-earned rest."

Absently, Paul sat down before the microphone, and
Kroner switched on the recorder. The official reaction to the
Ghost Shirt Society was the official response to so many
things: to ignore it, as pressing and complicated matters were
ignored in the annual passion plays at the Meadows. It was as
though the giving or withholding of official recognition were
life or death to ideas. And there was the old Meadows team
spirit in the reaction, too, the spirit that was supposed to hold
the system together: the notion that the opposition wanted
nothing but to win and humiliate, that the object of competition was total victory, with mortifying defeat the only alter-
native imaginable.

"Now then," said Kroner, "who's really at the head of
this monkey business, this Ghost Shirt Society?"

Here it was again, the most ancient of roadforks, one
that Paul had glimpsed before, in Kroner's study, months ago.
The choice of one course or the other had nothing to do
with machines, hierarchies, economics, love, age. It was a
purely internal matter. Every child older than six knew the
fork, and knew what the good guys did here, and what the
bad guys did here. The fork was a familiar one in folk tales
the world over, and the good guys and the bad guys, whether
in chaps, breechclouts, serapes, leopardskins, or banker's gray
pinstripes, all separated here.

Bad guys turned informer. Good guys didn't—no matter when, no matter what.

Kroner cleared his throat. "I said, 'who's their leader,
Paul?'"

"I am," said Paul. "And I wish to God I were a better
one."

The instant he'd said it, he knew it was true, and knew
what his father had known—what it was to belong and believe.

32

"Do you swear to tell the truth, the whole truth, and nothing but the truth, so help you God?"

"I do," said Paul.

The courtroom television cameras dollied back from his face, to reveal on fifty million television screens the tableau of the Ilium Federal Courtroom's south wall. There, beside and above Doctor Paul Proteus, sat the judge—the Sky Manager, Paul thought. The accused, seated on the witness stand, resembled less a man than an old-fashioned switchboard, with wires running from temperature-, pressure-, and moisture-sensitive instruments at his wrists, armpits, chest, temples, and palms. These, in turn, ran to a gray cabinet under the witness stand, where their findings were interpreted and relayed to a dial a yard in diameter over Paul's head.

The indicator needle on the dial, now pointing straight down, was pivoted so as to swing easily between a black *T* on the right and a red *F* on the left, or to a series of arbitrarily calibrated points between them.

Paul had pleaded guilty to conspiring to advocate the commission of sabotage, but was now being tried for treason, three weeks after his arrest.

"Doctor Proteus," said the prosecutor nastily. The television cameras closed in on his sneer and panned to the beads of sweat on Paul's forehead. "You have pleaded guilty to conspiracy to advocate the commission of sabotage, isn't that so?"

"It is." The needle swung toward *T*, and back to the neutral position, proving that, to the best of Paul's knowledge, it was indeed true.

"This conspiracy, of which you are the head, has as its
method, and I quote from your famous letter, 'We are prepared to use force to end the lawlessness, if other means fail.'
Those are your words, Doctor?"

"They were written by someone else, but I'm in sympathy with them," said Paul.

"And the word, 'lawlessness,' refers in this case to the
present mechanized economy?"

"And future."

"Your goal, as I understand it, was to destroy machines
in order that people might take a more personal part in production?"

"Some of the machines."

"What machines, Doctor?"

"That would have to be worked out."

"Oho! You haven't worked *that* out yet, eh?"

"The first step would be to get Americans to agree that
limitations be placed on the scope of machines."

"You would get this agreement by force, if necessary?
You would force this artificial condition, this step backward,
on the American people?"

"What distinguishes man from the rest of the animals is
his ability to do artificial things," said Paul. "To his greater
glory, I say. And a step backward, after making a wrong turn,
is a step in the right direction."

The television cameras looked deep into the prosecutor's righteously angry eyes, and backed away, awed at the
still unloosed mighty lightning there.

Paul looked too, and saw that the prosecutor knew a
great deal more than he had yet revealed. But Paul doubted
that the prosecutor knew his secretary was a member of the
Ghost Shirt Society, and that Paul's answers, while registering
as heartfelt on the lie detector, were a synthesis of the best
thinking and phrasing of Lasher, Finnerty, and Professor von
Neumann.

Paul was at ease, filled with the euphoria of well-publicized martyrdom for a cause in which he believed. There was no more question in his mind than there was in the prosecutor's that what the Ghost Shirt Society proposed to do was treason. The machines and the institutions of government were so integrated that trying to attack one without damaging the other was like trying to remove a diseased brain in order to save a patient. There would have to be a seizure of power—a benevolent seizure, but a seizure nonetheless.

The only old acquaintances in the room were Kroner, who seemed close to tears, and the fat, pig-eyed Fred Berringer, who was present, Paul supposed, to see the murder of Checker Charley avenged.

Anita hadn't come to court, nor had Shepherd. The two of them, presumably, were too busy mapping future campaigns to give more than a brief, pious prayer for those caught on the barbed wire of the battlefield of life. There was no need for Anita's coming to court to show the world how she felt about her erring husband. She had made that clear in several interviews with the press. She had married Paul, she'd explained, when she was but a child, and she thanked God things had come to a head while she was still young enough to salvage a little real happiness for herself. "Salvage" seemed a particularly apt term to Paul, with its implications of picking over city dumps and dragging harbor bottoms, for Anita had announced in her next breath that she was going to marry Doctor Lawson Shepherd as soon as she could get a divorce from Paul.

Paul had read her public declarations with ennui, as though they were gossip about someone else, about a television starlet's accusations against a middle-aged producer, say. The thing he concentrated on now, a far more entertaining and consequential enterprise, was the saying of as many poignant, antimachine, pro-Ghost Shirt Society things as he could over a nationwide television network.

"This *use of force*—you don't regard that as a levying of war against the United States, as treason, Doctor?" wheedled the prosecutor.

"The sovereignty of the United States resides in the people, not in the machines, and it's the people's to take back, if they so wish. The machines," said Paul, "have exceeded the personal sovereignty willingly surrendered to them by the American people for good government. Machines and organization and pursuit of efficiency have robbed the American people of liberty and the pursuit of happiness."

Paul twisted his head, and saw that the needle pointed at *T*.

"The witness will keep his head to the front," said the Judge sternly. "His concern is with telling the truth, the whole truth, and nothing but the truth. The indicator will take care of itself."

The prosecutor turned his back to Paul, as though finished with him, and suddenly wheeled to shake a finger at him. "You are a patriot, are you, Doctor?"

"I try to be."

"Your chief wish is to serve the American people well?"

"It is." Paul was puzzled by this new line of questioning, for which no one had prepared him.

"That is your basic reason for serving as nominal head of the Ghost Shirt Society—to do good?"

"It is," said Paul.

A ripple of whispers and a creaking of chairs under shifting bottoms told Paul that something had gone wrong with the lie detector's indicator.

The judge hammered with his gavel. "Order in the court. The court engineer will please check the tubes and circuits."

The engineer wheeled his steel cart up to the witness stand, and impersonally tested the connections to Paul. He took meter readings at various points along the circuits, slid the gray box out from under the witness stand, took out each

of the tubes and tested them, and put everything back together, all in less than two minutes. "Everything in order,
your honor."

"The witness will please tell what he considers to be a
lie," said the judge.

"Every new piece of scientific knowledge is a good
thing for humanity," said Paul.

"Object!" said the prosecutor.

"This is off the record—a test of the instrument," said
the judge.

"Swung to the left, all righty," said the engineer.

"Now a truth," said the judge.

"The main business of humanity is to do a good job of
being human beings," said Paul, "not to serve as appendages
to machines, institutions, and systems."

"Swung to *T*, O.K.," said the engineer, tucking a metal
clip just a little deeper into Paul's armpit.

"Now, a half-truth," said the judge.

"I am contented," said Paul.

The spectators chuckled appreciatively.

"Square in the middle," said the engineer.

"Proceed with the examination," said the judge.

"I will ask the good patriotic doctor the same question," said the prosecutor. "Doctor, your part in this plot to
overthrow the—ah—machines: you say it was motivated
solely by your desire to serve the American people?"

"I think so."

Again the telltale restlessness in the courtroom.

"You *think* so, eh?" said the prosecutor. "Do you know
where the needle pointed on that one, Doctor, patriot, latter-
day Patrick Henry?"

"No," said Paul uncomfortably.

"Squarely between *T* and *F*, Doctor. Apparently you're
not sure. Perhaps we can dissect this half-truth and remove
from it a whole one—like removing a tumor."

"Um."

"Could it be, Doctor, that this hate of what you describe as an injustice to humanity is in fact a hate or something a good bit less abstract?"

"Maybe. I don't quite follow you."

"I'm talking about your hate for some*one*, Doctor."

"I don't know who you're talking about."

"The needle says you *do* know, Doctor—that you *do* know your red-white-and-blue patriotism is really an expression of hate and resentment—hate and resentment for one of the greatest true patriots in American history, your father!"

"Nonsense!"

"The needle says you lie!" The prosecutor turned away from Paul in seeming disgust. "Ladies and gentlemen of the jury and the television audience: I submit that this man before you is little more than a spiteful boy, to whom this great land of ours, this great economy of ours, this civilization of ours, has become a symbol of his father! A father whom, subconsciously, he would have liked to destroy!

"A father, ladies and gentlemen of the jury and the television audience, to whom we are all in debt for our lives, for it was he, more than any other American, who mustered the forces of know-how, and brought civilization to victory!

"But this boy chose to resent, to hate this brilliant apparition on the pages of history, out of whose loins he had sprung. And now, as a man, he has transferred this hate to what might very well serve as a symbol for his father, your land, ladies and gentlemen of the jury and the television audience, and mine.

"Call it Oedipus complex, if you will. He's a grown man now, and I call it treason! Deny it, Doctor, deny it!

"Deny it," he said again, his voice little more than a whisper.

The cameras about-faced, and closed in on Paul like dogs closing in on a coon shot from a tree.

"Apparently I can't deny it," said Paul. He looked down helplessly, wonderingly, at the wires monitoring every

data bears me out on that. Sordid things, for the most part,
are what make human beings, my father included, move.
That's what it is to be human, I'm afraid.

"What the prosecutor has just done is to prove what
everything about this world we've made for ourselves seems
determined to prove, what the Ghost Shirt Society is determined to disprove: that I'm no good, you're no good, that
we're no good because we're human."

Paul gazed into the television camera lenses and imagined the millions now watching, now listening, and he wondered if he'd made sense to any of them. He tried to think of
some vivid image that would bring his point home to them
all. An image came to mind; he rejected it as indelicate, could
find no other, and so blurted it out anyway.

"The most beautiful peonies I ever saw," said Paul,
"were grown in almost pure cat excrement. I—"

Bagpipes and drums howled from the street below.

"What's going on out there?" demanded the judge.

"Parade, sir," said a guard, leaning out of the window.

"What organization is it?" said the judge. "I'll have every last one of them hauled in for this outrage."

"Dressed like Scotchmen, sir," said the guard, "with a couple fellas up front that look kind of like Injuns."

"All right," said the judge irritably, "we'll stop the testimony until they're past."

A brickbat shattered a courtroom window, showering the American flag to the judge's right with bits of glass.

33

THE STATE DEPARTMENT limousine, bound for New York City, crossed the Iroquois River at Ilium once more. In the back seat were Mr. Ewing J. Halyard, the Shah of Bratpuhr, spiritual leader of 6,000,000 members of the Kolhouri sect, and Khashdrahr Miasma, interpreter, and nephew of the Shah. The Shah and Khashdrahr, languishing with nostalgia for the temple bells, the splash of the fountain, and the cries of the *houri selano* in the palace courtyard, were going home.

When the expedition had crossed this bridge before, at the beginning of their trip, Halyard and the Shah, each in the fashion of his own culture, had been equals in splendor, with Khashdrahr coming off a poor, self-effacing third. Now, the hierarchy of the travelers had shifted. Khashdrahr's function had been extended, so that he served not only as a language bridge between the Shah and Halyard, but as an intermediate social step between them as well.

Wondering at the mechanics of being a human being, mechanics far beyond the poor leverage of free will, *Mr.* Halyard found himself representing the fact of no rank as plainly as *Doctor* Halyard had once represented a great deal of rank. Though he had told his charges nothing of the physical-education examination that could mean life or death to his career, they had sensed the collapse of his status the instant he'd been brought back from the Cornell gymnasium and revived.

When Halyard had recovered, and changed from the ruined shorts and tennis shoes into street clothes, he had seen in the mirror, not a brilliantly fashionable cosmopolite, but an old, overdressed fool. Off had come the boutonniere, the contrasting waistcoat, the colored shirt. Accessory by accessory, garment by garment, he'd stripped away the symbols of the discredited diplomat. Now he was, spiritually and sartorially, whites, grays, and blacks.

As though there were anything of Halyard left to crush, one more crushing blow had fallen. The State Department's personnel machines, automatically, with a respect for law and order never achieved by human beings, had started fraud proceedings against him, since he had never been entitled to his Ph.D., his classification numbers, or, more to the point, to his pay check.

"I'm going to bat for you," his immediate superior had written, but it was, Halyard knew, an archaic incantation in a wilderness of metal, glass, plastic, and inert gas.

"Khabu?" said the Shah, without looking at Halyard.

"Where are we?" said Khashdrahr to Halyard, filling the social gap for form's sake, though the Bratpuhrian word, God knows, was familiar enough to Halyard by now.

"Ilium. Remember? We crossed here before, going the other way."

"Nakka Takaru tooie," said the Shah, nodding.

"Eh?"

"Where the *Takaru* spit in your face," said Khashdrahr.

"Oh—that." Halyard smiled. "I hope you don't take that home as your chief recollection of the United States. Perfectly ridiculous incident, isolated, irrational. It certainly isn't any indication of the temperament of the American people. That one neurotic *would* have to manifest his aggressions in front of you gentlemen. Believe me, you could travel this country for the next hundred years and never see another outburst like that."

Halyard let none of his bitterness show. With a melancholy spitefulness he continued, for these last days of his career, to perform his job impeccably. "Forget about him," he said, "and remember all the other things you've seen, and try to imagine how your own nation might be transformed."

The Shah made thoughtful clucking sounds.

"At no expense whatsoever to you," said Halyard, "America will send engineers and managers, skilled in all fields, to study your resources, blueprint your modernization, get it started, test and classify your people, arrange credit, set up the machinery."

The Shah shook his head wonderingly. *"Prakka-fut takki sihn,"* he said at last, *"souli, sakki EPICAC, siki Kanu pu?"*

"Shah says," said Khashdrahr, " 'Before we take this first step, please, would you ask EPICAC what people are for?' "

The limousine came to a stop at the head of the bridge on the Homestead side, blocked this time, not by a Reconstruction and Reclamation Corps crew, but by a phalanx of Arabs. They were led, as though the significance of the banners and costumes weren't confusing enough, by two men wearing Indian shirts and war paint.

"Dinko?" said the Shah.

"Army?" said Khashdrahr.

Halyard had his first good chuckle in many weeks. That anyone, even a foreigner, could look on this colorful tangle of banners, sashes, and toy weapons as an effective fighting force! "Just some people having a little fun dressing up."

"Some of them have guns," said Khashdrahr.

"Wood, cardboard, and paint," said Halyard. "All make-believe." He picked up the speaking tube and spoke to the driver: "See if you can't ease past them and down a side street, toward the courthouse. Things ought to be quieter down there."

"Yessir," said the driver uneasily. "I don't know, though, sir. I don't like the way they're looking at us, and all that traffic on the other side looked like they were running away from something. Maybe we should turn around and—"

"Nonsense. Lock the doors, lean on the horn, and go on through. Things have come to a pretty pass if this sort of monkey business has the right of way over official business."

The bulletproof windows slithered to the top, the door locks clicked, and the limousine nosed diffidently into the apricot, green, and gold ranks of the Arabs.

Jeweled dirks and scimitars stabbed and slashed at the limousine's armored sides. Above the howls of the Arabs came crashes of gunfire. Two great pimples appeared suddenly in the side of the car, inches from Halyard's head.

Halyard, the Shah, and Khashdrahr threw themselves on the floor. The limousine plunged through the raging ranks, and down a side street.

"Head for the courthouse!" cried Halyard to the driver from the floor, "then out Westinghouse Boulevard!"

"The hell with you!" said the driver. "I'm bailing out right here. The whole town's going nuts!"

"Stay at the wheel or I kill you!" said Khashdrahr savagely. He was shielding the Shah's sacred body with his own poor flesh, and he held the point of a golden dagger against the back of the driver's neck.

Khashdrahr's next words were lost in an explosion nearby, followed by cheers and a hail of rubble on the limousine's top and hood.

"Here's the courthouse!" said the driver.

"Good. Turn left!" commanded Halyard.

"My God!" cried the driver. "Look!"

"What's the matter?" quavered Halyard, prone with Khashdrahr and the Shah. He could see only sky and building tops and passing skeins of smoke.

"The Scotchmen," said the driver hollowly. "My God, here come the Scotchmen." The limousine stopped with a shriek of rubber.

"All right, back up and—"

"You got radar down there on the floor? Take a look out the back window, *then* tell me we should back up."

Halyard raised his head cautiously above the window sill. The limousine was trapped by bagpipers ahead, and, behind, by a squad of gold-epauleted Royal Parmesans, who had sallied from an Automatic Market across the street from the courthouse.

An explosion hurled the market's conveyers and clips of canned goods through the windows. An automagic cashier rolled into the street, still miraculously upright on its round pedestal. "Did you see our special in Brussels sprouts?" it said, tripped on its own wire, and crashed to the pavement by the limousine, spewing cash from a mortal wound.

"It isn't us they're after!" called the driver. "Look!"

The Royal Parmesans, the Scotchmen, and a handful of Indians had joined forces and were ramming the courthouse door with a felled telephone pole.

The door burst into kindling, and the attackers were carried inside by the ram's momentum.

A moment later they emerged with a man on their shoulders. In the midst of their frenzied acclamation, he was marionettelike. As though to perfect the impression, bits of wire dangled from his extremities.

"To the Works!" cried the Indians.

The host, bearing their hero aloft like another banner beside the Stars and Stripes, followed the Indians toward the bridge across the Iroqois, cheering, skirling, smashing, dynamiting, and beating drums.

The limousine stayed where it had been trapped by the Royal Parmesans and Scotchmen for an hour, while the dull thunder of explosions walked about the city like the steps of drunken giants, and afternoon turned to twilight under a curtain of smoke. Each time escape seemed possible, and Halyard raised his head to investigate a lull, fresh contingents of vandals and looters sent him to the floor again.

"All right," he said at last, "I think maybe we're all right now. Let's try to make it to the police station. We can get protection there until this thing plays itself out."

The driver leaned on the steering wheel and stretched insolently. "You think you've been watching a football game or something? You think maybe everything's going to be just the way it was before?"

"I don't know what's going on, and neither do you. Now, drive to the police station, do you understand?" said Halyard.

"You think you can order me around, just because you've got a Ph.D. and I've got nothing but a B.S.?"

"Do as he says," hissed Khashdrahr, placing the point of his knife in the back of the driver's neck again.

The limousine moved down the littered, now-deserted streets toward the headquarters of Ilium's keepers of the peace.

The street before the police station was snow-white, paved with bits of punctured pasteboard: the fifty-thousand-card deck with which the Ilium personnel and crime-prevention machines had played their tireless games—shuffling, dealing, off the bottom, off the top, out of the middle, palming, marking, reading, faster than the human eye could follow, controlling every card, and implacably protecting the interests of the house, always the house, any house.

The doors of the building had been torn from their hinges, and within were rolling dunes of dumped files.

Halyard opened his window a crack. "Hello, there," he called, and waited hopefully for a policeman to appear. "I say, hello!" He opened his door cautiously.

Before he could close it again, two Indians with pistols jerked the door wide open.

Khashdrahr lunged at them with his knife, and was knocked senseless. He fell on top of the quivering Shah.

"I say," said Halyard, and was knocked cold, too.

"To the Works!" ordered the Indians.

When Halyard regained consciousness he found himself with his aching head on the limousine floor, halfway out of the open door.

The car was parked in front of a saloon near the bridge. The front of the saloon had been sandbagged, and inside were men operating radios, moving pins on maps, oiling weapons, and watching the clock. By the head of the bridge itself were crude breastworks of sandbags and timbers, facing the pillboxes and turrets of the Ilium Works across the river. Men in every conceivable type of uniform wandered about the fortifications in a holiday spirit, coming and going as they pleased, on missions seemingly best known to themselves.

The commandeering Indians and the driver were gone, while Khashdrahr and the Shah, bewildered and frightened, were being castigated by a tall, gaunt man who wore an Indian shirt but no war paint.

"Goddammit!" said the tall man. "The Knights of Kandahar are supposed to be manning the roadblock on Griffin Boulevard. What the hell you doing here?"

"We—" said Khashdrahr.

"Haven't got time to listen to excuses. Get back to your organization on the double!"

"But—"

"Lubbock!" cried the tall man.

"Yessir."

"Give these men transportation to the Griffin Boulevard block, or put 'em under arrest for insubordination."

"Yessir. Ammo truck's leaving now, sir." Lubbock hustled the Shah and Khashdrahr into the back of a truck, atop cases of handmade grenades.

"Brouha batouli, nibo. Nibo!" cried the Shah piteously. *"Nibo!"*

The truck meshed its gears and disappeared into the smoke.

"I say," said Halyard thickly.

"Finnerty!" cried a short, fat man in thick glasses from the door of the saloon. "The state police are trying to break through the Griffin Boulevard roadblock! Who've we got for reinforcements?"

Finnerty's eyes widened, and he ran his hands through his hair. "Sent back two stragglers, and that's it. The VFW and the Knights of Pythias wandered off, and the Masons never did show up. Tell them we haven't got any reserves!"

A geyser of flame and shattered masonry spouted from the Ilium Works across the river, and Halyard saw that where the Stars and Stripes had flown over the works manager's office, a white flag now snapped in the smoky wind.

"For chrissake!" said Finnerty. "Get the Moose and Elks on the radio and tell them to quit it. They're supposed to occupy the Works, not atomize it."

"Baker Dog Three," said Lasher into a microphone. "Baker Dog Three. Protect all equipment in the Works until decision can be made as to proper disposition. Can you hear me, Baker Dog Three?"

The crowd by the saloon fell silent, to hear the reply of

the Moose and Elks above the shushing noise of the loud-speaker.

"Baker Dog Three—did you hear me?" shouted Lasher.

"Zowie!" came a faraway cry in the speaker, and another volcano erupted in the Works.

"Lubbock!" said Finnerty. "Take over. I'm going over there to teach those babies a little discipline. We'll see who's running this show!" He climbed into a car, and sped across the bridge to the Works.

"Salt Lake City is ours!" shouted another radio operator inside the saloon.

"Oakland and Salt Lake and Ilium so far!" said Lasher. "What about Pittsburgh?"

"No reply."

"Pittsburgh's the key," said Lasher. "Keep trying." He glanced to the south over his shoulder, and a look of horror crossed his face. "Who set the museum on fire?" He shouted into his microphone desperately, "All posts! All posts! Protect all property! Vandalism and looting will be punished by death. Attention all posts—can you hear me?"

Silence.

"Moose? Elks? Knights of Pythias? VFW? Eagles? Hello! Anybody—can you hear me? Hello!"

Silence.

"Proteus!" called an Arab, staggering up to the saloon door, brandishing a bottle. "Where'sh Proteus? Give us a word."

Paul, haggard and aged, appeared beside Lasher in the saloon door. "God help us, gentlemen," he said slowly. "God help us. If we've won, it means that now the hard part begins."

"Jesus—you'd think we losht," said the Arab. "Shorry now I ashked for a word."

"Lou!"

"Right here," said the drunk Arab.

"Lou, boy—we forgot the bakery. Still poopin' out bread like nobody's business."

"Can't have it doin' that," said Lou. "Le'sh go knock the crap out of it."

"Listen, wait," said Paul. "We'll need the bakery."

"Machine, ain't it?" said Lou.

"Yes, sure, but there's no sense in—"

"Then le'sh go knock the crap out of it. And, by God, here'sh ol' Al to go with us. Where you been, y'ol' horse-thief?"

"Blew up the goddam sewage 'sposal plant," said Al proudly.

"'At's the shtuff! Give the friggin' worl' back to the friggin' people."

34

"I DON'T UNDERSTAND about Pittsburgh," said Finnerty. "I knew Seattle and Minneapolis were touch-and-go, but Pittsburgh!"

"And St. Louis and Chicago," said Paul, shaking his head.

"And Birmingham and Boston and New York," said Lasher, smiling sadly. He seemed curiously at peace, inexplicably satisfied.

"Pfft!" said Finnerty.

"Ilium came off like clockwork, anyway, and Salt Lake

and Oakland," said Professor von Neumann. "So I think we can say that the theory of attack was essentially valid. The execution, of course, was something else again."

"It always is," said Lasher.

"What makes you so cheery?" said Paul.

"Would a good cry make you feel better, Doctor?" said Lasher.

"Now all we have to do is close ranks with Salt Lake City and Oakland, and strangle the country into submission," said Finnerty.

"I wish now we'd sent one of our Ilium people out to get EPICAC," said von Neumann. "EPICAC was worth three Pittsburghs."

"Too bad about the Roswell Moose, all right," said Lasher. "D-71 said they were crazy about the idea of getting EPICAC."

"Too crazy," said Paul.

"Nitro's tricky enough stuff, without having crazy men trying to get it into Coke bottles," said Finnerty.

The four thought-chiefs of the Ghost Shirt Society were seated about what had once been Paul's desk, the works manager's desk in the Ilium Works.

The revolution was not yet a day old. It was early in the morning, before sunrise, but here and there burning buildings made patches of Ilium as bright and hot as tropical noon.

"I wish they'd attack, and get it over with," said Paul.

"It'll take them a little while to get their nerve back, after what the Knights of Kandahar did to the state police on Griffin Boulevard," said Finnerty. He sighed. "By God, if only we'd had a few more outfits like that in Pittsburgh—"

"And St. Louis," said Paul, "and Seattle and Minneapolis and Boston and—"

"Let's talk about something else," said Finnerty. "How's the arm, Paul?"

"Not bad," said Paul, stroking the makeshift splint. The Messiah of the Ghost Shirt Society had had his left arm broken by a rock while exercising his magnetism on a crowd interested in seeing the power station blown up. "How's the head, Professor?"

"Ringing," said von Neumann, adjusting his bandage. He had been struck by the Sacred Mace of The Order of the Aurora Borealis while giving a crowd reasons for not felling a two-hundred-foot radio tower.

"Glockenspiel or carillon?" said Lasher. "And how are your own contusions and abrasions, Ed?"

Finnerty twisted his neck and raised his arms experimentally. "Nothing, really. If the pain gets any worse, I can simply kill myself." He had been floored and trampled by stampeding Moose and Elks while explaining that the Works should be kept intact until a cool decision could be made as to which machines should be destroyed, which retained.

Fire spurted skyward from Homestead.

"Keeping the map right up to the minute, Professor?" said Lasher.

Professor von Neumann looked out at the new blaze through field glasses, and made a black *X* on the map before him. "Post office, most likely."

The map of the city had been clean and crackling at the start of the campaign, with a dozen small red circles indicating the primary objectives of the Ilium *Putsch:* the police station, the courthouse, communications centers, sites for roadblocks, the Ilium Works. After these objectives were taken, with a minimum of bloodshed and damage, the plan of operations declared, the systematic replacement of automatic control devices by human beings was to begin. The more important of these secondary objectives were circled in green.

But now the map was smudged and limp. Overlying the scattered constellation of red and green circles was a black, continuous smear of *X's* that marked what *had* been taken, and, moreover, destroyed.

Lasher glanced at his watch. "I've got 4 A.M. That right?"

"Who knows?" said Finnerty.

"Can't you see the City Hall clock from there?"

"They got that hours ago."

"And they're likely to be after your watch any minute," said Paul. "Better put it back in your pocket."

"What gets me are the specialists," said Finnerty. "Some guys seem to have it in for just one kind of machine, and leave everything else alone. There's a little colored guy going around town with a shotgun, blasting nothing but those little traffic safety boxes."

"Lord," said Paul, "I didn't think it'd be like this."

"You mean losing?" said Lasher.

"Losing, winning—whatever this mess is."

"It has all the characteristics of a lynching," said the professor. "It's on such a big scale, though, I suppose genocide is closer. The good die with the bad—the flush toilets with the automatic lathe controls."

"I wonder if things would have been much different if it hadn't been for the liquor," said Paul.

"You can't ask men to attack pillboxes cold sober," said Finnerty.

"And you can't ask them to stop when they're drunk," said Paul.

"Nobody said it wasn't going to be messy," said Lasher.

A terrific explosion lifted the floor and dropped it.

"Boy!" said Luke Lubbock, standing guard in what had been Katharine Finch's office.

"What was it, Luke?" called Lasher.

"Gasoline storage tanks. Boy!"

" 'Ray," said Paul dismally.

"People of Ilium!" boomed a voice from the sky. *"People of Ilium!"*

Paul, Lasher, Finnerty, and von Neumann hurried to the opening where the floor-to-ceiling window had once been. Looking up, they saw a robot helicopter in the sky, its belly and blades reddened by the fires below.

"People of Ilium, lay down your arms!" said its loud-speaker. *"Oakland and Salt Lake City have been restored to order. Your cause is lost. Overthrow your false leaders.*

"You are completely surrounded, cut off from the rest of the world. The blockade will not be lifted until Proteus, Lasher, Finnerty, and von Neumann are turned over to the authorities beyond the Griffin Boulevard roadblock.

"We could bomb and strafe you, but that is not the American way. We could send in tanks, but that is not the American way.

"This is an ultimatum: surrender your false leaders and lay down your arms within the next six hours, or suffer in the ruins of your own making for the next six months, cut off from the rest of the world. Click.

"People of Ilium, lay down your arms! Oakland and Salt Lake City have been re—"

Luke Lubbock aimed his rifle and fired.

"Beeby dee bobble dee beezle!" said the loudspeaker shrilly. *"Noozle ah reeble beejee boo."*

"Put it out of its misery," said Finnerty.

Luke fired again.

The helicopter floundered off clumsily, still haranguing the town. *"Beeby dee bobble dee beezle! Noozle ah reeble beejee . . ."*

"Where are you going, Paul?" said Finnerty.

"A walk."

"Mind if I come?"

"That's a small matter these days."

And the two walked out of the building and down the broad, littered boulevard that split the plant, past numbered façades that had nothing but silence, rubble, and scrap behind them.

"Not enough of it left for this to be like old times, eh?" said Finnerty, after they had walked some distance without speaking.

"New era," said Paul.

"Drink to it?" said Finnerty, taking a pint from the pocket of his ghost shirt.

"To the new era."

They sat down together before Building 58, and wordlessly passed the bottle back and forth.

"You know," said Paul at last, "things wouldn't have been so bad if they'd stayed the way they were when we first got here. Those were passable days, weren't they?" He and Finnerty were feeling a deep, melancholy rapport now, sitting amid the smashed masterpieces, the brilliantly designed, beautifully made machines. A good part of their lives and skills had gone into making them, making what they'd helped to destroy in a few hours.

"Things don't stay the way they are," said Finnerty. "It's too entertaining to try to change them. Remember the excitement of recording Rudy Hertz's movements, then trying to run automatic controls from the tape?"

"It worked!" said Paul.

"Damn right!"

"And then putting lathe group three together," said Paul. "Those weren't our ideas, of course."

"No, but we got ideas of our own later on. Wonderful ideas," said Finnerty. "Happiest I ever was, I guess, Paul; so damn engrossed, I never looked up to notice anything else."

"Most fascinating game there is, keeping things from staying the way they are."

"If only it weren't for the people, the goddamned people," said Finnerty, "always getting tangled up in the machinery. If it weren't for them, earth would be an engineer's paradise."

"Let's drink to that."

They did.

"You were a good engineer, Paul."

"You too, Ed. And there's no shame in that."

They shook hands warmly.

When they got back to the former works manager's office, they found Lasher and von Neumann asleep.

Finnerty shook Lasher's shoulder. "Master! *Maestro! Maître!*"

"Hmm?" The squat, homely man fumbled for his thick glasses, found them, and sat up. "Yes?"

"Doctor Proteus here has asked me a very interesting question," said Finnerty. "I was unable to supply him with a satisfactory answer."

"You're drunk. Go away, and let an old man sleep."

"This won't take long," said Finnerty. "Go ahead, Paul."

"What became of the Indians?" said Paul.

"What Indians?" said Lasher wearily.

"The original Ghost Shirt Society—the Ghost Dance Indians," said Finnerty. "Eighteen-ninety and all that."

"They found out the shirts weren't bulletproof, and magic didn't bother the U. S. Cavalry at all."

"So—?"

"So they were killed or gave up trying to be good Indians, and started being second-rate white men."

"And the Ghost Dance movement proved what?" said Paul.

"That being a good Indian was as important as being a good white man—important enough to fight and die for, no matter what the odds. They fought against the same odds we fought against: a thousand to one, maybe, or a little more."

Paul and Ed Finnerty looked at him incredulously.

"You thought we were sure to lose?" said Paul huskily.

"Certainly," said Lasher, looking at him as though Paul had said something idiotic.

"But you've been talking all along as though it were almost a sure thing," said Paul.

"Of course, Doctor," said Lasher patronizingly. "If we

hadn't all talked that way, we wouldn't have had that one chance in a thousand. But I didn't let myself lose touch with reality."

Lasher, Paul realized, was the only one who hadn't lost touch with reality. He, alone of the four leaders, seemed unshocked by the course of events, undisturbed by them, even, inexplicably, at peace. Paul, perhaps, had been the one most out of touch, having had little time for reflection, having been so eager to join a large, confident organization with seeming answers to the problems that had made him sorry to be alive.

Finnerty was covering his initial surprise at Lasher's statement, so perfect an apostle was he. Most of all, apparently, he wanted to remain intellectually as one with the dynamic Lasher, and he, too, now looked at Paul as though surprised to find that Paul wasn't sure what was going on.

"If we didn't have a chance, then what on earth was the sense of—?" Paul left the sentence unfinished, and included the ruins of Ilium in a sweep of his hand.

Lasher was fully awake now, and he stood, and paced up and down the room, apparently irritated that he should have to explain something so obvious. "It doesn't matter if we win or lose, Doctor. The important thing is that we tried. For the record, we tried!" He walked behind Paul's old desk and faced Paul and Finnerty across it.

"What record?" said Paul.

Suddenly Lasher underwent a transformation. He showed a side of himself he had mentioned, but which Paul had found impossible to imagine.

And, with the transformation, the desk became a pulpit.

"Revolutions aren't my main line of business," said Lasher, his voice deep and rolling. "I'm a minister, Doctor, remember? First and last, I'm an enemy of the Devil, a man of God!"

35

A<small>S THE SUN</small> arose over Ilium, and the embers of the town seemed gray in the light of the eternal fire ninety-three million miles away, the State Department limousine, flying a ghost shirt from its radio antenna, crept through the streets.

Bodies lay everywhere, in grotesque attitudes of violent death, but manifesting the miracle of life in a snore, a mutter, the flight of a bubble from the lips.

In the early light, the town seemed an enormous jewel box, lined with the black and gray velvet of fly-ash, and filled with millions of twinkling treasures: bits of air conditioners, amplidynes, analyzers, arc welders, batteries, belts, billers, bookkeeping machines, bottlers, canners, capacitors, circuit-breakers, clocks, coin boxes, calorimeters, colorimeters, computers, condensers, conduits, controls, converters, conveyers, cryostats, counters, cutouts, densitometers, detectors, dust precipitators, dishwashers, dispensers, dynamometers, dynamotors, electrodes, electronic tubes, exciters, fans, filers, filters, frequency changers, furnaces, fuses, gages, garbage disposers, gears, generators, heat exchangers, insulators, lamps, loudspeakers, magnets, mass spectrometers, motor generators, motors, noisemeters, oscillographs, panelboards, personnel machines, photoelectric cells, potentiometers, pushbuttons, radios, radiation detectors, reactors, recorders, rectifiers, reducers, regulators, relays, remote controls, resistors, rheostats, selsyns, servos, solenoids, sorters, spectrophotometers, spectroscopes, springs, starters, straingages, switchboards, switches, tape recorders, tachometers, telemeters, television sets, television cameras, testers, thermocouples, thermostats, timers, toasters, torquemeters, traffic controls, transitors, transducers, transformers, turbines, vacuum cleaners, vacuum gages, vacuum tubes, venders, vibration meters, viscosimeters, water heaters, wheels, X-ray spectrogoniometers, zymometers . . .

At the wheel of the limousine was Doctor Edward Francis Finnerty. Beside him was Doctor Paul Proteus. In the back seat were the Reverend James J. Lasher and Professor Ludwig von Neumann, and, asleep on the floor, lay Mr. Ewing J. Halyard of the State Department. In a world of ruins and deep sleep, Halyard's form on the floor was hardly cause for curiosity, comment, or remedial action.

The brains of the Ghost Shirt Society were touring the strongpoints on the frontiers of their Utopia. And everywhere they found the same things: abandoned weapons, abandoned posts, mounds of expended ammunition, and riddled machinery.

The four had come to an exciting decision: during the six months of blockade threatened by the authorities, they would make the ruins a laboratory, a demonstration of how well and happily men could live with virtually no machines. They saw now the common man's wisdom in wrecking practically everything. That *was* the way to do it, and the hell with moderation!

"All right, so we'll heat our water and cook our food and light and warm our homes with wood fires," said Lasher.

"And walk wherever we're going," said Finnerty.

"And read books instead of watching television," said von Neumann. "The Renaissance comes to upstate New York! We'll rediscover the two greatest wonders of the world, the human mind and hand."

"No quarter asked, no quarter given," said Paul as they contemplated the entire furnishings of an M-11 house, dragged into a vacant lot and hacked to bits.

"This is like the Indians' massacre of Custer and his men," said Lasher reflectively. "The Little Bighorn. One isolated victory against an irresistable tide. More and more whites where Custer came from; more and more machines where these came from. But we may win yet. Well! What is that noise? Somebody awake?"

A faint hubbub came from around a corner, from where the railroad station had been, where it still was after a fashion. Finnerty turned the corner for a better look at the celebrators.

In the station's waiting room, carnage was everywhere. The terrazzo floor, depicting an earlier slaughter of Iliumites by Oneida Indians, was strewn with the guts and internal secretions of the automatic ticket vendor, the automatic nylon vendor, the automatic coffee vendor, the automatic newspaper vendor, the automatic toothbrush vendor, the automatic shoeshine machine, the automatic photo studio, the automatic baggage checker, the automatic insurance salesman . . .

But around one machine a group had gathered. The people were crowding one another excitedly, as though a great wonder were in their midst.

Paul and Finnerty left the car to examine the mystery, and saw that the center of attention was an Orange-O machine. Orange-O, Paul recalled, was something of a *cause célèbre*, for no one in the whole country, apparently, could stomach the stuff—no one save Doctor Francis Eldgrin Gelhorne, National Industrial, Commercial, Communications, Foodstuffs, and Resources Director. As a monument to him, Orange-O machines stood shoulder-to-shoulder with the rest, though the coin-box collectors never found anything in the machines but stale Orange-O.

But now the excretor of the blended wood pulp, dye, water, and orange-type flavoring was as popular as a nymphomaniac at an American Legion convention.

"O.K., now let's try anotha' nickel in her an' see how she does," said a familiar voice from behind the machine— the voice of Bud Calhoun.

"Clunkle" went the coin, and then a whir, and a gurgle.

The crowd was overjoyed.

"Filled the cup almost to the top that time; and she's nice and cold now, too," called the man by the machine's spout.

"But the light behind the Orange-O sign didn't light up," said a woman. "Supposed to."

"We'll fix that, won't we, Bud?" said another voice from behind the machine. "You people get me about three feet of that red wire hanging out of the shoeshine machine, and somebody let me borrow their penknife a second." The speaker stood up and stretched, and smiled contentedly, and Paul recognized him: the tall, middle-aged, ruddy-faced man who'd fixed Paul's car with the sweatband of his hat long ago.

The man had been desperately unhappy then. Now he was proud and smiling because his hands were busy doing what they liked to do best, Paul supposed—replacing men like himself with machines. He hooked up the lamp behind the Orange-O sign. "There we are."

Bud Calhoun bolted on the back. "Now try her."

The people applauded and lined up, eager for their Orange-O. The first man up emptied his cup, and went immediately to the end of the line for seconds.

"Now, le's have a look at this li'l ol' ticket seller," said Bud. "Oh, oh. Got it right through the microphone."

"I knew we'd be able to use the telephone out in the street for something," said the ruddy man. "I'll go get it."

The crowd, filled with Orange-O, was drifting over to encourage them in their new enterprise.

When Paul and Finnerty returned to the limousine, they found Lasher and von Neumann looking extremely glum, engaged in conversation with a bright-looking teenager.

"Have you seen an eighth-horsepower electric motor lying around anywhere?" said the youngster. "One that isn't busted up too bad?"

Lasher shook his head.

"Well, I just have to keep looking, I guess," said the youngster, picking up a cardboard carton jammed with gears, tubes, switches, and other odd parts. "This place is a gold mine, all right, but it's tough finding exactly what you need."

"I imagine," said Lasher.

"Yep, if I had a decent little motor to go with what I got," said the youngster excitedly, "I'll betch anything I could make a gadget that'd play drums like nothing you ever heard before. See, you take a selsyn, and—"

"Proteus! Finnerty!" said Lasher irritably. "What's been keeping you?"

"Didn't know you were in a hurry to get anywhere," said Finnerty.

"Well, I am. Let's go."

"Where to?" Finnerty started the car.

"Griffin Boulevard. The roadblock."

"What's going on out there?" asked Paul.

"The authorities are waiting for the people of Ilium to turn over their false leaders," said Lasher. "Anybody want to get out? I'll drive myself, if you like."

Finnerty stopped the car.

"Well?" said Lasher.

"I suppose now *is* the time," said von Neumann matter-of-factly.

Paul said nothing, but made no move to get out.

Finnerty waited a moment longer, then pressed down on the accelerator.

No one spoke until they reached the concertina of barbed wire, the felled telephone poles, and the sandbags of the Griffin Boulevard roadblock. Two brown men, elegantly costumed—Khashdrahr Miasma and the Shah of Bratpuhr—huddled together, asleep in a slit trench to the left of the barricade. Beyond the barbed wire, their wheels toward heaven, were two riddled, abandoned state police cars.

Professor von Neumann looked out over the country-side through his field glasses. "Aha! The authorities." He handed the glasses to Paul. "There—to the left of that barn. See?"

Paul squinted at the three armored cars by the barn, and the police with their riot guns, lounging, smoking, chatting cheerfully.

Lasher patted Paul on his shoulder as Paul handed the glasses on to him. "Smile, Doctor Proteus—you're *somebody* now, like your old man was. Who's got a bottle?"

Finnerty produced one.

Lasher took it, and toasted the others. "To all good Indians," he said, "past, present, and future. Or, more to the point—to the record."

The bottle went around the group.

"The record," said Finnerty, and he seemed satisfied with the toast. He had got what he wanted from the revolution, Paul supposed—a chance to give a savage blow to a close little society that made no comfortable place for him.

"To the record," said von Neumann. He, too, seemed at peace. To him, the revolution had been a fascinating ex-periment, Paul realized. He had been less interested in achieving a premeditated end than in seeing what would hap-pen with given beginnings.

Paul took the bottle and studied Lasher for a moment over its fragrant mouth. Lasher, the chief instigator of it all, was contented. A lifelong trafficker in symbols, he had cre-ated the revolution as a symbol, and was now welcoming the opportunity to die as one.

And that left Paul. "To a better world," he started to say, but he cut the toast short, thinking of the people of Ilium, already eager to recreate the same old nightmare. He shrugged. "To the record," he said, and smashed the empty bottle on a rock.

Von Neumann considered Paul and then the broken

glass. "This isn't the end, you know," he said. "Nothing ever is, nothing ever will be—not even Judgment Day."

"Hands up," said Lasher almost gaily. "Forward March."